Wadmalaw

A GHOST STORY

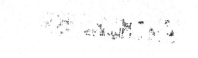

Wadmalaw
A GHOST STORY

Bart Bare

Canterbury House Publishing

www.canterburyhousepublishing.com
Imprint of Dudley Court Press

Canterbury House Publishing, Ltd.
www.canterburyhousepublishing.com
Imprint of Dudley Court Press

First Printing March 2011

Cover Illustration by Joe Burleson
Book Design by Aaron Burleson, Spokesmedia
Cover Concept Photography by Mike W. Burnett
Author Photography by Ree Strawser

AUTHOR'S NOTE: This is a work of fiction. Names characters, and incidents are either the product of the author's imagination or are used fictiously, and any resemblance to actual persons living or dead, business establishments, events, or locales is entirely coincidental.

Library of Congress Cataloging-in-Publication Data

Bare, Bart.
Wadmalaw : a ghost story / Bart Bare.
    p. cm.
ISBN 978-0-9829054-0-1 (paperback) | ISBN 978-1-945401-17-6 (ebook)
1. Dwellings--South Carolina--Wadmalaw Island (Island)--Fiction. 2.
Family secrets--Fiction. 3. Wadmalaw Island (S.C. : Island)--Fiction. I.
Title.
PS3602.A77533W33 2011
813'.6--dc22
                            2010049859

Caroline

Acknowledgements

The struggle from idea to paper is a long and tedious journey. The trip may be fraught with rough places, anxieties and pain, and, as the ancient maps cautioned for the unknown: "Here There Be Dragons." However, when the destination is reached, the pleasures of the goal and the path traveled become apparent. The greatest measure of contentment seems always to come from *people*—the shared experience of those met, and accompanied, along the way. Yes, the struggle is conducted by the singular writer over a waiting medium— paper or electronic. Yes, there are solitary periods at 2:00 a.m.. But, alone? No, never. There is ever the urging of friends and family. There are memories— happy, sad, or merely extant. I look down the long and dimming hall of my memories and I note a sea of faces, each representing a soul who has become a part of the "I" that is me. Some faces shine ever bright, some dimming but always there. Some hidden, yet perhaps exerting a sure force on that "I."

I bow my head in thanks to those many who are me. We are legion. These fingers would lie mute without their influence. So, thank you. Thank you Ethyl (High Test) Sheffield—school librarian Maven—for my intellectual life. John Palm (a bright face) for lighting the fire and fanning the flame. Kurt Palomaki for pushing me over the edge and making me think I could write. High Country Writers of Boone, NC.—Thank you for being the kind of family that benefits all who join. It would be sheer folly for me to think that I could lay claim to being an "*auther*" without your guidance. And always, Caroline, you are not gone.

Finally, there are the makers of this book—a book held in the hands of you who were drawn to its cover. A cover resulting from the talents of Mike W. Burnett (photographer), Joe Burleson (artist), Aaron Burleson (designer), and Ree Strawser (photographer). It was they who put this book in your hands. I only did the word part—a part that benefitted considerably from razor sharp editing skills of Sandy Horton and Patti Wheeler. I've never enjoyed a love-hate relationship so much. And finally, the book would never have made the shelves but for the marketing talent of Wendy Dingwall, owner of Canterbury House Publishing. To be the recipient of such talents as those above is humbling. Thank you.

—Bart Bare

Wadmalaw: A Sea Island Place

Wadmalaw is a Place. America still has Places—but the number dwindles. Development, chainsaws, and bulldozers are claiming our Places. But we still have some. It is noteworthy that people seem to enjoy our Places: There are the Smokies, Yellowstone, The Everglades, The Outer Banks—all Places where people go to visit and renew. Wadmalaw Island is one such Place, albeit one with limited appeal. If you like sunrise over the salt marsh, fecund estuaries teeming with promise of shrimp, crab and oysters , swamp life, and thick wild woods, then Wadmalaw might be a Place to you. If, on the other hand, you are for bumper-to-bumper traffic, hordes of tourists, acres of golf courses, and blocks of bars—I point you to Myrtle Beach. Don't come to Wadmalaw, for it is a Place, and there are those who would like it to remain a Place. It is one of the Sea Islands of South Carolina. One of the few—one that has yet to fall to the developer's axe, or the builder of bridges.

Native Americans discovered and settled the Sea Islands thousands of years ago. Despite the mosquito, sand flea, the cottonmouth, hurricanes and huge gators, the tribes survived and flourished, living off the bounty of the sea and surrounding estuaries.

17th century Europeans "discovered" and claimed the Sea Islands. The British and Spanish quarreled over who could most quickly displace the native population. England won. Native Americans lost. For a couple of centuries the Sea Islands were held in only modest regard. They were remote places, difficult to reach, and even more difficult to live on. Africans were enslaved and forced to endure labor in rice, indigo, and tea plantations under conditions that would be nearly impossible to make worse. The Civil War ended that blight on our history. The land was sort of settled by default to ex-slaves who developed a culture known as Gullah. And they thrived for over a hundred years. However, someone discovered screens, macadam, air-conditioning, and on-demand bridge building. The Gullah are slowly being replaced by wealthy vacationers, but will probably not go the way of the Native Americans—the Gullah have good public relations people, heavy federal and state funding, and a surrounding merchant population who spell it $ullah.

Yet, Wadmalaw remains a Place. There is America's only tea plantation, the Angle Oak grows nearby, now there is a winery, and—oh yes, the salt marshes still prevail. There are slave graves at the edge of the salt marsh. At the south tip of the island is the tiny community of Rockville where fresh seafood is brought in daily by people who live close to the water. "Close" in both the geographical and intimate sense. People who know who they are and who earn their way. So, yes, visit Wadmalaw. Come—if you only leave tracks, take pictures and then make track, maybe Wadmalaw can remain a Place.

—Bart Bare

Chapter 1

"Did you hear that?" Liv sat up in bed.

"What?" Autis disengaged himself from the early stages of sleep.

"Voices."

"No. I was asleep."

"Well, I did. There's someone in the basement."

"The dog would let us know."

"Maybe."

"He would, trust me. Go back to sleep." Autis rolled over and covered his head with a pillow.

"I'm going down there," Liv turned on her bedside light.

"Oh hell, I'll go." Autis rose from their bed naked, and moved toward the doorway.

"Put on some clothes."

"What, you don't want to embarrass the burglar?"

"Shit." Liv flounced from the bed and, wrapping herself in a sheer robe, strode to the doorway. Autis followed, his nakedness shining in the full moon that hung over the Carolina Sound. He carried his large Mag-Lite like a club.

As soon as they descended to the first floor Liv turned and whispered to Autis, "They've stopped."

"Good, let's go back to bed," Autis turned to head back upstairs.

"I'm going down to the pub." Liv insisted, opening the door to the cellar.

Autis followed his wife down the long stairwell to the basement. They had christened it "The Pub" on their first night. "Twenty steps." It was the first thing Autis complained about after they sealed the purchase of the home overlooking the salt marsh. "What were they thinking? Twenty steps. Jesus."

"They didn't have to think about steps," Liv answered. "They had slaves, and I doubt that the master or mistress of the house went up or down these steps once a week. They sent the servants if they needed something."

When they reached the pub Autis flicked wall switches, lighting an array of neon bar signs, "This Bud's for You!" "It's Miller Time!" and a variety of slogans intended to invoke thirst. Their sleepy English Pointer raised his head from the leather-covered couch, one of a pair that Liv rescued from Goodwill for use in the pub.

"See, sleeping canine. No bogeys, burglars, or haints."

"Wow, look at the moon over the marsh," Liv said, standing in front of the French doors. Autis didn't fail to notice her body outlined under the sheer gown. He moved up behind her, wrapped her in his naked arms, and buried his face in her perfumed hair, then moved to her neck where he placed a wet kiss. Liv chuckled under this attention.

"What is this thing at my back?"

"Here alone at night with a beautiful woman in a scary place. Old Blue just gets excited."

"Mother of God. You men are all goats. Don't you ever think of anything else?"

"Uh...No."

Liv chuckled warmly. "Suh, Ah'm a married woman, with a sacred honah to protect. You certainly don't intend to dis-honah me, do you, suh?

"In every conceivable way, Miss Magnolia. In every way."

"That sounds like a promise, suh."

"Let us hope it is." Autis moved closer to demonstrate his sincerity.

"Not here. Let's go back upstairs."

"Why not here? There's the moon, an empty couch in the corner, and Blue is loaded."

"Not here, Autis."

"What is it—the voices? Is that it? We did it here our first night."

"We christened all three floors on our first night as I recall. But not here, not now."

"Okay. You name the place, I got the time—and the tool."

"C'mon. Let's go to the bedroom. I promise to make it worth the climb."

"I'm yours. Lead on, Miss Magnolia."

She took Autis' hand in hers and lifted it to her lips, saying softly, "Let's put Old Blue to bed—proper. Walk this way." She led him to the stairwell.

Just as she reached the landing at the top of the stairs, Liv sensed a murmur of soft laughter from behind her. She turned to look at Autis, but then realized with a jolt that the laughter had not come from him.

"There it is again," Liv said. "Did you hear it?"

"I didn't hear a thing," Autis answered, head cocked as he paused before closing the cellar door with a solid 'thunk'."

"Right."

Chapter 2

The spring sunlight through the windows wakened Autis, who responded to the wakeful state with a long stretch, arching his back. Rising, he put on his undershorts, picked up his faded jeans and went to the window where he closed the sheer curtains to keep the bright light from waking his partner. As he pulled on his jeans he smiled at Liv's form sprawled on her back in complete surrender to the comfort of their bed. His smile broadened as he reflected on the passions of the night before.

After a quick trip to the kitchen, Autis returned with the coffee tray. He could swear his wife was smiling in her sleep. He wafted the aroma of steaming coffee near her face, and watched as she stirred. As always, she came gently out of sleep. He kissed the tip of her nose.

"It's time to make the doughnuts, Babe," He said, in reference to a television commercial they had found amusing.

"Cruel, cruel."

"Yes, I know how hard it is to have to endure your lover bringing you fresh hot coffee and biscotti in bed after a love marathon of the night before. You should write to 'Dear Abby.' Maybe she can ease your plight."

"Divorce."

"See my lawyer, but first you might want to try the coffee."

Liv sat up in bed, took the mug from his hands and made a slurping sip.

"Ah." Liv said feigning pleasure. "Okay, I'll keep you," another, longer draw, at the coffee. "That was some session last night. I don't know what we did to do what we did, but let's do that did again—soon."

"I'm free tonight, darlin'."

"You're on, sailor—just don't let my husband know about us."

"Our secret," Autis said with a grin as he piled back into bed, and moved to help Liv eliminate some of the pastries on the tray.

Liv looked at the sheers billowing in the morning breezes from the sound. Her gaze moved beyond the curtains and out to the sound waters glistening to the sunrise. She was silent for several moments, and then turned quickly to Autis. "It was the voices."

Autis shrugged at his love. "Like I said, I didn't hear them. However, I'm pleased to have them if they provide entertainment like we had last night."

"Goat."

"Guilty."

Liv signaled for a coffee refill. "I heard them. I couldn't make out what they were saying, but I know I heard them."

"You know, sound carries very well over water, and it was dead calm last night—at least until we returned to bed. I might add that the windows were open."

"I know what I heard, and I know it came from downstairs, dammit. I didn't hear some fishermen out on the sound."

"I'm not disputing that you heard something. I'm just in a quandary as to what it could be." He took a bite of biscotti. "What's on your agenda today?"

"I'm sending some October articles I promised to Southern Living and Southern Home. I'm finishing another one for the Charleston Magazine. I had lunch with their editor last week and we cut a deal for this fall. She sent me searching all over Charleston County for just the right setting. I've found a couple of homes that are nearly perfect. One of them is only a couple of blocks from the battery in downtown Charleston. I had no idea how steeped in history this town is."

"Are you still using a pseudonym?"

"Of course. I don't want the public infringing on our peaceable kingdom out here in the sticks, and I don't need the ego trip. I'm in it for the money, remember? I write kitchen kitsch, and they send checks. It's a lovely arrangement."

"And you had me convinced that I was marrying an *artiste*. Here you are, just another money grubber." Autis dunked the last of his biscotti scrap, and then quickly popped it into his mouth before it could dissolve.

"Pot calling kettle…"

"I beg your pardon. I'm a successful, albeit humble, architect, striving to provide a good, useful product for a public in need of same. I mean, someone has to design hospitals; who better than me? Can I help it if they want to lavish fabulous sums of money on me?"

"Use that argument again if you want, but I've seen your work, mister. How do you keep your sanity? I mean, the detail, the unbelievable amount of detail. I ask once more: How do you do it?"

"Focus, my love, focus. Remember, once more, 'there is no force on earth superior to the focused human mind.'"

"Maybe so, but eight hours a day, five days a week, week after week. It's not human."

"I like it. It's challenging, and the time flies by… plus I work with a great staff. It's a series of never-ending puzzles that we have to face up to and solve every day. We have fun, and we build hospitals. The hardest part is keeping the voices out of the basement."

"You funnin' me, Bub?" Liv said, with raised eyebrows.

"Just a little. Anyway, what else do you have laid on today? Maybe we could have lunch?"

"Sorry, I've got a luncheon meeting with a gal named 'Bambi.'"

"Bambi?"

"Right. Carole 'Bambi' Bamberg. Glass blower extraordinaire. We're meeting at her house where she is going to demonstrate her glass-blowing skill and artwork for an article to be published in a North Carolina magazine. She gets the publicity, and I get a check. Sorry, you'll have to dine alone."

"Alone hell, I'm going to take out that new draftsman we hired. She's twenty-four, right out of college, and has great…"

"Focus," Liv said wryly.

"Yeah, that's what I was going to say. Focus."

"Well, keep it under zipper, sport."

"I'm saving it for homework, dear."

"Liar."

"Ah, the sounds of a contented woman," he said on the way to the shower.

Chapter 3

The hand-painted sign showed a picture of an open hand, fingers spread—the universal sign of a palm reader, or palmist, as some prefer. Under the sign in elegant letters were the words: *Spiritualist and Psychic Advisor.* Liv checked the address in her notebook. It was the right place.

Liv opened the picket fence gate and walked the flagstones leading to the front of the house. As she approached the porch she noted the plantings of herbs and leafy vegetables surrounding the front and side porch of the house. There were birdfeeders, and an army of concrete and metal yard ornaments.

A fluffy, yellow tabby watched her approach from its perch on an old wicker chair beside the doorway. Liv bent and scratched the top of its head, effectively turning on its motor. The cat stood, stretched, and then lifted its front paws to rest on Liv's shoulder, bringing more stroking while it flexed its claws. After spending some time with her new friend, Liv rose and pressed the doorbell. She waited, stroked the cat, and then sounded the bell again. She could hear the bell from outside so she knew it was working. No answer. *Damn. I hate irresponsible people—probably another temperamental artiste.*

Liv went around back to see if her hostess might be tending the garden or some such thing. She found a good size vegetable garden in the middle of a large yard surrounded by oaks hung with Spanish Moss. These massive oaks grew all over Charleston and the neighboring communities, except for the sections where developers had discovered that it cost 10% less to develop if all greenery was stripped from the land.

This healthy, well-tended garden was crowned with a large stand of collards. *What is it with Southerners and collards?* No Bambi to be found. *Another afternoon gone to hell; maybe it's not too late to catch Autis for lunch.* Then she heard the motorcycle. She couldn't see it from the back yard, but she could tell it was coming fast. By the time she returned to the front of the house, the bike and its rider came to rest behind her car. A lanky woman in shorts and halter dismounted and peeled her helmet away, letting a cascade of golden hair fall to her shoulders. She shook it loose, and then hung the helmet from a handle bar of the Ducati road bike she had flown in on. As she strode up the walkway toward her luncheon guest, every part of her body seemed to move in a symphony of syncopation. *Damn!* Liv's next thought had to do with never wanting Autis to meet this woman. Then the woman smiled. *Oops, no problem.*

"Good mornin'. You Liv Oakley?"

"Yes. I take it you're Carole Bamberg."

"That's me. I go by 'Bambi' though."

"Okay. Nice place—Bambi. I like your cat."

"Spot? He's a piece of work. No mice in the house or rabbits in the garden though."

"He's a tabby…"

"Right, but when he lifts that tail of his'n he shows his spot, and he shows it right much. C'mon in the house. Hits a mess, but that's always so."

As Bambi spun toward the doorway, Liv noticed the price tag hanging from a rear belt loop.

"Wait a second…" She reached for the tag.

"Leave it be," Bambi said, showing a snaggle-toothed grin.

"Oh, I didn't mean to…"

"You didn't. If you notice," she thrust her shapely posterior at Liv, "they's no price on the tag."

Liv's puzzled expression morphed into a broad grin. "Priceless?"

"You got it, hon. It can't be bought, and it won't be sold."

Liv tipped her head back with an amused chuckle. "I like it."

"Howsomever, it might be given freely — to the right man."

"Damn, I like that. I think the world would run a lot smoother if more women wore one of those—and meant it."

"Maybe so, but it sure does keep me in trouble. Let's have a cup of tea, and I'll explain." Bambi led the way into her living room. Liv stopped in the open doorway; it was the sixties all over, complete with lava lamp and incense.

"Patchouli."

"You like it? That aroma annoys some people. Doesn't bother you, does it?"

"No. I like it. It reminds me of my childhood. We used to visit an aunt, my mother's sister, Aunt Olivia, in Southern California." Liv passed around the room, her gaze taking in the many articles, and artifacts of a bygone era. "I loved that time, and I loved Aunt Olivia. She owned a Vespa, and the two of us tooled all over town with it. This room reminds me so much of her living room. It's a trip back in time for me, a trip to a really good place." Liv paused in front of a Jimmi Hendrix poster that hung over a table holding the working lava lamp.

"That's authentic, it cost me an arm and a leg." Bambi came to stand beside Liv, adding softly. "It also made me violate my price tag rule, but I think it was worth it. That poster's worth ten times the cash money I put out."

Liv leaned close to her new friend. "Interesting choice of words 'put out'."

"Hayel, gal, I like you. You're quick, and you speak your mind. I got a feeling we're goin' t'be friends. God knows, I could use one in this place. Yeah, you've probably already noticed that gals 'put out,' while guys 'get some.'

"Yes, I have. But the way I see it, it lets you know who's really in charge." Liv said with a sardonic smile.

"Liv, you must be my long lost sister or some such thing." Bambi circled a lean tanned arm around Liv's shoulder and gave her a quick hug, then stepped away, flashing a broad grin, revealing her teeth at their worst.

"Yeah, I paid for that poster with pennies and pleasure—a lot of pennies, and a little pleasure. It was worth every penny and…" She stopped at that juncture, flashing the protruding teeth again.

Liv smiled back. "I won't ask."

"Well, let's just say he was a handsome remnant from the Hendrix era, and very grateful. We can leave it there."

"Good enough. Anyway, I like the poster, and, in fact, I like the dŽcor altogether; it's comfortable and has its own elegance. It'll certainly add to the story I want to do about you and your glass-blowing."

"Look around, make yourself at home while I brew us a pot. You like tea?"

"Yes. Mind if I take some pictures of this room?"

"Go right ahead," Bambi said over her shoulder as she moved toward the kitchen.

"Thanks, I'll run out to the car and get my equipment."

Twenty minutes later the ladies were settled on an overstuffed couch, tea at hand on the heavy wooden coffee table. Beatles played in the background.

Liv took a sip of tea, and paused over the cup, inhaling the aroma. "This is the best tea I've ever tasted, where do you get it?"

"Right here on the island, Hon. Just down the road a ways, in fact." She sampled her cup, and then tilted her head at Liv. "You never heard of the Charleston Tea Plantation? How long have you lived on Wadmalaw?"

"We've been here just under a couple of months, but we've been busy re-modeling, refinishing, repainting—and sometimes regretting our choice. The Nobles were no doubt nice people, but they were well into their retirement and just not up to the work that was necessary to…"

"The Nobles—you bought the Maxton Manor?" Bambi said as her eyes grew wide with a mixture of incredulity and horror. She quickly placed her tea cup on the coffee table, sloshing tea onto the wood. Liv reached for a napkin and cleaned the spill. After a couple of swipes she looked up to see her host staring wide-eyed at her.

"Yes. Is there anything wrong with that? I mean, you really look surprised. No. Worse than 'surprised,' you look scared."

Gathering her composure, Bambi leaned back into the soft cushions of the couch and looked evenly at her guest. "The place is carsed—really carsed." Bambi's pronunciation revealed her Scotch-Irish ancestry. "No one's been able to live there for any length. I moved here from the hill country of Virginia eight years ago—mountain girl born and bred am I—and that house has changed hands three times since then." She paused and mumbled, "You're number four."

Liv thought of the voices she'd heard the night before. "We don't believe in such things."

"Now's as good a time as any to start, darlin'. You and your man has bought you a mess of trouble. That house is hexed."

Chapter 4

"Hexed?" Autis said over his dessert.

"Well, first she said 'carsed,' then later 'hexed.'"

"The only 'carse' is that damn crappy finish the Nobles had done to those beautiful oak floors. I've *carsed* them more than once—the last and loudest time was when I had to write the check for the total floor re-finishing we had to do on every wood floor in the place."

"Bambi said..."

"Jesus, does she really want to be called 'Bambi?'" Autis interjected in something like disgusted amusement.

"Yes, she does. It works for her." Liv paused. "Don't give me that superior look; I like her. She's honest, says what she thinks, and doesn't tolerate any bullshit. What you see is what you get with her. Okay?"

"Okay, okay. What did you two do, bond or something?"

Liv looked closely at her mate. "Yes, we did. We bonded. But you don't have anything to worry about—as long as you keep Old Blue in good working order."

Autis leaned back from the supper table and laughed a deep full laugh.

"So, the secret is out; that's all I am to you, your boy toy. You're a hard-hearted, over-sexed wench." Autis sipped his Shiraz. "I like it."

"I promise not to change. Anyway, Bambi said the story goes that no one has been able to tolerate living in this house since the end of the Civil War. Many people have tried, some stayed for a number of years, but they always reported being unhappy with the place—at best."

"Unhappy 'at best?'"

"Yeah. At worst some were said to flee in terror, and a couple of people have died unexpectedly here."

"The Nobles didn't mention any of that."

"Bambi said that Mrs. Nobles was the one who really wanted to leave—apparently her husband didn't have any quarrel with it. Mrs. Nobles won."

"I've puzzled over why we were able to pick this place up at such a great price. What you're telling me explains it. If what you say is true, we've got a white elephant, and we'd better learn to cope with it because we sure aren't going to be able to sell it."

"I don't plan on selling," Liv said. "Remember when we first saw this place? We spent the better part of the afternoon looking it over, then we wound up on the little dock out back. We sat on the dock looking out over the marsh and the sound. You asked if I thought we could live here."

"I remember it like it was last night," Autis said. "I also remember that we didn't think we could afford this place. It was my brother who convinced us to come back with an absurd counter-offer." I was sure that the Nobles would tell us to get lost."

Liv smiled as she recalled how ecstatic they were on the way home from signing the sales agreement with the Nobles. "Yes, well, the question I'm wondering now is: Do you think we could *die* here? I don't want to leave this place—ever."

"Be careful with death wishes, darlin'."

"I mean 'die here' in the far distant future."

"I can go with that. But where does that leave us with the voices in the basement? From what Bambi has told you, this place has the haints."

At that moment, the doorbell rang. Liv and Autis looked at each other, then at the clock on the wall.

"Who the hell drops in unexpectedly at 9:30?" Autis rose to go to the door. He turned on the overhead porch light, and peered through the beveled panes of the door. "There's no one there," he called back over his shoulder. He opened the door and was greeted only by an uncommonly cool wind coming from the dark forest. Hearing a deep growl, he quickly turned and saw that it was Bob, their English pointer, standing a few feet behind him.

"What's out there, Bob?"

The muscular hound came forward, walked stiff-legged onto the porch, and focused on something in the dark. Autis turned out the light so they could better see into the quiet gloom of the soft southern night.

He opened the screen door leading out onto the steps. "You want to go have a look, Bob?" The pointer slowly descended the steps, all the while looking steadfastly into the dark. Autis followed him and sat on the bottom step. He put an arm over his friend, who responded by wagging his tail once. The animal was intent on something at the edge of the wood. Autis sensed a brief flash of white in the wood. The two sat unmoving for a time before Liv came to the doorway.

"What is it, Autis?"

"I may have seen a movement out there, but Bob sure is sensing something—it seems to be in the woods. He's looking at the big old loblolly pine, the one with low branches lying out on the ground."

"That would be a good place to stay concealed."

"I'm going out there. C'mon, Bob." The dog didn't move.

"Come, Bob. Let's go look."

Bob didn't respond, didn't wag, and refused to take his gaze away from the giant pine.

"Autis, don't go out there."

"I'm going. C'mon, boy, let's go." The dog wouldn't budge.

"Dammit, Autis. Can't you see the dog won't go out there? It seems like you'd have better sense than to go wandering around in the dark, unarmed and with no light. Use your head."

"There's nothing to be afraid of."

"Think so? Look at Bob."

The powerful canine's hindquarters were trembling like he was just about to go into a sprint. "Bob? Are you okay? C'mon, boy, let's go in the house." Bob turned and followed Autis up the steps. Once in the foyer, Autis knelt next to his companion. "It's okay, boy." He put his arm around the dog's neck and gave a gentle squeeze. The dog was trembling slightly and continued to stare as though he could see through the door.

"Stay, boy." Autis rose and headed to the basement stairwell, saying over his shoulder, "I'll be right back." Liv heard him opening the heavy doors to his gun cabinet. He returned shortly with a .45 automatic and his Mag-Lite.

"What are you doing?" Liv demanded.

"I'm going to find out what's out there."

"Why?"

"If you have to ask I can't explain it."

"Don't be such a damned manly prig. There's no good reason to go out clambering about in the dark of night."

"No good reason for a woman—all good reasons for a man," Autis shot back.

Liv reacted like she'd been slapped. "Damn you, damn you to hell, Autis Oakley." She yanked the door open and marched out onto the porch.

"What are you doing?" Autis demanded.

"What does it look like, you mule-headed jerk. I'm going with you." She seized a stout walking stick and said, "C'mon, Bob, let's go for a walk."

The hound leapt athletically past his master and to the side of his mistress. The twosome started down the steps.

"Okay," Autis said, and joined the rest of his family as they made their way to the dark form of the loblolly that draped low over its own shadows. Autis felt for the automatic's handle jutting from his belted waist as he stabbed the bright halogen light into the misting world of the night-time forest. Swamp peepers raised a chorus from a nearby slough as the threesome moved into the perimeter of the branches that rested on the forest floor. Bob crowded close to his mistress. Autis sensed that the dog had pushed his fear aside to protect her.

Autis pointed at the dog, "Look at that—he leaps at your slightest wish after ignoring my command, and he was my dog before we married."

"I'm the one who feeds him—and the sad truth is that I married you for your dog." Liv said, giving Autis' ribs a gentle poke. She loved the fact that he was outrageously ticklish—a trait she often used to her advantage.

They reached the trunk of the tree and watched as the flashlight illuminated the hidden places within the tree's grasp. Just as Autis pointed the beam up into the giant branches of the old pine the flashlight failed. It dimmed once, came bright again, and then extinguished.

"Shit." Autis exclaimed, as he slapped the flashlight head against his palm, hoping to jar it back to light.

The light from the house illuminated the lawn between them and the porch some 100 yards distant.

"Take my hand and follow me out of these branches." Autis said.

"Why? This is beautiful here."

"What?"

"It's lovely, Look around you. It's—its own quiet kingdom under this tree. I could sleep right here on the ground tonight. Smell the pine needles. Listen to the peepers. This is paradise." She moved up behind Autis and, running her hands inside his tee shirt, wrapped her arms around him, feeling his muscular chest. "You feel good. How do you stay in such good shape working behind a desk all day?"

"It's the push-ups I do over my sweet love every night that keeps the muscles toned. Where is all this amorousness coming from?"

"I don't know, but I don't want it to go away. Let's make love, right here, right now."

Autis' tee-shirt and trousers and Liv's skirt served as a blanket against the pine needles as they made quiet fierce love beside the revolver and flashlight. Bob had walked away from the sheltering branches, laid down and curled up as though bored with the whole thing. He never closed his eyes.

Half an hour later the lovers returned to the house, barefoot and naked. Liv carried their bundled clothing, and Autis carried shoes, automatic, and the flashlight. When they reached the porch over the front steps they stopped and looked back at the pine.

"That was some tree." Autis said.

"Yes, it was." Liv ran her hand down Autis' back.

Autis flicked the switch on the flashlight. It blazed its bright beam out to the concealing branches of what they would name *Lover's Loblolly*. "Damn," Autis exclaimed at his flashlight.

Once inside the foyer, Liv reached up tippy-toe and kissed her man softly on the lips. She tousled his chestnut curls, tapped the tip of his nose with a forefinger, then said, "But who rang the doorbell?"

Chapter 5

The voices continued, male and female, a small group. There was disquiet to their sound. There was never laughter, just a muttering — as of discontent. And then there were the dreams, not unpleasant, no intent of evil, but slightly disturbing nevertheless. Echoing with people who came and went softly, faces obscured. Clothed in rags. They were reaching to her.

Liv would waken on quiet windless nights to the shadows of conversation that drifted up from her cellar. She couldn't make out the words, but they sounded angry. Autis slept like a babe. After their outing under the loblolly pine, they made love every night. In the mornings over coffee and biscotti, they would muse on the passions of the night before. They came to the conclusion that the house and grounds possessed aphrodisiac qualities.

"You know, we could open a bed and breakfast and make a killing." Liv smiled. "You would never have to work in an office again. You could host and I would hostess."

"Right, I can just see me whipping up batches of homemade marijuana scones for smiling clients after a night of vigorous sexercise. Something my degree in architecture has prepared me to do."

"Don't knock it; four hundred dollars a night, and complimentary condoms on the pillow. We'd need a good name though."

"'Death by Coitus' would be my first choice," Autis said. "No one under fifty allowed; all clients would have to pay in advance and sign a release. But what would we do about the voices."

"We'd probably be okay there. I seem to be the only one who hears them. You don't, and Bob doesn't seem concerned. It's not likely our clients would hear them."

Liv finished the last bite of her second biscotti, set her coffee cup on the bedside table and pulled herself across the king-size bed to her man.

"This may surprise you—I know we both made the decision about the vasectomy—but I'm beginning to feel maternal.

"Bad timing, dear, the scalpel has fallen."

"I know. Maybe we acted in haste. It would be nice to have little you's and me's running around; and this would be a great house for a couple of kids."

"We could adopt."

Liv shook her head of dark curls. "Too expensive, to lengthy, and too risky. I hear nothing but horror stories about the process and results."

"You ain't wrong there."

"Don't they have a procedure for putting those tubes back together?"

"I hear it's doable, a little complicated, expensive, and kind of iffy, but doable."

Liv stretched herself out full length against Autis and threw a leg over his legs. Autis set aside his coffee.

"Under these conditions I would agree to almost anything — wench."

Liv ran her hand under the covers and up Autis' leg. Smiling, wickedly, she said, "See, Old Blue agrees."

Autis pulled Liv close and held her warm body close. She rested her head on his shoulder.

The doorbell rang.

"What the hell…?" Autis looked at the bedside clock. "At this hour of the morning. Jesus Christ."

"Pretend we didn't hear it." Liv pulled herself up.

The bell rang again.

"Shit." Autis leaned up on his elbows. "Hold that thought. I'll be right back. I'll run off whoever's there." With a low groan, Liv fell away toward her side of the bed so he could slip away.

Autis rose, danced his way into his jeans and was maneuvering the zipper, when Liv said, "Careful."

Zipper in place, Autis moved to the bedroom door.

"Hurry back, everything's warmed up and running here."

Autis made for the front door.

He returned in less than five minutes.

"There was no one there," he said with a puzzled frown. "I walked Bob all the way around the house, and there was no one." He retrieved his coffee cup and drained the last of it. "That's it. I'm going to get an electrician to check out the wiring."

Liv had pulled herself securely under the light coverlet. "Good idea, but how's your wiring? Mine's still sparking."

Autis chuckled as he slid under the covers. "My wiring's good. Now where were we?"

"I believe I was about to demonstrate the procedures involved in making babies."

Each pulled the other into an eager embrace. They began where they left off.

Leaving for work, Autis asked from the doorway if Liv wanted to try for lunch with him.

"Sorry, I've been invited to a luncheon tea."

"Luncheon tea?"

"Yes. It seems the good ladies of Wadmalaw Island are eager to meet this new person in their midst—this writer of clever kitchen kitsch articles. In those circles I'm a celeb."

"Sounds like women of good sense and impeccable taste."

"They are."

"It's your enduring modesty that drives me to such heights of passion."

"I'll try not to change." Liv pretended to hang her head in embarrassment.

"Say hello to the ladies for me. Tell them I look forward to meeting them."

"You will soon. There's talk about gathering at *Saloon Sandi* this Saturday."

"Good, we'll get to meet neighbors. We've been living like hermits for nearly three months now, what with getting the house decent and setting up housekeeping."

"It has been a chore," Liv said, "but the place looks great—inside and out. I like what you've done with the grounds and yard."

"Thanks, six acres of grass is a lot to mow, but that new mower does the job."

"I like it. I also like the little viewing dock you've placed at the pond. There is so much wildlife here."

"Yeah, well, with the surrounding acreage of old forest, and the extensive waterfront, there's bound to be a good supply of critters. That pond provides a source of freshwater for the wildlife. Whoever laid out this property knew what he was doing—and he certainly had a plan in mind."

"I'll bet he was a farmer," Liv said.

That night came with the most vivid dream yet. A woman, not much more than a girl, tall, erect, with elegant African features and beautiful slender hands. A single gold ear ring pierced her right lobe. She spoke a melodious voice while pointing at Liv, "You. You are. We are." The woman reached out with both hands open, then brought them back and crossed them over her breast. She repeated the gesture, then lowered her head over her clasped hands, much as a woman holding a child she loved.

Liv sat up in bed, she felt warm, calm—and loved. She sat for a short time before realizing that her hands were crossed over her breasts.

Chapter 6

Saloon Sandi, a favored watering hole for those who live south of Charleston, shares a corner building with *Salon* Sandi at the intersection of Maybank and Main. The intersection is a southern gateway to several residential areas on the surrounding islands, and a major crossing to South Charleston. It is about two miles from the bridge to Wadmalaw Island. While most of Salon Sandi's customers were women, a number of men wouldn't go anywhere else for a haircut—or a drink. Locals marveled at the level of energy and skill Sandi put into the management of a pair of unrelated businesses.

Liv and Autis Oakley parked out front and followed the signs to a nondescript side door that opened to another world. Leaving behind the traffic sounds, it took several seconds to accustom their eyes to the hushed dim interior. Sandi had hired professionals to sound-soften the room. Voices were heard but they were muted by screens, hanging tapestries, and sound-absorbent wall and ceiling coverings. Soft music—a part of the background—came from several sources overhead. Wall hangings, pictures, draperies, and panels featuring shoreline and salt marsh scenes, everything was understated. Cocktail tables had at least one panel to shut conversation in or out. It was an ambience that approached the spiritual, causing more than one resident to remark "If Sandi closes, I'm outta here." One such wit settled on calling the place Chapel Sandi. It was an oasis; a quiet place where patrons could retreat and lick their wounds from the bruising catastrophes of modern living.

Loves were started and cemented at Saloon Sandi's, hurts healed, and vows exchanged. No less than three marriages had been performed there. She boasted that all three are alive and well. Two daughters and one son of patrons carried the name Sandi or Sandy. Rarely a month passed that Sandi didn't get a proposal of marriage. Local males swore that they would lynch any man who tried to take away "Our Sandi."

"Good managers," Sandi said to her guests when they put the question regarding her successful businesses. "I couldn't run either of these operations without smart, hard-working managers. Billie Mae runs the Salon like it was a destroyer and she's the commander. Her husband handles the Saloon with a skill I'd never be able to match; if Wilson were to quit, I'd have to shut down. They both make as much money as I do, and that's the way it should be."

Wilson and Billie Mae Edisto, seated at the opposite end of the table from Sandi, beamed under the praise.

Wilson interjected, "Don't forget Jonas. Neither of us would have a job if it weren't for him."

"Jonas?" Liv asked from her place across the long table.

"He's our chef. He's Thai, and there's nothing he can't do with food. He's got the chef gene. You keep on coming here and you'll see what I mean. He's a genius—a pain in the ass to work with—but a wonderfully talented cook. We have a lot of return trade from Charleston just because they want to discover what he's whipped up on any given night."

Liv and Autis were introduced around by one of the ladies from the tea event that Liv attended earlier that week. The membership of the group went from young middle-age professional people, up to and including recent retirees. They were congenial, polite and, to a person, appeared to be manifestly competent. Conversations were terse, pointed, and given to edgy humor. Most of the group seemed to like most of the group—and to be like most of the group.

As Liv joined the discussion of the dozen or so community members she felt a growing sense of warmth and acceptance. It was almost too easy. And then she saw Bambi.

Liv realized that she had been aware of the couple stashed away at the far corner of the bar, but it was only when she excused herself to the restroom that she came close enough to identify her new friend.

"Hi, Bambi. I didn't know it was you over here. Good to see you."

"Hey, Liv. How's it going?" Bambi's partner turned to face Liv, showing a very tan face and a shock of almost-white blond hair that hung straight to his shoulders.

"This is Gar Hanson. Gar, Liv."

"Hi, Gar. Good to meet you."

"Back at you, Liv. Bambi told me about your magazine article."

"Yes, I got some great shots at Bambi's place—to show the editors. They'll send a professional photographer later. The magazine's going to love the article. I'm looking forward to going back to her house. We didn't have time to go into the glass-blowing process though. I'm hoping to see her in action next Wednesday. I did see the finished product of some of her work—beautiful."

"Yeah, the lady' got talent. Looks, brains, and talent. It's just not fair for the rest of us."

"Why don't you join Autis and I at our table? There's room for more."

Bambi shook her head. "No, we're good here. Thanks though."

"You sure? It's a pretty friendly group, and I'd like for you to meet Autis."

"Some other time," Bambi answered.

"Okay. I'm on a mission right now. Where's the ladies' room?"

"Second door on the left." Bambi waved a spangled arm in the direction of a hallway.

"See you Wednesday. Good to meet you, Gar."

"Likewise," he raised a glass in salute, flashing a bright smile.

Finishing up in the clean well-appointed ladies' room, Liv checked her makeup and hair before returning to the group, as two women entered chatting happily. They each smiled at Liv and introduced themselves as Sally and Eilene. After determining that Liv was a new property owner, they inquired as to her husband's line of work, how many children they had, and so on.

"I see you met the community entertainer." Sally ventured.

Liv responded with a puzzled look.

"Bambi—the glass blower; we saw you two talking at the bar," Sally said.

"Yes, I'm doing a piece on her."

The women broke out in hilarious laughter as though Liv had shared really funny joke.

"That's great," Sally said, "A piece on the community piece."

"I don't know what you mean."

"Nothin' much, except that she's the town slut." Eilene answered. "It's said she blows glass during the day and other things at night. Anyway—she blows."

Liv felt herself redden. She took a deep breath and said, "I don't know you. But I do know her, and I like her. So far, I can't say that about you, ladies, so if you'll excuse me, I'll be on my way."

"Well, *excuse me,* Miss Hi-tone, holier than thou. We didn't mean to offend your tender sensitivities over your new friend," Eilene shot back.

Liv forced herself to remain calm as she responded in a low, soft voice. "I've only met her once, at her house where we shared a pot of tea and discussed a magazine article I'm doing. I found her to be honest, friendly, and with nothing bad to say about anybody. I wish I could say the same about you two." Liv turned and exited to the sound of derisive comments.

After the two ladies attended to their toilet and left, Sandi came out of a stall, washed up, and smiled into the mirror. "Well, we seem to have a solid citizen for our new neighbor. " When she returned to her guests she took a seat beside Liv.

"Tell me, is that hunk of yours as good as he looks?" she said, leaning into Liv's line of sight.

"Better."

"Not up for loan is he?"

"He tells me he's happy at home."

"Good for you, gal. Well, I guess I'll just have to remain unrequited." She leaned back in her chair and looked at Liv with a quizzical expression.

"What?" Liv's confrontation in the ladies room was still rankling.

"Grab up your man and follow me, I've got something I want to show you." She moved to the back of the room, away from line of sight, and waited as Liv disengaged Autis from an animated discussion with a cluster of new acquaintances.

When Liv and Autis caught up with her, Sandi was standing in front of a door with the sign "Neptune's Reef" over it. Emblazoned in red under the sign was the word "Private."

Sandi nodded at their approach and opened the door saying, "Welcome home."

They entered a small barroom made to look like an undersea version of a reef. The ceiling over the bar revealed what appeared to be the underside of a small boat. Sky and clouds were painted to appear as if the viewer was seeing them from the ocean floor. Fishing lines dangled from bobbers. Stuffed fish hung from invisible lines; coral and sea fans were scattered about. The viewer saw a fish-eye view of floating seagulls and a pelican. Neptune sat on a coral throne attended by a couple of mermaids. Cocktail tables and chairs were clever mock-ups of sea-floor objects—coral, sunken flotsam and jetsam, rubber tires and pilings lent an air of authenticity. The room revealed an abundance of planning and energy. The small bar was backed by a smoked glass wall surrounding a life-size oil of a standing nude. She was facing forward, hands on hips, feet nearly shoulder-width apart, looking directly into the eyes of the viewer.

Autis moved to the bar and gazed at the painting, then at Sandi, then back at the painting. "Wow, you really *are* a red-head aren't you?"

Liv heaved an exasperated sigh. "My husband—the Goat."

Sandi laughed a low husky chuckle. "That's where they all look first, dear—men and women alike. But then who wouldn't?"

"What a beautiful painting. Who's the artist?" Autis asked.

"I lived in a small village in Umbria for a couple of years—in another life. He was a struggling artist at the time. He pretended I was his muse, and I pretended he was right. But it wasn't meant to be."

"What happened?" Autis asked, still gazing at the painting.

"He found fame and fortune, and then lost the need for a muse. Our parting was poignant, tearful, and tender—but there were fish to fry..."

After a long pause, Autis turned away from the painting and looked directly into Sandi's eyes saying, "I'm sorry—truly. He must have loved you greatly to have done such a masterpiece. This painting could hang anywhere with pride."

"Thank you. He sent it to me after I returned to the states. I wrote him that I'd opened this bar and described it to him. Six months later I received this painting. He painted it from memory."

Autis stood slowly shaking his head.

"What?" Sandi asked.

"I only hope that someday I can do something like that painting to show Liv how much I love her. How many people in the world possess such an offering?"

Sandi covered her mouth with her hand. Her eyes began to tear as she shook her head in silence. Finally, she said softly, "Thank you." Turning to Liv, she added, "Guard him with your life, for if someone else doesn't steal him from you, I will."

Liv moved to join Autis at the bar. "He's covered."

Dabbing at her eyes with a tissue, Sandi nodded in acknowledgement.

The door opened and a couple entered, and Liv was surprised to see Bambi and Gar. Sandi gave a familiar wave as the newcomers came to join the threesome under the painting. Liv introduced Autis, as Gar moved behind the counter. "Drinks on me. Name your poison."

After the drinks were served they all settled at the bar. Sandi glanced from Bambi to Liv. "This room is private to friends only—and on occasion, to a guest of a friend. Liv, I've never invited anyone to join on such short notice. In fact, some have pointedly asked for entry after a year of patronage and been refused. Usually, they stop coming altogether after that. There's no bartender, you fix your own drinks and settle up at the end of the month. I figure most people probably pay me more than is owed, but that's the nature of the kind of people I've invited to join us. You and Autis are welcome members."

"Thank you," Liv responded. But I wouldn't trust the goat around open bottles of whisky with beautiful women around. You might want to reconsider."

"Oh, I think he'll do just fine. She leaned against Autis and placed a kiss on his cheek."

"Watch her, Liv. She's a shark around other women's men." Bambi flashed a gat-tooth grin.

"Yeah, she tries to steal me from Bambi every chance she gets, but I remain true blue." Gar smiled.

Liv raised her glass in toast. "I don't know what kind of coven we've gotten mixed up in, but it looks challenging."

Chapter 7

Liv sat in wonder as Bambi heated glass tubing over a blue flame. The glass glowed and moved under the tools and breath of the artisan. The glass did Bambi's bidding from the moment she turned on the burners.

Liv watched and photographed Bambi as she turned out small glass trinkets and figures: birds, palm trees, automobiles, and action figures of children.

"My God, this is a perfect example of controlled chaos. You manage the glass as it tells you what it wants to be."

"That's one way of looking at it," Bambi answered. "Yes, controlled chaos; that's what my life is."

Liv paused with her camera up, but away from her face. Most of us live like that, at least sometime. We balance will and fate."

"Maybe, but it seems like Fate kicks the crap out of Will most of the time," Bambi leaned to turn off the gas lines leading to her burners. "Let's take a break. I could use a Firefly."

"A what?"

"A Firefly." Seeing the look of puzzlement on Liv's face, Bambi added, "It's a drink."

"What's in it?"

"Wait here," Bambi called over her shoulder as she headed to her kitchen. Sounds of glassware, the refrigerator ice crusher, and glasses being filled from a bottle drifted up the hallway. Bambi returned with a tray holding tall glasses of iced tea with a lemon slice on each glass; a bowl of cheese straws, and a dish of large strawberries.

Liv received one of the glasses and took a sip through its straw.

"Ice tea? You promised a drink and you bring iced tea?" Liv said in mock indignation.

"Take another drink."

Liv sampled her drink again, and then her face morphed into a broad smile.

"What is this, really?"

"It's Firefly, a vodka drink made by the Firefly distillery who shares the property with Irvin House Vineyards on Wadmalaw Island. Locals call it 'Plantation Tea' after the Charleston Tea Plantation. It's made from Charleston tea, Wadmalaw vodka, and Louisiana cane sugar. Pure South it is. The distillery and vineyard invites visitors and offers tours. You and Autis should break loose and give 'em a try."

"It's a wonderful drink," Liv took a long pull at her straw. "Where do you get it?" Another pull brought the liquid to the halfway mark in the glass.

"At the liquor store next to the Pig."

"The Pig? Oh, the Piggly Wiggly Grocery."

"Yeah. After we finish our drinks I'll blow some glass for your article."

Half an hour later Bambi put on tinted goggles followed by a plastic shield that covered her entire face.

"Why do you use goggles and a shield too?" Liv asked.

"These goggles protect my eyes from the ultraviolet rays that glowing glass gives off, while the shield protects my face in case of accident or a splatter." Bambi donned protective clothing as well.

She quickly turned out a pair of stemmed wine glasses and presented them to Liv. "Tonight you and Autis can drink from these."

"Thanks. I'll treasure them. I have nothing to give in return."

"You already have—these are my payment." Bambi began working on a vase as she talked with Liv. She heated, blew, and shaped with effortless competence.

"Payment? For what?"

Bambi fixed her work in a clamp where it could stay over the heat, and then she turned to Liv.

"For accepting me as I am, and for just being who you are. For friending me."

"Thank you, but why would I do otherwise?"

"You and Sandi are the only ones who have—oh, and Gar, but he seriously wants to get in my pants. Actually, he wants to make my pants a part of his life—permanent-like."

"I don't believe that. I mean, I believe the part about Gar, it's obvious he's head over heels for you, but I have a hard time with the idea that you lack friends."

"You know, you're the first person I've met who didn't glom on to my teeth and stare at 'em the whole time we talk. Seems like everybody else—that's all they see is this mouth full of snags and gaps. And everybody feels free to tell me right off that I ought to go see a dentist."

"That's none of their damn business," Liv said, holding up an empty glass.

"You're about the only person in the world who feels that way. Everyone I meet sees themselves as a missionary; mouth missionaries is what they are. Damn them to hayel." Her eyes flashed with anger as she refilled Liv's glass from a small pitcher, and replaced the lemon slice.

"What about Sandi and Gar?"

"We had our rocky moments, but they quickly came to understand what was going on. When they saw everybody giving me mouth advice, and laughin' about me behind my back, they came down on my side."

"Hell, Bambi, I've laughed about you, but it wasn't about your teeth."

"What did you find so damn funny about me?" Bambi sat her glass down and focused on Liv with narrowed eyes.

"Well, you're so beautiful. I don't think I've ever seen a more lovely body than yours—but it's more than that. It's the way you move. The confidence you own. You have a way about yourself that—frankly—turns me on. If I was that way, gal, I'd come after you."

"Well, dayem me. Here I was beginnin' to get pissed off at you." Tears welled up in Bambi's eyes, and she blushed. "Thank you." She moved to sit beside Liv and gave her a hug and a light kiss on the cheek. "That is sweet. No female's ever said things like that to me. Guys do all the time, but they want to get their knob polished, is all. The gals only want to put me down."

"What is that? What's going on there?"

"You heard what Sally and Eilene said. I blow glass during the day and anything else I can find to blow at night."

"How did you know that?"

"Sandi heard 'em. She was in one of the stalls. 'Said she heard you telling those two off."

"They were acting like jerks—probably had too much to drink."

"I'll tell you my side, if you care to hear it."

Liv gave her a wicked grin. "What you blow is your business."

Bambi tipped back in a rich laugh that came all the way from her toes.

"Dayem, gal. You are a piece. Now I want to tell you for sure."

"Refill first. But, right now I need a pit stop. Point me to the powder room." Liv rose, a little unsteady.

Bambi pointed the way to the rear of the house.

Liv moved down a hallway to the back of the house while Bambi returned to the kitchen. She made two more Plantation Teas, this time cutting Liv's glass half and half with iced tea from her refrigerator. She had a worried frown.

The two settled on the settee, doffed their shoes and shared a cushioned stool.

"Okay, here's the deal. I was at Sandi's late one night when I met this fine looking gentleman. We talked. He was a good listener—a huge plus in today's world of men. I had another drink, and another. Make a long story short—we wound up in his apartment. It wasn't really his but he said it was, along with some cock and bull story about getting divorced.

"We got in the sack and tried to get it on, but the gentleman couldn't get it up so I helped him out. You might say I talked his little friend into coming to attention for the task at hand. We did get it on but it lasted maybe ninety seconds before he got it off. In about another thirty seconds he was sound asleep. I took a hot shower, dressed and went home.

"Seems that the gentleman only remembered himself into thinking he got a complete blowjob—by a girl he picked up in the bar; seems also that he likes to brag around, which he did. It was some time before I could face going back to that bar. I only started going back after Sandi invited me. However, all the guys were lining up for blowjobs. Married men were the worst of all. Incidentally, my lover boy wasn't getting a divorce, didn't own the apartment— it belonged to an out-of-town friend—and he turned into a good listener only to con me into thinking he was something he wasn't. What he *was* in fact, was Sally's husband, Freddie. Word got back to Sally, and she has since told the world that I'm an easy lay and a cocksucker."

Liv took her friend's hand in her own.

"And that's the whole story. 'Cept for the part where Sandi made the Saloon off-limits to Freddie, and the fact that she called up Sally the night after you told her off, and let her know that she and Eileen were no longer welcome in either the Saloon or the Salon."

"I didn't mean to get anyone kicked out. I just don't want to hear people put down my friends." Liv frowned at this new information.

"I have to tell you this: The way you answered those bitches, and the way Autis responded to Sandi's painting, was what got you accepted into Neptune's Reef on your first visit. Autis passed the test. Most guys act like jerks when Sandi shows them the painting. That's some feller you got there, lady."

"You ain't wrong there, gal. He's a rock."

"You're a lucky woman."

"We're happy." Liv glowed under the praise for her man. She looked thoughtfully at her new friend and said, "I think we should get to know each other better; how about if you and Gar come over for dinner one night next week?"

"You're on. But you'll have to ask Gar separately. We don't date." Seeing Liv's raised eyebrows, Bambi continued. "I won't go there right now. I've already told you more about myself than I have anyone else 'cept Sandi. I'll fill you in later."

"Not my business."

"Good. Ask Gar separately, and let me know what night. What's the attire?"

"Dress blues and tennis shoes good for you?"

"Good 'nuff." Bambi pointed at Liv's empty glass. "I'm going to cut you off here. Can you drive okay?"

"Like Autis is fond of saying after too many drinks: I can drive the Cuckin' Far."

Chapter 8

The following week-end, Liv and Autis hosted Bambi and Gar on the high deck overlooking their back yard.

"Nice view of the sound from here," Gar gazed out past the yard to the salt marsh and beyond to the water. Weekend boaters were trying the spring winds with crisp white sails. "This deck looks new," he added. "Was it here when you bought the house?"

"Autis designed and built it." Liv smiled with apparent pleasure. "I can't imagine this house now without this split-level decking. I think we spend more time here than in the house."

"I sure do admire it."

"Thank you," Autis said. "It opens the house to the outdoors, and there's so much to see from this high deck. There's heavy woods to both sides all the way from the road to the salt marsh. We have all kinds of birds, and there are rabbits, deer, squirrel, raccoon. Bear live on the island too, but we've never seen one. They pretty much stay back in the woods."

"Well, you've got about the nicest, most livable house I've been in," Gar said. "I like it more than my Four Aces."

"Four Aces?"

"Yeah, that's my sailboat. It's a Morgan Out-Island 41, ketch-rigged. I won her in a poker game."

"Four Aces."

"You got it. The man didn't need his boat, and I needed a place to live."

"How do you like living on a boat?"

"I like it fine. Some would find it cramped, but I was raised around boats, and I don't mind the close quarters. Besides, with an ample larder, full tanks, and a clean hull I can go anywhere in the world that has a deep saltwater port. Four Aces has a blue water keel, which doesn't make it much suitable for sailing in the sound like those fellers out there." Gar pointed at the small sailboats working the wind in the distance. "But I do love blue water sailing. In this fine weather we should go out one weekend. We can catch an early morning outgoing tide and get through the pass pretty easy." He polished off the last of his lunch, saying to the hostess, "Mighty tasty." Liv smiled with a nod in his direction.

"I been eating pork all my days," Bambi said. "I grew up on pig. But this pork roast is the best I've ever eaten. How did you do that?"

Gar rose from the table and went to the downwind side of the deck and lit up. He smoked with an intensity that was unflattering.

"It's a nasty habit he won't even consider quitting," Bambi said to her hostess. "And I can't abide bein' around him when he stinks of stale cigarette smoke. Don't people know how bad that smells? My pappy and grand pappy smoked, but mama made 'em do it outside. They never smelled of stale smoke," she said as she rose to help Liv clean off the table. Carrying a tray of dishes back into the house she said, "And could you please tell me how you fixed those beets? I've never had them fixed in orange sauce like that. Lord, I'm stuffed." She patted her tummy.

When Gar was finished he snuffed his cigarette on his heel, stripped the paper and scattered the left-over tobacco to the wind, putting the filter back into the cigarette pack. Only then did he join the others at the glass deck table.

"This is some place you've got here," he said. "It's not just the view, it's the way things are laid out. I like how the lawn slopes out to the marsh; hardly any slope at all, just enough for rain water to drain away. Whoever laid out these grounds knew what he was doing. It looks like the house is built up against and into a shell mound—putting it way above high water. And then you're protected from the north wind by the pines, and from the summer sun by those big maples on its south side. It seems to me that some thought went into this house." Nodding a thank you to the fresh beer Autis handed him, he turned to Liv who had returned to her chair after clearing the table. "But you were about to confess your pork cooking secret. I'd like to hear it because it was grand tasty, and, living alone, like I'm apparently doomed to do the rest of my natural life," he said glancing at Bambi, "I need to know how to make toothsome dishes such as that."

"Listen to you, sucking all the sympathy you can get out of your stubborn ways," Bambi scoffed. "Go ahead, darlin'," she turned to Liv. "Just ignore my pitiful friend here—who's lying in a bed of his own making."

Liv and Autis smiled with enjoyment at the banter between their guests.

"Cooking a pork shoulder that way for the first time is an act of courage," Liv said.

"How's that?" Bambi asked.

"Here's the recipe. Preheat your oven to five hundred degrees. Dredge—and I mean dredge—the pork shoulder with powdered cinnamon. Cook it uncovered at five hundred degrees for fifteen minutes, and then turn the heat down to three fifty and let it cook out the rest of the time depending on the size of the roast. Don't put any salt on it, and don't poke any holes in it. What happens is that the high heat sears the cinnamon, killing most of its flavor and making a sort of a crust. That seals the roast and locks in the juices—there won't be any juice on the bottom of the roasting pan. You end up with a very juicy pork roast with just a hint of cinnamon flavor. It needs salt, but your guests can do that to their own taste."

"I've got it." Bambi tapped her temple with a nicely manicured finger. I'd like to try it sometime, if I knew anybody I care enough about to cook for."

"To the quick she cuts. See how she treats me?" Gar intoned. "And all I've ever done is place her on a pedestal."

"Yeah, that's where...Who's that?" Bambi said pointing to the heavy woods bordering the north side of the property.

They all turned to look just as a white figure wearing a large straw hat vanished into the undergrowth.

"That's the mystery lady who lives in an old mansion next door." Liv answered.

"Mystery lady?" Bambi sidled close to Liv.

"Yes, Freedom Covers is her name, and the only reason we know that is because my nosy husband took it upon himself to violate federal law, and snoop in her mailbox beside the road. We tried visiting her but she never comes to the door."

Bambi looked puzzled. "You say that like you know she was home."

"We did, one time, because we were in the woods near her house and saw her at her back porch stoop. She spotted us and quickly ducked into the house. She has a lot of cats and was feeding them at the stoop. We went right to her front door and rang the bell. No one came. Autis went to the back door and knocked—no luck."

"I'm gettin' goose bumps," Bambi said, briskly rubbing her arms. "What does the house look like?"

Autis grinned. "Hell, Bambi, it looks almost exactly like the big house on the hill above the Bates Motel—you know, the one where Anthony Perkins kept his mom." He paused in amusement over Bambi wide-eyed attention. "Except it's in worse shape than the Bates home, shutters falling away, some roof shingles missing, torn screens, long vanished paint. It's a handyman's de-light." Autis and Gar were enjoying the effects of his description.

"Knock it off, you moron, can't you see that Bambi is frightened." She took Bambi's hand. "Sorry, Bambi. Now you see what I have to put up with. If I..." She was cut off by the sound of a barely perceptible high sound coming from the direction of their neighbor's house. It was somewhere between animal and human.

"Shit, what is that? Autis moved to the railing nearer the wood just as there came an answering wail from the west woods"

Bambi walked quickly to the door leading into the house, and turned to look from the opened door back at her companions who were standing with silent parted lips.

"Swamp birds." Gar scoffed as he withdrew a cigarette from his pack.

"Really? What kind?" Autis turned from the woods to face Gar.

"Hell, who knows, there's so many. I know there's a lot of birds, and they make a lot of strange sounds."

"That didn't sound like anything with feathers I know of." Liv said as she went to join Bambi.

Autis headed to the doorway. "How about a beer, Gar.?"

Sunday afternoon passed in soft friendly banter and joking among the foursome who found they were rapidly cementing a good friendship. The easterly winds held true, keeping the mosquitoes and no-see-ums to a tolerable level.

Around three o'clock Autis invited Gar to the basement bar for a game of pool. He called upstairs to Liv, who had taken Bambi to demonstrate her grandmother's 1903 peddle sewing machine. On the way to the basement door, Gar's glance fell on Autis' gun cabinet standing in a corner. He went to the cabinet and studied the row of gleaming weaponry.

"This is quite a collection you've got. Is that an M-1?

"Yes. It was my grandfather's. He was a paratrooper with the 82nd when they dropped in during the Normandy invasion. He said he cussed, cleaned, and cradled it all the way across Germany. His best buddy was in supply and he helped Grandpa get some items home after the war. Grandpa kept an 8 millimeter Mauser Model 1898, a German officer's Luger, and a B.A.R.— Browning Automatic Rife."

"You've got a B.A.R?"

"Yes. I grew up with these weapons. I've been firing them since I was six. Mom was really antsy about that, but Dad was a Special Forces officer in Vietnam, and between him and grandpa, Mom's objections didn't stand a chance."

"That's quite a story."

"That's nothing; Grandpa's dad fought in World War I. He was a dough-boy. Grandpa was in World War II, Dad was in Nam, and I was in Desert Storm. It's a long tradition; I've got ancestors who fought in the Civil War." As Autis unlocked his gun cabinet, Gar called out, "Hey, Bambi, you need to see this. Your best friend's husband is a gun-nut."

"There are worse things—he could be a ne'er-do-well sailboat bum." Bambi called back.

Gar turned to Autis, who had snapped the lock shut and returned the key to his pocket.

"I was yanking your chain, Autis. I've been a squirrel hunter since I was six. Rifle, shotgun, bow, I can use them all. I haven't hunted since I was in my early twenties—I just don't want to kill anything else, but I still enjoy target practice. How about showing me that M-1? I've always wanted to shoot one of those."

"Sure." The keys came back out.

The cavernous living room had a high ceiling and a side stairwell that led to the second floor walkway that opened into the upstairs rooms. The women had finished with the sewing machine and were standing at the railing which overlooked the living room. "Oh, God, they're going to start a gun club," Liv said to Bambi. "We're about to become Weapons Widows. Oh no, it's too late," Liv said as Autis withdrew his grandfather's weapon from its lock-up in the gun rack.

"Let's you and me go out to the pier," Liv said to Bambi. "We've got a nice view over the marsh."

"I'd like that. I need to walk off some of that roast."

Turning, Liv said to Gar who was trying the action on Autis' M-1. "Gar, don't let him talk you into betting over pool. The man's a shark—a sure sign of his misspent youth." She turned back to Bambi and led her out the French doors. They descended the stairs to the yard and trekked the hundred yards where the lawn met the saw grass and scrub at the edge of the salt marsh.

"Watch out for fire ants," Liv cautioned. The damned things are every-where. Autis sprays for them, but they put up new nests overnight." They crossed the lawn to the edge of the salt marsh and were just about to step up onto the board walkway, when Bambi stopped cold in her tracks and turned to her right. "Something is out there," she said.

"What is it?"

"I don't know what it is, but it's under that cluster of palms," Bambi said, pointing to an area about thirty yards from the trail.

They walked over to the small island of palms and small cedars.

"There, what is that?" Bambi pointed at a large flat rise in the ground.

"Oh, those are some kind of rock formations. Autis discovered them the first day we walked the grounds. We think it's some coral formation washed up during a violent storm."

Bambi took a board that was left by the tide, and scraped a layer of leaves away. "See. It's rectangular like—oh my God, it's a grave. This is a grave cap-stone. This ain't coral. It's tabby. Man made. Look close, there's another," she said pointing to a similar one. "Oh, here's one." She turned to Liv and said, "Honey, you got you a slave graveyard here."

Chapter 9

"Tabby? What's tabby?" Liv asked as they hastened back—the trip to the dock being forgotten.

"I keep on forgettin'— you're not from around here," Bambi said. "Tabby is a construction material, sort of like concrete; it's made from crushed shell, lime, and ash, mixed with water. Oh yeah, and sand. It's been used around here for centuries. Tabby was cheap, easy to make, and there was plenty of shell about."

They reached the top deck where they had just finished lunch earlier. Liv said, "I need a drink. You want a Firefly?"

"Sure wouldn't hurt none." Bambi leaned against the railing looking back at the site they had just investigated.

Liv returned shortly with tall glasses of Firefly over crushed ice.

"I called down to the pub for the men to come up." Liv said, joining Bambi at the railing. "Are you okay? You're pale as a ghost?"

"Lord, honey, don't say ghost. That's a fearsome thought."

"Sorry. I was just concerned for you. Why Bambi, you're shaking like a leaf in a storm. Let's sit down."

"I'm all right. I'm good here at the rail."

Liv put her arm over Bambi's shoulder and pulled her close.

"You're not all right. You're pale and shaking, and you feel cold. Let's go in. Come on." She took Bambi by the arm and led her through the sliding French doors and to a couch in the living room. She was just putting a throw over her shivering friend when the men came up from the pub.

"What's up?" Gar asked. Then he saw Bambi on the couch. "Good grief, what's the matter?"

"She's had a scare, and it's put her in a state of shock."

"Call 911." Autis said.

"No. No. I'm okay. I just had sort of a dizzy spell there."

Gar seated himself near Bambi. "What frightened her?" he asked, lifting her legs and putting them across his lap, and then seeing that her legs and feet were carefully wrapped with the comforter.

"On the way to the boardwalk, she sensed something, a presence it seems, off to the right of the trail. When we investigated, she identified what she is sure is a slave graveyard. That distressed her very much—so distressed we nearly didn't make it back up to the deck. I think we need a doctor."

"No doctor. I'm getting better. I just felt a little faint, but I'm getting my senses back. That Firefly helped, Liv. Thanks."

"Your color's starting to return. You were pale as...white as a sheet," Liv said.

"It wasn't just the shock of finding graves," Bambi said. "There's something else there—a sad, angry presence. Didn't you feel it?"

"Not at all. Autis and I have walked by that site several times, day and night, and I've never sensed anything other than the beauty of the marsh around me. I've never felt anything sinister about this house or grounds. Oh! The voices." Liv shot a quick look at Autis who was standing behind the couch where Bambi lay. She and Autis stared at each other for a moment.

"What voices?" Bambi asked.

Autis spoke up. "Liv has heard voices coming up from the pub late at night. I've never heard them, but Liv hears them whenever she wakes up in the middle of the night. Like I said, I've not heard them, but I don't doubt that Liv has. She's no fool, and is about the most commonsense person I know. I mean, the woman's got to have good sense—look who she married," he ended with a grin.

Liv shook her head and rolled her eyes. One mistake, I make one mistake, and the world never lets me forget. Mother tried to tell me..."

"My gal's dying of fright here, and you guys are making jokes." Gar said with a smile. He added. "I guess you-all know that Bambi is psychic as well as a palm reader. I've seen her come up with some stuff about people so dead-on that it gave me chill bumps. She's supersensitive to what most folks would call 'paranormal happenings' around us. I've seen her in action enough to believe that what she does is honest and true."

"I'm okay now," Bambi said, removing the comforter and standing up, a little unsteadily at first. She took a deep breath, saying, "Let's go back outside. Fresh air and sunshine..."

From the deck the foursome stood side by side looking out at the site where the graves lay. The breeze seemed chillier than earlier, and the creatures of the forest and sky were silent.

"What makes you so sure they are graves?" Autis asked Bambi.

"I've seen the likes of them before, and they're always located at water's edge, just like those you've got."

"That makes no sense, why would they do that? I mean, high tides and storms would wash them away."

Gar answered Liv's query. "I've got this archeologist friend, Buff Shellman, who tells me that the slaves wanted it that way so they could be at the water's edge when the boat came to take their souls back to Africa. If they couldn't reach the boat they would be trapped in the place that enslaved them, never to return home. They would be in purgatory, locked forever between heaven and hell. There are waterside graves all over these islands, must have been thousands at one time. Storm and tide have claimed most of them. A few remain in protected coves like we have here." He started toward the steps leading to the lawn. "You want to show them to me, Autis?"

The ladies watched as their men tracked to the little rise in the land that had protected the graves for over a hundred and fifty years from flood tides and storm-driven waves.

Bambi took a sip of Firefly. "This place is so beautiful. You've got high forests, you're hidden from the road, a quarter of a mile away, by trees and shrubbery, and then you're up high overlooking the sound and salt marsh. I envy you. I don't ever expect to have a place this grand."

"We were lucky. The Nobles were desperate to leave. In fact, Mrs. Nobles had already packed up and left for her mother's. Mr. Nobles was batching it here until he could unload the property. We still can't believe that he grabbed up our counter-offer. The realtor told us he would laugh in our face when we offered it up, but it was really the best we could do."

"Well you done good, hon. Most people would give an arm to live here." Bambi set her drink aside on the deck railing. "I'm sorry about my giddy act just now. I feel that I've made myself look like a fool."

"Only in the eyes of fools. You're our friend, and I feel I know you well enough to say that you're no fool. Who of us hasn't at some time been scared to the point of fainting? I know I have in the past, and expect I will at sometime in the future. No apologies among friends and, I might say, it ends here."

"Thank you."

The ladies watched as the men poked and probed around the grave sites. They stood a while and talked. Gar pointed several times out to the sound, gesturing during his conversation.

"Gar seems a really decent fellow. I think you've got a good one there."

"Thanks, but I don't *have* him, and I won't until he grows up. I don't know what happened that locked him forever into an adolescent state, but something has. He's intelligent, hard-working, and thoroughly decent, but he has almost no sense of direction or personal responsibility for his decisions. He's like a feather in the wind. I can't accept his proposal. I've heard it said that when a man marries he gets a wife, but when a woman marries, she gets a life style. I'm not interested in Gar's life style. I grew up a poor mountain girl, and I seen poverty. I grew up in a house full of brothers, and never learned much lady-like ways until I went off to college. I know empty stomach, no shoes, and sharp ways. All my life I tried to push away from that. I can't even abide to make a visit to my growing up place in Virginia, as much as I want to see my folks; and I can't get them to leave the mountains to visit or stay with me. So, no Gar for me, thank you. He is what he is, and I won't ask him to be something else just to please me. To make it worse, he says he won't bed down with me outside of wedlock. So we're at what some would call an impasse. We're impassed all to hayel and back." She paused, took a deep breath, then added. "And that's all I'm going to say on that."

"I didn't mean to pry. Like I said before, what you blow is your own business." This brought a laugh from the both of them.

Bambi took a drink of *Fly*, then asked. "Now, what's this business about voices in the pub?"

Chapter 10

"Like Autis said, I hear them late at night. There's no pattern to it. If I waken in the middle of the night, which I sometimes do, I can hear them. It sounds like people talking, just talking, downstairs in the pub. When I go down to investigate, as soon as I get to the head of the stairs, they stop."

"Gal, you scarin' the poop out of me. Sounds like you got a coven under your house. Damn, you got a graveyard in your lawn, and a coven in your basement. Are you trying to run me off? That's it, isn't it? You want to get rid of me, so you set me up."

"That's right, I placed those capstones out there just to make sure you won't be coming around anymore," Liv said, grinning.

"Well, it's not workin,' darlin.' I been doing some asking around, since you told me you bought this house, and let me tell you what I've found out."

"Seems like a psychic wouldn't need to 'ask around.' Couldn't you just dip into some psychic powers and come up with whatever information is needed?"

"It doesn't work that way, smart ass. Here I am tryin' to be a friend, and I get all this crap." Bambi placed a gentle hand on Liv's forearm. "You know, that's one of the reasons I like you; we can talk this way to each other and still keep the friendship. It's like havin' the sister I've always wanted. I've only had brothers, and they're no one to talk to."

Liv placed her hand over Bambi's and nodded in understanding. "Okay—Sis—what did you discover?"

"Jason Maxton started this creaky old house of yours in 1830 and it was finished by his son, Alexander Maxton, in the 1840s or there-abouts. The Maxtons grew indigo and rice. They also raised cattle, horses, and hogs—everbody raised hogs back then. Jason's holdings went into several thousand acres and almost a hundred slaves. He even had major interests in shipping out of Charleston Harbor. But most of all, he was one ornery son-of-a-bitch. Everbody feared him. Those who didn't fear him, hated him. Three times men tried to kill him but got themselves killed. He got wounded once but survived."

"Jesus, where did you get all this?"

"I got a friend who has a friend. She wrote a paper on the indigo trade in the South. It don't paint a pretty picture. I keep on hearing about how most of the plantation owners were kind to their slaves, but think about that just a second. What's wrong with the phrase, 'kind to their slaves'?"

"I get it. But I got it a long time ago."

"Well, I was raised in the South and didn't get it until I could think for myself. My daddy and his kin were all Kluxers at heart if not deed."

"I've got to stop you here. I need to know why you're doing all this. You've put some work into getting this information; I need know why you're so interested."

"Damn. You Yankees are hard-hearted folks. But here it is. Number one: I like you a lot—Sis. Also, this house has a local reputation that gets gossiped about a lot. It has a lot of history, most of it bad. It's been called 'haunted,' 'carsed,' 'vengeful,' and generally fearsome. Number three: As a spiritual person I'm interested in such things. But most of all, because you're my friend I want to help protect you—and Autis—from harm."

"Okay, I'm sorry I sounded like an ungrateful bitch. My public life as a writer frequently puts me in contact with a lot of materialist types. People who like to think of themselves as 'realists.'"

"I understand. Where I come from we call them 'Yankees,' but that's another story. Let's get back to this hexed house of yours. You see, as a spiritualist, I believe in such things. I know most folks say they don't, but when you get right down to it, most do believe in mysterious forces that nobody understands. With the reputation this house has, there has got to be a reason for it. It may not be a reason that we can understand, or even see clearly, but it's there. As a spiritualist I want to find out what it is."

"Reason number five."

"Bambi nodded agreement. "You counted?"

"Well, from my 'Yankee' point of view, you are curious about such things and you want to satisfy your curiosity about this house."

"Yes."

"Why in the hell didn't you say so instead of doing this dance around your sacred Southern roots? Let's find out what makes this house tick. I'm curious too—Sis. What else did you find out?"

"Well, now it goes to rumor—as handed down by slaves—that Alexander Maxton killed his mean bastard of a father and two older brothers who'd been making his life miserable."

"He killed off his family?"

"Not exactly. The slave version is that he didn't prevent an Indian attack until it was too late to save his family.

"Why would he do such a thing? Weren't families supposed to be close back then?"

"Your guess is as good as mine, but who do you think wound up the owner of a few thousand acres of farmland and over a hundred slaves?"

"Oh. I see. Alexander went from being the youngest son and family goat to the head of the house and all the holdings—all in one day."

"Yep. Good old Alexander Maxton who, it turns out, was really one mean, sadistic bastard. His pappy was only mean because he came from hard circumstances. Alexander, on the other hand, had a hobby."

"You said this is rumor."

"I've talked to local historians who told me that there's a lot of support for Maxton's sadism in the form of neighbor's letters, notes, and court proceedings. It would take some digging to assemble the true story. That's the bad news."

Falling for the leading statement, Liv asked: "What's the good news?"

"The good news is that this gal had found her way to a community college that helped her get a high school diploma, and a two year college degree, where I graduated top of my class. That got me a scholarship to Virginia Polytech that led to a bachelors degree in research."

"Research? What...?"

"Historical research. I was a good ol Southern girl who was interested in our glorious past. I needed to find out things."

"What did you discover?"

"A lot. I found that the past wasn't glorious. I also found that a girl could screw her way to any number of assistantships and scholarship funds and worked my ass off doing just that. I was too insecure to realize that my brains would have gotten me just as far—probably farther. And I also found that the greatest phonies in the world are college professors."

Liv reflected a moment and said, "I've often wondered why I didn't get a couple of assistantship positions that everyone knew I deserved."

"'Assistantship positions?' That's a hoot, honey. The favored 'assistantship position' is on her knees. And I don't see any calluses on your knees, Darlin'."

"I came close once. He was a handsome devil. Smoked the prerequisite pipe, wore tweeds, and affected a British air. But I caught him in the act in his office with a freshman coed. I can still see the scene, him with his pants down around his shoes."

"If you'd been at VPI, I might have been that coed."

"Okay, so you've got background in historical research. I guess that brings us to number six on your list."

"I guess it does. I need to know not only what's here, but what's been here. Personally, I don't believe you can know the present until you understand the past."

"I agree with that sentiment. So, it sounds like you're going to make me your next research project."

"That too."

"Too—as in 'also'?"

"Yes. I want to write a paper, and maybe a book about this area."

"All this is blowing up in my face. We just bought a house—a place that we wanted to make into a home. I thought we were well along the way, and now this *slave graves* thing comes up. I don't know what to do about that. I have nightly discourse taking place in my basement, and a spooky doorbell…"

"Doorbell? What's going on there?"

"The doorbell rings on its own. No pattern. It just rings when it feels like ringing. I go to the door, and there's no one there. It's kinda fun, actually." Seeing that Bambi was about to say something obvious, Liv added. "We checked out the wiring."

Bambi nodded, and then asked, "Do you have a digital camera?"

"All of sudden you have the urge to photograph something? What does that have to do with what we're talking about?"

"Maybe a lot. Have you heard of orbs?"

"No, is that another Southern tradition?"

"Orbs, smart ass, are faint spheres of light that can be photographed at night. They are mostly found over graves."

"I get it. You want to check out our orbs?"

"I want to see if there are orbs over your slave graves."

"They're not *my* slaves. Stop calling them that."

"Sorry. *The* grave sites."

"We have a digital camera. Autis has been taking a lot of 'before and after' shots of the house. Some are pretty impressive. It's a cheap camera, but it does the job. Point and shoot."

"Well, Gar is a camera buff. In fact, he ought to go professional. He's got some good equipment. Can we come out one night and do some photography?"

"You're going out there at *night?* Look at what visiting the graves in broad daylight did to you."

"A body's got to confront her fears. Besides, I'll be prepared; and nothing bothers Gar." She thought on what she had just said. "I don't know if that's a good thing or a bad thing."

Later that week, Liv couldn't resist the temptation to test Bambi's notion about orbs. She took a beach chair, a flashlight, camera, and Bob out to the graves and waited for something—she didn't know what. Autis was away at an elevator convention. Liv laughed out loud as she recalled their conversation two days past.

"Elevator convention—that's how architects get high? You guys really live on the edge."

"I don't need elevator highs, I'm married to a woman I love." Autis snapped his suitcase latch.

Sitting in the salt marsh mists, Liv reflected on the exchange with Autis. "Bob, we'll stay until I finish my wine, then we're outta here." The pointer wagged at hearing his name, then went back to sleep.

Fifteen minutes later, Liv drained the last of her chardonnay, stood, folded her chair and took one last look around. "C'mon, Bob." The muscular dog rose into a stretch and moved to Liv's side as she started to follow her flashlight beam to the house. She sensed a faint sound behind her after she had taken a couple of steps. Liv wheeled around, and illuminated what appeared to be six columns of clear air in the fog. Five were adult-size, and one was the size of a six-year-old that seemed attached to one of the columns. Liv dropped her folded lawn chair and reached down to touch Bob's head. Sensing unease, Bob moved to lean against his mistress. A minute passed, then two.

"Who are you?" The apparitions appeared to quiver at the sound of her voice. They bunched closer together.

Liv took two steps toward them and asked, "What do you want?" She took another step, bringing them to within six feet. Another step. They faded back, and the spaces they occupied filled with mist. Gone. Liv turned and began the walk to the house. She tripped and fell over the lawn chair, scraping a shin.

"Damn," she rose quickly and ran to the Pub door.

Inside she slammed the door and threw the latch. Her breath was coming in gasps as her heart pounded. Bob was excited from the dash to the house. He was ready for a romp in the yard. Liv leaned against a support column and placed a hand over her thudding heart.

"Damn." She knelt beside Bob and wrapped an arm around his neck. "You're good company, you know that?" Bob pushed against her. Liv waited for her heart to stop pounding before standing up. She rose, took a deep breath, and exhaled. It was only then, she realized that there was something else in the dimly lit room. She couldn't see or hear it, but it had a dank, earth odor. Liv started, collected herself, and walked to the center of the room.

"I'm here. Where are you?" Slowly, the odor vanished. Liv felt emboldened. "Come out, I mean you no harm." Bob was looking at her with his head cocked.

Liv went to the fridge and poured another glass of wine. She sat on a bar stool and waited, her eyes accustomed to the dark. Bob climbed onto, and became one with the couch.

Liv sat and waited, growing confident in her fearlessness. Finally, she drained her glass, got down from the bar stool and made for the stairwell. Bob followed. When she reached the stairs, she stopped and looked into the gloom.

"Well, if you change your mind, you know where I live." She ascended the stairs, closed and locked the cellar door, and went up to her bedroom, Bob in tow.

I doubt I should tell Bambi about this.

More dreams that night. A soft flow of gentle voices swept through her. Again, she dreamt of the African woman with the earring. She stood before Liv, weeping with downcast eyes. She lifted her head and looked directly at Liv. Her eyes were pale hazel. They beseeched her. Liv felt the woman's need, a time-worn desire, tired, yet intense like a burning flame. The woman placed gentle hands on Liv's shoulders, and Liv experienced deep love.

Liv wakened, sobbing. She quieted her unease by planning for the coming evening of photographing orbs.

Chapter 11

Autis stepped carefully while flashlighting the fog in front of himself and Gar. He turned back to Gar, "Watch out, the damn fire ants are everywhere. The spray I use must be an ant aphrodisiac." The fog over the marsh was so thick that the men made their way at a very slow walk so as to not run into trees and shrubs.

"Could we have picked a worse night?" Autis said.

"Here we are, let's locate the ant nests before we start photographing. The orbs have to be photographed in the dark, no lights, no flash."

"Do you feel anything?"

"No, do you?" Gar chuckled.

"Nope. I guess we're a couple of hopeless clods. We're probably surrounded by ghostly critters, and don't have brains enough to be scared. Listen, there's our resident great horned owl. Maybe that's a sign."

"Yeah, he sounds pissed. I am scared though—of the ants. Use the light. I don't want to find myself taking pictures while standing in the middle of a fire ant nest."

"I think we're in the clear. There's one and there's one," Autis said, pointing the flashlight. "I don't see any more near where we'll stand."

"Okay, let's do it."

Ten minutes later the two men headed back to the house. Liv turned on the outside lighting when she saw the flashlight returning.

"See anything?" She asked.

"Everything we saw or heard was alive—it's a quiet night," Gar replied.

"Did you get any pictures of orbs?" Bambi said, sharply.

"I don't know, and won't know until we get to look at the pictures. We's tryin our bes', Miz' Bambi."

"Up yours. Let's download what you've taken, and check it out on the computer."

"That's the plan, lady." Autis said, as the men reached the top level of the deck. "I've got the memory card right here in my sweaty hand." The foursome trooped into Autis' home office and gathered around the monitor. Autis slipped the memory card into the card reader and then sat at his desk as the computer worked up the data.

The computer screen showed a series of black photos. "Nothing," Bambi said in disgust.

"Patience, oh ye of little faith," Gar answered. You can't see anything from the thumbnails. I've got to pull them up one at a time." He clicked on the first thumbnail. As one, the small group leaned over the monitor.

"Nothing," Bambi said.

"We're so glad you're here to keep score," Gar said, clicking the next thumbnail.

"Ditto."

"Well, Miss Glass-Half-Empty, these first several were of areas nowhere near the graves. I'm using them for comparisons, and if you want to...Oops!"

"Dayem," Bambi breathed. "Dayem."

"There's two right there. One is apparently closer than the other. Shit." Liv moved her face closer to the monitor.

"We got orbs." Bambi nearly screamed as she grabbed Gar and gave him a kiss.

"Look, there's more," Autis said, pointing to another frame with four orbs. Perfectly round blobs of what looked like white soccer balls of mist.

The group grew silent as Gar moved from frame to frame, showing clusters of orbs. "Oh my God," Bambi said. We've got a community. No wonder I reacted so the other day." She looked at Liv, and said softly with a pained expression. We've got a community of—of," She stopped.

"I know," Liv said softly. "Dozens of slaves—people who lived short brutal lives under terrible conditions, and died, God only knows how—away from home, family, and community. No wonder you were faint with emotions the other day; you sensed what was here." Liv shook her head slowly. "I wouldn't want to possess that ability."

Autis turned around in his desk chair and said evenly. "All right, what now, guys?" The group fell silent, each looking at the others uncertainly.

"I—I—don't know what to do here," Liv said. "I mean, are we going to tell somebody? Who? Why?"

"I think the regional historical society would want to see this," Gar said. "I reckon black folks would be more than slightly interested, especially those from the island. The University of South Carolina will surely send investigators."

The group fell silent again.

"Sheeit," Bambi said. Do we want all that traipsing about taking place here? I mean, those poor souls have been here nearly one hundred and fifty years. Leave 'em be, I say. I'm not hot to satisfy some academics' idle curiosity. I can see teams of well-meaning archeologists poppin' off those caps and stirring around those bones. What happened here was awful enough. I don't know that it needs play in the media. Like my grandpappy says, 'Don't stir shit.' I think we ought to leave them poor souls in peace."

Liv and Bambi were both tearing up.

The men looked at each other in confusion and puzzlement before Autis broke the impasse. "Let's get a beer."

Gar smiled nodding, while the women broke out in laughter through their remorse.

"Of course you would," Liv shook her head as in disbelief as Bambi looked on chuckling.

"Men," Bambi intoned, shaking her blonde mane.

Autis took the lead, guiding them down the stairwell to the pub.

Liv hadn't gone seven steps when she heard a slight sound behind her, and turned just in time to catch a fainting Bambi.

Chapter 12

"I can't go down there."

"That's okay, Bambi. You don't have to go there," Liv answered, folding a moistened towel over Bambi's forehead. "You're burning up, honey."

"I feel like I'm on fire, and I can't catch my breath. I'm suffocating."

"Take deep breaths," Liv said, and then turning to Autis, "Bring me some crushed ice in a towel." Autis departed for the kitchen, followed by Gar.

"How about bringing some beers from the pub refrigerator?" Autis asked.

"Beers on the way," Gar said, turning to the stairwell.

The towel-wrapped package of crushed ice was applied to Bambi's face, neck, and shoulders. Her temperature started to drop, her breathing became smoother, and she relaxed. Bambi took Liv by the hand, and pulled her close, "Gal, are you ever going to want to have me back to your house? I mean, I'm either freezing or burning up, and all in all making a plumb fool of myself. I've never been so embarrassed in all my life."

"You don't need to talk like that. You've had a bad fright from something, twice now. I'm worried about *you*, not how things look. You're with friends."

"I think I've pushed friendship about as far as a body ought to. Some would say that I'm not worth the trouble."

Gar entered carrying bottles of Bud Light. "Well they would be wrong now, wouldn't they? I can't speak for everyone here, but I love you, and I have no patience with notions of anything other than concern for your welfare."

"I'm still not going to marry you."

"Damn, woman, who's askin' for marriage? I just want you to get right." Gar handed out the beers.

Later that week, Bambi and Liv sat over tall glasses of Plantation Tea in Bambi's living room.

"I don't know what brought on my faintin' spell, but whatever it was is in that basement, and it's angry—very angry." Bambi said, rubbing a shin scrape from her collapse in the Oakley's staircase. "Also—I—I sensed more than one."

"Great, I've got an angry mob in my basement." Liv took a long pull on her drink. "You know, this stuff should be banned. If the nation discovers Firefly this summer, we're doomed as a country."

"Yeah, but we'd go down smiling,'" Bambi said.

"Anyway, what can I do about the critters in our pub?"

"Do you have to 'do' anything?"

Liv thought a moment. "No, I don't 'have' to do anything." She folded her hands in front of her face, steepled her forefingers and pressed them against her lips. "But—I feel the *need* to do something about it; a strong need."

"Good," Bambi seized Liv's forearm and squeezed.

"Why 'good?'"

"Whatever's down there is angry. It's angry because of the pain it feels—I did sense that." Bambi ran her hand over her eyes. "I think it was the pain that overtook me, more than the anger. You saying that you feel the need to do something about it means that you're willing to try to bring an end to the pain."

"Okay. That's acceptable to me. But that brings me back to my question: What can I do?"

"Let's begin with what can *we* do?" Bambi said.

"Loyalty to friends has its limits; I've seen—twice—what those spirits do to you," Liv said.

"I can prepare myself. Both times I encountered them I was unprepared. There are things I can do, mental and physical, that can protect me—some."

"Some? *Some* sounds like not a good idea to me," Liv said, shaking her head while tonging more ice cubes.

"I think I could work my way up to confronting whatever, or whoever, is in your basement. It might take a while, but I believe I can do it." Bambi was scanning the room as though looking for a thing or an idea as she talked. Then she refilled Liv's glass. "That's all for you, slugger. I've seen the effect this stuff has on you."

Liv took a small sip and put her drink down. "I have an idea. The basement has a ground level entryway that opens directly into it. A set of French doors that open wide. If we were to…"

Late that afternoon, the two women stood in front of the French doors leading into the basement of Liv's house. Bambi was wearing a black robe and a dark hat with a wide brim. She held a chain from which hung a brass incense burner. A ring of sand was laid on the landing outside the doors, and Bambi stood inside the ring, swaying and chanting a slow incantation of words foreign to Liv's ear. Liv stood at the door, waiting for a signal from her companion. Bob sat on his haunches in the grass beyond the landing, head cocked.

Bambi swung the burner first east and west, then north and south, and then she let it hang before her, its fumes curling up and around her hat. She nodded silently to Liv, who turned the door handle and opened the right side door, then the left door. The only light in the cavernous room came from the open doorway.

Liv stepped over the threshold and into the room. She turned to look at Bambi, who was intoning softly, eyes closed.

For the first time, Liv felt like an interloper in her own house. Ironically, she also felt drawn to the center of the room—to the billiard table. As she stood looking down at its green surface, she felt a rush of cold air. She turned to look back at her helper outlined by the doorway. As if following instructions, Liv sat on the edge of the table, and then slid to the middle. She swung her legs up and over the edge, and then stretched out on her back. She rolled her head toward the doorway and saw Bambi standing still and silent, eyes wide, lips apart. And then the doors slowly closed as her friend stood helpless. Liv heard Bob barking and scratching at the door before she passed out.

Chapter 13

Liv woke up from a dream of being kissed, over and over. She looked directly into the face of her pointer who was licking her face. The big dog was standing with his paws on the edge of the table and Bambi was standing next to him.

"Enough, Bob. That's enough, you've done your job. Good boy." Bambi pulled the straining animal away from the table.

"What—how…" Liv started to rise but was pressed back by Bambi.

"Stay still for a few minutes and get your bearings," Bambi held Bob by his collar.

Liv laid her head back down on the pool table and looked up at the maze of wires, pipes, and ductwork in the high ceiling.

"There was a man," she reported. "A big man, tall, handsome, but his face was tight with anger. It seemed like anger *at me*. Why would he be angry at me?"

Bambi stood in wide-eyed silence looking at her friend. She had let go of Bob's collar, but kept her hand on his head in a mild restraint.

"Oh!" Liv exclaimed. "You—how did you—you're here, in the pub." She abruptly sat up and swung her legs over the side of the table, bringing her hands to her forehead and rubbing her eyes with the heels of her palms.

"The door was stuck shut," Bambi said. "So I ran into the house and came down the stairwell. I could feel the presence in this room, stronger than any I've ever felt. My heart was poundin', but I was able to break through to get to you. When I got to the bottom of the stairwell I could make out what looked like a sort of vapor coming from under the table and hanging over you. I shouted at it and Bob lunged past me to get to your side. The vapor figure turned to look at me, and then it vanished. Hayel, it was the damndest thing I've ever seen."

"Oh. He spoke to me." Liv cupped a hand over her open mouth.

"What did he say?"

Liv frowned in concentration. "I think he said, 'Why so long?'"

"Dayem." Bambi's vivid blue eyes were wide as saucers.

"Yes, that's what he said, 'Why so long?'"

"Now I'm really ready to go upstairs," Bambi said, looking around the room.

Bob put paws on the table and tried to nuzzle Liv again.

"That dog of yours—he stopped about halfway to the pool table, looked back at me, and then walked stiff-legged like up to the table. He was ready to do battle, and I'd say he'd give his life for you." Bambi took Bob's head between her hands and fluffed his ears. The dog wagged twice but never took his eyes off of Liv—who slid from her perch on the edge of pool table and stood leaning against it to steady herself.

"He's a good fellah," Liv said stroking his head. "The other night he acted like he was afraid to go out in the dark to look for intruders with Autis. But when I went out, he came along and stayed with us."

"He's protective of you. He probably thinks that Autis can take care of hisself, but you—the damsel—needs looking after. He's a Southern gentleman."

Liv looked closely at her friend. "So you're okay down here in the pub then?"

"I'm not loving it, and I'm glad the light switches are handy at the steps. I can stay as long as you want. But—this room does have a feel to it." Bambi looked around the room. "You don't feel it, do you?"

"No, I don't," Liv answered. "What does it feel like?"

"It feels purely like someplace that don't want me about," Bambi said. "And I'm willing to oblige it as soon as you feel ready to go upstairs."

Liv stood erect. "Let's go then," she started toward the stairwell, then changed her direction and went to the French doors—the ones that Bambi could not open. She turned the handles on the doors and they swung easily open. The women glanced at each other, and then walked into the late afternoon sun.

"Damn, I couldn't get them to budge once they closed. At the last minute I tried to stop them from closing, but it felt like there was a Mack truck pulling them. I don't know when I've been more scared—seeing those doors shut themselves, and nobody or nothing was going to stop them. It was a fright."

"But you came on down the stairwell anyway."

"Hayel, yes. But don't you think for a minute I wasn't scared shitless. Anyway, Bob was behind me, and he would've run me over to get down here. That dog loves you. If I could find a man that'd love me that much I'd give him a family of children."

"Gar loves you. He loves you more than you are willing to admit."

"You say *love*. He loves that damn tobacco more than me, and probably that ratty sailboat of his, too. I'll not play second fiddle to weed nor watercraft. To hayel with him, I say." She stood looking out over the sound, and then turned to Liv. "Damn him to hayel, damn all men to hayel." Liv realized that her friend was in distress. She moved to embrace Bambi just as the brave woman in her gave up, and the little girl in her sank to the ground. Liv followed, holding the terrified woman in her arms as the dam that held her terror in check, cracked and broke. Bambi sobbed in Liv's arms. Her breath came in gasps, and she made a mewing sound between sobs. Liv held and rocked her as she would a child with a hurt.

"I was so scared, so scared." Bambi gasped between sobs and panting breaths. "I wet myself." My clothes are soaked under this gown." She cried and moaned. Liv swept the tear tracks from Bambi's cheeks.

"I'm so ugly. I can't abide to look in a mirror with my mouth open. I don't see how people can stand to be around me—let alone a man want to have anything to do with me, except do me in the dark, and then run like hell when the lights come on. Why did God give me this mouth? Why does he hate me? I didn't do nothin' to him—and damn it, I ain't going to do nothin' for him neither." Years of anguish, driven by the release of terror, bubbled up in the woman Liv held in her arms.

They embraced each other for several minutes as Bambi got control of her breathing and composure. Soon the two women were sitting side by side gazing out over the sound, each with her arm around the other.

"It is a lovely evening," Liv said softly.

"You know," Bambi said, sitting up, breaking away from her state, "if we're sitting on fire ants we're purely screwed." They shot to their feet giggling and brushing at their bottoms. Bambi wiped at her face with the backs of her hands.

"Let's go upstairs and put those wet clothes of yours in the washer," Liv said, smiling.

Bambi grabbed Liv and hugged her close. "I love you, Sis. I love you like no one I've loved since I was a little girl. Thanks for being my friend." She held Liv for a short time, then let go. This time Liv was weeping.

"Ain't we a pair of ghost hunters though?" Bambi said, laughing as they mounted the steps to the upper deck. "A trio," Liv said, pointing out Bob at their heels.

The Oakleys' laundry room shared a spacious pantry adjoining the kitchen. Bambi stripped as Liv put her clothing into the washer. She added detergent and softener, adjusted the settings, and hit the start button.

"Ever since I's a little girl I wet myself when I got excited, but I don't generally make a flood."

"Go upstairs and take a shower. I'll get you a towel, and a robe to wear while your clothes finish."

Bambi, in the nude, strode out of the kitchen and almost ran into Autis coming up from the pub, cold beer in hand.

Without breaking stride he said, "Hi, Bambi," and came into the kitchen. "This looks like something I don't want to know about."

"Up yours, pervert." Liv smoked a look at her husband.

"Hey, I'm not the one with a naked girlfriend in my kitchen," Autis said grinning.

Bambi turned around and stood in the doorway with her fists on her hips. "Autis Oakley, that's about the most insulted I've ever been in my life. Here I am, naked as the day I was born, and you walk by me like I was wearing my Sunday-go-to-church best."

Autis took a pull at his Budweiser. "Well hell, Bambi, what would you have me do? I came home, saw the doors to the pub open, followed a trail of wet spots up the steps, heard the washer start up, and heard Liv tell you to hit the showers. And finally, I saw you in the nude before you saw me. I had time to retain my composure. Do you want me to ogle you? I can do that, but I'd rather do it when you're wearing revealing clothes. Right now you're leaving nothing to the imagination."

"Men!" Bambi turned and stalked off.

"Honey, I'm home," Autis said, turning to Liv and gathering her up with a kiss.

"You walked by her like she was fully clothed. She didn't impress you at all."

"Are you kidding, lady? You're going to get laid tonight like you've never been laid. Juices are flowing."

"Ah, there's the horny old goat I've learned to love." Liv placed a soft kiss on his lips.

Autis walked out of the kitchen and into the living room where he yelled upstairs, "Hey, Bambi. Only your hairdresser and I know for sure."

"Up yours," came her shouted response.

Autis laughed, and returned to Liv. "Now, you want to tell me what's been going on around the nudist colony today?"

Chapter 14

Monday morning a week later, Liv had just finished kneading the dough for loaves of her mother's oatmeal-marmalade bread, when her phone rang.

"Hello." She gingerly held the phone between a dough-coated finger and thumb.

"Hey, Sis. Are you busy this afternoon?"

"Hold on, I'll be right back." Liv went to the sink to take care of the dough problem, and then returned to the phone.

"Okay, Bambi, what's up?"

"I got someone I'd really like you to meet," Bambi said. "She might help us some with the orb and voices problem."

"I'm clear, but I have bread rising, so can't leave until after lunch. What's this about?"

"Amazing! She's beautiful, a writer, intelligent, and she cooks too. Martha Stewart, watch out." Bambi said with a giggle.

"Okay, smart-ass, once more: What's it about?"

"The island librarian told me about this black lady that lives near the south end of the island, name of Sweet. You need to meet her."

"And this is because…"

"Cause she's a descendant of the slaves that used to live on your property. Her ancestors are likely buried in your back yard." Bambi said softly.

"Come for lunch, and we'll leave from here, after I take bread out of the oven."

"You got it, Martha."

*   *   *

The handsome clapboard cottage sheltered under ancient oaks near the edge of the salt marsh, and beyond the marsh lay a wide waterway that opened to the sound. Aronte 'Sweetgrass' Weaver had purchased the waterfront wood-land in the fifties, at a time when everyone considered it a worthless swamp at the edge of a backwater. Every year since the late nineties, Miz Weaver had to turn away developers eager to sink millions into her land. And every year, 'Granny Sweet' refused kinfolk looking for a gift parcel of land on which to park their doublewide. None knew of the papers filed in the offices of an attorney, or of The Nature Conservancy. In not too many years, her immediate family would receive a small inheritance of cash and a great surprise.

Her driveway curved through a grove of pecan trees laden with promise, and then circled to the front of the house that faced the sound.

Sweetgrass sat on a porch rocker weaving a piece that gave her name a ring of honest declaration. She rocked as two attractive white ladies parked their car under the old live oak that shaded her home from the afternoon sun. A limber brown hound descended the porch steps and sauntered out to greet the visitors. Some dogs approach people with a graceful joy that says "I'm so glad you could come." Goody was such a dog. After stooping to pet the greeter, the girls waved to the coffee-and-cream-colored lady on the porch before they reached the steps.

"Good morning, Miz Weaver. I called yesterday. You said I could come by this afternoon. This is my friend I told you about, Liv Oakley."

"Morning, ladies. Come and sit. I'll not rise if you don't mind. I'm ninety and my knees don't need the aggravation. There's some tea and glasses on the side table. Ice in the bucket." Liv saw that the elderly lady was staring at her intently. "Help yourselves. There's lemon in the dish. I don't brew my tea so sweet, and I take it with lemon." All this was said while not missing a stroke on the large basket she was weaving. Sweetgrass Weaver spoke with the soft cultured accent so often found among well-educated Southern ladies.

The women fixed their tea, pulled chairs close, and settled in.

"I understand…" Liv started, but was silenced by Bambi placing a hand on her knee.

"Lovely day," Bambi said.

"True, it is. The Lord has graced us with one more day."

"Yes, He has. You have a beautiful place here, Miz Weaver," Bambi said.

"Thank you. I've been blessed all my life, and now I'm blessed with the comfort of such weather. Sunny days like this don't bother my arthritis but little much."

"That's quite a stand of pecan you have," Bambi continued.

"It does look like a good crop this year. Last year was only fair." She rocked some, and weaved some. "I put in those trees 43 years ago. My plan was for them to support me and my man—God rest his soul—in our old age. Now, I call them my tax trees."

"How's that, Miz Weaver?" Bambi asked, taking a sip of tea.

"Taxes. Those trees pay my property taxes and then some. The taxes go up each year—but then, so does the price of pecans. I sell them direct to a company in France. Seems there's a fondness for the likes of these nuts over there. A Monsieur Jaynes comes personal each year, inspects the crop and sees to its shipment. He buys baskets while he's here, and I fix his supper.

That man does like his shrimp and grits. He brings a bottle of white wine. I'm not much of a drinking lady, but who could resist sharing a glass with an elegant French gentleman? And him with such manners." She took a sip of tea. "You can call me Sweetgrass—everyone does. Some just call me 'Sweet,' your choice. My name is Aronte Wells, but so many people were drawn in by the sign," she pointed out a derelict sign leaning against an outbuilding that read "Sweetgrass Weaver" in flowing faded lettering. "They came in asking to see 'Sweetgrass Weaver' that I finally just gave up and took the name as my own. That was back in the sixties, I'd say. My man—rest his soul—he didn't mind as long as I knew I was Aronte Wells, and as long as those rich tourists continued to lay down cash money for my baskets and pecans."

"I take your point, Miz—Sweetgrass. And you're right, it is hard to turn down a true gentleman, rare as they are." Bambi turned to Liv, who was about to speak, and gave a tiny shake of the head.

Miz Weaver continued, "Monsieur Jaynes' company makes some kind of cake with them. He brings me one every year. It's good. I give him a tin of pralines. He seems fond of such. Some say I make a decent praline."

"I wouldn't doubt that."

"There's some in that wood box on the table. You help yourself."

"Thank you." Bambi picked up the cigar box, selected a praline and handed the box to Liv.

"Bambi crunched a small bite, savored it a while and rocked, and then said, "This is the best praline I've ever eaten. You do have a gift."

"Thank you. If you call ninety years of *trying* a gift, I reckon you're right. My grandma taught me how to make these. You've got to stand over them and control the heat. It takes a few minutes, and it takes some tending, something that young people now-a-day don't much care to do. Nobody wants to tend what needs tending. They seem to think things should be done automatic like. I've got an old toaster that does my toast as I watch it. My grandchildren push their toaster handle down and walk away while the machine does the work for them. My toast is better."

"I'm sure it is, Miz Weaver." Bambi looked around the property. "You lived all your life on this island?"

"Can't say, ain't dead yet." She paused for this to sink in, and then went on. "When the Lord comes for me—on that day I can say I lived all my life on Wadmalaw."

"I reckon it's changed right much since your childhood."

"It's changed right much since my *late adulthood*," Sweetgrass said with a short laugh. "Everybody's in such a hurry."

"It must seem that way to someone who has seen what you've seen in ninety years of seein'," Bambi said.

"It does. Now, you take the way young people go about courting. If it can be called courting at all. In my day such behavior as I see in my grands would be met with the hard back of a mama's hand. And the way they talk, such looseness. I'd not want to think that we got free from the slavers so we could carry on like farm animals, and talk gutter talk, but that's what some of the children do hereabouts. And I'm not talking about colored children only. Why the whites is sometime worst of all. Seems to me that parents today 'raise kids' instead of 'bringing up children' and that makes all the sorry difference in the lives of their offspring. Goes to 'tending' it seems—like pralines."

"I can see your ninety years weren't wasted, Miz Weaver." Liv added.

"Thank you. I hope they weren't, because they were in the service of Our Lord Jesus." Turning her gaze to Liv, she asked, "Were you brought up in the service of Our Lord, young lady?" Caught off guard, Liv stammered, "Uh, I, uh, I was raised in the Methodist church."

"Well that's a good group, the Methodists." I have friends who go that way. Do you read the good book, daily?"

"No, I don't. I haven't been active in the church since I went off to college."

"I see. Education seems to have that effect on children," Miz Weaver said with a concerned frown. "Why do you suppose that is? It seems to me that more a body learns, the more they'd know."

"That's so," Bambi intervened. "I've often wondered about that myself. Do you suppose the churches could do something about that?"

Liv, realized that she'd been rescued from heathendom. She sat demurely holding her tea in her lap, as Bambi lavishly demonstrated the swamp of Southern protocol.

Sweet turned attention to her basket. "I'm at a turn here that takes some watching. So I'm going to ask your patience while I work through it, but before I do I want to ask Miz Oakley a thing," she looked intently at Liv, who responded by leaning toward her slender host.

"Miz Bambi tells me that you come from a town in O-hi-o."

"Yes, Hilliards, Ohio. I was born and raised there."

"Where in O-hi-o is Hilliards?"

"In the middle. It's just outside of Columbus; it's sort of a suburb of Columbus."

"I see." Sweet returned to the basket in her lap.

Shortly, Sweet paused again from her work and looked at Liv. "Do you know of any members of the Jolly family in O-hi-o?

Liv frowned over the question. "Jolly, that name rings a bell." But I can't quite bring it to mind. Why?"

"I knew some folks up there by that name and I was just wondering." She returned to her basket.

The two young ladies sat in silence as the black lady worked her way past a tedious part. Her hands moved with a mind of their own, and a deftness that belied her ninety years. When finished, she looked directly at Liv and softly said, "I'm glad you came home, child."

Liv tried not to show her confusion. Then Sweetgrass added to that confusion.

"You've been missed."

"I—I don't know what you mean."

"Well, I'm fixin' to show you." Sweet rocked hard three times and on the fourth cycle thrust herself to her feet. When she came erect, Bambi was at her side. "Thank you, child." It took a moment for her to set her balance.

"Hand me that cane," Sweet said, nodding in the direction of a staff leaning against the porch wall. "I'll not be but a moment." She disappeared into her house as Bambi held the screen door.

When she closed the door, Bambi turned to Liv and gave a slight shrug. She stood watch at the doorway.

Sweet returned with a thin leather photograph album that showed signs of age and use. A long cloth sack hung weightily from a cord she had looped around her neck. She sat in her rocker and handed her cane to Bambi who leaned it against the wall. Once settled, Sweet placed the album in her lap and removed the loop of cord from around her neck, "Ladies, we have some business before us, but before we begin let me suggest a change of beverage." She withdrew a bottle of Firefly from the cloth sack. "Miz Bambi, would you do the honors."

"Certainly," Bambi answered with a broad smile. She set to the task.

"Miz Bambi," I'd like mine cut with tea from my pitcher, about half and half would do fine, and make it most ice. This old body of mine don't take much beverage abuse."

"Good notion, Miz Weaver, I think I'll follow your lead. Liv?"

"Me too. That stuff goes down way too easy."

Sweetgrass made a light chuckle. "You've noticed that too. After I had twice to spend nights in this rocker, cause I couldn't maneuver my way out of it and into the house, I came to realize that I had to use this tea weak and slow."

Bambi laughed. "I like that, 'weak and slow.' Sounds like some of the men I've known." This brought surprisingly rich laughter from the ninety-year-old lady.

Drinks were served up, and a tin of Miz Weaver's cheese straws passed around, and passed around once again. "Sweet" sat back in her rocker and looked up at the early summer clouds forming in the distance. "This is fine," she said. "The Lord is good to us." Bambi nodded in accord and shot a glance at Liv that elicited a concurring nod.

Sweet took a good pull from her glass and then set it on the table beside her rocker, saying, "Miss Liv, it would appear that you and I may be blood kin."

Chapter 15

"Distant kin, but kin for sure."

Bambi and Liv sat in stunned silence for a short period. All rocking ceased, the sound of a nearby mockingbird hung in the still air. Liv broke the silence. "How did you come to that conclusion?"

Wordlessly, Sweet opened the album and handed it to Liv, who looked down at a single large tintype. It was like looking into a mirror. Liv's focus was broken when she heard a gasp from Bambi who had come to stand behind her."

"Who is this?" Liv asked.

"That is Camille Maxton, daughter of Alexander Maxton, the son of the man who built Maxton Manor. He owned my great-grandmother, and was known among his slaves as *Monster Maxton*. He was a hard man like his father Jason Maxton, but he was also a cruel man. He enjoyed the power that comes from holding pain and death over the heads of others." Sweetgrass dabbed at the corner of an eye with her kerchief, rocked a few cycles, then added, "He thrived on the fear of others."

"How does that relate to me?" Liv asked.

"Alexander Maxton had two sons and a daughter. Both boys died during the fighting, and Camille took charge of the plantation in the last years of the war because of her father's health—he suffered from gout. When he realized the war was lost, Alexander Maxton sent Camille, along with much of his wealth, to stay with her mother's relatives in Columbus, Ohio. He stayed behind to protect his property, saying that he would die at the gate rather than watch Union soldiers occupy his land. Camille was carrying a load of grief and a load of love. She remained to live in O-hi-o, coming back to visit after the war. You look at that picture of her, look into a mirror, and tell me where it leads your mind. She—moving to Columbus, and you coming from nearby there—it puts pieces of a puzzle in place."

Sweet took a long sip of her tea, and leaned back in her rocker with an air of completion.

Liv sat looking at the photograph in her lap. "I've not been able to follow all you've told me, and I don't know of the name *Maxton* in my family, but then I'm not familiar with my maternal ancestors beyond my grandma's mother and father. My father's family traces its roots to eighteenth century

Germany, but I don't know much about them beyond daddy's parents. Also, my family has always worked with the future in mind, and hasn't concerned itself with much family history."

Sweetgrass clasped her hands over her breast and said, "My people have word-of-mouth sense about who we are, who we were—and where we came from. Most slaves couldn't read or write. They had to go on stories handed around and down. I know stories from a hundred years before I was born. Late at night, by the light of the fireplace, family stories and tales were passed, usually from mother to daughter. I've told the stories and legends to my children, grandchildren, and even on to greatgrandchildren—though very few wanted to hear them. My youngest granddaughter tape-recorded the stories passed by me and others who knew the island history. I'm one of the few left. Copies of those tapes are on file in the university library."

Liv sat wide-eyed through the gently told story. "I don't know what to say. You're talking about events I can't comment on because I don't have any frame of reference. You could be right, or you could be wrong. I don't know." She reflected a moment, and then added. "Not only do I not know if you're right, but I know of no way to confirm it. I mean, what's the proof of what you say?"

Miz Weaver sat and rocked in thought, and then she began speaking, still in her soft manner. Her eyes were shut, and remained so as she continued, "Camille Maxton was a lady. It is true that she did have—a dalliance with her lover, but it was a fine love and a pairing that would have become a marriage but for Camille's father and the evil ways of her society. Just before the end of the war—at her father's command—she fled to Ohio, taking a servant and much of the family wealth in the form of jewelry, silver, and gold coin. Her father knew better than to trust confederate paper money.

"During the war she and her father corresponded by mail. There was a falling out, and she did not return to Maxton Manor for nearly two years. When she did return she found both her father and her lover dead, and the manor had been burned, and partly rebuilt. She saw to the rebuilding, sold most of the property, and then returned to Ohio. She forsook the name of 'Maxton' and took the maiden name of her mother. She became Camille Jolly, and her daughter, 'Janey Jolly.'" Miz Weaver stopped rocking, opened her eyes and leaned toward Liv saying, "There is more, much more, but that is the main part of the happenings at the time." She gathered up a woven palmetto fan and stroked some air over her face. "I'm tired and need to take a lie-down. Will you ladies help me to my couch?"

Bambi and Liv assisted the fragile lady to her living room couch, and saw to it that she had a glass of water on the table at hand.

"Is there anything we can do for you, Miz Weaver?" Bambi asked. "Anyone we can call? I mean, are you going to be okay?"

"Oh, I'm fine. I'm ninety, is all. I generally have had a short nap by this time."

Bambi held onto her hand. "Are you sure?"

"Miz Weaver, could we stay awhile with you?" Liv asked.

Sweetgrass gave out a soft chuckle. "You're sweet, child. I'm quite all right, and I generally don't drink spirits this time of day. I have enjoyed your company, and you must know that you are welcome to visit any time at all. No need to call—just drop in."

"Thank you, Miz Weaver." Liv placed the phone on the table beside Sweetgrass."

"Why yes, that would be good." Sweetgrass pulled the phone closer. She chuckled to herself. "My granddaughter set it on a thing she calls speed dial. All I have to do is turn it on and push number 'one' for her phone, number 'two' for her mother's or number 'three' for her brother's phone." She smiled and said softly to herself, "speed dial," and then she was gone, her chest rising and falling slowly.

Bambi released the long, delicate hand, placing it over the ladies' breast. She rose from beside the couch and turned toward Liz, her eyes glittering. "Lord, that I could have had such a grandmother."

Liz put an arm around her friend's shoulder, "That anyone could."

In the car they rode in silence for several miles while Bambi gathered herself. Finally, she said, "What do you think?"

"I sure do admire that lady." Liv answered.

"Yes. What's not to like? She's the most gracious lady I've ever met, and I surely plan to visit her. But what do you think about her story?"

It could all be true and accurate, but what does that have to do with the orbs and with the voices I'm still hearing in the pub. I've enjoyed meeting the lady, and might possibly have a trace as to my ancestry, but it doesn't change anything, or affect my situation at all."

They rode in silence, then Bambi spoke up. "Here's the Tea Plantation—pull in here."

Liv wheeled in past the sign that read Charleston Tea Plantation and took the driveway to the plantation parking lot.

"You ever been here?" Bambi asked.

"No, we've talked about visiting this place, but we've both been too busy. We've only recently gotten the house how we want it. We've been to the beach just once since moving here."

"I swear, you and that man of yours live like monks. Let's get a cup of tea, I'll show you around. I come here often. I like the tea and I like the place. There's peacefulness about a working farm that's kept the natural beauty around itself. When I'm feeling down, I come get a cup of tea and walk among the tea plants. It's calming."

As they got out of the car, Bambi pointed to long rows of chest-high plants. "Those are the tea plants."

"Looks like hedges."

"They are—tea hedges. The leaves are harvested mechanically and then processed in this building here; first they're wilted, then they're dried," Bambi said, leading her friend toward a large, low building.

After cruising a well-stocked gift shop and buying "The Freshest Tea in the USA," the girls sat over their complimentary cups and discussed the events of the afternoon.

"How hard would it be for you to check out Miz Weaver's story about her relationship to you?" Bambi asked.

"I don't know. I could make some phone calls. My grandma has passed away, she would have known. However, her brother, Uncle Wiley, lives by himself in his farm north of Columbus. Maybe I could pay him a visit. I haven't seen him for nearly a year, and I miss him. We used to visit his farm when I was little. He and Aunt Sue had apple trees, a big sugar pear in the front yard, chickens, pigs, and milk cows, everything a farm needs to stay alive. He sends a card, with a new twenty, every holiday occasion: Christmas, Easter, and Valentine—he never fails. Uncle Wiley might know something about our distant ancestors. Like I said, my family has never been interested in ancestry. We just don't care about those things. What's past is past; we look to the future."

"Damn, you people in the north never cease to surprise me. How could you not care about your family history? Even as broke-off as I am from family, I still keep photographs, letters, and memorabilia from them. My cousins have stuff that goes back before the war."

"The war? World War II?"

"Dear God. The war between the North and the South. The Woah, honey."

"Oh, the Civil War."

"Nothing 'civil' about it, dear; there were more Americans killed in that war than all the other wars before or since combined. Americans killing Americans, it was. I have kin in Virginia who're dead serious when they call it 'The War of Northern Aggression.' Yes, the 'Civil War' if it suits you. Anyway, in the South we pay attention to roots—and you being a transplanted Southerner need to learn the ways of your adopted country. Get on it, Gal."

*   *   *

That night, Liv and Autis made love. They fell asleep in each other's arms. Shorty after, Liv wakened and disengaged herself, rolled over, and was gone again to deep sleep. The girl with the golden earring came with others—a dozen or more crowded Liv's sleeping hours.

"Tige. I'm called Tige, and I raised you. Why don't you remember me? I loved you."

Tige stepped aside and waved her arm back to the others assembled in silence behind her. They stood in anticipation, clothed in rags, hands down at their sides. They seemed to breathe as one.

"You must help us, you know us. You're one of us." Tige said and then faded with the others.

Liv awoke covered in sweat. She rose and went to draw a glass of water from the bathroom. She downed the first glass standing before the lavatory, then drew another and took it to the open window overlooking the sound. The night air cooled her as she sipped her water. A gold crescent moon hung over the water as Liv looked down at the site of the grave caps.

Who are they? Who am I?

Chapter 16

Liv wheeled her rental into Wiley Sheets' driveway, and returned a wave from the slender gray-haired man sitting with his newspaper in the shade of his covered porch.

She leaned out of the window and said, "Good afternoon, sir. Do you have any sugar pears for sale?"

The wiry man picked up a small wicker basket beside his rocker and hoisted it with a broad grin and whoop of pleasure. "Too early, but I've got pear preserves" he called back.

Liv rushed from her car into the arms of her favorite relative. He planted a soft kiss on her cheek and said, "Look at you," as he handed her the basket that held her favorite childhood treat. He stepped back from her and smiled. "You've grown so beautiful." Blushing, she was once again the darling little niece of "Uncle Wiley."

"You've always told me that." She saw that his eyes were red-rimmed. *Had he been crying?*

"I speak the truth. Meanwhile, there's a pot of Russian Tea." He turned and slowly made his way to the car, saying over his shoulder, "I'll join you in a cup as soon as I get your luggage."

"This is just like I remember it, Uncle Wiley," she sipped the fruity spiced tea. "You've got to give up Aunt Sue's recipe."

"I will. One more way to remember an aunt who loved you like her own. It's really simple. Brew a pot of strong black tea, add orange and pineapple juice in equal parts, three or four cloves, a stick of cinnamon, and heat for a while. I'll write out the whole thing before you leave. Oh, and some lemon slices."

"Thanks. By the way, I've brought you some tea that's grown just down the road from our house on Wadmalaw."

"American tea? I've never heard of such a thing." His skepticism showed through in his voice and manner.

"Don't judge, Uncle. You always told me: 'Don't judge.' I'll only say that it's the tea that's been served in the White House since 1987. I think that speaks to its quality."

"Thanks for the lesson, Liv. I'll give it a try. Now, what's this"—he sat his tea cup aside— "about your relative on—on—"

"'Wadmalaw'. It's pronounced 'law' with a 'wadma' in front of it; probably an Indian name. There's a slight accent on the first syllable."

"Certainly an odd name."

"Yes, but it's a lovely island, and we have a spacious home just waiting for your visit—if you could be pried away from the farm long enough to come spend some time with your favorite niece."

"I'll do it. I promise I'll come for a visit." She knew he wouldn't.

"I remember when I received that brochure in the mail addressed to your grandmother. I thought that strange because she was long dead—even stranger that I wound up with it. I sent it on to you because I knew you were looking for a house. It was a 'For Sale by Owner' brochure, stating 'Owner Must Sell.' Your letters said you were looking for a house, and I thought I might give you a hand. Apparently it worked. Just think of it as a gift from your grandmother— through me." Uncle Wiley laughed as though he was pleased with himself.

"That brochure came from you? There was no note or return address; we just assumed that it came from a realtor. We got a number of brochures in the mail once the word was out that we were serious house-hunters. But that brochure had no return address, only the location of the house. We went to look at it, fell in love with it—and now it's ours. However, we did go through a realtor. Autis wanted to do it that way because our headaches would become the realtor's headaches—'to share the grief,' he said."

"I'm getting so forgetful in my old age I probably forgot to put on one of the dozens of return address stickers we get from charities who want us to support them."

"I do the same thing sometimes, Uncle Wiley, don't feel bad. But I wonder why the brochure was sent to my grandmother?"

Wiley shrugged his shoulders and took up his tea again. "Who knows? I frequently get strange mail. A lot of it seems to come from South Carolina. You must have some peculiar folks down there."

"We've got our share, Uncle Wiley."

"Now, what did you need to know?"

"Uncle Wiley, I mostly came just to see one of my favorite people. And I was hoping you could tell me the family names of your parents and grandparents."

"That's easy enough. My father's name was Allen Sheets, my mother was Rose –Rosalind – Bell and…"

"Bell? Her maiden name was Bell?" Liv asked, writing in a notepad.

"Yes. Her mother was Janey Jolly, her father Harmon Bell." He paused, and then said, "Why the frown, Liv? You look as though you disagree with what I've said. I'm quite sure that I am correct in this matter."

"No. It's okay. Go ahead."

"I've dug out an old wooden box. I think everything in the attic was stacked over it. The box contains ledgers, letters and notes from the estate of a distant relative. It was a gift from Janey Jolly to her granddaughter, Iris. Because of Iris' auto accident it was passed back to her mother— your great grandmother—Rose, and then to me, as her nearest relative, after she died so unexpectedly in her sleep. I thought it strange, but an autopsy was voted down by relatives. I let it go. I've never given much attention to such things. You've acquired a passing interest in ancestry, so I'm giving the box with its records to you. I've perused some of the documents, but haven't actually taken the time to read or study them—I'll leave the task of uncovering our families' past to my favorite niece." He rose from his rocker. "I'll get the box." He returned with a rectangular wooden box about the size of a small footlocker. "I think you'll find some of these documents quite interesting—they had marvelous handwriting." He sat the box on a coffee table and turned the latch that un-locked it.

"What a beautiful box," Liv exclaimed. All this carving and inlay. What kind of wood is this I wonder?"

"I have no idea, but I would guess it to be one of those exotic foreign woods, like teak or ebony or some such thing. It's lovely, and quite heavy. I've long admired it, but what would I do with it?" He ran his fingertips gently over the old wood.

"I'll be thrilled to own it, Uncle Wiley. It will have a place of honor in our home. Thank you."

"My pleasure. Well, like I was saying, Janey Jolly married Harmon Bell. I can't recall the parents of either Janey or Harmon, but it's written out in some records I've set out for you to take with you. I have no need for them, and you're the nearest relative I have." He took a deep breath as in thought, and then said. "You know, some day, not too long from now, this farm is going to be yours."

"Oh, Uncle Wiley, I had no idea. Are you sure you want to do that?"

"I'm quite sure, child. You've been my favorite all along. For years, you've maintained correspondence and visits, while everyone else in the family has all but forsaken this old man. Sue and I talked about this before—before she—left this world. The decision to give you the property was mutual years ago."

"Thank you, Uncle Wiley. I've always loved you and Aunt Sue. At times I think I cared more for you two than I did Mom and Dad."

"Say not such a thing, child. It is unbecoming."

"I'm sorry. Tell me again, what was Harmon Bell's wife's name?"

"She was Janey Jolly." The man thought for a moment. "That's as far as my recollection goes, but I'm sure there will be more in the records I've trusted to your keep." The old man stood and stretched. "Ah, these bones of mine are getting old. I can barely manage this farm—couldn't do it at all without hired help. I've got a couple of neighborhood high school boys who are a big help." He regained his seat and leaned toward Liv. "Do you and Autis plan for children? I do hope so. It would be a shame to end it all in your generation."

"Just the other day Autis and I talked about how nice it would be to have a couple of little ones running around the house," Liv said, deliberately overlooking her husband's vasectomy.

"Good. These records I'm giving to you will have a home, and perhaps mean something to someone some day. Sue and I never recovered from the accident that took our boys. Just the other day I was… Oh! I just remembered another name. Janey Jolly's mother was named Camille. Yes, Camille Jolly."

Chapter 17

"Mother-of-pearl."

"Yeah, that's it, mother-of-pearl." Bambi stroked the inlay and carvings. Why didn't your uncle want to keep it?"

"He said he had no need for it, and wanted me to have it as his niece. There were a number of small family things he sent back with me. It was sad to hear him lay out the history of many artifacts and photos around his house. I've promised to return and take notes, some of the items were very meaningful to him—and he's my nearest and dearest relative."

"This is some fancy box," Bambi said as it rested on the coffee table in front of her. "It's carved and inlaid with that iridescent mother-of-pearl stuff. Just the box alone would be worth a sizable sum for those interested in such. I'm still surprised he gave it up. Most older folks seem to want to hang on to family heirlooms."

"Ancestry is not his long suit; he's a here-and-now kind of man. He said I would likely find the box and its contents interesting. It was sealed shut with some kind of wax; Uncle Wiley said it was probably bee's wax. He had cut the seal and examined the contents but didn't spend much time with them until my visit."

"Find anything interesting?" Bambi asked as she lifted a single page that was folded in half.

"That note." Liv answered, nodding at the paper in Bambi's hand. "Look closely and you'll see it's made out to someone. Look at the back of the note."

"'Iris.' Bambi said, "Who is 'Iris?'"

"Uncle Wiley's sister. Actually, Uncle Wiley is my father's uncle. He's my great uncle, and Iris is my grandmother—my father's mother. The note is for her, but it doesn't make much sense."

Bambi gently unfolded aging paper and read out loud from its faded script.

Dear Iris,

You know where to look. Everything is where I promised. Remember—reward comes to those who know how to get to the bottom of things. My letter will answer the many questions you asked me when you were a young lady. Don't forget.

Love,
Your Granny Janey

"'What' is where she promised?" Bambi asked, holding the note in front of her with both hands.

"I don't know. I've looked carefully through the stuff in the chest; it's all records, ledgers, and personal letters. The letters—I've read all of them—were mostly between Alexander Maxton and his daughter Camille Jolly, who was Iris' great-grandmother."

Bambi and Liv spent the afternoon poring over ledgers, notes, bills of lading, receipts, and letters written in a beautiful hand. The box was packed with history. Liv had the presence of mind to begin a chronological ordering of the random paperwork. Each scrap of paper had been meticulously dated in a clean, legible hand. They came to the realization that most of the record-keeping had been done by Camille Maxton—later Camille Jolly.

"Forty three." Bambi laid her pencil down on the lined note pad. "That's the most number of slaves working the plantation at any one time, not counting children, of course. Dear Lord, such sadness." During her count she made a listing of the names of slaves.

"Liv, honey, if it's okay with you, I'd like to try to make some sense of this list of names. I think I can show who is related to whom."

* * *

The door bell rang at 11:20 that night. It rang again, and rang again.

"Dammit. Goddamn it." Autis said. The bell rang again.

"Shit, who would come by at this hour." He pulled on his jeans and headed to the door.

"Be careful," Liv said, suddenly wide awake and sitting up in bed. She reached for Autis' shirt and pulled it on by the time Autis was halfway down the stairs. Bob was standing at the door wagging his tail.

"There's someone out there, Autis said over his shoulder, and flicked on the light just as Liv came up behind him, handing over a stout walking stick.

"Open the damn door," Liv and Autis recognized a familiar voice.

Bambi stood barefoot in a nighty—over which she had thrown her jeans jacket.

As Bambi brushed by him, Autis said, "Well, this is better than *completely* naked.

"I got to thinking—we got to get to the bottom of things."

"I'm just about to put a hand to your bottom, lady," Autis said gruffly.

"Promises, promises," Bambi smiled back. "In the meanwhile, let's take a look at that box. I've got an idea." Taking Liv by the hand, she led her into the living room where the box sat on a coffee table.

Bambi opened it and removed the contents to the coffee table. She sat down and placed the box upside down on her knees. Thumping the bottom of the box, she exclaimed. "It's got a hollow bottom." Then, looking at Liv standing with her arms akimbo, with Autis' white dress shirt hanging open, she said, "You both sleep in the nude? Damn, that's fine."

Liv pulled her shirt closed and began buttoning. "You better be right about that hollow bottom, or I'll get Autis to take a big stick to *your* bottom."

Bambi grinned her toothiest evil grin. "I won't go there right now. Look," she beckoned her friends closer and pointed to a very faint line running about an inch and a half above the bottom of the box. The line was concealed by a layer of wax but was nevertheless visible under close inspection.

"I need a knife," she said, looking at Autis.

Typical man, he patted his back pocket for his pen knife. "Wait, I've got a better idea." He went into the kitchen and returned with a slender plastic box cutter in one hand and a toolbox in the other. Bambi held the box up for him as Liv slid the contents of the box to the end of the coffee table.

"No," Autis said. "Let's take this to the kitchen table. It'll be easier to see and work on there." He turned to Bambi. "Damn, woman, don't you ever sleep?"

"I do, but I got to thinking about you near naked in your jeans, and bare-foot, and I just tossed and turned."

Autis, shaking his head, carried the box to the kitchen. "Liv, remind me to talk with you sometime about your choice of friends."

It took the three of them, working with a larger box cutter than Autis had initially presented, a scraper, and a rubber mallet, to stir the sliding bottom loose from a position of over a half century. Bambi was surprisingly careful and persistent in her effort to dislodge the false bottom without damaging it; Autis was ready to take a hammer to it. Liv came up with the idea of using her hair dryer to soften the wax, thus making it easier to remove. Finally the bottom slowly and grudgingly gave way and was placed on the table top. Three tousled heads leaned over the contents of the wooden tray—several cloth and leather pouches resting on a leather envelope. Autis looked up at his wife with raised eyebrows. "I believe it's your place to do the honors," nodding at the pouches.

Liv carefully lifted a small dried-up leather pouch from the tray and gently worked open the string that held it closed. She peered into the pouch, then took Bambi's hand in hers and poured the contents of the pouch into her friend's open palm.

"Lordy. Lordy, be-Jesus," Bambi said in soft reverent tones as she gazed at the handful of cut diamonds nestled in her now-shaking hand.

"Here, take these, I can't hold 'em, I jus cain't," Bambi said with tears in her eyes. "Oh, God, Lordy be-Jesus. I've never even dreamed of such, let alone hold it in my hand." She poured the diamonds into Liv's hands, rapidly shaking her head in small jerking cycles. Autis slid over to Bambi and pulled her head onto his shoulder as she wept her tears onto his naked chest. He looked at Liv who was standing with her hands cupped around a modest fortune. She closed her hands into fists, splitting the cache of gems into two equal parts. She poured one palm of diamonds back into the pouch. Then, reaching to her weeping friend she wordlessly poured the right hand of gems into Bambi's breast pocket.

Bambi looked up with a startled expression that immediately stopped her sobbing. She sat blinking and panting.

"You'll not say 'no' to this," Liv said. "We've come to this because of you. My history, these valuables, I owe it all to you. It's payback time—and we love you.

"I can't..." Liv placed two fingers over Bambi's mouth, and shook her head in dismissal.

"You can, and will. That's a Ph.D. in your pocket. I'll tell you what my Grandma Iris used to tell me—just say "Thank you.""

"Yes. Yes. Thank you." The sobbing resumed, softer this time. "No one has ever give me this kind of love, except my granny. Everbody's always wanted somethin' from me—never give somethin' to me. I—I don't know what to say or how to act."

After a short while Liv said, "Let me know when you've finished wetting my husband with your tears. We've got work to do."

Bambi separated herself from Autis and sat wiping her eyes with the back of her hand. Autis held out a box of tissues; Bambi selected one, and then wiped his chest. "There. All good now." She smiled at Liv.

Liv opened the next soft cloth pouch and retrieved a line of pearls that kept on coming as she lifted them from the pouch.

"Careful," Autis said. That's old thread. We don't want to spend the morning retrieving pearls from the kitchen floor."

Liv smiled at the very long string of black pearls she laid on the kitchen table. "Sometimes, you are such an old woman."

Autis chuckled, shaking his head. He gathered the pearls in his hands and looked down on them with a bemused expression. "Black pearls; these must be worth a fortune. Look," he said, spreading the necklace on the table. "They're sized from middle to end—look at the size of the one in the middle." He looked up at Liv with a smile. "Can we keep 'em, Mommy?"

Liv chuckled at his wide-eyed expression. "Well, okay. Just don't play outside with them."

Another leather pouch contained more diamonds, a larger pouch held a variety of set stones, precious and semi-precious. The remaining pouches held gold coin, some silver, and a pouch of emeralds. All were laid on the table in front of the totally silent trio.

Autis, Liv, and Bambi remained frozen before the fortune that lay on the table. Bob sat on his haunches, head cocked quizzically at the uncharacteristic stillness of his friends.

"Anyone for a beer?" Autis broke the silence.

Liv and Bambi looked at each other laughing. Bambi shook her head slightly. "I declare. Y'all *are* a different species, you men."

"Was that a yes?" Autis responded nonplussed.

"I would kill for a cup of strong coffee about now," Liv volunteered, rising from her chair. "Guard the swag, Bambi, no telling what 'The Man' might do in the face of such wealth." She moved to the coffeemaker on the sideboard.

"Yeah, he's got that polygamous look they all take on when they get rich."

"Bambi, darling." Autis said softly.

"Yes, dear," she responded with widened blinking eyes.

"Go upstairs and swipe some of Liv's clothes. I'm getting eyestrain trying not to look at your nipples under that sheer nightie."

"You're right, Liv," she said rising, "He *is* a goat." As she reached the doorway, she turned to Autis and said, "You put on a shirt, I'm getting a hard-on." Liv laughed from her post at the coffeemaker.

Into his second jelly-filled Krispy Kreme donut, Autis asked, "Well?" He pointed at the envelope in the bottom of the wooden tray.

Liv put down her coffee cup and gingerly lifted the vellum envelope, and placed it on the table. She moved her cup and a dish of donut crumbs, then gave the table a swipe with her shirttail. The envelope was not sealed, but its flap was secured in place with a string that looped from the flap to a button in the middle of the envelope. She carefully unwound the string and peered into the envelope. She withdrew a sheaf of fine writing paper.

Laying the stack of paper on the table she said, "Have you ever seen such beautiful handwriting?" The letters were long and gracefully slanted, each word written as though placed on an invisible straight line. It was done in a faint purple ink.

Liv lifted another—thicker—envelope, opened it, and removed some tintypes. Faces—people frozen forever in time, leaving indelible impressions on the viewers who knew them not the slightest. Blacks, and whites and grays fading into obscurity.

"Look at these people," Bambi whispered.

Autis took a tintype, studied it and flipped it over. "It's named and dated on the back—looks like pencil. This man was named A. Maxton. The date is—looks like 1864." Autis laid the photo on the table. Alexander Maxton was a robust figure sporting a wide-brim straw hat at an angle on his head. He was standing beside a large, big-boned stallion; the reins were in the master's fist. Maxton was wearing an elegant, loose-fitting white shirt open at the neck, and a pair of somewhat tailored dark trousers, which ran into his riding boots. He held his chin elevated, and his shoulders were thrown back. His legs were spread as if to say, "I'm in command here." A pistol thrust in the cummerbund that served as his belt.

"What's he holding in his left hand?" Bambi asked viewing the picture upside down from her vantage point.

"A whip," Autis answered. "It's lying uncoiled on the ground in front of him."

"What an asshole," Bambi said, taking the photograph and turning it so she could see it. "So that's Alexander 'Monster' Maxton. God, I'll bet he was despised by all. It makes me angry just looking at him."

Liv took the photo. "His vileness reaches across a hundred and forty years." She studied the picture while Bambi looked away, frowning as though in thought. She looked back at her friend. "I—I'm sorry."

Liv returned her look, nodding in understanding.

"What is this about?" Autis said.

Bambi looked at him, she was biting her lower lip. "Seems that Sweetgrass Weaver was right. We're probably looking at a picture of one of Liv's distant ancestors.

"Damn," Autis said.

"Yes. Damn," Liv answered. She slid another photo to Bambi and Autis who had moved to sit side by side. "Here's Camille Maxton, his daughter."

Bambi made a sharp intake of breath. She looked at the photo, then at her best friend, and back to the photo. "It's you. She looks exactly like you, and she's standing in front of this house."

"My Lord, she's beautiful." Autis said softly. If I got you one of those dresses, could I get you to strike that pose for me? I've never seen such elegance leap off a piece of metal." He paused and stared at the photo and back to his wife. "I've come to take your beauty for granted—it being so over-shadowed by your character and your brains."

Bambi looked at Liv with glistening eyes. "Can I have him? I'll give back the diamonds."

Liv shook her head. "I'm keepin' that fool."

"Look," Autis pulled a larger tintype toward himself and Bambi. "Slaves." It was a group picture of a large number of black men and women dressed in little more than rags. Maxton stood triumphantly in the forefront, legs straddled, coiled whip in hand.

"Damn, I hate that man. I want to hurt him. I've never said that about another human; but him I would hurt—bad." Bambi's hands shook as she held the picture up for inspection. "I wonder how many were like him." She swiped at the corner of an eye. "It's so obvious that the right side won the war. Bastards. Bastards, all."

Autis withdrew a tintype of a trio of light-skinned African-Americans. He flipped it over and read: "Mongo, Tige, and Sugar." He turned the picture over and looked again. "What a handsome man—and big."

Liv and Bambi exchanged looks. Liv shrugged, He's one of my ancestors."

Autis handed her the photo. "Well, that's one to be proud of."

"Alexander Maxton was his father, Tige his mother, and Sugar his sister."

"It's a good thing he takes after his mother and not his father in looks." Autis looked at Liv. "Wait a minute. You're almost acting embarrassed that he was an ancestor. Where's that coming from?"

"I'm not embarrassed. I was just worried about you."

"Me?" Autis said, his voice hardening. "Now where's *that* coming from? You just insulted me."

"I'm sorry. I underestimated you and I shouldn't have."

Bambi jumped in the middle of the tension. "See now. If you were mine we wouldn't be having these kinds of misunderstandings. I would be your willing, unquestioning slave."

Liv threw back her head and laughed. "Bambi, who could not love you?"

"Apparently, all the men in the western world."

Autis raised a forefinger and a questioning eyebrow.

"'Cept this one," Bambi said. "Pleez can I have him—maybe just on loan for a while. I won't wear him out, and I promise to return him in better condition than when I got him."

Liv rose and got the coffee pot. "Refills?"

Cups filled, Liv returned to the table. "I guess I better read this material. It looks like a very long letter or a sort of a journal."

Autis raised a hand and said. "I'm drained. Let's knock off for a while, have some breakfast and return to the task at hand. And for Chrissake, Liv, put on some britches."

Chapter 18

Breakfast was a group effort, made and enjoyed with speculation over Liv's ancestry. The dishes were stacked in the dishwasher and a fresh pot of coffee started before the group settled in the living room, seated around the sizeable fortune on the coffee table. Liv took up the papers and began to read.

August 20, 1942 Anno Domini

Dearest Iris,

If you are reading this letter you have taken possession of the chest I promised, and have followed my instructions regarding the false bottom therein. The jewelry, precious metals and stones are all that is left of the considerable wealth once known as Maxton Manor. I have deemed it fit that you should be the possessor of this record of the Manor because of the nature of your lively and precocious intellect and manner. I remember the day of your birth like it was yesterday, and now sixteen years have passed; sixteen of the most satisfying years of my life due in large measure to our relationship. You, dear Iris, are the best and boldest hope for this family. I believe you to be a person of keen character who will mature into a woman of great force and influence. My days are numbered, I know, and I am satisfied with a moderate life, well-lived. However, I find myself wanting to linger so that I may observe, and in some way, however small, participate in your flowering, full womanhood.

Bambi interrupted the reading. "I don't understand this. Why didn't Iris open the chest? I mean, it's never been opened."

"Uncle Wiley told me that Iris was killed in a car wreck in the early 1950s, leaving no one else to accept the chest, and no one knowing the secret of the false bottom. Iris held the chest for several years, but I don't think she was aware of the value of the contents in the false bottom. The chest eventually passed on to Uncle Wiley." Liv paused, looking at the array of jewels and precious metal on her coffee table. "And now it's mine—ours," she said as she grasped Autis' hand.

Bambi shrugged. "I got lost in all that, but go on. We'll sort it out later. Incidentally, we've got to get these pictures to Sweetgrass."

"Definitely. Shall I continue?" Bambi and Autis nodded.

...I rest in comfort with the knowledge that you will never be exposed to the horrors that I experienced as a young child on the frequent visits to Maxton Manor with my mother, your great-grandmother, Camille Jolly. She was born and raised on that manor, and grew up playing with the children of slaves. My mother visited the estate every year, sometimes as often as a dozen times a year to try to set aright the horrible injustices visited on those unfortunate souls enslaved by her father, Alexander Maxton, and by those of his malevolent kind. Mother hired a competent estate manager to try to bring about a productive wage-producing farm and was moderately successful. I believe she could have made it work to perfection had she not possessed such a strong loathing of the memory of the place. She was able to secure employment for many ex-slaves, both on and off her estate. Mother also brought some of the more willing members of the Negro population to the north where they could find good jobs and a community in which they would be accepted. She had a school built for Negro children, and saw to its furnishings and staff. Last, and not least, mother parceled out much of the land to Negro farmers and their families, that they might earn a decent living. It is not untrue to state that there are now a very many Negro people who owe their livelihood and station in life to Camille Maxton. Perhaps she has repaid some of the debt created by her tyrannical father, although I doubt it will ever be possible to make up for the terrible travails visited on several generations of those undefended human souls. If ever angels weep it must be over those awful times.

I have enclosed all the tintypes of the family in my possession, and tintypes of the slaves. Alexander Maxton, prideful beast that he was, saw to it that he was recorded, and, as long as the photographer had been called to his presence, he might as well make a record of others—as his property—on the estate. His hubris has provided us with a snippet of those times. Even so, I hope that God will forgive him because neither mother nor I can do so. We have both witnessed the evil of that man's work. She saw it first hand, and I, after the fact.

In 1864 mother was dispatched along with the family valuables to live with her mother's relatives until the war was over. Maxton had the good sense to convert most of his wealth to precious metals and stones rather than trust Confederate paper. Apparently, he was ever the shrewd opportunist—one who professed allegiance and confidence in the Confederacy, while simultaneously squirreling away his belongings in the event of failure.

Mother told me that, by late eighteen sixty three, Alexander Maxton was sure the South was going to lose—a belief that precipitated the collection and concealment of his resources. Many times he was approached by local leaders with pleas for assistance, to which he responded with beggarly pittance. In the meanwhile, he sold and saved. Late in the war he was able to purchase the valuables of his fleeing neighbors who were desperate to evade the approaching defeat. My mother witnessed how he so cruelly treated those who thought him friend, later boasting of his advantage in their sorry plight. It was the beginning of a true alienation from him. However, it was the death of her loved one, by Alexander Maxton's hand, that fanned the fires of my mother's dislike of her own father to intense hatred. It saddens me to report that your great-grandmother Camille had such an intense negation of her Maxton ancestry that she strove to prevent knowledge of its path and pattern. It has been her influence that dampened my desire to pass on the family history. However, falsehood will serve no end here. Truth must out, as they say.

Continuing this tack, I am impelled to reveal the nature of our background. But first I must outlay some conditions of their situation. When a man and a woman are thrust together, working day after day, side by side, it is near to impossible for strong feelings to be shunted aside. Those who share common goals, struggles, and enemy, are given to harboring emotions in common. And so it was with my mother, daughter of the plantation world, and with Mongo Maxton, a slave on that plantation. There is little need to skirt issues on this topic. Again, falsehood will serve no end. Mongo was the son of Alexander Maxton and Tige, a mulatto slave, who was herself the daughter of Jason Maxton, Alexander's father, and a slave house servant, making her in effect Alexander Maxton's half-sister—by whom he had two children, Mongo, and a daughter, Sugar. Mongo was then, in fact, my mother's half-brother, out of his mother who was half-sister to his father.

"Dear Lord Almighty!" fell from Bambi, who sat with her hand over her opened mouth. She then hastened to add: "Go on. Go on."

Autis rose and went to the kitchen. "More coffee?"

Liv continued as the coffee was poured.

...Dear Iris, you must be thoroughly shocked out of your wits by now, and it is at this juncture that I hasten to support why I chose to put this information in your hands, rather than those of your mother. I have my reasons. You are far enough removed and can remain dispassionate and therefore, less judgmental on such a delicate matter; and I see in you a very practical and rational streak, so lacking in those about me.

Also, I invite your attention to the enclosed tintypes. You have pictorial evidence of the appearance of your great-grandparents Camille and Mongo Maxton, and of their father, Alexander Maxton. Look at Mongo Maxton, and look at your great-grandmother. Place the images side by side. I challenge you to assert that you have ever seen a more handsome couple. In your world, that pair could enter any drawing room arm in arm, drawing only gasps of admiration.

My mother, Camille Maxton Jolly, whom you resemble in appearance and kind, more than you might guess, was a beautiful, spirited lady of great grace and excellence of character. All my life I have striven, unsuccessfully I might add, to emulate her manner and being. But you, my dear Iris, are her youth returned. I remember her as she was from my childhood, and I look up from my needlework and see her in your face and figure. There are no words to relate the feeling of gratification I experience in the light of such occurrence.

Mother and Mongo fell hopelessly in love. In a saner world they would have been allowed, nay, encouraged, to exchange vows, but theirs was not such a world, and they had to satisfy their love in secretive ways not condoned. Mother waited until I was well into adulthood before she shared this confidence, and even then, close as we were, she did so with great reluctance. It took her no less than four conversations over the period of a week to fully reveal the nature of her love, and my subsequent appearance on this earth. I love my mother all the more for showing the courage to reveal those events in her life, events known only to herself and to Mongo's sister, Sugar, who became as a sister-in-law to her after The War.

Mother strove to bring Sugar into her life up north, and Sugar tried to accommodate mother's wishes, but she could not thrive without the community of Negroes with whom she grew from childhood. She finally returned to Maxton Manor as an employee, and eventually took an overseer position. I knew and loved her as Aunt Sugar. She married a fine fellow and gave me many cousins with whom I played as a child, and visited well into my older years. However, we kept our ancestry secret from all others—until now, dear Iris. I have included a family chart with this letter to help you clearly see the relationships I've discussed.

Would that we could be together at your reading of this note. I now know that I should have confided this tale to you in person, and that these revelations would have found acceptance in your fulsome heart. Oh, how I do so love you, dear Iris. Please know that much of my thought, on the occasion of my passing, will dwell on you. As I fade from consciousness the vision of your loveliness will be there to urge me on to a better place, and I shall pass with a smile from this world.

I am ever yours,
Janey Jolly

The three friends sat silently around the table as Bambi handed the box of Kleenex to Autis.

Chapter 19

Sweetgrass Weaver read and rocked, read and rocked, while her guests strolled the grounds of her pecan grove. Goody, the redbone hound, served as guide and companion.

"Now you know, if I's to have a dawg it'd be this'n," Bambi said, lapsing into what Autis had come to call her 'Mountain-Mojo'. "I mean, he's handsome, smart, and willing to be a good friend, without making too many demands." She paused and thought a moment. "Come to think of it, that'd be a good design for a husband too."

Their musical laughter drifted among the leaves of the burgeoning pecan trees.

"Bambi, you are a case," said Liv.

"Dayem, girl, when'd you learn to speak Southern?"

"I've had a good teacher. Do you suppose—*reckon*—Miz Sweet's had time enough with the materials we've given her to look over."

"Yes," Bambi said with a grin. "I *reckon*." The twosome headed slowly back to the house, their summer frocks flowing in the breeze from the sound. Their guide and companion strayed at their heels.

They found Sweetgrass sitting motionless. Her dress front was wet and her face tear-streaked. She remained still as the girls approached and regained their rockers. The silence held for several minutes; a heavy void that spoke volumes.

"I know," Sweetgrass began firmly, "that you ladies properly think you have some idea how much this…" she ran her hands over the box of papers and tintypes on her lap, "these pictures, these words, mean to me. But I can assure you that you aren't even close." She silently rocked in affirmation of her statement.

She resumed, "I would have traded this house, this land, and those pecans for these pictures of my ancestors. They give me a comfort, a fullness, a sense of completion…" She stopped rocking, and gazed out at the sound. "What has transpired on this island, these lands—what has transpired?" She held up the photo of the group of slaves surrounding their *Master*. "Look at these faces, those rags falling off their bodies. Look at the children, most of them naked as the day they came into their terrible world." The girls sensed the anger underlying the soft language of their black friend.

The silence grew leaden.

Bambi was the first to speak. "Granny, you're going to have to tell us your thoughts. If we are to be, and keep, as friends, we have to be honest with one another. Like my Granny back in Virginia says: Your friends tell you the truth."

"Child, I know what your Virginia Granny says is true. But truth may bring pain in tow."

"Yes, and pain is sometimes needed." Bambi answered.

Sweetgrass nodded and rocked a few cycles before speaking, "I was feeling pain for you. You came to me with these pictures of my ancestors as slaves under the absolute control of a tyrant. I can't help but feel embarrassment for you. How must you feel when, with these images, you are saying, 'This is how white people treated black.' Your actions say this, knowing that you are white and I am black. You are braver than me—I would have sent the pictures in the mail and possibly never returned to this place."

"I don't believe that, Miz Sweet," Liv said. "In my heart, I know that you're stronger than me, and probably braver. I think you would have done what we've done because it was done out of love. When we found these pictures, some of the first words out of Bambi's mouth were, 'We've got to bring these to Sweetgrass Weaver. I immediately agreed. We wept when we saw those children in rags and naked, and we know we cannot grasp how they lived and died. The horror of that life—if it can be called 'living' at all. But you're right. It was difficult to bring these images of such an evil time to such a fine and gracious lady whose ancestors were the victims. If that has brought pain to you, I can only offer my sincerest apologies, and hope you know that I want to commiserate."

Sweet turned to Bambi with a toothy grin and said, "Our friend sure does lawyer up good, doesn't she?" This brought a round of laughter and clasping of hands among the three friends.

"Yes, she does," Bambi said dabbing the corner of her eye. "But she's smart and I hold out good hope for her."

"Well, I've studied here what Miz Janey Jolly wrote. It was so good to see her hand, and good to listen to her voice come off the page like it does. My mother knew her well, and I have had the pleasure of meeting her. Yes. She passed away when I was twenty years old. She had visited us a number of times during my childhood, but old age prevented her traveling by the time I reached my teens. I remember her as a fine and gracious lady. My mother remembers Janey's mother, Camille Jolly, as a near saint. My mother also knew that she and Mongo were lovers, and that Janey was their love child. Alexander Maxton was my mother's great-grandfather. That man, that evil man, also fathered Sugar Maxton, who started my line. She was my great-grandmother. She died when I was in my teens. Janey didn't learn of Sugar's death until after the burial, but she came and saw to a fine granite stone over that grave. I'll take you to it. Most of my earlier people wanted burial by the sea so their souls could be washed or wind-driven back to Africa. But Sugar put away the old ways, and tried to lead us to a new world. I have stories I will put to you sometime. But for now I want to tell you the story of Alexander Maxton and his children, Sugar, Mongo, and Camille. Do you have time for a long tale?"

The girls nodded in assent. "Yes, do. Go on," Liv said.

"I'll have to start with Alexander's Maxton's father, Jason Maxton. He fathered Tige, who was Alexander's half-sister and later sex-toy. Tige was Sugar's mother. This information is important because much of this history came from Tige and Sugar who lived in the house all their lives. Sugar was first a slave child and later a house servant, and finally, Alexander Maxton's—her half-brother, you recall—unwilling sex partner. What I'm about to tell you was handed from Sugar to her daughter—my grandmother, to my mother, and then to me.

It is ample evidence of the low regard the Maxtons held for their slave property. It is greater evidence, however, of their evil. Jason Maxton was a hard man, a cruel man."

Chapter 20

Maxton Manor 1836

"I'm not a cruel man, Alexander. I just want what's right, what's due us as white people. In order to get your due, you got to be hard. That's all it takes—some firmness. I'm trying to make you hard, but I swear I can't do it if you come running to me every time one of your brothers looks cross-eyed at you."

"I know that Daddy, but they are both at me all the time, they never give me a minute of quiet. They tease, and push, and trip, and hit me ever chance. Both of them seem to have nothing better to do than make a hurt for me. It's not fair. I could do with one of them, but two is too many…"

"Okay, I'll giv'm a good talkin' to. But you're going to have to learn to look out for yourself in this world. Do you hear me good? Look out for yourself. You're goin' on seventeen and already bigger—and smarter than your two brothers. But I'll not abide a whiny son; be a man, my boy." Maxton rose to get his tobacco jar as Alexander went to the door. "Here, take my whip. I wish you'd do everything as well as you do that whip. I swear; you could take out a fly's eye at ten paces. Be as strong in all things as you are with that leather."

"Yes, Sir" Alexander said, taking the braided coil.

"Now go check on the niggers in the North Quarter. Old Jedson's a good nigger but he'll let'm get slack if there's no one about to push him. We got to get the crop in before the cold comes. And take the flintlock, they's word of outriders about."

"Yes, Sir." Alexander headed for the door, thinking, *Look out for myself. Yes, I'm going to look out for myself.*

He passed by the barn on the way out, and took the short trail to the back wood. At the edge of the wood he found his brothers laid out around a cook fire.

"Why, howdy little brother, we's just finishing a bite—too bad you couldn'a been here to join us. It was mighty tasty."

Alexander knew that his oldest brother, Elson, was up to no good, so he kept walking in silence.

"Yeah, you know that little bunny you been petting up since it was a foundling?" The brothers laughed raucously. "Well, all that grain and green you been feedin' him paid out fine. He cooked up real good."

"Yeah, he were tender." Ambrose, the middle brother, sneered.

Alexander stopped, turned in his tracks and walked back to his blood kin.

He stood over them, gripping his musket.

"You killed Meadow?"

"Yep, and et him," the older boy said around his beech twig toothpick. "They's the bones," he pointed to a small stack of bones next to some fur and a familiar head. "The dogs hadn't found 'em yet."

Alexander stood over his outstretched brothers with silent, pursed lips. It was at that moment he realized the depth of his cold hatred for his own flesh and blood.

"What are you goin' to do, little brother? You goin' to go runnin' to Pa?"

"I'll make you pay for this."

Ambrose rose to his feet. "Now how you goin' do that, little twig? You gonna whip us? Hell, boy, the only thing you can whip is hanging between your legs. Now git, before I take this blade," he withdrew a large sheath knife, "to that little puny whip of your'n."

Alexander stood his ground.

"Git, I said." The brother thrust a fist into Alexander's chest, sending him reeling. He tripped and fell on his backside. The brothers hooted with glee.

Alexander rose and walked away, toward his assigned task. He'd gone no more that six paces when a well-thrown rock struck him in the back of the head.

"Damn you. Damn you both to hell. I'll get even, you wait." He fled from them in haste, rubbing the back of his head. His hand came away with a smear of blood.

I'll get even. Tears of anger and shame ran down his cheeks. *You'll see. I'm looking out for myself.*

When Alexander arrived at the work field, he found the slaves stooped over their labors, softly murmuring a rhythmic song. He strode into the field of growth and swung his whip in an arc, then brought it to an abrupt *crack*.

"Now hear up. There'll be no slackin'. Cold's coming, and this crop better come before it does, or there's pain enough to go around." He cracked the leather again. "Jedson, you hear me, boy?"

"Yes, Mistah Alexandah. I do indeed."

"Then get on it, damn you."

The old black man moved among the field hands urging a quicker pace.

Alexander faded into the woods. He stopped to relieve himself against a tree, then walked further into the brush in order to watch without being seen. Jedson knew this was so, and he continued haranguing the straw hats bending to their work.

As always, Alexander felt the pleasure with the power he exerted over others. He felt an erection coming on and decided it was as good a time as any to take care of business. He sat down and handled himself. He was soon underway when he remembered what his brother had said about his whip, and he lost his erection.

"Damn him." He stuffed his limp member back into his breeches, and made to stand when he heard soft movement off to his left. He slowly turned his head in time to see a file of men moving quietly toward the house. They were carrying guns, knives, and hatchets. After they were out of sight he rose, went back into the field and skirted its edge until he found a quick path back to the farm. He ran with a light jog over the familiar terrain. He would get to the house to warn his father of the coming attack. A quarter of a mile away from the house he stopped and caught his breath—and his thoughts. An idea came to him with a suddenness that caused him to make a sharp intake of breath.

"Yes!" He exclaimed out loud, and once again. "Yes." He leaned against a tree and waited. Moments turned to minutes, and the minutes seemed to drag. Then he heard a gunshot, then another, and another. He walked at a good clip toward the home where he was born and raised.

He made the clearing in time to see Elson facing three marauders who were circling him. Alexander's musket ball caught the nearest between the shoulder blades. The boy swiftly reloaded his musket as his brother struck a vicious slice across the belly of one of his assailants. The two attackers, seeing the oncoming rifleman, fled. One of them cast a lot of blood about him as he ran.

"Just in time, Alexander. Pa kilt one. Ma got another before she fell next to Pa. I got one, but..." He was pointing at the fallen figure of Ambrose when Alexander's musket ball struck him in the chest. Alexander reloaded as he walked up to his brother.

Elson, lying on his back, struggled up on his elbows. "What..." He fell and never again stirred.

Alexander went to look at Ambrose, who had caught a ball in the head. He realized that he was now an only child and smiled to himself. *I said I'd get even.*

He went to the house and found his mother slumped over the kitchen table, dead. His father was at the fireplace with a pistol in his hand. His father showed four bullet holes in his clothing. There was a dead outrider in the kitchen and one laid out on the front porch. Alexander took the pistol from his father's hand, loaded it, put some shot in his pouch and walked back out into the scene of carnage. He saw a slight movement at the edge of the wood. The slave girl, Tige, seeing him, turned to flee back into the wood.

"Stop." His sharp command halted the frightened girl. "Come here. Now!"

The violently shaking girl stood before him, tears in her eyes, and a rivulet of drool running down her chin.

"Tige. Catch yourself up, girl. I need your help. Run and tell Jedson to come quick with the hands. Tell him to send a boy on muleback to fetch the sheriff. I'm going after those other two men. Now git, girl, run!" She turned and fled.

Alexander caught up with the wounded man less than a half mile from the house. The blood trail made easy tracking. The man was sitting on the ground with his back to a chestnut tree as Alexander approached.

The hunter smiled to himself with thoughts of avenging his family, and then he stopped and ducked behind a tree. *This is too easy,* came his thoughts. He would reflect on that scene and grudgingly admit that one good thing had come of his brothers. They had played at Indians for hours on end, stalking and "killing" one another in mock attack. Many tricks are available to the minds of young boys. He knew that this trick—this time—was deadly. He knew also, that had he been playing the trick, he would have let the pursuers pass him and come up from behind in a sneak attack. He turned to look back, and at the same time dropped to the ground. He waited, rifle at ready.

The figure came quietly from tree to tree. The wounded marauder was white, but this one stalking from behind was indeed an Indian. At just about the same time the stalker realized that his ruse had not worked, Alexander's musket ball shattered his right hip and spun him to the ground.

Pistol in hand, Alexander approached the writhing man. He took away the Indian's weapons and fired his pistol into the man's left knee. Then Alexander went to take care of the man at the chestnut, reloading his pistol as he walked.

The man at the tree could barely lift his musket as death approached with a loaded weapon. Alexander's ball blew away his right shoulder.

Standing over the bleeding figure, Alexander slowly reloaded, and then fired into the man's abdomen.

"If you two are still alive when Sheriff gets here, he'll see to the rest."

The boy then turned and strode back to the house. Half an hour earlier he had been the youngest son, due to accept short shrift all his life. Now he was a plantation owner. He owned land, livestock, and a large crop of indigo to bring in. He hummed to himself as he made his way through the wood. He was a slave owner.

Chapter 21

The sheriff appeared late in the afternoon.

"I came on them too late, Sheriff. They'd already killed Daddy and Momma, and my two brothers. There was three left standing. I killed one outright. Elson had struck another with his knife before he was shot dead; that one and his partner took off for the wood. I chased them down and killed them. One was an Indian."

Sheriff Hudson, a giant of a man, was said to be sheriff because "he can whip any man in the county," and had seen more than his share of mayhem at the hand of marauders and outriders. Nevertheless he stood in silence for several minutes as he surveyed the two rows of bodies laid out on the Maxton front yard. He spoke briefly to the two neighbor sisters, Nell and Cassie Watson, who were tending the bodies of the Maxton family. The outrider corpses were left as they were, bloodied and unkempt. After viewing the corpses he walked to his horse, withdrew a metal flask and took a good pull at it. He capped the flask and put it back in the saddle bag, and then returned to the scene in the front yard of the Maxton property. Alexander was standing silently over the bodies of his family. The sheriff walked up to Alexander, placed a ham-size hand on the boy's shoulder and softly said, "You done a man's work today, son. Your pa would be proud."

Without taking his eyes off the work of the Watson sisters, Alexander said, "Daddy and Momma killed two of them in the house before they went down themselves. I don't know how it happened 'cause I wadn't here. I was out looking after the fields, and seeing to the hands."

"No doubt you're a man now. This farm is a big responsibility—and it's all on your shoulders."

Alexander feigned surprise. "I…Yes, I guess it is."

"I know you can handle it. Your pa brought you boys up good, and your momma saw to it that you could read and cipher. She told me in town one day this spring that she picked you to do the book-learning 'cause you were the quickest of the lot. You'll learn fast. If'n I's you, I'd go see my neighbors real soon, and get them to help you figure your way through the coming harvest. This ain't no time to be proud; ask for help." The sheriff paused, took out a rag and wiped his brow. "Lord, this is a mess," he said, surveying the bodies that had been laid out. "I'll help you with burying of these outriders."

"Nossir, they ain't goin' to foul my land. I got my field hands to making a pile of fat pine wood. We're going to have us a big bonfire tomorrow night. I need for you to go with me to see to the other two critters I left dying in the wood. We'll bring a couple of mules to drag 'em back. Sheriff, I'm hoping you'll stay to supper and the fire. I'll put you up in daddy's room."

The sheriff nodded assent, "My wife's family is visiting from the North, so I can't stay long. You send a boy on mule to tell her to come tomorrow for the burning; tell them to make ready to attend the funeral too."

Alexander frowned in thought. "Sheriff, you won't need me to find the other two men—just follow the blood trail." Alexander pointed the direction. "I've already started some niggers digging graves over where granddaddy and mammy are buried. I want to see to that work. And I need to be alone for a while. I sent riders to neighbors with word of the funeral come Sunday. I put my carpenter to building boxes." Alexander stopped and ran his hand over his face.

The sheriff stood with his mouth open. "Damn, boy, your momma was right. You *are* quick."

"Sheriff, you know better than me what to do. What else is needed for the next coming days?"

"I'll get Preacher Engles out here to help plan the funeral. He'll say the words."

"Pa don't church."

"No matter. A body's got to have a decent burial. It wouldn't hurt none if you's to grow the church fund some."

"I can do that. How much, you reckon?"

"Well, you got four to bury. I'd say a dollar a head, and one thrown in for good measure. Five dollars would be fair."

"I'll do that."

"I'd commend you to the church, son. They are good folks with strong beliefs. A man can use neighbors like that."

"I'll take your heed, sheriff. Now I need to spend some alone time. I'm going to walk the wood trails that my momma taught me as a child. She had her favorite places. I know I'll find her there." The mention of his gentle and kind mother finally brought tears to the boy's face. The sheriff walked off to the side as the boy wept. It was the last time in his life that Alexander Maxton would shed tears.

The sheriff proceeded to the barn where a pair of mules were being bridled and made ready by the field hand. Alexander headed to the site where graves were being made.

"Mistah Alex?" Tige approached with a handful of garden greens.

"Yes. What is it?"

"I knows you is busy, so I picked some garden green for your pet rabbit."

Alexander turned to look at the light-skinned slave girl. She had an odd look on her face, and a triumphant set to her jaw.

"I... " Alexander looked closely at the girl, sensing a kind of understanding. "Is he okay then?"

"Yessir, he fine. I jus looked on him. But he hongry. Can I feed him? I know you so caught up and all with—with—" She waved in the direction of the front yard.

Alexander's jaws tightened as he remembered his brother's jeers. "Feed him. Does he have water?"

"Yessir he do." The girl took a deep breath then said. "You so kind to him, Mistah," she said averting her eyes. "An Mistah Alex, I be proud to help with everything."

Alexander nodded. "Tige, you look after the kitchen help, and get a couple of the field girls to wash up and come in to clean the house and set things straight. We got a lot of folks coming the next four or five days, and I don't want to shame my momma with a dirty house."

"Yessah. I feed your rabbit, and git on it right away. Okay do I pick the helper girls?"

"You do that Tige, now go." Alexander waved her away. He watched her young, healthy body move under the flimsy cloth of her cotton shift as she moved away with a grace that said, *I know you're looking.*

"...And Tige."

"Yessah." She stopped and turned back to the new master.

"You wash up good yourself."

"Yessah, Mistah Alex." She hurried away, filled with a new air of self-importance.

"One more thing." Alexander said, turning the girl again.

"Pick out four field hands that can be trusted to spread the word by muleback. I want the whole county here for the funeral. Tell them to see me for orders." The girl stood nodding with a growing understanding of her new position of power on the plantation.

"Go do it."

"Yessah, Mistah Alex. I'll do it *all,*" she answered with a bold confidence.

Over the next week, Tige was good as her word. At first she brought in two girls from the field—scrubbed and combed. Mastah Alex don't want no 'smelly field trash in his house.' She added two more on the next day, and by the funeral she had a staff of six women and two men ready to serve at a moment's call. The Watson sisters, both experienced in running a household, oversaw Tige and added considerably to her growing knowledge of how to manage. They were impressed, and not a little put off, by the fact that Felicia Maxton had taught this slave girl to read, but they soon set aside their reservations when they discovered the intensity of the girls' desire to do good work without once complaining. It was also a pleasure to be able to leave written instructions—thus assuring that nothing would be forgotten or easily misunderstood.

By week's end they had taken Tige's cotton shift away and replaced it with some gingham frocks. "Child, even a servant can't walk about nearly naked in a house full of guests." Massive quantities of food appeared—delivered by horse and mule from outlying neighbors. Tige saw to it that no food was wasted; some went to white guests, most to grateful blacks. In the evening dark, dishes and platters found their way to the slave quarters where they were joyously accepted. No food spoiled in the autumn warmth.

Neighbors came to help. They sent servants, field hands, and skilled craftsmen. Nothing was left unattended or in need. No less than a dozen field hands were loaned to help "keep the crop." Jedson, the old slave overseer, rose to new heights of authority on the farm, and responded well to his modified position.

Word of the coming spectacle and of the Maxton funeral spread like a storm throughout the county. On the night of the bonfire, surrounding neighbors and the Maxton slaves stood in awe at the sight of no less than five corpses burning over fat pine timbers. Flasks were handed silently among the white men. Not a few of the older women were emboldened with a nip or two by evening's end. Most there would never forget the odor of burning human flesh. Nightmares were passed in the coming weeks, especially by the black people who had watched in silent terror from the forest. The fire burned all night as more logs were added. Many folks simply joined their children and slept on the ground until dawn. Tige saw to it that all were fed before going home.

For years to come, children of the region related the spectacle to any who would listen. The name "Maxton" was heard throughout the South. By year's end, the rumor was that the fifteen-year-old boy had single-handedly hunted down and killed the five men who murdered his family, and then burned the bodies. Alexander Maxton was impelled to grow into a force.

In the days after the bonfire, Tige oversaw washing, cooking, mending, and repair. She put in sixteen-hour days, and was surprised by the ease with which she managed to do so. Each day she silently thanked Felicia Maxton for the guidance and instruction she had quietly extended to the light-skinned child of Jason Maxton and a servant girl. She quickly selected a bright young barn hand called Toby to help with the physical work. His reward was a new pair of breeches and a store-bought shirt. Toby's father, Dack, with help from two of his sons, managed the barns and outlying buildings. Dack was made overseer of the caskets and grave digging. He carved wood markers that would serve until more proper stones could be ordered and placed. The Watson sisters etched out the lettering for Dack, who carved them on fine-grained old cypress blocks.

Tige was worried. It was the house that bothered her the most. At the end of her first day's work as house manager, Tige came to Alexander with a request. He was in his father's study, puzzling over how to become a plantation owner and manager.

"Mister Alex."

He looked up from his desk, "What is it now, Tige?"

"I know you want to set your best out for the services."

"That's true."

"Sir, I have a worry I can't shut."

"Say it, Tige, I got work to do. I can read but I can't cipher good. Say it out, girl."

"Mistah Alex. Toby says that, if we start tomorrow, and set enough help to it—Dack showing how—we could have the house painted by buryin' day." This came out in a rapid gush.

"Toby said that, did he?"

"Yessir. He also say that he and Dack could paint the parlor walls—if'n we's to start tomorrow."

"The parlor walls."

"Yessir, Mistah Alex. The guests—they only see the outside of the house and the parlor walls. We have it all done before they come."

Alexander leaned back in his chair and looked closely at his house manager. "Where did you get such ideas, Tige?"

Had her skin color been darker, Alexander would not have seen the strong flush that came to her face.

"I turned on it all day."

"Why so, Tige?"

"Mister Alex," tears welled in the girl's eyes. "I's studying… I's…I's…"

"Say it out, Tige. I won't hurt you."

"If Miz Maxton be here, she'd want the house…" Tige fell prostrate to the floor and sobbed openly—her face scant inches from Alexander's muddy boot.

"My momma would want the house to look fine. Is that what you're about, Tige?"

The weeping servant raised her head and pushed herself up to sit on the floor. She nodded as she tried to wipe her tears away with her palms.

"Miz Maxton was the kindest, best mistress a body could hope for, and I..." Tige knew that she was skirting a serious breach of protocol. It was not the place of a slave to judge her master or mistress. She was thus prevented from saying out loud the extent of her love for a lady from whom she had known only kindness. Tige had lost the one ray of sunshine in her life. Hers was probably the greatest loss of any on the plantation—and she was forced to stifle it.

"Tige, you're right. That's what Momma would want. You're right, and you were smart coming to me like you did. Now get yourself up, and go tell Toby that you and him are going to town tomorrow to buy the supplies you need. Tell him not to skimp. Better yet, take Dack along with you, and let him decide what's needed. Now go wash up and fetch me Dack."

"Thank you, Mistah Alex." Tige turned and fled from the room as though chased.

By the day of the services the house looked the best it had looked in Alexander's memory. The outside walls and colorful trim fairly sparkled in the autumn sun, the roof shingles were scrubbed and given a coat of oil, the lawn was scythed and then raked clean, and the parlor was hung with new wallpaper, per Dack's suggestion to Tige, who seized on the idea immediately.

"Dack—he say that paint won't dry good in time, and that wallpaper will be up and hung and dry in plenty o'time. And the Watson Miz's, they picked out a pretty paper with flowers and apples and grapes. It look like walking in a big orchard it do."

Alexander gave approval, and it was done. The farm was a beehive for four days. Neighbors came to pay respects and stayed on to help. Slaves were recruited from all parts of the county. Jedson was hard-pressed to keep everyone working. Food was brought in and cooked on makeshift outdoor fire pits. Everything centered around the women who were under Tige's management with the authority of the Watson sisters behind her.

The bodies had been put in their coffins and stored in cool earthen caves.

On the day of the funeral, the entire south county emptied itself onto the Maxton property. Extra outhouses had been built. It was the first time any had seen separate outhouses standing side by side—one for men and one for ladies. Long pit trenches were dug in the woods for the slaves.

The funeral was talked about for years after the event. No less than four preachers had their turn at the pulpit, each earning an extra dollar. More than one man was heard to say: "It's the best damned buryin' this county has ever seen."

The day of the services, Tige wept and worked, wept and worked. She risked serious violation of etiquette by allowing herself to approach too close to the services. More than one white Christian looked her way from under a puzzled brow. But she wanted to hear her mistress buried proper. Sally Maxton's grave was never in want for flowers while Tige lived. On warm moonlit nights, the slave girl could often be found stretched out face down across the grave of the white woman she loved—her cheek pressed to the grass, and her tears watering the earth.

Decades later, when Tige passed, she was heard to say the last words, "I's coming Missus. I's comin." She left this earth with a smile.

Before the sheriff left the services he brought his family and his visiting in-laws to meet Alexander. He was especially interested to put forth his wife's young cousin, Kathleen Jolly—a young lady who, within the year would become Mrs. Alexander Maxton; a decision she would soon regret, but be helpless to correct.

Chapter 22

Sweetgrass leaned back in her rocker. "Now that's the story as Tige told Sugar, who told it to her daughter, Mizelle, who told it to Mattie, her oldest daughter. Mattie Jones was my mother, and she passed the story to me. You see, what Alexander Maxton never knew was that Tige had followed him all the way from where he saw his brothers eating rabbit to where he polluted himself, and where he shot his older brother. Tige was a house servant and was given a lot of freedom to do her work in her own way. She was smart, quiet, and she kept to herself. The tales about Tige went on to say that she could see around corners, and hear what was meant, instead of just what was said. She listened outside of a lot of doorways."

"'Polluted himself?' What..." Bambi said with a furrowed brow.

Sweetgrass, tight-lipped, rocked herself in small quick cycles, finally breaking her silence. "That's what the nuns used to call masturbation; self-pollution. They said it came from the Latin."

"You're Catholic?" Liv asked.

"No, but I was privileged to attend a Catholic school for girls. My momma used some of the last money that Miz Camille gave the family to send me there. It was difficult at first, but turned out to be the best thing that happened to me. I'm forever grateful for my mother's choice—and for Camille Maxton's gift."

Liv and Bambi exchanged glances over the evaluation of masturbation. Bambi was leaning into a question when she realized that Sweetgrass was just before nodding off. She and Liv rose to help Sweet to her living room couch.

"You ladies come back tomorrow, and I'll finish the telling of how it all ended up after the War. It's a story I've carried all these years."

Once again, a glass of water was placed along with the telephone beside the frail sleeping figure. Bambi pulled an afghan over her adopted grandmother.

"We'll come back tomorrow?" Bambi asked Liv.

"Would you miss it? I wouldn't."

Bambi laughed out loud. "Gal, you're getting interested in your history— sounds like you're turning into a southern belle."

Liv smiled. "Let's stop by the Tea Plantation. I need a strong cup of tea."

"All that history wearing you out, darling?'"

"That, but I've got to wake up also. Autis is out of town for a couple of days, and I can use the time to catch up on my writing. I can put in a good six hours before I crash."

"Yeah, I guess I'll work on my glass this evening," Bambi said.

"Can't find anything else to blow, huh?" Liv chuckled as she wheeled into the Tea Plantation parking lot.

"Yeah, now that Autis is out of town, or as long as I know how to pollute myself." Bambi shot back with a wicked grin. The closed car windows prevented the other visitors from hearing the raucous laughter that rang inside the car.

Liv worked four frustrating hours trying to develop a piece about farm kitchens titled "A Farm in Your Condo." Her head was spinning with uses of natural pine, copper pots, and Blue Willow crockery, but she kept flashing back to recent events—her recent fortune, Tige, and Sweetgrass were thoughts that peopled her mind and would not be denied. After a hot shower, she crawled between the sheets and opened the latest John Grisham novel. She read for a while as she finished off a tumbler of Yellowtail chardonnay, knowing that it would put her to sleep. "Second best sleeping pill I know," Autis had maintained.

She dozed off with the book laid across her stomach. Bob was breathing deeply from the floor at the foot of the bed. His soft, repeated "Bruff" awakened Liv at three a.m. *The voices.* "Damn." Liv threw aside the bed covers and slipped into her clogs. She pulled a terry robe around her and headed to the pub, Bob in tow.

"Sounds like they're having a goddamn convention downstairs, Bob." She opened the door to the stairwell leading down to the pub. "Hey! Knock it off down there. I'm trying to get some sleep." The voices grew silent, then Liv heard that same chuckle she'd heard the night that Autis and she investigated the voices. She descended the stairs and hit a light switch—nothing happened. She made her way to a corner of the room and found a table lamp. It gave out enough light for her to see her way around the room. "All right, people, this is the last time I'm telling you. Keep it up and I'm calling in a witch doctor. You're going to find yourself out on your spooky asses." Silence. "Okay, I'm going back to bed now, and I don't want to hear any crap from you people. If you must talk, keep it down."

Bob started whining. Liv turned to see him pawing at the French doors to the patio.

"Jesus, Bob, why didn't you take care of that earlier? You've been out all evening." She opened the door, and Bob took out barking.

"Oh, I see—a deer out there with your name on it."

Liv left the door ajar and went to the cooler to get a glass of table wine, which she set beside one of the day beds where she stretched out. Halfway through the glass of wine she dozed off. She didn't hear the door softly close as she drifted off.

Her dream started almost immediately. She was in the clutches of a man, a large man whose face she couldn't see. She fought him, her hand pushing against his naked chest. She found him muscled and powerful. She gasped helplessly as he entered her. He was big, very big, and he thrust into her with what had to be anger. He thrust and thrust. She soon found herself reaching for him with her body, giving as good as she got.

His face materialized briefly. "I waited, where have you been?" he demanded. She reached up to pull his face to hers, but he wouldn't let her, and he continued driving fiercely into her. Then he stopped, and shuddered with a moan. She could feel his orgasm—and he was gone.

Bob was barking outside the door.

"Damn." Liv rose from the day bed and staggered a step or two before she caught her balance. She opened the door and Bob danced into the room.

"Pumped from the chase, huh, boy. Well, I just had me one hell of a dream—glad you weren't here." Liv went to the day bed to get her wine glass. Just as she reached for the glass the lights came on. She reflexively turned to see if there was someone at the switch. Nothing. As she picked up her glass she saw a large wet spot on the day bed where she had been dreaming. She smelled a familiar mushroomy odor hovering over the day bed. Bob came up and sniffed at the spot, backed away, and looked at her—she thought—accusingly.

"Don't look at me like that; I was only dreaming," she chided her companion, then added, "I hope."

*　　*　　*

"Hayel's bayels, gal; what was the name of that wine you were drinking? I'm goin' to get me a bottle," Bambi said.

Seated at a quiet corner table of Salon Sandi's, Liv rolled her eyes at the ceiling. "I knew I shouldn't have told this tale. It just makes me look like a damn fool."

Sandi said, "Now, don't go getting your back up. In fact, I believe what you've told me to be true and accurate. I mean, you're no flake to be scoffed at. Now Bambi here…" The three had a light chuckle.

"Seriously though," Sandi continued, "this region is filled with tales of boo-hags and evils spirits and such."

"Boo-hags?" Liv said.

"You haven't told her about boo-hags?" Sandi said to Bambi, who shook her head in response.

Sandi drained her glass, refilled and started. "A boo-hag, or hag is what my friend Buff would call a ghostly apparition. It's the soul of someone who has left this world. Sometimes they take over the body of someone living. Most would call them demons or wicked spirits intent on harm."

"'Buff? Is that Buff Shellman—Gar's friend?" Liv asked.

"Yeah, Buff is a retired archaeology professor from the University of Georgia. He lives in a one-room shack on poles over the salt marsh. He gave up his position and professorial lifestyle after his wife passed—he won't say how. Some would say he's a hermit, but that ain't so. He just wants a simple life, and he's got it. He's probably Gar's best friend—sorry, Bambi, I know you thought you were."

"Hell, we're not 'best friends,' we're in love is all."

"Oh."

"Well, we are. Everone knows that. Everone also knows that Buff's a great sailor, and he and Gar sail together whenever they can."

"Anyway," Sandi continued, "A boo-hag is not something to mess with; they are usually bent on mischief and mayhem. Ask any local. Some say they are witches, and some know them to be shape-shifters that occupy the skin of living people. Rumor has it that most boo-hags can't go out by day—but some can."

"Do you believe in the existence of these—these boo-hags?"

"Why do you think I've painted all my window frames such outlandish blue? It's to keep out the boo-hags."

"What's that about?"

"It keeps out the evil spirits; seems that boo-hags won't cross blue windows and door frames."

"Is it working?" Liv asked tongue-in-cheek.

"If you looked at my checking account you would say it is."

"Your bank balance is a result of good sense and hard work, Sandi."

"Blue window frames can't hurt."

"Okay, so I've got a boo-hag, or hag—whatever." Liv shrugged. What can I do about it?"

"Rent him out."

"Hayel yes, pimp him," Bambi said. "If he's as good as you say, I want dibs on first."

"Vaudeville. My basement running over with boo-hags, and I get a comedy act from my best friends," Liz scoffed.

"Okay, okay." Sandi feigned resignation. "I have a—friend, a good friend who can probably help you. Let me make a phone call." She rose and went into her office, signaling the bartender to keep an eye on things.

The girls ordered sandwiches with a side salad, and they split an order of shrimp and cheese grits. One of Bambi's favorite sayings was, "A day without grits is a day without sunshine." Liv realized that Bambi lived by that code.

Sandi returned to the table nearly thirty minutes later.

"Those grits were fine, Sandi." Bambi gave a deep sigh, adding, "That Thai cook of yours should be cloned."

"If Jason said he wanted me to double his salary, I would do it without question, and he's one of the highest paid chefs in the region already. That's not an invitation to blackmail, ladies. Anyway, my friend's name is Elethea Gaines, and she says she can meet you at the Angel Oak for about an hour on Thursday. She may know something—or someone—who can help you with your boo-hag problem."

Chapter 23

"Why 'Angel Oak?' I've never heard of that species," Liv said.

"It's not a species," Bambi said. "It's a huge oak, named after the family that once owned the land it's on, and it's a big tourist attraction hereabouts."

"Named after a family called 'Angel?'"

"Yep, why you grinning so?"

"I was just thinking, it's a good thing the Humperdink family didn't own it."

"You got too much time on your hands, gal, and too much in your head."

"Yeah. Here we are." Liv slowed for the sign that pointed them into a sand driveway. They parked next to the Angel Oak gift shop and went to look for a lady wearing a bright yellow scarf, per Sandi's instructions.

"Oh, my God," Liv said as she rounded the gift shop and saw the enormous life form before her. Like so many first time visitors, she stood mute, as in the presence of a deity of nature. She turned to look at her amused companion.

"I come here sometimes, just to sit on one of these giant branches low-lying on the ground."

The 300+ year-old oak spread over an area about the size of a football field. Its lower limbs lay on the ground, some larger than a man's waist, and running prone for fifty or sixty feet before curving upward.

"I've never seen anything like this before. This isn't just a tree, it's a city," Liv said in a whisper. "Autis has got to see this."

"Sometimes Sandi comes here with me for lunch. We sit on a branch and eat our sandwiches; afterward, we both come away from here renewed. It's like God was really serious when he made this tree. I could never take this place for granted."

"I believe that," Liv said. "There, the yellow scarf. Oh!"

"What? Oh."

The lady was sitting on a large root branch with her back against the tree. Her eyes were closed. The vivid scarf and white dress offset against her ebony skin.

"She's beautiful," Bambi whispered.

"Yes, but I wonder why Sandi didn't tell us..."

"No matter, she's here, we're here. Let's go introduce ourselves," she said as she walked toward the tranquil scene of the lady in repose.

"Elethea?"

The woman opened her eyes, took a deep breath, and rose to her full height, towering over Bambi, who was by no means small.

"Yes. Do I have the pleasure of speaking to Liv Oakley?" The woman's voice had the same cultured manner heard in Sweetgrass.

"No, I'm Carole Bamberg, and this," turning to her friend, "is Liv Oakley."

"So, I finally get to meet the infamous *Bambi*." Elethea gave a soft chuckle. "I've heard so much about you. Sandi considers you about her best friend."

"Well, she's certainly tops in my book."

"Miz Oakley, my pleasure." The lady extended a slender hand and gripped Liv's in a handshake.

"Please—call me Liv, and the pleasure is mine." Liv studied the black woman's finely chiseled features, wondering what part of Africa her ancestors came from

"Won't you join me on my root? There's room for the three of us. I was just listening to the Angel Oak. I come here often. The tree has much to tell those who would listen."

"What does it say?" Liv found a perch on the tree root.

"It doesn't 'say' a thing," Elethea answered. "The communication is in the listening, not the telling. If your next question is, 'What do I hear?' I have to say that I hear a different message than either of you might hear, and that each of us would be correct." Elethea sat down and pulled her knees to her chin, tucking her skirt around her, much like one would see a little girl do. "We—I come here often. Sometimes for ten minutes, sometimes for lunch. It is, at times, a sanctuary. Do either of you have a sanctuary?"

The newcomers were silent. Bambi spoke up. "In Virginia—I had one on the mountainside above my grandparents' cabin. It was a rock ledge with an overhang from the rain and sun. I would go there for hours as a little girl. I would watch and listen to the forest and its critters. Storms would come and I'd go to the back of the ledge and stay dry while I watched the tumult. It was the most secure place I knew as a girl. Someday I'll go back and take the trail behind that cabin up to my sanctuary."

Liv could see that her friend was moved by the memory.

"Mine was a sugar pear tree in my Aunt Sue and Uncle Wiley's front yard at their farm in Ohio," Liv added, in an attempt to distract Bambi from her sadness. "I would climb the tree, it was very large, and I'd find the biggest sweetest pears up high. From there I could see the neighboring farms and fields. I could see the dairy cows in my uncle's field, the bull in his pasture, and the forest out behind them. I still remember what it looked like from that height. There was one big branch I could sit on while I rested my feet on another just below it. I'd stay so long that Aunt Sue would come out to see if I was okay. I did so love those sugar pears. I'm like Bambi—someday I'd like to go there and climb that tree to that branch, and just sit."

"Then I'm talking with people who have soul, aren't I?" Elethea said.

"If that's what it takes, then that's me," Bambi answered. "But I see beauty all around me—every day. I think some folks carry a 'sanctuary kit' with them, and are prepared to take it out when needed."

"Oh my," Elethea said. "That is good. Thank you for that thought gift. I'll take it with me for the rest of my days, and when I use it, I'll think of my friend Bambi who gave me a sanctuary kit. Sandi told me that you were one of the most gifted people she knew. I know what she means now."

"Thank you, but she's no fool herself. Look at what she's been able to do with her businesses. Don't you just love that saloon of hers? I mean, it's near perfect."

"I've never been there, but I've heard her talk about it—she's filled with love for that place—and I've heard others discuss it with pleasure."

"I see," Bambi said softly.

Elethea turned to Liv. "Now, you have a problem I'm told."

"I don't know, do I?"

"From what Sandi has told me, I would say you do—a serious problem. Your house is, what shall we say, 'inhabited' by someone other than you and your husband?"

"That would be one way of putting it."

"Sandi told me of your…experience with a spirit in your basement recreation room."

"Yes, I—I experienced a spirit."

"In what way did you interact with the spirit?"

"We had sex. I thought it was a dream, but I'm not at all sure that it was, in fact there was evidence to suggest that the sex was real."

"Physical evidence?"

"Yes on the couch, and—my body."

"It happened this one time only?"

Liv paused, and looked at Bambi. No, I've been back twice since, while my husband was out of town. Both times it happened again after I fell asleep."

Bambi looked startled at this news. "You never said…"

"I didn't want to look foolish or stupid. And…"

"And?" Bambi said.

"I enjoyed the sex. It was like having a wonderfully erotic dream."

"What you described to me before was like a rape."

"I know. In a way it is, but there's something more, something that makes it not a rape." Liv blushed intensely. "I hadn't meant to go into this. It's so personal, and now, talking about it, I feel like a slut—and an adulterer. I enjoyed what I did. On the one hand I would go back tonight; on the other, I want it to stop. It could easily become an addiction."

"You're falling in love with a ghost," Bambi said.

"No. No. I'm in love with my husband—in all ways, mentally, emotionally, physically. He is all things to me, and I hope that he feels that way toward me. But..."

Liv's companions leaned into her hanging sentence.

"But the sex is unbelievable."

Bambi scoffed. "Now you're pissin' me off. I love that man of yours like he was my own, and you're telling me that you're willing to continue being unfaithful to him."

"I'm not unfaithful." Liv turned to face Elethea. "You must think I'm some kind of nut, or no better than a two-bit whore. I'm sorry. I'm not this way. I've led a normal life up to this point, and now I'm in over my head with this—this 'thing.'"

"Bullshit," Bambi said in a strong whisper. "If you really loved Autis, you would walk away from this ghost, this spirit, and not even look over your shoulder."

Liv nodded and bit at her lower lip. When was the last time either of you had three orgasms during a single act of sex?"

Liv heard a sharp intake of breath from Elethea. "But you said you don't love this spirit."

"That's right, I don't."

"I have orgasms, but they come from love. I can't image experiencing an orgasm with someone for whom I hold no love."

"I can't account for what you do. I can only say what is happening to me."

Bambi took her friend's hand in hers. "I'm sorry. I judged you when I shouldn't have. I love you, and I don't ever want to hurt you or abandon that love. You're my dearest friend. Can you forgive me?"

"There's nothing to forgive between best friends," Liv answered. Then she turned and leaned toward Elethea. "Can you help me? I have to get out of this macabre relationship."

"I know someone," Elethea said. "I have a great-aunt who is Gullah."

"What is Gullah?" Liz asked.

"I'm Gullah on my mother's side of the family," Elethea said. "My father immigrated here from Ethiopia and has nothing to do with Gullah. The Gullah are African Americans who speak their own language, a derivative of Eastern African languages and English. They have their own variation of Christianity and customs that are specific to them only. They occupy some outer islands on the South Carolina and Georgia coasts. In Georgia they are called Geechee, and they are dying out."

"Why—why are they dying out?"

"Until very recently, they lived a secluded life on their islands. There were no bridges and not that many boats. Now...everyone seems to want a piece of them. They are regarded as quaint fare for tourists by people who want to make money peddling quaintness." Elethea's voice showed her anger. "People just won't leave them alone. Then, of course, there are the developers—there are always developers—who view the land as worth millions. Rest assured that in this county there are people who will go to bed tonight with visions of condominiums rising along the beachfront of lands that are presently owned by people who have little money of their own and no knowledge as to how to defend themselves from predators with lawyers. The Gullah are smart, capable people, but they lack the deceits necessary to cope with the ways of people who regard making money as the ultimate good."

"Hayel, honey, it's the same as in the mountains. My kin sold their land for next to nothing, only to watch it subdivided—each lot selling for more than they got for the whole damn parcel."

Liv joined in. "I have a cousin who grew up near Orlando, Florida. She has the same horror story to tell. She says her little home town was eaten by a rat some call Mouse. Is there no stopping it?"

Elethea shrugged. "Who knows? Anyway, the number of Gullah grows smaller each year—some of them just leave to be a part of the larger community off the island. Like everywhere, their young people crave excitement and novelty. It is only when they get older that they realize the beauty they fled. My great-aunt, Books Wrenn, is one of the last of what some might call a 'shaman,' or more commonly, a 'root doctor,' or even 'witch doctor.' I hate that term, but it connects with most people. Aunt Books would probably say that you have a hag in your basement."

Chapter 24

"I am of two minds on the Gullah," Sweetgrass said. "They are my people, but our ancestors went two different ways after The War. The Gullah froze themselves in time, drawing from their African roots and languages. My side followed the path set out by Sugah and her family. They strove to cope with what was then the modern world. At first, that world held great promise, and it looked as though people of color were going to join the mainstream of America. But in ways most profound and evil, the South won the war after all. Southern politicians were able to pass laws that worked against black people and their culture. Those laws would have been ineffective if the courts refused to back them, but that was not the case. Southern politicians and federal judges put black people in a place of second class citizenship and kept them there until the 1960s. It took a hundred years of misery and woe for America to begin to fulfill its promise to people of color.

"While this was happening, the Gullah moved back in time and stayed there, choosing isolation—protected from the world at large by living on islands that no one else wanted, until now.

"The Christian religion of the Gullah is much influenced by African nativism and has a powerful draw to its practitioners. It is not my place to say they are right or wrong. They are merely different from my way."

Bambi took a sip of tea. "I understand that, Granny. Liv wants to know what you think about using a Gullah shaman to locate and, maybe, remove the spirits from her basement."

Sweet rocked, looking steadfastly at Liv. "Locate, yes—but remove, I doubt.

It's going to take more than that to remove your spirits."

"I see," Liv said. "Do you believe in this Gullah religion, Miz Weaver?"

Sweetgrass pursed her lips in reflection. "Belief *of,* and believing *in* are different things. I believe the Gullah faith works for them. However, I believe in my own way, not theirs. It's not my place, nor yours, to question another's belief. I feel I must respect the beliefs of other people, and what they believe in, even if—no, especially if, I disagree with them. That said, what I believe in is belief. I don't think that we can live in civility without belief. Does that answer your question?"

"Yes—yes it does. Thank you. It wasn't my intent to pry."

"I understand that, child; no offense taken." Sweetgrass patted Liv on her forearm.

"Miz Weaver, do you think that boo-hags exist?" Liv said.

This was a seven rocker-cycle question. "Yes, as much as I believe that Satan exists, and, from what I read and hear, every society has its own ideas of Satan. Those creatures might just be another of Satan's many forms." Sweet reached to a shelf under the side table and withdrew a Bible. "This is what I have to protect me from my Satan. This is my armor, my shield," she said in a firm, raised voice, while she rocked in short brisk cycles. After nearly a minute she slowed and lengthened her rocking and asked Liv in a soft voice. "What is your Satan, my child, and what shield have you?"

"I don't know that I have a shield, Miz Weaver," Liz answered after some thought.

"Then my dear, I say that what you appear to have is a Gullah demon. I think you need a 'Gullah' shield."

High in a pecan tree, the neighborhood mockingbird sang, triumphantly marking his domain.

Chapter 25

The following day found Liv and Bambi back at Sweetgrass Weaver's home. As before there was tea and mockingbird. This time the bird caught Liv's attention. "Miz Weaver, that mockingbird's got one all-white wing."

"Yes, he does. He's been hanging around for going on three years now. I think he likes the company. I call him Marcel."

"Marcel?"

"After that French mime fellow, Marcel Marceau. I'll make myself clear on this later. In the meantime, I've asked you back because there's history that needs passing on, and, Liv, you're the one that needs to hear it."

"Thank you Miz Weaver. You've gotten me interested in my ancestry, and my life has become complicated beyond anything I would have imagined. Bambi is trying her hardest to convert me to a southern belle, insisting that knowledge of ancestors is a good starting place in my education."

"Good as any, Liv," she smiled thoughtfully, then added, "Would you ladies care for some cheese straws?"

The tin was passed around, leaving each of the ladies with a small pile of cheese straws in a napkin on her lap.

"Will you pass on your recipe for these, Granny Sweet?" Bambi asked.

"I'll do better. You come over one day soon and we'll make up a batch together."

"Just say the day," Bambi said, crunching one of the cheese morsels.

"Liv, you said that you had no evidence of what I've told you about our common ancestry, and I can understand your skepticism. I'd raise an eyebrow, if I was in your shoes. Course, now we got us pictures and letters..."

"Miz Weaver, I didn't mean..." Sweetgrass halted her with a wave.

"No offense taken, child; I admire your need for proof." She rocked a few cycles. "I'd like to offer the following as some support for what's been said so far. Recall that I told you about Alexander Maxton fathering the children, Mongo and Sugah, through his slave housekeeper, Tige." The girls nodded in understanding.

"Sugah was my great-grandmother. She was born in 1846 and lived until 1936. I was born in 1920, which means that I was sixteen years old when Sugah passed. I also knew Janey Jolly, Camille Jolly's daughter from Mongo. Recall that she was Alexander Maxton's granddaughter, and Sugah's niece.

Camille visited Sugah frequently, and was the benefactor whose money paid for my education. I was a teen when she passed, and I remember her quite clear from her visits." Sweet's hand went to a jeweled brooch pinned to her shirt collar. "She gave me this brooch, and I have worn it with love and pride since I was sixteen. Like Sugah, she told me stories of the lives of people living in and around Maxton Manor. She did not bring me into her confidence, but told Sugah to do so when I came of age. As I've said most of this story came from Sugah, and some from Camille Maxton. I think the starting place has to be about the love that came about between Camille and Mongo." Sweetgrass rocked for a while as she collected her memories.

"One spring day Camille was riding the mare that had been given her on her sixteenth birthday a month earlier. The mare was named *Goldie* because of her beautiful color. She stood at sixteen hands, and was a gentle and kindly mount for a lady. Returning home they were accosted by two uncouth men who grabbed at Camille and were very explicit in making their intentions known. Camille lashed her riding crop at the face of the man attempting to grab her reins and took off with them in pursuit. Goldie quickly outdistanced the sorry mounts those highwaymen were riding, and Camille arrived home safely. Camille went immediately to her father, who gathered his sons and went in search of the outriders. The boys took up arms and went looking; their aim was murder."

*   *   *

"We didn't catch them this time," Alexander Maxton said, "but we'll get them soon. They can't stay hid forever. Meanwhile, I forbid you from riding off alone like you did today."

"Pappy, that's not fair. You're punishing me for something that someone else did."

"Ain't punishment; I only want to keep you from harm."

"But I like to ride, and Goldie loves the long runs we take. She is so beautiful."

"Child, you're worse than those sorry brothers of yours. You'd live on that mare if I's to let you."

"I'd rather do that then be cooped up like a layin' hen."

"I've been getting complaints from all over, about you taking off in men's breeches, riding all over this county and nearby. I forbid you from riding far off, and when you do go out you'll be escorted."

"Daddy, that's wrong."

"No, it's right, and it's good sense."

Tige entered the room, carrying a tray of refreshments.

"Tige, you tell her what those ladies from the church said to me in this very room the other day."

The command caught the slave girl unawares. "It's...it's not my place, Mistah Alex."

"It is, dammit, if I say it is. You tell her."

Tige turned to the girl she had raised as her own. "Miss Camille, your daddy right. Those fine ladies from the church they say that you look..." Tige was starting to perspire under the risk of violating the rigid codes of the time.

"That she looked like what? Say it, damn you," Maxton demanded.

Had the women been alone they would have been able to say what and how they wished. But, before the master of the house, they both knew that strict protocols had to be observed.

Camille broke the tension by saying. "I know what they said. I've already been made aware of that gossip, and I don't care. I'm not going to ride about side saddle like some doll in four layers of finery. I can ride as good as any man, and I'm going to ride like a man. And I'm going to ride when and where I want." She stamped her foot and slashed at a stuffed chair with her riding crop.

Tige, began to back out of the room.

"Tige, go get Mongo. Now!" Maxton commanded, and then turned back to his daughter, "You're right, daughter. I never did understand all the finery you women wear, and I know that it must be a lot easier riding like a man than it would, perched side saddle like a parrot. I would say that you should take one of your brothers with you, but I know how poorly you get along with them, so I won't even bring up that subject."

"Daddy, all they want to do is tease and torture."

"I know that, child. I've seen you with them and it rends me, but I've long given up trying to mend those fences. So..." He stopped and walked over to an open window that looked out at his fields.

"Yes, Daddy?"

"I've decided to let Mongo accompany you on your rides. You can tell everyone he is your manservant."

"Daddy, that is outrageous. Women don't have menservants. Men have menservants."

"Well, I can't very well send you off with a maid because she won't be of any help. Mongo is big and strong, and he's smart as hell for a darkie. Now, y'all have played together since you were in diapers and he running around near naked." Maxton laughed loudly to himself. "More'n once I've had to scold you about not wearing clothes when you were nothing more than a pippin. I remember how mad you used to get when I made you wear clothes while the little pickaninnies were running around naked as the day they came into the world. You wanted to be just like them. I used to find your clothes all over the damn farm. In the summer you were nearly as brown as some of them. I remember that one time I let some visitors to the farm think that you were an octoroon, rather than let them know that I let my little girl run naked with the nigger children. You really embarrassed me when you came running up and called me 'Pappy' in front of those ladies. They had the preacher come try to lecture me."

"Daddy, I'd still rather run naked with them, than have to dress up and put on like those helpless, simpering fools I see in town and at gatherings. If I could wear men's clothes all the time I would."

"Well, you can't. You're turning into a lady, and you blessed well better start acting like one, or..."

"Or what, Daddy? You let those idiot brothers of mine do as they please. But me? I've got to act like some kind of fool toy. There's hardly a day that goes by that those sons of yours aren't out there rutting on those poor field women like—like some kind of boar hog. It's shameful is what it is. How come you to be embarrassed of me as an innocent little child, but not ashamed of grown sons who act like animals in the field?"

"A man's got to do what a man's got to do. It's different with men, and I don't expect you to understand. Besides, what are you doing spying on your brothers? You shouldn't be watching such spectacles as that. It's not something that ladies do."

"How can I miss it, Daddy? They're out there in broad daylight in the middle of the field."

"Well, they're improving the breed, I'd say."

"Shame, Daddy, shame. Those are people. What a terrible thing to say."

"Those are Africans. They're barely more than apes and..."

"I'll not hear such talk." Camille put her hands to her ears. "Daddy, you are wrong. They're my friends, and I consider them family."

Maxton's face grew livid. He grabbed his daughter fiercely by the arm and yanked her down into a chair. "Now you listen to me. This is *my* house, you are *my* daughter, those are *my* slaves. I own them, I own this house, and dammit, I own *you*. I will say and think and do as I please."

Camille wrenched her arm away from her father. "You don't own me. No one owns me. Daddy, you are so wrong, that you are evil on this."

Maxton back-handed her in his rage; it was the first time he had struck her since she was a little brat in need of a paddling. She looked at him in astonishment.

"You hit me."

"You damn right I did. Someone has got..." Maxton wheeled about to find his giant slave Mongo standing immediately behind him. He had the distinct feeling that the light skinned servant was about to grab him.

"What are you doing sneaking up on me?"

"Sorry, Mister Alex, I took my boots off at the door. They were field muddy."

"I don't like people sneaking up to me."

"Sorry, Mister."

Maxton walked over to the side table where there was a tray of food and fixed himself a glass of rum and water; then, he turned back to Mongo and Camille. Maxton had the uneasy feeling that Mongo had moved closer to Camille as if to protect her.

"I've got a new job for you." Mongo stood silently in attention.

"Tige has done a good job raising you, and you are one of my best hands. I trust you more than any of the others. Camille wants to ride her mare around the county on long trips, but she was almost attacked by outriders today." Mongo was mute.

"You ride behind her on those trips. Take Banner. He's our biggest gelding, and is strong and fast. I've seen you ride him in the field, and you have good control of him. You're the only one that does." Maxton took a long pull on his rum. "Dammit, boy, are you listening to me?"

"Yessir."

"Dammit to hell, I never know when you're listening. You never speak."

"Nossir. I don't want to speak unless told to."

"A good rule I suppose. But sometimes it's irritating."

"Sorry, Mister."

"Mongo, I swear, there is an uppityness about you that...If you weren't..."

"Daddy, that's a fine idea." Camille finally found her tongue. "I'd like to have company on my rides."

"Mongo is not 'company.' He is our property, like Goldie."

Camille pursed her lips and threw a glance a Mongo. "Yes, Daddy."

"I trust Mongo. You two grew up pretty much together until he had to go to the fields. You and he and Sugah spent entire days with your heads buried in books. That tutor I hired said that Mongo picked up ciphering faster than anyone he's ever seen. Tige wanted him to stay in the house, but he got so big that it was like having a draft mule stomping on the floor. Anyway, he's our best hand." Maxton turn to face his slave. "Mongo, I'll tell you this. You're my most valuable darkie . I wouldn't take three for you."

"Why, that's kind of you to tell him that, Daddy." Camille said, covering Mongo's silence in the face of the praise.

"One more thing, daughter," Maxton said, frowning at Mongo's failure to thank him for the praise.

"I want you to take this with you on your rides." He handed her a small twin barrel derringer. "The next outrider that makes a grab at you, I want you to keep this handy and blow his brains out with it. You know how to use it as well as any man. Don't hesitate. That's the difference between men and women. A woman will hesitate, and a man will act.

"Now," Maxton continued. "Mongo, you can't carry a gun, but I want you to have a good knife, a tomahawk, and a stout club with you at all times when you're following my daughter. I am giving you permission—no, I'm commanding you to protect her, no matter the cost."

"Daddy, what if the attacker is white?"

"I told him to protect you; I don't care if they are blue with lace frills. Do you understand that, Mongo?

"Yessir."

"You protect my daughter, and I'll protect you."

Chapter 26

Camille, astride Goldie, broke through a line of pines and onto the long expanse of green field that lay out ahead. She lightly touched her spurs to the mare, who took off like a shot. Banner and his rider followed, galloping at what appeared to be great ease as Mongo lightly held the reins, always making sure that they didn't overtake the woman in the billowing white shirt. Camille was wont to burst into a run at every opportunity, often scattering livestock, people, and whatever stood in her path.

Mongo watched in amusement as Camille's black hair streamed in rhythm with her gait until she veered off toward a small vale with a stream of clear water running through it. At the edge of the wood she slowed to a canter, then a walk. Goldie was breathing hard when Banner pulled up next to her.

"There's a stream up ahead. Let's water the horses and take a rest in the shade," Camille said to her silent companion.

Ever watchful, Mongo turned in his saddle and surveyed the area before they ducked into the wood. He felt for the tomahawk at his belt.

In the shade the horses sidled to the stream where they drank deeply. Camille swung a leg over the saddle horn and dropped lightly to the ground.

"I could do this all day, every day." She shook her locks and combed them into a semblance of order with her fingers. She turned and grabbed Mongo by his shoulders, attempting to shake him. "Let's run away, you and me. We'll ride forever. We'll explore where no one else has ever gone. We can take to the plains and then cross the mountains to the land beyond. No one will ever find us." She tipped her head back in a loud burst of joy, showing a strong chin and flashing white teeth. Mongo smiled, knowing that he would remember the moment.

"What would we eat?" he asked. "Where would we sleep?"

"You could shoot us game, and we would sleep under the stars. Banner would stand guard over us." She impulsively reached up and clasped her hands behind Mongo's neck and pulled herself to him, and him to her. She planted a light kiss on his mouth, laughed and spun away, leaving him to stagger dumbfounded. But for the stout tree trunk behind him, he would have fallen backwards to the ground.

Camille walked to her horse, leaned her head against the palomino's flank, and turned to cut her eyes at her astonished protector who was wiping his mouth with the back of his hand.

"What, you'd wipe away my token of affection? How rude." Camille feigned indignation.

"Miss Camille, don't do such things," Mongo blushed scarlet.

"Why Mongo Maxton, you're embarrassed. I've never seen such. Here you are a looming hulk of a man thrown completely off your stride by a little peck on the mouth." She strode up to her giant protector and moved to pull his head to hers again, but was stopped as Mongo took her by the wrists and restrained her. "Please, Miss Camille. If we are seen like this it will go hard on your reputation, and I'll see a noose."

"Who's to see us, silly man? We're miles away from everybody—we can do what we please, and it pleases me to kiss you."

"No, it ain't right."

"Who's to say? Aren't we best friends?"

"Yes, but..."

"And haven't we been best friends since I was a naked little girl running with the pickaninnies? You used to call me an Indian."

"I was a boy and you were a baby."

"You were only two years older than me. But I thought you were a grown man then. You've always been a grown man to me."

"Good. But you can't keep acting like a little girl."

Camille flushed crimson. "I'm not a little girl. I am a grown woman."

"You're the size and shape of a woman, but sometimes you..."

"So, you have noticed my shape then?" Camille said as she snatched a blanket from behind her saddle. She spread the blanket, sat down and commenced to pull off her boots.

As an astonished Mongo watched, Camille shed her boots and britches and waded into the clear stream. He gathered the horse's reins and led them away from the stream, refusing to look at Camille splashing in the water.

"Come on in, the water's fine."

Mongo hobbled the horses in a down-stream grassy spot where they could graze, and then he sat down with his back against a tree, looking back in the direction from which they had ridden. His hand fell to the tomahawk at his side. He wiped his lips once again, but not before he ran his tongue over them, tasting. Only then did Mongo realize that he was trembling. He scanned the horizon for intruders. It was midday, midweek, and most people were in their fields or working their farms in a variety of endless tasks. Mongo knew this, but he was also aware that some people were able to move out and about; vagrants, children, farm hands on errands and so on. Then there were outriders, a threat to all. They stole, pilfered, and menaced rural counties throughout the South. Constant vigilance was the order of the day. Lynching and whippings were typical of the swift justice that kept the scourge at bay in most communities. As the meanest, toughest man in the county, the sheriff was expected to give no leeway to outriders, and he was good at doing what was expected. The county sheriff was often the one with the rope.

Mongo knew that he would be given no quarter if Camille came to harm while under his protection. He also knew that, as a black man, he had few choices available to him in defending his master's property or family. These thoughts abruptly halted when a dripping Camille Maxton came to stand next to him. She had removed her shirt and was wearing only a once-piece undergarment that she used for bathing. If Mongo hadn't so quickly averted his eyes he would have seen how the thin garment clung to his mistress, revealing breasts and curves that were much considered but rarely seen by men of the South.

"Come swim with me," Camille half-commanded, half-pleaded.

Mongo shook his head with his eyes fixed on the ground between his boots.

"But why? We're best friends. We've always been best friends. You taught me to swim, to fish, to ride. Almost everything I know outside of books I learned from you, and Sugah. Isn't it true?"

"Yes, we've always been friends, and you've always been like..." He stopped, refusing to look up.

"Like what?"

Mongo shook his head. "Nothing."

"Nothing? I've always been like nothing to you? I certainly can't take kindly to that, Mongo Maxton. Most men seem to find me attractive."

"No, it's not that. It's..."

"What? What is it, Mongo?" Camille said softly as she sunk to her knees beside the light-skinned Negro.

Mongo looked into her eyes. "Everything. You've always been everything to me. I've watched you grow up from a pippin to the grown lady you are now. I remember when you were born and your mother died. I thought my momma was going to go with her."

"Yes, Tige still weeps over my momma's grave, and over Grandma Sally's grave. It was your momma that taught me what a fine lady my momma was. If it weren't for her, I'd know next to nothing about my family. It was your momma who caused me to know that you and I are brother and sister."

"I don't want to hear that."

"Well, it's true, but it doesn't matter to me. I'd love you like I do, no matter what. We got the same daddy, just different mommas is all. Same as with Sugah and me. We're sisters. We get together and talk sister-talk. There's nothing I wouldn't tell her about me, and nothing she wouldn't tell me about herself—or you." Camille's eyes sparkled with glee. "She knows a lot more about you than you realize, I can tell you that."

"Now you're making trouble for sure."

"She told me, Mister Mongo Maxton, that Daddy is trying to make you into his prize stud."

"This is trash talk," Mongo said.

"No, it's not. She heard him command you to put yourself to any or all of the slave women you wanted. She said he said it was so because you are so big and strong." She twisted her torso and looked directly at Mongo.

"You're a lady, and you can't listen to such."

"I'm a woman, and I want to listen to all I can about you. Sugah said that the women try to put themselves to you because you've got—a tool like that yard donkey that runs with the horses."

"Stop now. You can't talk like this," Mongo said.

"Why not? Who says?"

"Everybody says, is who," Mongo said. "And everybody knows why."

"Why? Why? I'm a grown woman and you're a grown man." Camille leaned low from her seated position and turned her head to look up at Mongo's downcast face.

He finally sat back and looked directly into Camille's eyes. "Because we are close kin and…because you're a white woman and I'm your nigger slave boy."

Camille shot to her feet, spun around and delivered a hard left-hand slap to the side of Mongo's face, hurting her hand more than his face. She stood directly in front of him, feet apart, hands on hips and said sharply, "Don't you ever say that again, damn you, damn you to hell, Mongo Maxton." She threw herself onto him straddling his lap and wrapping her arms around his head. The side of his face that had received the slap was pressed against her firm breasts and he could hear her heart pounding.

She would not release her hold. "I love you, Mongo. I've always loved you, and I'm going to until I die." She could feel him shaking under her, and then she kissed him again. And again. These kisses were not like the light peck she had placed earlier; they were the released passion of a grown woman who would have her way. At once she felt his manhood rise under her, and it excited her all the more, to know that she was in command of this giant man she had adored from childhood.

A lesser man couldn't have done so, but with a muscular effort Mongo rose to his feet with Camille clinging to his body.

"We can't do this." He pulled her arms from around his neck.

"You love me, I know you do," she said. "I see it in your eyes, I know it in the way you speak to me and treat me. You've always loved me."

"That's true, but they's nothing we can do about it."

"Why? That's wrong." Camille's breathing was quick and heavy like she had just run up the steps from the cellar.

"It may be wrong—but it's right. That's just the way things are, and there's no need to torture ourselves over it. I do love you. I'll go to my grave loving you, but if we get seen like this I'd see that grave tomorrow. Now, get dressed and we'll head back to the farm."

Mongo shook uncontrollably as he unhobbled Goldie and Banner, and then led them back to Camille just as she was rolling up the blanket she had thrown down.

"You've not heard the last of me, Mongo Maxton. You just haven't, that's all."

Chapter 27

Sweetgrass rocked in thought, as her eyes wandered to the mockingbird singing from the highest branch of a pecan tree.

"No one knew how close Sugah and Camille were. They confided everything to each other. They were close in age, both raised by Tige, and lived and played together all through that big old house. Tige was a tall, handsome woman—some said elegant, and she had hopes that Alexander Maxton would accept her children by him as his own, but that wasn't to be. In that man's dark heart they were his slaves, his property. Oh, he treated them fair enough, but that was because he considered them play toys for his daughter. But for Camille, it was another matter. She saw Sugah and Mongo as her sister and brother. That's why what happened later between Camille and Mongo might be hard for some to accept if they's to know about it."

The mockingbird was running his trills. "Listen to old *mimus polyglottis* up there. Isn't he a sight?" Sweet's eyes seemed to cloud over.

"Miz Weaver, are you okay?" Liv asked.

"I'm fine, child. I was just thinking, if I's to come back, I believe I'd like for it to be as a mockingbird. That way, I'd set up at lovers' homes and lighten their lives with music."

She clasped the hands of the ladies on each side of her.

"To go on," she said. "Camille told Sugah about her feelings for Mongo. And Mongo, of course, told Sugah everything about himself. He and Sugah weren't white and they weren't Gullah. Because of their condition of limbo, Sugah, was the only one Mongo could give his confidence to. Sugah and Mongo mought just as well of been shipwrecked on an island; all they really had was each other, Camille, and their mother. Everything went along okay like that until Camille and Mongo became lovers; it happened as you would expect it to happen..." The mockingbird was on a pattern of two notes, a trill; two notes, a trill; two notes, a trill.

The horses, tired from a long ride, were slowly walked by their riders. Camille was seated on Goldie, but Mongo had gotten off Banner and was walking between the two mounts. Every so often he would reach up and stroke Banner on the neck or run his fingers through the gelding's thick mane.

"You like that animal, don't you?"

"None better. If he was mine, I'd set him free. I'd let him run to the plains and join the wild herds out there. I would have never cut him. He's too valuable an animal to give up the line. He should be covering all the mares here-about."

Camille laughed. "Like you're doing with the colored women on the farm?"

"I'm not wanting to do that. It's your daddy that's forcing that done."

"Now how's he doing that? Seems to me that you're the one that's getting the women heavy."

"Your daddy is giving a sow for a girl child and three sows for a boy. More than one man has come to me asking to give his woman a try. One man I'll not name asked me with tears in his eye. We were both shamed."

"I don't believe that."

Mongo stopped in his tracks. "You think I'd make that up, like it was something to be proud of? Mister is shaming us all."

"Sugah says that the women like having you treat them."

"They like the doing of it, I do too, but when the *after* sets in, it makes a body sick in the heart and the head. I can't look in the eyes of about half the men on the farm. Times I feels I's the slaver. I don't sleep good nights. Do you think I'd lie about such?"

"I'm sorry. I apologize. It's just so contemptible, that I don't want to think my own father would…"

"Hey, nigger," rang out from behind, causing the rider and her companion to look back.

"Get your black ass away from that white woman." Two men approached from the woods on a single run-down roan.

"You heard me, step away." The man with the reins said, pointing an ancient muzzle loader at Mongo.

"He's my servant, and he does what I tell him, not what you say," Camille said sharply.

"Seems to me ya'll is right friendly for a white woman and a nigger." The muzzle-loader spoke through tobacco stained teeth.

"What I do or say with my servants is no concern of yours. Now be on your way."

"I'm tellin' that black nigger last time to step away. If he don't I'm blowing his head off his shoulders." The man slid from his bareback perch onto the ground and walked up behind Banner just as Mongo drove his thumb into Banner's withers. The gelding responded with a kick that sent the outrider flying as his partner was getting off their nag. He was the older, tall and lean. He drew a large sheath knife from under the rope that served as his belt. Mongo walked up to the man as though the knife didn't exist. He brushed away a futile attempt at a slash and hit the man with a blow that sent him sprawling. As the man struggled to rise to his feet, Mongo's boot caught him on the jaw, laying the man out on his back. Then Mongo bent down and lifted the man to his feet, and snapped his neck between his forearm and the opposite hand. It sounded like a dry branch breaking.

The gunshot so startled Mongo that he dropped the dead man in his arms and spun away to face the first man—who was standing with his musket in his hands, and a startled look on his face as a large red stain appeared in the middle of his chest. He staggered, then fell forward with a grunt and was still.

Mongo looked up at Camille who sat with the derringer in hand, the second barrel cocked and ready. The breeze fanned her hair out to a massive black wreath surrounding her face. Her breast was heaving against her light cotton shirt. She looked at the dead men, then back to Mongo as the results of their actions dawned on her. She leaned forward over her mount and sagged against the golden mane. Banner had bolted at the pistol report, but did not run far.

"Go chase down Banner," Mongo commanded. Responding almost automatically, Camille sat up in the saddle and trotted Goldie toward Banner, who stood grazing in the middle of a pasture.

By the time she returned, Mongo had slung both corpses over the back of their horse and was in the middle of tying them in place with strips of cloth he made from their shirts.

"What are you doing? Let's just leave them here," Camille said.

"No. If we leave them here, they're sure to be found."

"That doesn't matter, no one will know it was us who—who killed them." Camille said, choking on the word.

"There's tracks," Mongo said as he used his boot to cover the blood stains on the dusty trail. "Tracks can be followed. That won't do." Swinging onto his mount, he said, "I know a place where they won't be found, leastways not by people."

Taking the reins of the packhorse, Mongo led him off the trail and into the grass. Camille followed. In less than half a mile, Mongo cut back toward a swamp where wild hogs were known to hide during the day. At the edge of the swamp he dismounted and handed Banner's reins to Camille.

"Meet me at the stream below the spring, where we were before; I won't be long." He turned and led the loaded pack horse into the swamp.

Camille reined Goldie in the direction of the familiar stream.

In the swamp, Mongo led the roan a short distance to a tiny muck island. He dropped the old musket and the sheath knife in the water just before he got to the island. Once there he dropped the bodies into the muck, then turned and walked the horse out. By the time they got out of the swamp, both were muddy most of the way up their legs.

When Mongo arrived at the stream he saw that Camille had already hobbled their mounts and laid out some oats on flat rocks for them. She was standing in her chemise in knee deep water.

"Give some oats to that roan, he looks starved," Camille said.

Waving acceptance, Mongo walked the roan into water deep enough to wash off the swamp, then he sponged away the blood of the man whose life Camille had ended. The roan was almost frantic in the way he took to the oats laid out for him. Mongo shook his head over the condition of the poor beast. "You're coming home with me, boy. You've got no brands or marks on you. We'll say you just took up with us on the trail."

As Mongo fed the starving animal, a doe cautiously stuck her head out from the brush on the opposite side of the meadow that led to the spring where Mongo and Camille were recovering. The doe carefully stepped from the shaded brush into the lush meadow. She was followed by a pair of gamboling fawns. After seeing that there was no nearby threat, the doe began to graze in quick snatches as the fawns chased each other about the meadow. She was alert to the presence of the humans.

When Mongo returned to the blanket he found Camille holding the derringer cupped in her hands; her widened dark eyes glistened. "We killed them both—you and me. We killed two men." Her breast heaved.

"Yes. But..." He was stopped by Camille's sudden movement to him. She flung the derringer to the blanket and threw her arms around his neck, pulling him to a fierce kiss. She pulled him to the ground and covered his face with kisses as she tore at his clothing. After she got him out of his shirt she dragged his boots off, then went for the fastenings of his trousers.

"I told you that you hadn't heard the end of me yet, Mongo Maxton."

The doe heard the sound of raised voices but continued to graze and watch. Her fear was ever present but so to, her hunger. There was milk to be made. Fawns to feed. She ate—and watched.

"We can't do this. We got to stop—now." He was holding onto his trousers, resisting her efforts to pull them off.

"No. Why?" She demanded as she flung his trousers away, then sat straddling the man she wanted.

"How many reasons do you need, woman?" Mongo said, knowing that he had lost the battle.

Camille tipped back her head with a burst of satisfied laughter.

"What is it?"

"You just sealed our fate, Mongo. For the first time ever, you called me a woman. Up to now, I've always been a girl to you."

"That's right, and you're still a girl."

"No. Today I'm a woman, and I need a thousand reasons to keep me from doing what is so rightfully ours to do. I love you, and you love me."

Mongo was silent as she struggled clumsily to enfold his member into her body.

"Help me. I can't do this alone, and you know how to do it." She attempted to sit back onto him. "It won't go in. Help me, dammit. Oh!"

The doe raised her head in the direction of the human sounds.

He rolled her over so that he was on top.

"Oh. It hurts."

"Yes. That's one reason right there. It hurts the first time."

"Sugah told me that. Ohh." She struggled to arch up into him.

"Don't do this. It's not too late to stop."

"It is too late. It was too late a week ago, last month, last year. I love you. Aagh. Push."

"It isn't working," Mongo said. "You're too young, too small."

"Get off."

The doe made quiet sounds that brought the fawns closer to her.

Mongo, relieved and pouring sweat, backed away from her open legs. Camille rolled away to reach for an embroidered satchel next to the blanket. She removed a sealed jar and handed it to Mongo saying, "Put this on your—yourself."

"What is this?"

"It's a salve. An oil. Sugah gave it to me, and said it would be needed."

"This is crazy, and it's just one more reason not to do this. I know we both want to do it. But that don't make it right."

"Right? Wrong? The *wrong* is in this horrid world. What is wrong is not consummating a love like ours, that's what wrong. Put it on, or do you want me to put it on for you?" Her eyes flared and flashed in near anger.

She averted her gaze as Mongo applied the salve and replaced the lid on the jar.

"Now. Now we can do it. Sugah told me what I need to do to make this work better." She crawled on all fours to a sweet gum sapling about the size of her wrist and took hold of it. "Now, let's try it this way. Sugah said it would work better the first time if you mount me like I was a mare and you a stallion."

"No. This ain't right."

"Do it."

Mongo shook his head in silence as he moved to accede to Camille's demands.

"Yes. Ah. Oh. Push. Push."

"I am pushing, but this is hurting you too much."

"Push!"

"No. This is wrong." Mongo moved to withdraw from her.

"Push, you damn nigger. Push."

Mongo paused, took Camille by the saddle of her hips and drove himself into her.

The high-pitched scream coming from the wood across the meadow brought instant reaction from the doe. She sounded a short whistle and dashed, almost in panic, to the forest. Generations of instinct brought her fawns to her heels as she fled. A second cry, more guttural, added to her impetus to seek the deep wood.

It was a long time before the breathing of the lovers calmed and their hearts stopped their rich *thud*, *thud*. They remained pressed together as one. Camille felt the man inside her grow less turgid and demanding.

"I—I—It's..." She breathed several breaths. "When—I'm—passing—on my death bed. I will remember this—this very moment. I'll run it over and over as long as breath will let me."

They separated briefly so they could gather into each other's arms—and time stood still. The creatures of the surrounding wood played out their many instincts. The doe had stopped her flight and stood braced in the shade as a fawn nursed.

Finally, Mongo slowly rose from their coupling. He looked down at himself, then to Camille. "We need to wash. Can you get up?"

He helped her to her feet, and then to the healing waters, where they rested and floated, each lost in silent thought. Through her diminishing pain, Camille's face shone with a bright smile of triumph. She had won.

They were silent during the slow ride back to the manor. Mongo placed a folded blanket on Camille's saddle to ease the ride back.

They were met at the back door by Sugah, who immediately sensed what had transpired, and what was needed. Swiftly and in tight-lipped silence, she helped Camille up the steps to the house and made ready to guide her sister-friend to her bedroom. As Camille entered the kitchen door, Sugah turned and looked spitefully at Mongo, and then she spat viciously in his direction. A dark storm cloud roiled in her stare.

As Mongo reined his horse about, he realized that he was in for a terrible tongue-lashing. Goldie and the roan followed him to the barn.

Chapter 28

The mockingbird was triumphant. His fluid notes floated over and mingled with Sweetgrass's telling of the love between Mongo and Camille.

"That is the story as it was told me when I was sixteen." Sweetgrass swiveled her head to look into the eyes of her friends. "And as I am telling it to you."

Liv and Bambi were both shocked into silence by the degree of intimacy and detail given them in the story; both women had what soldiers call a 'thousand yard stare.'

The threesome sat motionless in their rockers, inhaling the Sea Island summer and exhaling memories of passions past. No thought of tea or cheese straws, only a turning in the mind of what had been revealed.

Finally, Liv broke the silence. "My mind keeps going back to the question of why? Why are you telling us the story, why did Camille pass it to Sugah, and Sugah to you?"

Sweetgrass nodded slightly. "A fair question, and one that I can answer. But only if you're willin' to accept the fact that we in the South do not live as islands, alone and separated from each other by tides and shoals. We colored folk especially, hold to a sense of place and history. There are some who feel that you can't know who you are until you know who you were. If you can accept that, then an understanding of what I've told you begins to grow. Remember, my ancestors were forcibly brought here as slaves and made to forget their past while they were made to live in ways that weren't even suitable to livestock in a decent society. Some may tire of hearing that message; some may over-burden themselves and others with that message, but the message cannot be allowed to disappear. Much like the message of the Jew Holocaust in Europe—it must stay in our awareness. The *reason* for that doesn't need to be said because what took place in that horrible time speaks for itself.

"I've got a granddaughter, Rebecca, who is a bright, capable young lady, well on the path to making her way in this world. She will become a professional person who will someday enable others. I have shared with her much of what I've told you—because it will help her appreciate all the more who she is, by knowing who she came from. This knowledge will help her to see her rise as meteoric. I can give her no better gift than the knowledge of who we were." Sweetgrass said this last sentence with a finality that indicated an end to her soliloquy.

Liv let a respectful period of time pass before asking, "And me? Why tell me the story of your ancestors?"

"Because they are your ancestors as well and because you have returned to your roots. The knowledge of what has taken place in your surroundings will help you become a part of those surroundings. Finally, I've told the story because I have a growing love for you ladies, and I hope we will become a part of each other's lives."

Bambi's faced reddened at this last thought as she pursed her lips and fought to hold back her feelings. Sweetgrass sensed this, and patted her on the hand saying, "That's okay, my child, let your feelings loose."

"Granny, I—I… people already think I'm some kind of flake because I cry over anything and everything at the drop of a hat, and here I go again. I'm about to lose it right now."

"I don't doubt that some people get all tear-eyed for nothing. But there are many who know pain all too well and, because of that, are sensitive to the pain of others. Those who thoughtlessly scoff at such kind souls diminish their own humanity. Your tears can fall fearlessly in this house; we are strong enough to love them."

Mimus polyglottis ran a symphony while the three ladies digested the events of that day.

* * *

Liv and Bambi returned four days later at Sweetgrass' request. She told them that 'the tale wants completion.'

"My mockingbird is entertaining elsewhere today," Sweetgrass said, pouring cups of fresh-brewed Wadmalaw Island tea. "I've made some shortbread from an old recipe. It goes so well with this wonderful tea."

"I've never had shortbread before, Granny." Bambi said. "These look like scallop shells." She took a bite of one.

"That's close. They were called Royal Fans when they came over from Scotland, but we call them Royal Fronds because they look so much like palmetto fronds. My grands just call them Fronds, and they can go through a platter of them in no time."

"You're right. They are wonderful with this tea," Liv said.

Bambi, on her second Frond, asked. Will you give up the recipe?"

"Of course. Why have a recipe if it can't be shared?" Sweetgrass said with a smile.

Sweetgrass had a scattering of folders, envelopes, and notepapers laid out on a card table before her rocker. She had been sorting through them when the girls arrived.

"I began making notes some fifty or so years past. So much to remember, and I find that my remembering isn't what it once was. Could you ladies remove this table for me? Just place it aside for now."

Liv and Bambi set the card table on the other side of the doorway.

"I need to finish the story while we enjoy our tea. There's more tea in the pot, so just help yourself. Bambi, I'm cutting your Fronds off at six." Sweetgrass gave a throaty chuckle that brought gleeful laughter from her guests.

The gentle lady leaned back in her chair with an authority that said she was about to resume the story.

"What took place between Mongo and Camille back then would be called a love affair today, or an affair of the heart. It would have been called another thing entirely in those times. No matter. They were in love; totally and completely in love. A love, no doubt, made all the more tantalizing with the knowledge that discovery would lead to ostracism for Camille and death for Mongo. Have you ladies ever had a love like that? A love so formidable that you would set aside all other considerations?"

Liv and Bambi glanced at each other. Bambi raised a finger. "I have."

Liv nodded. "I—I'm not sure, but I think I am growing to understand."

"How did they hide their love?" Bambi asked around her fourth Frond.

"Sugah. She protected them, hid them, acted as a lookout, and applied whatever old wives-tale remedies that kept away pregnancy. She loved them both and would have given her life on their behalf. Tige was helpful at times. The thing that saved them from discovery was the onset of the war; a war that became an all-consuming preoccupation among the men and women of the South. But, more important for Camille, it took away the prying eyes of those sorry brothers of hers. Sugah told me how they both rode off to war together, officers with feathered plumes waving over their uniform hats." Sweetgrass made grand gesture over her head. "They were both dead by the end of the first year. Rumor has it that one was shot by his own men. For all his bluster and bravado, Maxton was never able to recover their bodies. They were officers in the army, yet they lie in unmarked graves, which says something of the low regard their men held for them.

"The boys were gone, Maxton was off partying around Charleston, holding himself up as a wealthy planter of some substance. It is true that his plantation was a financial success right up until the end of the war. That success came not from Maxton's skill, but from his daughter's shrewd money sense, and Mongo's capable management of the colored people who worked the farm. Mongo saw to their care, housing, and feeding like no plantation owner even thought of doing at the time. They responded by giving him an honest day's work. Camille saw to the building of a church, which was actually a school, for the workers. She and Mongo tutored the children to read and write and cipher. The slave quarters were improved, outhouses installed, wells dug, and a good supply of cloth for clothing was brought in.

"Camille and Mongo did the best they could, considering that they were still working in a society that demanded slavery. They were banking everything on their belief that the South would lose the war, ending slavery and the plantation way of life, and they were equally sure that a literate black population would be necessary after the war was over. Camille and Sugah and Mongo would stay up late nights trying to figure ways to improve conditions on the farm. They also laid out plans for what to do with the plantation after the war. They pictured provisions where the plantation owners would be allowed to keep the plantations if they would hire on the slaves as employees, eventually selling off their land to the employees.

"It was too good to last, and it didn't. As the tide of the war began to change in favor of the North, and as the extent of the carnage became common knowledge, the merry-making mood of the South was replaced by a sense of apprehension. Sherman's march through Georgia made the war's outcome clear to all. Maxton ended his prodigal ways and returned home to resume the management of his property. The nature and amount of change he found at home sent him into a rage."

*   *   *

Alexander Maxton stood at his study window. As he watched the work going on between the house and the barn, he finished his third toddy of the morning, a fact that only served to bring his simmering indignation to the surface. He wheeled to face Camille who was seated by a table that held a cup of tea. A large volume rested in her lap; she had come prepared.

"What in God's name were you thinking, Daughter?" Maxton's voice echoed through the house. "You've turned the farming operations over to the niggers."

Camille sat looking down at the ledger.

"Well, explain yourself," Maxton demanded.

"What you say is true, Father. I have turned the farming operations of this plantation over to the people doing the work."

Maxton's jaw dropped open. "Then you don't deny it?"

"No. Why should I want to?"

"Dammit, woman." Camille smiled at being called a woman by her father. "This is my property, those slaves are mine, they do what *I* want them to do, not what they want to do. They do what I want, when I want it, and the way I want it. You don't know what they are like. If you give them the slightest reason, they'll turn against you and take over. And that, daughter, is why you should care about my concern. We're fightin' a war in which thousands of our boys have give their all, a war to protect our way of life. What you've done here flies directly in the face of everything we stand for and die for. You're no better than a common traitor to our cause." Maxton swayed and stepped back, unsteady on his feet. He hobbled with a cane to an easy chair and fell backward into it. "You've destroyed everything I've worked for—my own flesh and blood."

"What have you worked for, Father?"

Maxton failed to notice that his only remaining child no longer addressed him with the endearing "Daddy," or "Papa." He had now become a formal "father."

Maxton rose and went to the window, slapping his riding whip against his leg. "I've worked to make a farm. I've tried to make Maxton Manor into the most productive plantation in these parts. I made a family—most of which those foul creatures from the North have taken from me. I support a way of life that is proper for our white race. Dammit, I wanted us to take our place in this world." He held his glass out to his daughter. "Fix me a toddy, my gout is killing me this morning."

Camille rose, laid the ledger on the chair, and retrieved her father's tumbler.

"No, Father. You've had enough to drink this morning. Maybe this," she held up the tumbler, "is the cause of your gout."

"Nonsense. Why live if you can't live according to your wishes?"

Camille smiled to her father and said, "I guess everyone's like that."

"Well then, it's settled. Fix my toddy."

"I'd rather not, Father. I don't want to be a participant in your suicide."

Maxton caught his breath at that disclosure. "Suicide?"

"Yes, that's what it is. You're killing yourself with your indulgences. I used to think that you were the strongest man I knew. That there was nothing you couldn't do if you set your mind to it. You were like a force of nature to me, and I feared and respected you."

Maxton smiled in satisfaction, again failing to note the absence of remarks of affection. "Well, I strove to provide for my family. There was no place for weakness. There is no place for weakness in this entire world. Strength is needed."

"Yes, Father. Strength is needed. The strength that is needed to cast off the indulgences you have been killing yourself with the past two years and more. That's all I'm asking for."

"You're your mother all over. I never could win an argument with that woman, and she would worry at me like a hound with a bone."

Camille placed the tumbler on the tray beside a decanter and returned to her chair to pick up the ledger. She knew better than to acknowledge that she had bested Maxton in the discussion of his health.

"Father, I want you to look at these figures, and then we will talk whether or not this farm is failing." She placed the ledger in his lap. "I'll leave you with this while I go get you a glass of water." She turned and left the aging man with her figures.

"Well?" Camille asked after her father had studied the ledger for nearly an hour.

"You have a beautiful hand." Maxton observed.

"Thank you, Father, but it's the figures that are done in that hand that matters. What do you think?"

"If these figures are correct..."

"You insult me, Father."

"And you interrupt me."

"I'm sorry, Father. Please continue."

"These figures show an increase in production over the past two years."

Camille was silent.

"Expenses were up considerably, however. Triple, I'd say."

"At least that," Camille said softly.

"So. You admit that you have spent far more than has ever been spent on the running of the farm."

"Yes, I do."

"And you have no defense for this?"

Camille moved to stand beside her father. She leafed through several pages of the open ledger, arriving at the tally pages.

"That is my defense." She pointed at a figure at the bottom of the page. "You are quick to note a tripling of the expenses, but you fail to acknowledge a doubling of our income in just two years—a figure that is some twenty times the increase in expenses."

"You have sacrificed everything to achieve that income."

"What have I sacrificed, Father?"

Maxton slammed the ledger shut with a loud report. "Everything the South stands for. That's what you've sacrificed. If things were run the way you've managed this plantation, we'd all be working for the darkie by the end of the century. There's places hereabout where we're outnumbered ten to one. They'd take over. We'd be the slaves, and they'd be the masters. Is that what you want?"

"No, Father. What I want is a world where there are no slaves, and no masters."

"Well, that's not going to happen. It never has—I thought you'd read those history books." He waved in the direction of the book shelves. "There've always been slaves, it's just a matter of who they are, not if there will be slaves. Besides, these Africans are not really humans after all. Science has proven that."

"That's just not true. You know it's not, but it's what you want to believe. You read that drivel that those rabble-rousers write, and you pretend it's science, or religion, or philosophy, whatever your fancy."

"I'm wrong, Daughter. I think you've read too much of those books." He gave another wave at the bookshelf. "You've filled your mind with such trash that you can't think clearly. This is a real world, with real people, not like those puffed-up prissy philosophers you've been reading. Put your feet on the ground, Woman. We have a plantation to run, and a war to win. Your soft indulgence will accomplish neither."

Maxton would have risen to his feet. But his pain prevented it.

"You're the one who gave me those books. You said you were going to lay all the knowledge of the world at my feet. Well, you did. I read the Greeks, the Romans, the French, Germans, English. I read everything you brought home, and I've come to the conclusion that the South is wrong. It is Sparta and Athens all over, Father, except we in the South think we are Athenian when we are actually the Spartans. We want to regard ourselves a moral and sensible people building a decent society, but we are only willing to use force to achieve that."

"Humbug." Maxton's complexion had gone from red to purple. "I'm hearing the ravings of an over-educated, idealistic girl who is just out of childhood. Get some years on you before you act as though you know what this world is about." Maxton rapped his cane on the floor. "This blather of yours is fit only for parlor conversation and has little to do with how the world works."

"That's my answer." Camille said, pointing to the ledger. "Do you want us to make money, or do you want to run this plantation as a playground for your dream world. That's what it's all about, isn't it; money or whimsy." She turned and walked from the room.

Sweetgrass pointed at her tea cup, which Liv refilled from the cozy-clad pot. A single sugar cube was added.

"Maxton and Camille never arrived at a settlement, 'cause the Yankee soldiers did it for them. Charleston was taken over by the North and placed under military law. The Yankee commander of the place handed out the land to the former slaves. Families were given land and livestock that would let them make a farm. Landowners fled in fear of payback from both the army and former slaves. Maxton Manor, 20 miles away from Charleston and protected all around by water, was one of the last places reached by the Yankee laws and rulings. Alexander Maxton took advantage of his neighbors by buying out their valuables at bottom prices. All they wanted was enough money to escape to a safer place. Many went from rich to poor in one day.

"Maxton was many things—but stupid was not one of them. He knew the war was lost, he knew the Yankees were coming. He saw the devastation visited upon his neighbors and was determined to avoid their fate. He did this by sending his wealth to a safer place—in safe hands."

"Ohio?"

"Yes, Ohio."

"Why must I go to Ohio, Father?"

"Because of what is in this satchel." Maxton hefted the heavy brocaded bag and let it return to the floor with a thump that registered its weight. "Most of our movable wealth will be in the baggage you carry with you. The light weight things you can carry on your person: coin, jewelry, and scrip. You'll be safe there with your mother's family."

Camille walked to the window and gazed out over the place of her birth and life. "This is the end isn't it, Father? Your words tell me that you know the war to be lost."

"For now, yes."

"For now?"

"Some of our units are mobilizing in the west and plan to continue the war."

"What utter folly! It is a lost cause—just as it was from the very beginning."

"You speak treason, Daughter."

"Eye of the beholder, Father. Eye of the beholder. There are some who would claim you and your friends are guilty of treason."

"Yes, and they are the enemy that we have fought, and who is now at the gate."

"And now you want to run from them."

"No, Daughter. I'll stay and stand. They will enter this property only over my corpse."

"Father!"

"Don't 'Father' me. It is what must be done. My granddaddy bought and laid out this land. Daddy took over from him and built a farm. I've fought and killed for this land, I've ripped it from swamp and bramble. I've turned muck and mire into profitable farmland, and I will not see it taken over by a bunch of Yankee rabble and niggers."

Camille left her post at the window and came to sit beside her father. She took his hand into hers. "Papa, why must we be so far apart on so many things?"

"I have no answer for that, Camille. I've spent hours frettin' on that and can only conclude that I have failed to bring you up proper. If only your mother hadn't..."

"Oh, Papa, it cuts to my very heart to hear you say those words—to think of myself only as your failure." Her eyes were brimming.

"I did not claim to not love you. I'm only saddened that you fail to see things as they are—that you fail to accept the natural order of things."

Camille started to—once again—address this issue but realized the futility and halted her tongue.

"As it stands, Daughter, you should leave in less than five days—the sooner the better in fact. The Yankees are in Atlanta and will likely come to Charleston next, and to do so they must pass by our very doorstep. I've had small trees and bramble planted to conceal the entry of our track from the road. In their haste to reach Charleston they will pass by us."

"And if they don't pass by us?"

"Then there will be a fight."

"You against the Yankee army, Papa?"

"No, Daughter. Me against the men who come to invade our property."

"You will die."

"I will die defending what is rightfully mine—and the principles in which I believe. There are worse things."

"And there are better. Come with me, Papa. We have enough wealth to start up a farm wherever we choose."

"Maxton Manor is my choice. Here I was born. Here I've lived. And, by God, here I will die. I will bury next to my kin—that is all I ask. No more talk. Begin packing and planning. I'm sending Sugah with you. She'll be a boon in the face of difficulties with Yankees. I'm also sending Romer and Loya. They're two of my best darkies—and they have wives and children here. They are to return when you reach the Ohio border. I've hired a trusted agent from Charleston to guide you to Ohio. He will be very handsomely paid upon his return—but take the derringer and keep it by your side at all times. We will discuss the route later, but there is much to do in packing and preparing the carriage and harness. Should you find it necessary to take other transport, the agent is charged with the return of the carriage and team. Much to do, Daughter. Now go."

Camille rose and left her father to his plans. Her thoughts were only of Mongo.

"I cut our mark on this tree," Mongo said pointing at lettering. It's small now, but the tree will grow and I'll make the letters grow with it."

Camille rolled away from her lover to look at the engraving on the narrow tree trunk she had held onto at their first joining. "It's beautiful."

"It's like us. The letter 'C' with an 'M' inside it. Like we were on that first time."

"Yes, like we were then—and many times since. I carry the memory of that day like a ruby on a pendant lying between my breasts. I can pull it out at will and hold it up to the light of consciousness. Everyone should have such a treasure at their bid."

The following morning the whole farm turned out to see Camille and Sugah off. Alexander Maxton was the only one not to weep. A wailing that was not to be denied began among the women. The feeling was that they were losing two of their loved ones, and they would never see them again. Mongo stalked among his people like a caged beast. He couldn't stand quiet and there was wildness in his glance. All shrank back in fear from him.

Camille had said her goodbyes to the people the night before, going from shack to shack. Many did not sleep at all that night, but tossed in fear for the two of their own who were leaving.

"Keep the pistol at hand, Daughter, and suffer neither fools nor foolishness."

"Yes, Father."

"When the war is over, we'll be back together and set this farm to work better than it ever worked."

"Let us hope, Father."

"Be off with you now—and—and..."

"Father?"

"You look so much like your mother—so beautiful..." Maxton looked quickly away at the ground, and then turned to make a quick check of the horses and harness. When he returned to Camille he was breathing as though short of breath.

"I'll miss you, Daughter. And I'll await your return."

"I will write—Papa."

"Up now." Maxton opened the door of the carriage and took the arm of his daughter as she stepped up. He closed the door and looked into his daughter's eyes. They both seemed to sense that it was the last time they would ever do so. Maxton gestured to the driver who slapped the horses with the reins as he released the carriage brake. Camille Maxton raised her hand in farewell. As she looked up to see Mongo standing alone behind the crowd, Camille had a terrible sense of foreboding that remained with her the entire trip.

Fall of 1864

As Sherman was planning a march to the sea, the last cash crops of Maxton Manor were being harvested. Maxton was confident that he would get top dollar for his rice, indigo, and cotton in the face of deprivation brought about by the war and the collapse of so many plantations in the region. In Fall of 1864 Savannah surrendered to Sherman thus saving the town from destruction, and permitting the Union army to quickly move on Charleston. And, that was when the hurricane hit. It must have been a big slow-moving storm because Maxton had time to collect some of his belongings and head for Charleston. He left Mongo in charge of the plantation with specific instruction not to let the workers into the house.

When the storm hit, it hit hard. Everything was right for an evil outcome. A full moon drove a high tide, and the storm came directly from the East, pushing the flood even higher. The only safe place for the Negroes was in the house, which rested on a high shell mound.

Mongo confined the crowd to the basement and first floor of the manor house. The terrified slaves huddled in the dry safety of the house until a young child knocked over a full kerosene lamp, at the foot of the basement stairwell. Attempts to put out the fire were futile because the house was built with fat pine lumber. Finally, out of desperation, Mongo had all the windows and doors opened. Those tall floor-to-ceiling windows saved the day, but ruined much of the carpet, upholstery and curtains in the house. By the time the storm ended, the house was severely damaged from a combination of fire and water. It was nearly a week before the water withdrew so the workers could return to what remained of their quarters. The slave quarters stood the storm fairly well as they were protected by the trees surrounding them. Once the water and mud were swept out of them, they were livable. Several workers had died either fighting the fire or drowned in the flood. A few took the opportunity to flee. The crops were lost and the livestock scattered.

Liv spoke up. "That would account for some of the scorched timbers in the basement. We wondered what had happened, and presumed that it was a fire that had been successfully put out."

"The blowing storm and buckets is what put it out," Sweetgrass said, and then continued. "When Maxton returned, he found his plantation all but non-existent. Loss of lives, livestock, crops, and the house itself was barely habitable. But that wasn't the worst of it." Sweetgrass was rocking slow and gentle between her guests who sat motionless, leaning forward in their rockers.

Finally, Bambi asked, "What could be worse, Granny? He lost everything."

"Fetch me that yellow envelope from the corner of the table." Sweetgrass pointed.

She opened the envelope and withdrew a letter written in an elegant slanted hand.

"This was worse. This letter from Camille was sent in another envelope to a trusted neighbor girl her age to be delivered to Mongo Maxton under the pretext that she was planning a surprise visit home and didn't want her father to know. The girl and her family took refuge in Charleston in the same hotel with Maxton. Somehow this letter found its way to Maxton's hands. I'll read the first few lines and let you ladies read the rest on your own." Sweetgrass read out loud in a soft voice:

My Dearest,

I hope this letter finds you well. I cannot tell you how much I miss you, but I don't feel the need to do so because I am confident that you feel the same pain of absence as sharply as do I. I can barely contain myself with the joy of this news I must impart. I am with child, your child, our child who grows larger each passing day, filling me with a glorious feeling of love for you.

My mother's family is wonderful to me. I've told them that I am wed to a distant cousin of the same name of 'Maxton.' They have been so kind and helpful...

Sweetgrass stopped at this point. "In the aftermath, Eulie, a slave girl, had found this letter, and later gave it to Sugah. I'll leave the rest of the reading to you ladies in private." She folded the letter and handed it to Liv.

"Meantime, I will relate the outcome of the discovery of the letter. Eulie, now the main house girl, was known to stand outside open doorways, and she was a good listener. The monumental arrogance of the slavers permitted them the false belief in secrets—while living in the midst of people who have centuries of oral tradition. Nothing transpired by day that wasn't heard around the fires of night. Alexander Maxton was given to a state of blind rage upon reading this letter..."

Chapter 29

Alexander Maxton, muddied by the ride home from Charleston, stood in the middle of his smoke and water-stained study. His gaze went from floor to bookcase, to ceiling. He looked out the window at his flattened fields and shattered forest.

"I'm ruined. You've ruined me, you black bastard." Maxton's face was rigid and purple. He stood with his legs braced while slapping his right leg with his riding crop.

"I couldn't stop the storm, Mister. I tried to save your property from the storm."

"How, by burning it to the ground?" Maxton flung the crop across the room.

"No sir. That was an accident. A child knocked over a lamp that fired the rugs and curtains. The fire spread fast."

"A child? Who's child?"

"A child of one of the field workers. I had to let them in during the storm. There was nowhere else for them to go."

Maxton moved to a window and grabbed a handful of rumpled curtain that had been washed and rehung. He turned to face his overseer. "After I gave orders to let no one in the house, you let them in."

"They would have drowned. The water came all the way up to the door of the house. Some drowned trying to get to the house as it was."

"Better they all drown than burn down my house." Maxton looked up at the soot covered ceiling. "You've brought an end to Maxton Manor—first the Yankees, and now you."

"Mama Tige died trying to save a child in the fire."

"Tige?" Maxton tried unsuccessfully to open a drawer in his desk. "No wonder the place is such a mess. Tige would have cleaned it up in short order. I'm ruined."

"I'm sorry, Mister."

"Your 'sorry' doesn't bring anything back. Who's doing Tige's work?"

"I brought in Eulie. Tige's been training her in cooking and housework. She's a good worker."

"She hasn't done much about getting this house clean; look at these walls and ceiling." Maxton waved his arms in an encompassing manner.

"She's had four women helping her since after the storm."

"Can she fix my favorite meals?"

"She's smart. She can quick learn how."

"What'll I eat while she's learning? Damn. If Camille hadn't taken Sugah off with her we wouldn't be having this problem." Maxton walked out into the hallway and looked around at the woodwork and rails on the banister. "Did you think I'd be happy when I got back from Charleston?"

"No sir." Mongo looked around at the disorder. "I did what I had to do to save your property. I tried to rescue the animals, the farm equipment, and your—your negroes. The crops were flooded, there was nothing I could do about that."

"Don't talk back to me, damn you."

"Sir, I don't mean to be sounding like backtalk, I'm trying to tell you what happened and why it happened. What I hear of folk from other farms, the ruining is everywhere."

"Everyone got their house burned down, too?"

"No sir, but right many of the houses hereabout are completely gone. You must have seen that on your ride back from Charleston."

"I didn't see any houses burned." Maxton retrieved his saddle bags from the floor in the hallway and carried them to his desk.

"Go see to repairs outside. We'll talk more later." He picked up a brass bell from his desk and rang it loudly. Eulie came to the door immediately.

"Yes, Massah Maxton?" She stood with her eyes cast down. It was her boy who had knocked over the lamp that started the fire.

"Bring me a basin of warm water and a pitcher from the well. I want to wash up and have a toddy."

"Massah." She turned and fled.

Maxton looked up at Mongo standing off to the side of his desk. "Go. I've got some mail to go through. The postmaster knew I was in town so he had it delivered to my hotel—along with a note from Cassie Watson's daughter."

"The Watson house was blown down by the storm," Mongo said.

"They've taken quarters in Charleston. I bought their holdings after the storm. He's a ruined man—like me. Go to work. Get out of my sight." Maxton opened his mud-splattered saddlebags as Mongo walked out of the room.

Maxton broke the seal on the first letter out of his saddle bag and hunched over its contents, beginning the laborious act of reading.

Mongo stood in the middle of the barn. In short order he had supervised the rebuilding of the damaged slave quarters and the farm outbuildings. Lumber was plentiful—as an aftermath of the storm. Mongo had sent riders and wagons out to retrieve materials. He personally rounded up horses and cattle left stranded. Later, he dispatched small groups of young boys to gather and herd hogs. By the end of two weeks Maxton's animal stock had quadrupled over pre-storm days.

The stalls and pens were filled and overflowing. Mongo's crews could barely keep up with the steady stream of farm animals coming into the property. He was formulating a plan for increasing the pasture acreage when Eulie came running breathlessly.

"Massah say you come to house—now. He say you meet him in the basement. He say now. He fussin' mad."

Maxton was standing in the middle of the basement floor when Mongo arrived. He was holding a coiled whip in one hand and a crumpled piece of paper in the other.

"Eulie said you wanted to see me, Sir."

"I wish I had never seen you. You son of Hell."

"Sir, I did everything I could…"

"I'm not talking about the farm; I'm talking about my daughter. The daughter that you ruined, you black bastard."

"Camille."

"Yes, my only daughter. The one you've given a permanent stain."

"Sir, I…"

"Shut up, damn you. I ought to kill you right here."

Mongo saw that there were several lamps burning in the normally dim-lit cellar. Maxton's eyes glittered in their reflected light, as he uncoiled and shook out his deadly leather cattle whip.

"In this sickening letter from Camille she whines about her great love for you and for the bastard nigger baby you put in her belly. There's not a man in this state that wouldn't put a bullet in you right now. But I'm not going to do that." He snaked his whip on the dirt floor of the cellar. "I'm going to give you the worst whipping any nigger has ever had in this state," Maxton said. "Get over here to this post."

Mongo stood his ground.

"After all I've done for you—and for that lazy sister of yours. You've been brought up near like family in this house. And this is the payment you give me. Get over here. Now!" Maxton demanded.

Mongo shook his head.

Maxton's face turned even darker. "Are you refusing my orders?"

"I'm not going to be whipped."

"Yes, hell you are, too." Maxton spun the whip and cracked it over his head. "Now, one last time. Get over here."

"I'm not going to be whipped."

Maxton lashed out with his leather and cut Mongo on the neck. "Get on your knees." He slashed again with the leather, but this time Mongo grabbed it and drew the stout white man to him. Maxton struck Mongo in the face with the weighted handle of the leather just before Mongo wrenched it from his grasp.

"Your slavin' days and whippin' days are over, Mister," Mongo said. "This island is crawling with Yankee soldiers, and it's just a matter of time before they come a-poundin' on your front door."

"I'll kill them as they come. I'll be put in a grave before I see this land taken from me. This is my land. I'll not have it turned over to a bunch of African monkeys."

"You won't have no choice."

Maxton was breathing heavily from his anger and from the struggle for the leather. "Yes, I will. I have a choice, and my choosing starts with how I deal with my property." Maxton withdrew a derringer from his belt, took one step toward Mongo and fired a round directly into Mongo's breast, then stepped back.

Mongo stood with a startled look, then placed his hand over the wound and looked down at the blood coming out.

"What have you done?"

Maxton stood in silence with the derringer held out in front of him.

Mongo fell forward against the slaver, who caught him and let him slowly slip to the floor. Mongo held onto Maxton and pulled him down to him.

"Father. What have you done?" Mongo took a deep breath and shuddered from the pain. "Why?"

Maxton was silent as he watched the life slowly leave his son.

Mongo took another breath then said softly before passing. "I can read..."

The slaver rose from the ground and returned the derringer to his belt. He bent to pick up his whip and then walked from the room out into the bright fall sunlight.

At no time was he aware of Eulie standing in the shadows, her hands clapped fiercely over her mouth to contain the scream in her throat. She crumpled into a heap in the corner and remained a helpless drooling soul filled with terror and confusion. She witnessed the death of the man who was idolized by nearly every member of the black community on the plantation. She could not imagine life on the plantation without Mongo Maxton.

Alexander Maxton returned with two slaves carrying shovels.

"I want him buried where he lay. Bury him deep and bury him quick."

"Massah."

The younger black man started to dig, but the older man stood looking down at Mongo's body.

"Why you holding back, Petey?" Maxton demanded.

"I was puzzling on how come we don't bury him with the others down by the salt marsh."

"That's not your place to ask. I want him buried here, and that's where he'll be buried. Now let me see some dirt fly, or I'll bury you with him."

"Yessuh, Massah Maxton." Petey bent to the task.

"When you're done I want a heavy floor laid over this dirt floor. Level the dirt first, put down a thick layer of crushed oyster shell then a layer of brick over it. On top of that I want it finished with heavy cypress timbers, cut and laid tongue and groove. I'll show you how I want it cut when the time comes."

Maxton walked to the doorway then stopped and turned. "I'll get a crew gathering brick from the ruined homes hereabouts, and another crew shaping the cypress timbers. You dig. I want those two that died from the house fire burns' buried with him. I'll get them carried here. Dig." He stalked through the doorway, slapping his quirt against his leg.

"Eulie. Damn your lazy soul, where are you?" he shouted as he went toward the outbuildings.

The grave diggers remained intent on their task as a quiet shadow slipped from the room to hasten to her master's call. Both of the men wept in silence as they dug. Petey's face was set rigid as he turned his helpless rage to the soil under his shovel.

Come a time. Rivulets of sweat ran down his face and body. *There will come a time…*

On the end of the twelfth day after Mongo's death, Maxton stood solidly on his new cypress beam floor, pleased with the work. He heard a shout from outside the open doorway. A young black boy came running up to the doorway.

"Massah Maxton," the breathless boy almost shouted.

"What is it?"

"Petey, he say go tell you that blue soldiers is coming up the pathway from town."

Sweetgrass stopped at this point because both of the girls were anguished and weeping.

Liv was the first to catch her breath. "That was so wrong, Granny Sweet. So wrong. How could…I mean what was…" She paused and caught her breath. "Dear God in heaven, how could one man be so…completely vile?"

Bambi, who couldn't speak, just sat red-faced and silent as tears streamed down her face.

"Would you ladies like a Firefly?" There were nods to Sweet's question.

Bambi found her voice halfway through her glass. "Granny Sweet, there is so much pain in this world. So much suffering."

"Yes, child, that's so. That's why we have to help one another, why we have to have faith, and maybe know why there's a God in heaven."

The three ladies sat and rocked in the summer shade of the porch. Sweetwater broke the silence after a while.

"I'd like to continue the story if it's acceptable."

Liv answered for the two of them. "Of course, Miz Sweet, go on with it."

"Well, it concerns Alexander Maxton and his meet-up with the enemy at the gate."

Chapter 30

Maxton rode to the Union soldiers. He met them at the gate a half mile from the house. There were four of them: A youthful lieutenant, two privates, and a grizzled sergeant whose facial scars were healing from combat wounds. The lieutenant was in dress-parade garb, complete with plumed hat and a scattering of bouillon across his chest. His mount was a dancing palomino stallion he could barely control. The enlisted men and the sergeant were dressed for work.

Maxton had a brace of pistols on his belt, and a carbine rested across his saddle when he rode to encounter the mounted detail. He reined his horse up against the gate to prevent it from opening.

"What is your business? he demanded.

"Are you Alexander Maxton?" the officer inquired.

"Yes."

"Then you, sir, are my business."

"State your reason for coming onto my property."

The slender young man leaned forward in his saddle. "That this is no longer your property is my reason." The lieutenant reined and prodded his stallion that started at any outburst of sound.

"This land was purchased by my grandfather and built up by my father and by me. I have the paper deed, and it is registered in the courthouse. This is my property, and I'm telling you to turn around that animal you can't control, and leave now." The sergeant dropped a hand to his holstered pistol.

"Maxton, you are impeding me in the carrying out of my orders. I must insist that you remove yourself from the gateway that we may enter."

"You, sir, are a damn Yankee trespasser. Now, git!" Maxton raised his carbine, and leveled it at the source of his anger just as the round from Sergeant Fell's pistol caught him in the chest, knocking him from his mount.

Lieutenant Payson's stallion reared at the gunfire, and deposited his rider to the dusty path. Payson had the good sense to roll away from the stomping hooves of his frightened mount. His roll landed him on a mound of fresh manure and in line of sight with Maxton whom he saw pointing the carbine at him.

Maxton's rifle ball made a furrow on Payson's youthful cheek and nicked off his left ear lobe. Wounds that in a score of years would become scars won in fierce combat with an army of Rebel soldiers intent on preventing a daring young officer from winning the war.

Maxton breathed his last while attempting to jack another shell into the chamber of his carbine.

Sergeant Fell, pistol pointed at Maxton, dismounted and went to the aid of his officer, helping him to a sitting position. Private Elger went in pursuit of the palomino.

"I've been shot," the lieutenant said, in what sounded like relief at being alive.

"Well, he burned your cheek and took part of your ear, but you'll do—sir." The sergeant tried to staunch the prolific flow of blood with a rag. He turned to the remaining soldier. "James, build us a quick fire." He gently leaned the lieutenant back to the ground. "Sir, we need to cauterize this wound, or you'll lose a lot of blood and get infected. I've seen smaller wounds kill men who left them alone. We ain't going to lose you, sir."

By the time a twig fire had been built, Private Elger had rounded up the lieutenant's mount and secured him alongside the others at the gate. After Private James opened the gate and secured Maxton's body across his horse, he presented a slender sheath knife to his sergeant.

"That'll do fine," Sergeant Fell said, holding the blade over the flame.

Lieutenant Payson stared at the blade with wide eyes. His glance went to his sergeant's as if to plea for mercy.

Narrow-eyed, and intent on his task, the sergeant said, "Sir, this is going to smart some, but it ain't nearly as bad as dying from blood poison." He turned to his men. "James, give me that kit you got slung over your shoulder. Elger, you come here and hold the lieutenant's head where I tell you." Fell took Private James' leather kit belt, folded it once and placed it between the lieutenant's teeth. "Sir, you bite on this. Elger, take his head just like it's turned, that's right. James you hold his arms. Lieutenant, you'd be a dang fool not to scream." The sergeant withdrew the glowing blade from the fire and swiftly placed it against the raw wound at the lieutenant's ear. The young officer screamed through the belt clenched in his mouth as the smoke and steam rose from the wound. The smell of burning flesh met the nostrils of the three men at their work. As Fell cauterized the cheek wound the lieutenant went limp. "Dang, Sergeant, you killed him," Elger said.

"Naw," James responded. "He just fainted is all. See, he's breathing."

Sergeant Fell thrust the knife blade into the dirt several times, cleaning from it the caked human flesh and blood. He left it buried in the cooling soil after pointing it out to Elger for later retrieval.

"He probly pissed hisself. I know I would have." The sergeant gave a slight grin. "James, scatter that fire, then you and Elger make a quick scout toward the Manor house. Don't go out of sight from here, and don't approach the house. Look for signs of ambush on either side of the trail. Check the barn and see if it's clear. Check the other outbuildings for Reb snipers, but be careful; don't go getting kilt. These trees and shrub are cut way back from the road-way, not leaving much cover, but you never know; these Johnny Rebs is crazy and crafty. I've seed em come up out of the sand, rifles firing. I'll 'speck you back in ten minutes; now go." He turned to the lieutenant and commenced wiping the blood from the cherubic face with a filthy wet cloth.

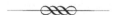

Sweetgrass Weaver seemed very satisfied with her telling of the story when she added, "That's the story of how Alexander Maxton died. I know it to be true and correct because Private Elger married a Charleston miss and settled down to farm not far from where Maxton was shot out of his saddle. Private Elger's wife penned the story and gave it to a newspaperman who later saw that it got to print in a book about the war around Charleston. I've got a copy."

Liv and Bambi had sat speechless and still through the tale of Maxton's death. It was as though he had become a part of their lives, and now he was gone. Liv broke the silence. "Far too merciful an end to such a cruel and vio-lent man. Ancestor or no, he got what he deserved—actually, better than he deserved. His passing was violent but it was quick." Her mouth and throat were dry from sitting with parted lips through the entire telling of the story.

"That's right," Bambi added. "There was no justice for the slaves that he'd treated with such meanness and cruelty. No justice for the death of Mongo."

Sweetgrass rocked a couple of cycles. "Justice—like Shakespeare's *beauty*—is in the eye of the beholder. The colored folk at Maxton Manor got their justice."

The next round of tea had just a splash of Firefly in it. "Justice," Sweetgrass repeated softly, and again, softer, "Sweet Justice." She ran slender fingers over her brow, and then down into a gentle pinching of her nose as though to draw out the memory. "In the eye of the beholder, the colored folk who worked for Maxton got their justice—as the story goes, their *sweet* justice."

Lieutenant Payson took so long to waken that Sergeant Fell finally had to splash some water on him.

"What? What?" The lieutenant tried to sit up and was stopped by the pain. He lay back on the grass and took a deep breath.

"Lieutenant, are you okay?"

"Damn, this hurts."

"I said it would smart."

"If that just 'smarts,' I'd like to know what you call pain."

Sergeant Fell looked at his commanding officer with narrowed gray eyes. "No, Sir. You don't." The silence that fell among the four men conveyed all the meaning that was necessary.

Lt. Payson rose to his feet with Sergeant Fell's help. He surveyed their situation.

"Sir," Sergeant Fell said, "Do you want to return to Charleston?"

"No, Sergeant, we've come here to do a job, and we're going to do it."

As the four riders approached the outbuildings of Maxton Manor, Sgt. Fell, in command of the palomino, began issuing orders, "James, check that barn and set yourself up with a clear field of fire from whatever opening you can find up high there. Elger, you give a look in those small outbuildings. Be sure to check the pig sty—them Rebs is crafty. The lieutenant and me will take the house. Sir, do you want the front door or the back door?"

"I'll take the front, Sergeant, and meet you inside."

"Yes sir. Okay, we'll dismount and walk our horses between us and the buildings until we get where we're goin.'"

In less than ten minutes it was determined that there was no immediate threat from anyone in the buildings. The sergeant and lieutenant gathered their mounts and the one carrying Maxton's body, and then walked into the center of the farmyard just as Elger appeared from the corn crib with an elderly black man in tow—hat in hand.

"Calls himself Petey; says he's the overseer of the darkies, sir."

Petey couldn't take his eyes off Alexander Maxton, slung dead and tied over his horse. Feet on one side, head on the other. Blood ran steadily from Maxton's chest wound and down alongside his ear. His hair was darkened by the blood that dripped from it to the ground at the horse's hooves. The horse was made skittish by the smell of the fresh blood.

Sergeant Fell looked at the wide-eyed slave, the pooling blood, and the dancing horse. "Elger, cut that man down." He nodded at Maxton's body. "Petey, put that horse where it belongs—and when you're finished, start gatherin' up the field hands and bring them here. We're Union soldiers here to protect you and your people. No harm will come to you—if you do as I say."

"Yes, Massah soljer." Petey took the reins from Sgt. Fell, and waited as Elger cut Maxton free and let him fall into the puddle of his own blood.

Lt. Payson removed his hat, adjusted the plume, and returned it to his head before mounting the bay that the sergeant had been riding.

"James—see anything?" Sgt. Fell shouted to the lookout in the barn.

"Darkies comin' out'n the wood to your right."

"Keep an eye, James. I didn't come through this whole damn war to get killed off by some ignorant fool after the peace was settin' in. Elger, watch our back."

Elger moved with his horse off to the side. He held his carbine at ready as he scanned the perimeter of the farming compound with practiced eyes.

"Elger, James, keep an eye." Fell's voice was terse and sure. "This is how people get killed. Don't let your guard down. James, you standin' right in the middle of that doorway up there would make a fine target. I want to see less of you." Both of the privates made affirmative sounds, and Pvt. James dropped to a crouch and then moved behind a stout door frame. The Sergeant held his carbine at ready as he scanned from between his horse and the lieutenant's.

"Sir, I don't know you ought to be settin' up there like that—Johnny Reb can knock you out of that saddle every time from three hundred paces."

"Thank you, Sergeant. I think we're pretty much in the clear now, and I have a good vantage point from up here."

Sgt Fell kept scanning through narrowed eyes. "Sir."

Petey had returned to the sergeant and lieutenant after securing Maxton's horse.

"Call 'em in, Petey"

"Yessuh, Massah soljer."

"No Massahs here, Petey. I'm Sergeant Fell, and this here's our commanding officer, Lieutenant Payson."

"Yessuh, Massah Sergeant."

"Call 'em in."

Petey raised a holler, and another. The woods slowly emptied its contents into the open compound.

"Lieutenant, I'm not likin' this. Let's move over next to the barn. That way we can have our back covered." Fell walked his horse and the lieutenant's to the barn.

"Elger, you move over to where you can see the other end of the barn so's no one can sneak in behind us. Put your back to the tool shed yonder, and keep your horse for cover." Fell pointed where he wanted his man. "James, you keep an eye out for Elger's back. That way we're all covered."

Over four dozen hands gathered in front of the sergeant and lieutenant. Each took a turn looking close at Maxton. An older woman laid him out on his back with his arms down at his sides and then kicked him in the head before joining the gathering in front of the soldiers. Petey motioned them to come closer.

"Sir." Sgt. Fell turned and looked up at the officer who was a lot older than he had been two hours earlier. Lt. Payson nodded and stood up in his stirrups, causing all eyes to turn to him.

"I am First Lieutenant Farnsworth Payson of the First Division, Eleventh Corps of the Army of Northern Virginia. We are Union soldiers, come here to free you. You are no longer slaves. You are free people. You can stay here or you can go. I would ask you to give yourself some time to make up your mind about what you want to do. The military governor of this and surrounding counties is authorized to parcel out land for those who want to stay and farm.

"A military contingent will come here in about two weeks. They will have maps and scribes. They will be able to give out the land in ten-acre parcels. Farmers will be given a mule or horse, two hogs, a plow, and other such tools for farming."

The lieutenant unrolled a scroll and read it to the group. None of the listeners, including his own men, understood a word of the formal language. When he was finished he rolled the scroll and returned it to his saddlebag.

"Sergeant, call Elger and James in. We'll set up in the house. Locate the house servants and have them make some coffee and food."

"Yessir." Sgt. Fell gave a sharp whistle and waved his men in. He turned to the older darkie. "Petey, see to our horses. They need feed and water. Brush 'em down good."

"Yessuh. Massah Sergeant, suh." Petey waited until the lieutenant was out of earshot, then he asked, "Dat man wid' de feather, what he say?"

"He said you are free. He said you can stay here." Fell pointed at the ground. "Or you can go." He pointed down the path to the gate. "He said you choose in two weeks." He raised two fingers.

"Yessuh." The beginning of understanding was growing in the black man's eyes—as were tears.

"Send the house servants to the house—we're goin' to need coffee and food." Sgt. Fell handed over the Palomino's reins.

"And Petey, Mr. Maxton there…" He pointed at the body. "…wants a grave."

"Yessuh, we see to his propah buryin' for sure. We know jus' how to do it, Massah Sergeant. An' I send Eulie to cook." Petey waited until the sergeant walked away, and then he turned and walked over to Maxton's corpse, leading the Palomino. He stood for some time looking down at the bloody, lifeless mound of hated flesh. He cleared his throat vigorously and spat handsomely into Maxton's face, and then he went to see to Sgt. Fell's demands. There was a new and confident spring to his step.

The soldiers ate and drank their fill that afternoon. The lieutenant decided they should stay the night and leave out in the morning. Pvt. James found the liquor cabinet and passed a bottle. Sergeant Fell took one drink and quit. "I'll take first watch. James, I'll wake you at eleven, and you wake Elger at two. Drink what you want, but you sure as hell better be sober for your watch. Elger, tell the darkies to have coffee ready all night."

They slept between clean sheets. They ate a huge breakfast and were gone while the sun was rising. The last sight the ex-slaves had of the four soldiers was a white plume dancing in the distance to the morning sunrise.

"We done strip Massah, and we dug a deep trench," a large field hand named Dunny told Petey after the soldiers left.

"He ain't 'Massah' no more. He a man like me and you. I don't never want t'hear 'Massah' again. I name him 'Satan.' An' today we buries Satan."

Maxton's final resting place was a hole in the swamp muck—as deep as could be made before surface water took over—a trench. A deep latrine as it were. Every man, woman, and child relieved themselves in Maxton's grave. Each was glad to spit into the mire as well. Maxton's whip was wound tightly around his neck and he was laid face down, naked, in the leavings of his ex-slaves. Each soul put a foot on Maxton's body and pushed it further into the sucking earth.

"Look at Satan there," Petey shouted out. "He look like one o' them big white grubs that come under tree bark." A shovel passed from hand to hand, and each slave took a turn at throwing earth in the grave. Bare feet trampled the soft swamp soil to firm flatness. For some time after, when a man or woman had to urinate, Maxton's grave was sought out.

The story of Maxton's burial was told and retold. It passed from community to county, and from county to state, and state to state. Each telling was relished and embellished. There was much laughter around candles, lanterns, and campfire—and much solace.

The land around Maxton's grave was never cultivated, never planted. Only grass was permitted to grow there. Nothing marked the spot but a small grassy clearing in the forest.

Descendents of the Maxton Manor ex-slaves grew to adulthood and old age. Some of their last memories were of that bare white corpse in the black muck, bringing a satisfied smile to their last few breaths.

Sweet took a sip of her tea. "That is the story of who we are as it was handed down from many who were there. We owe it to Sugah who collected most of the tale by asking and asking again those there at the time. And, of course some of it came from the newspaper article by Mrs. Linda Elger—Private Elger's wife."

Bambi and Liz had long given up their tea to parted-lip silence in awe of the story.

Liv broke the silence. "You said you had something to tell me. Something important. Why is this so, Miz Sweet?" Bambi looked at her friend in amazement.

"It is so because you need to know that burying place—there are few who know it. You need to know it because Maxton was your ancestor. And it is so because Maxton's grave is on your property."

Chapter 31

Arriving at 2 a.m., Autis didn't expect Liv to be up, but he knew something was wrong as soon as he rounded the last curve before his driveway. Every light, inside and out, was burning. He sped up the quarter-mile driveway and wheeled up the rise to the parking area in front of the house. The haphazard parking of Liv's and Bambi's cars was another tip-off that something was going on. When he got out of his car he saw large dark stains on the concrete steps leading up to the front porch. Blood. He literally ran into the house.

"Liv! Liv!"

"In the kitchen."

He rushed to the kitchen, and found Liv and Bambi sitting over coffee. They were both red-eyed and puffy-faced.

"What's with the blood on the driveway? He demanded. Then he looked around. "Where's Bob?"

"At the vet's. He's okay. Hurt, but okay. We got a call from them about an hour ago. They just finished stitching him—he was a mess.

"Stitching him? Did he get hit by a car, he never goes down to the road, how could..."

"It was a panther."

"A panther?"

"Yes. A black panther."

"Did you see it?"

"Yes, it almost attacked me, but Bob got to it first."

"Where did—how...?" Autis asked in growing agitation. He took a deep breath.

"Sit." Liv stood up and took control. "Coffee?"

"Coffee? I want a drink." He thought a moment. "No, no, I'll take coffee. He dropped into the chair Bambi had pulled out.

"What happened?"

"About nine o'clock I decided to walk out on the pier and check out the moon over the water. It was such a clear night, with enough of a breeze to keep down the mosquitoes. Naturally, Bob went with me. I was out there about half an hour, and I was considering waiting up for you, but you'd said that your flight wouldn't get in until after midnight, so I thought I'd climb into bed with a book. I'm reading a new novel by..."

Autis' raised hand stopped that direction of thought. "Anyway, we headed back to the house. I'd already checked out the path for fire ants on the way to the dock, so I didn't have the flashlight on. About halfway back to the house, Bob stopped and came out with a really fierce growl. I've never heard him make a noise like that. I switched on the flashlight and beamed it ahead of me, and there in the pathway was a big black panther, crouching, looking right at me. As soon as the light hit him, he opened his mouth and made a fierce noise somewhere between a hiss and a growl. Bob didn't hesitate. He ran right at the damn thing. It took off in the direction of the Big Loblolly Pine, where we..." She glanced at Bambi. "Where we went one night." She blushed visibly.

"Dayem. I want to hear that story." Bambi grinned.

"Unfortunately, Bob caught up with him, and they went round and round. I ran at them screaming and waving the flashlight. By the time I got to them, they were both bleeding all over the place. The cat ran off toward the road. I grabbed Bob by the collar and dragged him back to the house. He fought me all the way. He wanted to go after the damn thing. He didn't stop struggling until I got him on the porch and closed the screen door. I've never seen him like that. He was so enraged that I was scared of him. He was bleeding badly from the cat's bite on his neck and some scratches on his side." Liv stopped and caught her breath. She was shaking and pale. Autis pulled his chair over and took Liv's hands in his.

"He had the cat by the throat when I got to them, but I don't think he gave as good as he got."

"You could have been killed."

"I would have been—if it hadn't been for Bob. That was a big cat."

The doorbell rang. Autis and Liv looked at each other. Autis rose, but Bambi was quicker. "That'd be Gar. I called him, but I didn't know he'd come over this time of night." She went to the door.

Gar came in dressed as for a safari: bush jacket, boots and rough clothing. He nodded at Autis and went to Liv's side. "Are you okay, darlin'? You look like hell."

"Thanks, Gar. I needed that." Liv smiled.

"Smooth, Gar, smooth." Bambi said.

"Well, you know, I mean... Hell. I'm sorry."

"You look ready for war, Gar," Autis said.

"I am. Get dressed, we're going hunting. I borrowed some hunting hounds from a friend; I've got my rifle, a good light, and I'm wearing my swamp boots. I'm ready to go when you are."

Autis rose wordlessly from his chair and went in the direction of the bedroom. "I'll be right back."

The women looked at each other in amazement.

"Got any coffee?" Gar asked. Bambi went to the sideboard for a mug.

"I know it's scary, but would you mind telling me what happened?" Gar spoke softly and took Liv by the hand. "And you don't really look like hell," he glanced up at Bambi who was bringing him a steaming mug. As she set the drink before him, he nodded his thanks and smiled. "Bambi looks like hell."

"Making points there, Sport?" Bambi shot back.

"How's Bob? Have you heard from the vet?"

"Bob's hurt, but okay. They've stitched him up, and he's sleeping it off. They said they would call first thing in the morning."

By the time Liv finished her story, Autis returned, armed and dressed for swamp work. He was carrying a sixteen-gauge pump and had a .45 automatic at his hip. He handed a Smith and Wesson revolver and belt to Gar, who rose and strapped the gear around his waist without saying a word. Gar removed the pistol from its holster and loaded its cylinder.

"Wait a minute," Liv said. "This is insane. You can't go out there in the dark, trying to find a black panther that has every possible advantage."

Gar looked at Liv, frowning in thought. "If it's hurt like you said, it won't go far. It'll tree up and tend its wounds. Now's a good time to go after it. I've got three good hunting dogs, and there's a blood trail. They'll find him."

"If you have to go, at least wait until the sun comes up. Gar, if you had seen that animal, you wouldn't be so hot to go out there in the dark to find him. I'll never forget those eyes, those evil eyes; they glowed a bright red in the spotlight..."

"Wait a second," Gar said. "His eyes glowed red?"

"Yes. They looked like they were lighted from within when the flashlight beam hit him."

"Cat's eyes are usually yellow or pale brown, and they reflect a bright emerald green. They don't reflect red. Deer eyes sometimes glow red, but not cats. Are you sure it was a cat?"

"I am. Just as sure as you are a damn fool for going out in the dark after it—dogs or no. It was big and it was black, and it was a goddamn panther." Liv said, raising almost to a shout.

"Okay, okay. It's just that I've hunted just about every North American game there is, including panther, and I know for a fact that cat eyes glow green—sometimes a little yellow. But I've never heard of a cat's eyes glowing bright red."

"Well shit, Gar, that's one of the problems I've had all my life—telling the difference between red and green, that and not being able to tell the difference between a deer and a large black panther."

"I bow to your experience. We're going after that red-eyed critter—and we're going now. You ready, Autis? Autis?" Gar turned to find his friend.

"I'm at the front door while y'all work out color scheme and species."

"Shit." Gar rose to join Autis.

"Don't forget to take a cell phone," Bambi said. "And remember, red eyes. Maybe he's got a hangover."

Autis turned to Bambi. "The eye color is important because sometimes, at night, that's all you can see."

"Exactly, therefore, a 'sane' person would wait until the sun came up."

"Look..." Gar replied.

"Go, dammit!" Bambi pointed at the door. "Go spread some testosterone around the swamp. Are all men stupid stubborn asses, or just you two?"

Gar responded by grabbing her in his arms and kissing her fiercely. Bambi answered by smacking him hard in the face. He laughed. "Thanks, now I'm ready to kill something." He turned and followed Autis to the truck where the dogs were yelping. He withdrew a .44 Ruger carbine from the cab, checked the safety one more time, slung the weapon over his shoulder and, carrying a tangle of leashes, went to the back of the truck.

"Walk 'em to the place where the blood starts, then we'll follow them leashed until the trail gets really hot. Be ready, 'cause it's probably gonna get quick once we strike the cat." They were gone; two beams of light outlined their figures in the murk.

"Asshole!" Bambi shouted loudly. She could barely see the outline of Gar's waved response.

She and Liv returned to the kitchen table. "Damn, I love that man," Her tongue glided over her lips tasting his kiss.

"You ought to marry him."

"Why ruin a perfect thing?" Bambi shrugged.

Chapter 32

"Do you have any stew beef?" Bambi glanced at the clock over the doorway leading out of Liv's kitchen.

"Uh, yes. I've got some in the freezer. Are you hungry? I could whip up some breakfast."

"No, I was going to make some stew."

"At four in the morning, you're going Martha Stewart on me?"

"Something like that. You have vegetables? Potatoes, carrots, celery, onion, and such?"

"I've got them all. I've also got some bay leaf, garlic, and a few other things that might dress up a beef stew." Liv smiled. "Sometimes, you're so transparent, Bambi. You knew the men would come home hungry for 'man food.'"

"Actually, I'm going to make 'dog food.' The men are going to think it's for them, and that's good cause they're going to come home hungry—but the dogs, they'll be coming home 'hongry.' I care about the dogs."

"Beef stew?"

"Dogs love it and it's good for them; meat and vegetables, and I'll cook up some brown rice—you do have brown rice, don't you—and pour a platter of beef stew over it for the hounds. The men'll think we've cooked it up for them. We get points."

"Bambi, you're truly diabolical, you know that?"

"It's a gift. You got rice?"

"Yes, I've got brown rice. 'Hongry?' What's that?"

"Hungry is when you want to eat. 'Hongry' is when you damn well better be fed. I was raised around dawgs and hunter men. Dogs want food. Hunter men want food, alcohol, and sex. If you get a lot of food in them first, you don't have to worry so much about the other two. Whatever you do, don't let them get to the alcohol first—they get intolerable. I need to make a big plate of cornbread too—and deep-dish fruit pie."

"Damn, Sis, you're not just diabolical, you're plumb dangerous," Liv said in a light imitation of Bambi's dialect.

Just before noon, they heard the dogs baying. Bambi moved to prepare dishes of food for the dogs. "Remember—food first. We don't want them drinking on an empty stomach—not with all that testosterone running through 'em."

Liv turned on the coffee maker and had plates ready to pile high with beef stew and cornbread. A deep dish apple pie was cooling on a rack in the corner of the kitchen counter.

"They didn't get him." Bambi looked out the window at the approaching men and dogs.

"How can you tell?" Liv asked.

"Men move different when they've got what they went out to get—whether it's game or women."

"Different? How?"

Bambi thought a second. "In either case if they'd hit what they's shooting at, they'd be jostlin' and jokin.' Them two coming our way look like a couple of city boys who shoulda stayed home." She walked out carrying bowls of stew and rice for the dogs.

Liv watched from the kitchen window as Autis and Gar closely inspected the dogs and put them into their kennels on the back of the truck. Bambi placed a bowl of stew in each kennel.

"We didn't get him." Autis entered the kitchen.

"No shit," Bambi said.

Gar ignored the sarcasm. "The dogs struck him about half a mile from here, and he led them on a long, slow chase. They treed him three times. It was like he let them tree him so he could rest until we got close, and then he'd take off again. That is one smart animal."

Bambi came in the kitchen. "You sure? You both look like you caught him—or he caught you, one."

"I've had a greater intimacy with swamp and briar than I'd ever hoped to have. We followed him in a large circle, coming back almost to here, then he went into a grassy slough and the trail just disappeared like it went up in smoke. The dogs are plumb tuckered. That stew smells good."

"We made it just for you, darlin'. "Bambi winked at Liv. Have a sit down, I'll get you a beer." She motioned to Liv who began ladling out the stew. The plan was for Bambi to bring up cold beer from the pub—very slowly, so that by the time she came back with the beer, the hungry men would have polished off half their stew and a slab of hot cornbread. It worked to perfection.

"This is the best stew I've ever eaten," Autis said as Gar nodded agreement with his mouth full.

Gar took a big swallow, then said, "I could have sworn we had him twice, and both times he vanished like he was a ghost." He put away another mouthful of stew. We've been puzzling on how a black panther came to Wadmalaw, and the only thing we can come up with is that some fool must have had him for a pet or some such thing and let him go, or he escaped. I mean, they're not native to this area. In fact, all the swamp panthers have been killed off from around here for years, so it has to be either an African or Indian panther or a jaguar. American cats don't come in black."

"Is that like they don't shine with red eyes?" Bambi chided.

"Sort of, I guess." Gar embraced a formal demeanor, and turned to Bambi. "What we have here is an anomaly, my dear."

"Thank you, professor."

"Well, your 'anomaly' just about had me for supper last night." Liv turned to Autis. "What are we going to do?"

"Do? We're going to hunt him down. I'll call in the state game warden. We can get a team out to track him. Maybe they can dart and capture him and not have to kill him."

"You think they'll believe a story about a panther, a black panther?" Liv asked.

"A red-eyed black panther," Gar jibed.

"They might not care about his eye or fur color when they see our dog and the pug marks he left. There are plenty of tracks. At least they will know that a very large, aggressive cat is on the island—one that apparently is not afraid of human beings."

"I have a confession," Liv said. Everyone fell quiet and motionless.

"Okay," Autis said.

"The eyes weren't red?" Gar added.

Liv raised her fist in Gar's direction. "Well, you know how much grief I've been giving you about that gun case of yours. And you know how I rail against the evils of guns."

"I'm familiar with that." Autis nodded

"The first thing I thought of when I got into the house with Bob was how to open the damn case so I could get to a gun, but it was locked, and I don't have a key."

Autis reflected on this a moment. "That's right, and you're not going to have a key until you agree to take lessons on how to use guns. There's nothing more dangerous than a gun in the hands of someone who doesn't know how to use it. Let me know when you're ready to learn." Gar nodded vigorously to that line of argument.

"He's right," Bambi said. "Where I come from, every year you hear about some yahoo blowing some part of himself, or someone else, off because they 'didn't know the gun was loaded' or some such stupid reason. I could shoot before I went to school."

"I can't argue with you, Autis. I'm ready to learn how to shoot."

"Tell you what I'll do, I'll get a pellet gun, and we'll have target practice on the back lawn. That way it won't bother the neighbors, and it'll be safe—and fun. We can work up to a .22 and take it from there. I'll locate a firing range and we'll do pistol work there. Fair enough?"

"I can do that." A wide grin crept over Liv's face. "But when do I get to kill something?"

Chapter 33

Two weeks later Liv was on the phone when she looked out her kitchen window to see Bambi's car coming at high speed.

"I'll call you back, Uncle Wiley. I've got a visitor coming up my drive. Yes, thank you, I love you back." She hung up and rushed to the door just as Bambi got out of her car.

"Get your handbag—we gotta go. Miz Sweet's been attacked by an animal, and she's hurt." Bambi jumped back into her car as Liv ran for her bag.

Liv dropped into the car seat and reeled out the seat belt. "What happened?"

"I don't really know, except that I was working in the yard when my phone rang. I wasn't able to get to it in time. Miz Sweet's granddaughter left a message saying that Miz Sweet had been attacked by an animal, was hurt, and that I should come—and bring you." Bambi ignored the speed limit to such an extent that Liv was fearful of a serious accident.

"You could slow down a little, and I'm sure we will get there. The way you're driving now, I'm not so sure."

Bambi eased off the gas. "You're right."

In less than ten minutes they were pulling into Sweetgrass Weaver's driveway; cars were haphazardly parked under the pecan trees. Men stood about in groups of three or four, watching as the two women got out of their car and ran to the house. Children were everywhere. There were dogs, guns, and pickups. It looked like a red-neck convention except that almost everyone there was black. Bambi and Liv raced to the house and found it filled with women of all ages. Many were crying, and all seemed angered.

"Where is she?" Bambi demanded.

"Are you Bambi?" A comely girl in her teens approached the newest arrivals.

"Yes, I'm Bambi, and this is Liv. Where is she? Is she okay?"

"She's in the bedroom. I think she's okay. We got a doctor coming."

"Can we go in?"

"Of course. She's been asking for Liv. I'm her great-granddaughter, Alicia, and she's told me about meeting you two. Come with me" she turned to go down a short hallway leading to the back of the house.

In the bedroom, Bambi knelt beside Sweet's four poster bed.

"Hey, Miz Sweet, it's Bambi. Can you hear me? Are you okay?"

"I can hear you, child, and yes, I'm okay. I've just had a bad scare and got the wind knocked out of me. Where's my dog? Is he being taken care of? He got hit bad by that black devil. Where is he?"

"Goody's at the vet, Granny." Alicia touched her grandmother's cheek. "He's in good hands."

"Bring some water." Sweet's request created a rustle of movement, and the sound of demands for water being passed to those in the kitchen. In seconds a glass of water was produced, followed by a pitcher, tinkling ice.

Sweetgrass pulled herself up on her elbows. "Help me to sit—I can't drink flat."

Alicia, Bambi, and another young lady, who surely had to be Alicia's relative, gently eased the elderly lady into a sitting position and propped her on pillows. She took a polite sip, another, and then nearly drained the glass. Alicia's relative added more water from the pitcher, stood and looked at the two white women.

"My name is Devon. I'm Alicia's little sister." She stood a good four inches taller than Alicia, and looked like she could have walked off the front cover of Cosmopolitan. Bambi nodded at the young woman.

"I'm Bambi, and this is Liv."

"You're the one she's been asking for. She had Bambi's phone number, but not yours." Devon said to Liv. "That's our mama at the door." Acknowledgements were made with head nods to a large-boned lady who was obviously the door guard. There was a sea of faces behind her.

"I'm Rebecca Wells, Miz Sweet's granddaughter," another Cosmo model said as she walked past the door guard and into the room.

"Child, thank you for coming," Sweetgrass said to Liv and handed her the glass. "Thank you both."

"Miz Sweet, is there anything we can do for you?" Bambi asked. "Please let us help."

Sweetgrass motioned to Liv, who then sat on the bed next to the lady and took her hand. "Yes, Miz Weaver?"

"There is more I need to tell you, and I want to tell it now—while I can. It is something you must know and promise that you will act on."

At that moment a doctor and a nurse entered the room. He was a stocky black man with a no-nonsense demeanor. She was a slender grey-haired white RN whose manner made the doctor look almost frivolous.

"I want the room cleared—now." He pointed to the door and proceeded to open has satchel.

"Come back when the doctor's finished with me," Sweetgrass said to those in the room.

"They'll come back when I say they can come back," the doctor said with soft assurance.

Sweetgrass smiled at the doctor. "I diapered you, spanked you when needed, suffered through your teens, and sent you to medical school with my savings. I'm going on ninety-one, and they will return when you are finished."

The doctor pointed at the doorway.

Rebecca hugged the guard at the door, then guided Bambi and Liv through the mass of humanity in the house, making introductions along the way. Liv sensed that the air was alive with a palpable intensity like she had never experienced before. They wound up in a surprisingly large kitchen. Food was appearing faster than space for it could be found—or it could be eaten. The ladies were organizing the set-up of tables in the yard, knowing that the men would address the food surplus issue.

Bambi took Rebecca by the hand. "Is it possible for one person to be loved more than this?" She waved an encompassing arm.

"No, it is not. Grandmother loves and is loved by the entire community. Everyone here has benefited from her Christian ways. Time will not permit me to tell you the number of people she has turned from the wrong path. She is love." The girl started to shake as she choked back her feelings. Bambi gathered her in her arms.

Liv looked in wonder about the room at the dozens of souls exposed to each other, seated, standing, squatting against a supporting wall, breathing together in near silence. Hands were clasped, shoulders embraced, and tender kisses exchanged. Liv knew she would never again see the likes of this.

While waiting for the doctor, Liv and Bambi made their way outside to one of the clusters of men standing and talking. Men with taut faces. There were guns.

"She said it was a big black cat."

"A black panther. I've not heard of such, hereabouts."

"Well, now you have."

"That's true."

"If we're going to go, we best go soon. There's a blood trail, and the dogs are ready. It's going to be swamp and briar. Go home and get your right clothes on. We will leave as soon as the doctor comes out. I don't want to go off not knowin'." The speaker was a muscular man of medium height and dark complexion. "I figure probably half an hour." The group thinned as men hurried off to make preparations.

The heavy-set man shouted to the men as they dispersed. "Bring machetes and don't come back not ready for huntin' the swamp. We're going to catch that thing, and we're going to kill it. Now go." He turned and acknowledged Liv and Bambi.

"Ladies." He touched the brim of his hat.

"I'm Liv Oakley, this is Bambi Bamberg."

"Clevis Wells. Granny Sweet's my grandmother."

"Do you know what happened, Clevis?"

"As best as I can make out from what Granny Sweet told me, she was working a basket on her front porch when she heard Goody barking. She saw this big cat—she said black—coming across the pecan grove. Goody went at it barking—he's not much more than a puppy. They went round and round at each other. The cat caught Goody with a hard swipe of its paw and sent him flying. Then the cat turned and headed to the porch where Granny Sweet was sitting. She got herself up right quick and went into the house, but she didn't close the door. She got Grand's double barrel twelve from off its wall rack and pointed it at the screen just as the cat made the porch. She leveled that twelve gauge at the cat just as Goody struck it from behind and turned him from charging. The cat bit hard on Goody and put him down. Then it got quiet. Granny Sweet couldn't see nor hear a thing and she moved toward the door." Clevis ran a callused hand over his face. "Just as she got to the screen the cat jumped up from the ground below the porch and came through the screen like it wasn't even there. Granny Sweet got off a single shot that only grazed the animal. It jumped on her and knocked her to the floor. Goody came through the hole in the screen and caught the cat by the haunch. The two of them went back out the door and at each other again, Goody getting the worst. Granny got up, went to the door and fired the other barrel at the animal. I think she got it good this time because it took off for the wood. Granny Sweet went in the house, reloaded, and then came back out to look after her dog laying on the ground."

Clevis was shaking with rage by the time he finished the tale; it would be retold hundreds of times by night's end.

"Where's Goody now? Is he still alive?" Liv asked.

"He's been taken to Dr. Jameson's place. When the doctor saw him, he said he'd not likely survive."

Bambi engaged Clevis in further conversation as Liv walked away and moved among the small clusters of men who were seething for action. They were talking softly among themselves, but as Liv approached, the men would stop talking, turn and quietly greet the white lady in their midst. It was known that the white women were there by request. Liv moved from group to group saying a soft word of greeting or concern. She was aware of being watched. Not all looks were approving. *So this is what it's like.*

Half an hour later the physician appeared on the porch and walked to the steps where he stopped and waited as the family gathered on the lawn below him. The doctor waited for the group to settle and cluster. Liv could swear that no one was breathing. Then he spoke.

"Our Granny Sweet is going to be okay." Everyone exhaled. Smiles were everywhere along with a collective sigh of relief. Any kind of outburst would be unseemly at this time. Many buried their face in their hands and wept in silence.

"There appear to be no broken bones. She is bruised, shaken, and has some small scratches where she fell. But she is going to be okay. She wanted me to tell you that you all are expected when the pecans come in." This statement was met with grateful laughter and sounds of affirmation. Liv looked on as the collective body of people slowly sank to their knees with prayer hands clasped.

An old man, obviously a preacher, took the porch. We shall offer up a prayer of thanks to our Lord Jesus..."

Liv saw Bambi in the midst of the crowd, swaying and rocking gently on her knees like the rest, hands clasped, and tears in her eyes. Liv fell silently to her knees, closed her eyes, and listened. "...and Jesus, Lord, we know you move in ways that we do not, cannot, and may not understand. And we know, Jesus, that it is not our place to ask, but only to accept..."

After a lengthy prayer session, people rose refreshed, and passed among themselves in joyous fellowship.

Liv Oakley absorbed many lessons.

The physician signaled Liv and Bambi, who came to him. "Ladies, I beg that you not overstay your visit with Miz Sweet. She needs her rest, but she insists that she has something she must tell Miz Oakley. Try to keep it short."

Rebecca was on gatekeeper duty, and she let the girls enter. Devon and Alicia were at bedside.

"Ladies, thank you for returning. I am going to follow William's bidding. After all, he is the doctor. I will be very brief, but perhaps you can return tomorrow so I might tell the whole tale that must be told." The girls nodded.

Liv sat next to Sweetgrass and gently held her hand. "Grandma Sweet, I have to ask before we go...How many grandchildren and great-grandchildren do you have?"

Sweet chuckled, "I have been blessed with seven children some fifteen years apart, twenty-two grandchildren, and six greats. Why do you ask, child?"

"I was just wondering. It seems like every time I turn around I'm introduced to another relative. You're a fortunate lady, Miz Sweet."

"As I said—I'm blessed."

Miz Sweet signaled for the water glass which was produced immediately. Taking a drink she held onto the glass in both hands. "Alicia, you and Devon can leave us alone now. This needs be said in private. Please close the door and don't fret. I'll not be long." She patted the bed for her friends to sit.

"What I am about to tell you will sound like the ravings of a mad woman, and I apologize ahead of time for that. You may judge my sanity if you wish." She smoothed the covers over her lap. "I told the story of being attacked by a black panther. That story is only half true. What I saw came in the appearance of a large black cat that was in fact—not. What I was attacked, and nearly killed by, was Alexander Maxton."

Liv and Bambi looked at each other in amazement. Miz Sweet continued. "Don't ask me how I know this—I just know it. Liv, you have an evil spirit dwelling on your land and you won't know peace until you rid yourself of that monster."

Chapter 34

"I hope you got more sleep last night than I did," Bambi said the next day on the way back to Granny Sweet's. "I feel like pure shit."

"It took the better part of a bottle of Chardonnay, but I finally drank myself to sleep. The last time I looked at the clock, it was three a.m."

"I could use a big, greasy breakfast about now; the kind doctors warn against, but hayel, what do they know anyway?" Bambi wheeled into a neighborhood diner near Fenwick Crossings, the intersection of Main and Maybank highways.

"Have you eaten yet?"

"No, Autis let me sleep. He knew I'd been awake most of the night. I got up just before you came. I haven't even had coffee."

"Good, let's go clog an artery." Bambi slipped out of the car.

There was still a crowd at Miz Sweet's. Later, the girls found that many had stayed all night, sleeping on couches, the floor or the porch where citronella smudges still burned. Men with guns were there, but in smaller number. Clevis was seated on the porch floor leaning against the wall. He rose as the girls approached. He shook his head. "We didn't get him—came close, but didn't kill him. He killed a good dog and injured others."

"Don't tell me," Bambi said. "He would tree, but when you men got close he'd take off again."

"Yes, how'd you come to know that?" Clevis asked with a puzzled frown.

"He did the same thing to our men a couple weeks back. And they came home looking just about like you do now—which ain't pretty, I might add."

Clevis winced with a small grin and a slight turning of his head. "Well, we'll come back. We'll get him, and we'll kill him. I got a cousin coming from New Mexico. I called him this morning. He's bringing a friend of his who hunts cougar and jaguar in Mexico. We'll get him."

"Clevis, I'd tell you what Granny would tell; you need a long bath and a short sleep," Bambi said. "And do something about those briar kisses before they go infected."

"Damn, are all white women as bossy as you?" Clevis grinned.

"No, only the good ones." Bambi shot back on her way into the house.

Sweetgrass Weaver was propped on pillows with attendants around her. Bambi went to her bedside. "Looks like a queen with her court."

"Court? *Keepers* would be closer to the truth. They won't let me get out of bed. I had to beg to get to the bathroom before I wet myself. They had a bedpan and were ready for me to use such. It was only when I lost my kindness that I got a reprieve. Court, indeed," Sweetgrass huffed.

"How are you feeling this morning?" Liv asked.

"Like I've been run over. My whole body aches. If I ever believed in doctor pills I'd take one now."

"I'd say this was the time to do so. I've got some Tylenol that should help your aches. I'll let you take two, but I won't leave the bottle, lest you get the habit." Bambi winked at Liv. She dug into her purse and came out with a small bottle. "Take these with a good drink of water."

"I'll violate my precepts for you, dear. We heard you out there, bossing Clevis about. We all got the chuckles. No one, I do mean no one, tells Clevis what to do. There's bets out that the man will never marry. He'll not find a woman foolish enough to put up with such a hard shell man."

"I don't know, Granny. I think the right woman will come along and crack that shell like it was an egg."

"How's come you to never marry, child? You being pretty and smart like you are."

"Because I'm not pretty, and I am smart, Granny."

"Oh, that was quick, it was."

"That's because I've had plenty of time to think it through."

"Don't listen to her, Miz Weaver," Liv added. "She's got a fine man who would marry her today if she'd say. And she loves him to boot."

"Is that true?" Sweetgrass asked.

"Granny, look at this mouth. What man would want to wake up every morning and face this ugly mouthful of teeth."

"You ladies leave us." Granny waved at her court.

When the room was empty and the door closed, Sweetgrass took Bambi by the hand. "Child, I've not got long for this world, so I'm going to say what needs saying, and I expect to be heeded."

Bambi slumped a little and nodded as her faced reddened. Liv could sense her friend tightening.

"Now don't go getting weepy on me. What I've got to say needs a clear-headed listener."

Bambi sat up and leaned close.

"Tomorrow or as soon as you can, I want to hear that you've made an appointment with a dentist to fix your smile. I've got savings. I'll help out and pay all if needed."

Bambi remained silent.

"Now, how's come you've not done such a simple thing? There's dentists everywhere."

Bambi waited for what seemed a long time before answering. "I've not told a soul what I'm about to say to you." She looked away. She glanced back at Liv before her eyes locked with Miz Sweet's. "When I was twelve, my ma took me to the dentist to fix this mouth." Bambi shuddered. "This is hard, Granny. stay with me though. She took me there and left me. He used some sleeping gas on me, and I wakened to find him on top of me with his—his ..." Bambi started to shake uncontrollably, and her breath came in short gasps. Liv put her arms around her.

"Stop, child. You don't have to go on." Granny's lips tightened and her jaw clenched tight.

"Yes, I do, Granny. He hurt me. There was blood. He cleaned me up and sent me on my way with the caution to be quiet. I never went back. Since then, I've tried to go to the dentist, but every time I get a severe case of nausea. A couple of times I fainted in the waiting room."

"Well, it's out in the open now, isn't it?" Sweetgrass said.

"Yes." Bambi took a big breath and exhaled.

"Why didn't you tell me?" Liv said.

"You never asked. Remember? That was one of the main reasons I made you my best friend. You took me the way I was and never said a word. Nobody'd ever taken me that way. Ever."

Nodding, Sweetgrass Weaver placed a hand over Liv's hand as Liv held Bambi's hand. "When it comes down to it, children, all we really have is each other. Everything else amounts to a pile of baubles. Without our Lord Jesus, and without each other, we are nothing. Love is our wealth."

Liv said, "Granny, do you realize how rich you are?"

Sweetgrass nodded. "I sometimes think that just the knowledge of that wealth is the greatest riches of all. Maybe that is what is intended in the saying, God Is Love."

There was a knocking at the door. "Are you okay, Granny?"

Liv went to the door and opened it. Sweetgrass spoke to the multitude at the doorway. "I'm fine, children. We are having a wonderful talk in here. Now leave us."

The door softly closed.

"I visit a woman dentist in Charleston. I want you to call her and make an appointment. Be sure to tell her that you are kin. I think a woman dentist is what is needed here."

"Thank you Granny, but we're not blood kin. I can't lie."

"Not blood, child, but kin nevertheless. You tell her I said so. No, I'll call her and let you know when to go."

"Okay, Granny, but I won't need your money. I got more than enough to take care of what needs be done." Bambi glanced at Liv who nodded in acknowledgement.

"I'll say one more thing, Bambi. I've heard tell that you have mischievous ways with men. I expect this has something to do with those teeth and your pain. I don't know the truth or the extent of it, but I want you to remember this." She paused and thought a moment as she looked with bright eyes into those of her friend. "No one will call you by a name you don't answer to."

The girls sat in silence. The mockingbird had returned, and was in an azalea bush just outside the window.

"That bird, he sings to me each day, all day long. There's no sweeter music. I looked him up in the dictionary word-book. Scientists call him in Latin *mimus polyglottis*. It means 'a mime with many voices.'" She chuckled to herself. "My neighbor has one of those cuckoo clocks from Germany. That mockingbird imitates her clock. Sometimes scientists are pretty smart."

"So, that's why you call him Marcel, because he's a mime," Liv said.

"Yes, child." Sweetgrass took a deep breath. "I do believe those doctor pills are helping. But I sure am sleepy right now. Why don't you come back this evening, and we can talk some more. I haven't told Liv what is needed." The ladies helped Sweetgrass lay out flat. As they rose to leave, Bambi planted a gentle kiss on Sweet's brow, and heard the lady softly say as she fell off to sleep with a smile, "mimus polyglottis."

Sweetgrass Weaver was breathing deeply while the girls slipped to the door.

Chapter 35

That evening Liv and Bambi were pleased to find Sweetgrass sitting up in a rocker next to her bed.

"We had to call the doctor," Rebecca said. "She was fussing so, having to lie in bed all the time. The doctor, William, he's my cousin, said that it would be better, her sittin' happy in a chair instead of fussin' in bed."

Bambi sat cross-legged on the bed while Liv pulled the dresser chair next to Sweetgrass, who took her by the hand. The others wordlessly left the room. Rebecca was asked to stay, and she joined Bambi on the bed.

"I want Rebecca to hear this story." Sweet nodded to her granddaughter. "She's already heard what I've told you up to this point, but now she needs to know the all of it."

The ladies settled in their respective places, intent on listening.

"Liv, first off, can I call you Olivia? It is such a pretty name."

"Yes, of course, that's my name, it just got shortened to Liv."

"Olivia." Sweet slowly savored each syllable. "You and I are blood kin. Distant, for sure, but blood kin from several generations past. Alexander Maxton—Monster Maxton—was our common ancestor. I've sketched out my ancestry on paper and will give it to you to copy. Rebecca should have a copy too." She tipped her head at her granddaughter who responded with a nod.

"I shall be brief because I'm tired and want to get to the point. We can fill in the details and answer your questions later." Granny Sweet smoothed a quilt draped over her legs, and began. "I told you last time that I know the black cat to be the spirit of Alexander Maxton. I know this to be true because it happened once before—to Camille Maxton."

"Miz Sweet..." Liv was silenced by Granny Sweet's raised hand.

"As I told you at the end of our last talk, Maxton was buried in a trench on the property, and for some time after that, the slaves would come to that spot to relieve themselves. It was probably made into some of the richest soil in South Carolina. The slaves scattered about the property and the island, some claiming a parcel as their own. Some moved away and went to the Promised Land up north. Maxton Manor stood as a jumbled heap of half-burnt and half-built lumber for a couple of years. After the war ended Camille Maxton returned. President Andrew Johnson, Lincoln's successor, rescinded the orders dictating the breaking up of the plantation properties. Most of the plantations were returned to those who owned them before the end of the war. Camille and Sugah took on the rebuilding of the manor house and they reestablished the site as a working farm. Her daughter played with the children of free-men—who were now employees of the farm and sharecroppers—just as her mother had done with slave's children some twenty years before. In three years' time a community grew nearby—a mercantile store, a smithy, stables and rooms for travelers. A year later, Camille Maxton took Janey and returned to Ohio, leaving Sugah in control and ownership."

Bambi stirred from her intense focus on the story. "Why did she leave, Granny? I mean, she seemed to have everything in hand. She was living on her family property, surrounded by friends and sharing a life with her half-sister. I don't understand. Why would she want to go?"

Sweetgrass motioned for a glass of water, and Liv handed to her. "Let me have a couple of those doctor pills of yours, Bambi."

Bambi dug in her purse. "There you go, Granny. Didn't I warn you? You're hooked—a doper for sure."

Sweet took the gentle ribbing with a smile. "Go ahead now; make fun of a helpless old woman." She downed the pills with a swallow of water.

"Helpless?" Rebecca almost shouted. "When did 'helpless' start up, Granny?" The beautiful girl leaned back and laughed a rich laugh from deep inside. "Wait'll I tell the rest that you've become helpless."

"You too, Rebecca? After all the diaperin' and cookies and fishin' togeth-er—you turn on me? Shame." Sweet grinned, enjoying the banter.

After the amusement faded away she turned back to Bambi. "Camille didn't choose to leave, she was driven out."

The long silence that followed was broken by Liv. "Driven out? Who could have driven her away from the home where she was born and raised?"

Sweet pursed her lips, and frowned in thought. "It wasn't a who. It was a what. She was driven out by Alexander Maxton."

"I thought he…" Liv started.

"By his specter." Sweet cut in. "By his spirit—ghost—boo-hag. Whatever name you care—it swept down on her at the end of her second year here, and it gave her no rest. It was a thing of vengeful evil that would not be denied."

"My God Almighty," Bambi said. "He never gave up, did he?"

"There's more," Sweet answered.

Bambi crossed her arms over her chest and rubbed them with her hands. "Granny, I'm gettin' goose bumps all over, and you're tellin' me there's more? What more could there be?" Bambi rose as to leave the room but was stopped by Liv who said, "Don't desert me, Bambi. I need you here with me."

Rebecca rose from her perch on the bed and came to stand beside Bambi, placing a gentle hand on her shoulder. "We'll all stay together because we'll all have to deal with this together. We need each other's strengths—and we each need to fill the gaps left by each other's weaknesses."

Sweet looked at her granddaughter in puzzled wonder. "Child, where does this profound wisdom of yours come from?" She clasped her hands over her breast and lowered her head as in humility before a superior force.

"Granny, I'm growing nothing you didn't plant," Rebecca said softly. Bambi's shoulders shuddered under the girl's hand. "Stay, Bambi. We'll all come away stronger for this."

"What more?" Liv broke in.

Sweet looked at Liv with softening eyes. "You are strong, Olivia. Strong like Camille." Then she turned to Bambi. "And you have passion—oh, how I envy that passion in you." She raised her eyes to her granddaughter. "And Rebecca—it is so easy for me to see you in diapers. My Rebecca, your wisdom must light the way. All three of you will be needed to defeat these terrible forces who strike from the grave." She turned her attention back to Liv. "Olivia, the more of which I spoke is Mongo Maxton."

Once more, silence blanketed the room. Liv reached for Bambi's hand.

"Mongo Maxton. Camille's great and only lover. It is rumored that, late at night, Camille and Mongo would couple in the basement of Maxton Manor. She would take to sleep on a daybed she had brought down to the basement. He would come to her and consummate the undying love they initiated that summer day beside the spring." Bambi and Liv exchanged the look of two people who simultaneously discovered something. Sweet continued, "It's further said that their late night love-making raised a vengeful Alexander Maxton from the grave. The spirit form he took began to threaten and torment Camille. At first it would only approach her if she happened onto the grounds at night. As the months passed it grew bolder and would appear before her at twilight, and finally it could be seen in broad daylight. It came after her and her child with malevolent intent. Priests were brought in—and a shaman. Spells and incantations were brought to bear against the evil force, but nothing worked. Nothing would do but Camille had to take her child and flee out of fear for the safety of her daughter. Afterward she would come to the Manor only for short visits, never staying overnight at the manor house. It is said that Mongo mourned her absence by torturing those who tried to live in the house. The only one to escape his wrath was his sister, Sugah. Workers came to the house by day, but none stayed overnight. Voices in the basement drove them in fear from the house."

"I've heard those voices, Miz Sweet," Liv said.

Miz Sweet sat in thought for some time before speaking. "Yes. Was there more you were going to tell me, Olivia?"

"I didn't think it was important." Liv didn't know how much she was blushing with those words.

Another long silence. "Your high color tells me there's more that ought to be spoken."

Liv heaved a heavy sigh. "I—Yes...There is...A lot more."

Miz Sweet raised a hand. "Rebecca, give us a few minutes, will you please?"

"No, Miz Sweet. I want her to stay. She needs to hear the story as much as any in the room." Rebecca settled back. Liv cleared her throat. Miz Sweet handed her the glass of water and she took a drink. "Thank you."

Bambi took Liv's hand. "Are you sure you want to go there?"

Liv nodded. "Yes. The story needs telling. I think it's important." She turned to her host. "I'll go directly to the heart of the matter, Miz Sweet. I have—in your words—coupled with Mongo Maxton."

"Then this is indeed a story that must come out," Sweetgrass answered.

Chapter 36

"Gal, you got some *cojones*." Bambi sipped her tea. "I would never have fessed up to what you just told Granny Sweet."

Liv looked out over the well-tended tea hedges of the Charleston Tea Plantation. "That's not the hard part."

"Dear Lord Jesus, stop. "Don't tell me about anything harder than what we've just been through."

"*We* went through? Where did this *we* come from? It happened to me—I'm the guilty party here. I'm the one who did the ghost in my basement."

"Dayem, gal. How long's it goin' to take for you to start understanding Southerners? Your pain is mine, darlin.' Get used to it."

Liv leaned back and laughed so hard that people at near tables under the live oak patio stopped talking and stared.

"What's so funny?" Bambi asked.

"I guess this means I'm going to have to share Autis with you."

"Damn straight. We start today, right?"

Liv shook her head in amusement. "You wouldn't do it. You know you wouldn't—no more than I would if the tables were turned. You Southerners with your arcane 'code of honah'—you wouldn't have Autis now if I handed him over on a platter and you know it. Come on now—in your words, fess up."

"Guilty as charged but that doesn't keep me from sportin' some wonderful fantasies in my dreams. That is some hunk you got—it's a pure shame him goin' to waste like he is." Bambi said with a wicked grin.

"You may have noticed through that hazy dream world of yours that Autis seems to be a happy man—very happy."

"Go ahead now—brag."

"There's no need to brag over the truth. But you've got Gar—and he loves you like sin. You two are made for each other."

"Truth is, I dearly love that lug, but he's breaking my heart with his prodigal ways. They's any number of things he could do to make a decent livin', but he's like a butterfly—bouncing from one thing to another. Unless he changes his ways, he's goin' to wind up an old man who has accomplished absolutely nothing with his life. He's going to be an old, bald, fat man filled with bitterness and regrets over a life of bad choices. I'll not be witness to that. I'll not be there to watch his promise die." Bambi was struggling with her feelings as Liv pulled close and took her friend in her arms as the dam burst. The other tea drinkers stared in silence.

On the way home from the Charleston Tea Plantation, Liv volunteered. "A good cry helps sometimes."

"It does that."

"I know you love Gar as much as a man deserves to be loved, and that's what hurts so much."

"My love of Gar wasn't the only reason for my tears. My tears were for you as well.

I was crying because I knew that you were going to have to tell Autis about your ghost lover."

Liv pulled over into the parking lot of a small clapboard church and turned off the engine. "I can't do that."

"You can and you got to."

"Why? It would only break his heart."

Bambi reflected into herself. "Even though you knew how this would hurt Autis, you still went back to get it again—twice."

"That's right. That's what I did. I can't explain it, I'm not proud of it, and I can't defend why I did it." Liv paused and then pounded the steering wheel with both hands. "The worst thing about it is that I'm scared to death that Autis will go on another business trip. I don't know if I can keep myself from going down to the pub."

"But you said it was like…"

"It's more than that—much more. There's an attraction I can't explain. It's like I'm under some kind of spell—and I have no control over it."

Bambi leaned away from her friend, placing her back against the car door as though to distance herself.

"You must think I'm real trash."

Bambi covered her mouth with her hand momentarily. "You're the sister I've always wanted, and I'm not going to throw you away because you did something wrong. You can't get rid of me that easy—Sis."

"I don't know how you can be that way, Bambi—as much as you love Autis, and as vile as my behavior has been."

"It's not that simple, darlin.' I've got my own cross to bear—and it weighs heavy."

"Let's go to my place, light some incense, pour some Firefly and I'll tell all. I'll give you a chance to do the rejecting."

Liv leaned back into the soft cushions of Bambi's overstuffed couch and drank in the odor of patchouli while her friend fixed drinks in the kitchen. Her eyes rested on the lava lamp and she became aware of soft sitar music coming from another room—Ravi Shankar.

"I mixed our poison half and half with iced tea—sober being the preferred state during confession." Bambi set down the tray of drinks and stretched next to Liv, sharing the cushioned hassock with her bare feet.

"'Confession' sounds seriously serious."

"It is." Bambi took a long pull on her drink. Those college professors I told you about that I used to screw my way to scholarships and work study jobs—not all of them were just a means to my end. One—his name was Evans. We did it everywhere, everyway, and anytime. I would have crawled over cactus to be with him. I risked expulsion and he risked his professorship. He had a beautiful, intelligent wife who loved him, and two boys who thought he was God—and he still couldn't stop himself. We lied, cheated, and stole our way to one tryst after another. Every time was like the first time." Bambi was struggling with herself. She took a deep breath and exhaled. "He went home at two in the morning one night and found his wife and children gone. It took a year and a half of therapy and lawyers for him to get his family back. That ended my sluttin' days in college—I was Miss Straight Arrow after that. I made it the rest of the way through college off my knees."

The two friends lay side by side staring at the ceiling—exhausted. The silence grew long but neither felt the need to speak. Finally, Bambi turned to face Liv. "You want to switch to the straight stuff?" Bambi said, holding up an empty glass.

"Yeah, I want to but I won't—because I want to."

"Dayem, gal, you're plumb admirable."

"Thank you, but I need a clear head because I'm not sure I know what your confession has to do with me screwing a ghost."

Bambi rose from the cushions and walked over to stand in front of her Jimmi Hendrix poster. She leaned her head back causing her mouth to open as she stared at her ceiling. Then she looked levelly at her guest. "If I hadn't experienced the total helplessness I felt for that man I would never be able to understand—or overlook your being swept away with the ghostly Mr. Maxton. As it is—it's not just livin' in a glass house—it's more like bein' totally aware of 'been there done that.' Like I said, darlin', your pain is my pain. My own dalliance has given me compassion I wouldn't have otherwise."

Another lengthy silence ensued as Ravi Shankar performed the seemingly impossible.

"Well, dayem," Liv gently mocked her friend.

Bambi ran fingers through the gold that surrounded her face. "Tell you what, sport. Next time Autis goes off, you call me and Sandi and we'll have us a pajama party. Meantime, you gotta promise me you'll keep away from 'the pub.'"

Liv hoisted her glass.

Chapter 37

Gar handed the small rifle to Liv. "It shoots BBs and pellets. I got both kinds here for you to try out."

Liv held the Crossman air rifle much like she might have grabbed a black snake.

Gar placed her hands in more appropriate positions. "It ain't going to fire just by holding it. Also, it's empty and not cocked. About all it would be good for is as a lightweight club."

"It's okay to hit him with it, Liv." Bambi observed Liv and Gar from a short distance. "Just hit him on the head—that way you can't hurt anything worthwhile."

"First off, we'll deal with safety—handling, carrying, loading, unloading and such. I'll get your loquacious friend here to demonstrate…"

Bambi tossed her curls in the sunshine. "I got your loquacious right here, Buster."

Autis watched from his deck chair. Grinning ear to ear, he took a sip of Bud Light. Rising from the chair, he walked to the opposite end of the deck and gazed out over the dark forest lowering at the edge of the yard. *I know it's watching us right now.* He raised a pair of binoculars just in time to see a dark shadow disappear into the underbrush. *We're running out of time.*

He glanced at the Glock resting on the table before he walked over to the threesome at the other end of the deck. "Let's go ahead with some target practice. Maybe we can get Bambi to run across the yard while we attempt to hit a moving target."

By the end of the week, Liv had fired hundreds of pellets and BBs, .22 shorts and rat shot. Over the weekend Autis and Gar introduced her to a .22 rifle and handgun practice at a local gun range. Bambi went along for what she called "immoral support."

"Dayem, Gal. You got a dead-eye. I been shootin' since I was just out of diapers, and you beat all."

Liv studied the pattern of her hits on the paper target that had been handed to her. The hits were clustered around the bullseye. "I've got good teachers. Plus the fact that it's fun. I never thought gunplay would be so enjoyable."

"Gunplay? We gotta work on that vocabulary, Darlin.' Our hairy-handed companions would be highly pissed if they's to hear you callin' their primal urges play. Men will tolerate most anything—but not mockery." Bambi pointed to Autis and Gar emerging from the forest.

"Ain't they a sight? They look like a couple of revolutionaries what with their armaments—shotgun, pistols, rifles. It's a good thing they can't find a source for hand grenades."

Liv frowned. "I'm worried. I've never seen Autis like this. I mean, I'm accustomed to his focus, but he's paranoid about this panther."

"Gar told me that Autis has seen the panther lurking at the edge of the wood—mostly early in the morning or evening, but last week he saw it in broad daylight in the branches of that big ol' loblolly. He took the 16 gauge and went out there, but the cat was gone. The cat had done a lot of digging and scratching under that pine."

"That's why he won't let me go outside alone. He told me he'd seen it, but he didn't give me any details. I think he's trying to protect me."

"Darlin,' he'd do a lot better protectin' by lettin' you know the whole story. That panther is serious—and it's gittin' bold."

"Autis is getting serious too. We've gone to indoor or outdoor gun ranges almost every day the past three weeks, and we've got loaded weapons stashed at nearly every doorway around the house and basement. I feel like we're under siege."

"You are, darlin.'"

"I need to learn how to shoot a shotgun—and that damned Glock of his."

"You're talkin' heavy artillery now. Get him to let you try out that little .410 shotgun of his. You can work your way up from there."

"I must be doing something right—Autis has given me a key to the gun case."

Three weeks later Autis presented Liv with a 20-gauge pump Remington and a 9mm Beretta. "Graduation presents, Hon. You've earned them."

Liv worked the action on her new pump gun. "Well hell, I never realized they'd be such fun. Good teachers helped. Can we try our hand at skeet shooting?"

"Yes, now that you're not dangerous with guns. Let's hope you never have to put your new knowledge to use."

Chapter 38

"You taped them?"

"Yes. Well—no. Not taped. I recorded them on a voice activated electronic recorder. Last night was the first time I was able to capture any sounds. Want to hear it?"

"Of course." Liv set aside her review notes for a future article.

Autis went to their sound system in the corner of the living area and began working button and dials. The soft fading explosion signaled an activated sound system. Liv leaned forward from the couch.

At first, the sound from the speakers sounded like any public building with people passing by—almost white noise. As Liv and Autis listened it became apparent that they were listening to human speech that sounded much like English in its pace and rhythm—but not quite. They heard laughter—a man laughing softly.

"What are they saying?"

Autis shrugged. "Your guess is as good as mine. I've listened to it a dozen times and I can't make out a sentence that I understand. I think I can pick out words that are familiar: 'swamp,' 'marsh,' and what I think sounds like 'loblolly.' It's like English but spoken in a different language."

Liv leaned forward and, with a deep frown, listened once again to the faint garbled sounds on the tape. "I think we need to get this tape to someone who can understand what's on it."

"Gullah." Miz Sweet leaned close to the recorder. "That's Gullah for sure, but a dialect unlike any I know. I can't make out what is said, but I can tell you there is a man, two women and, I believe, a child. If I could study it some I think I might be able to understand bits and pieces of what is said, but I think you'd do well to take it to Books Wrenn. She's a master of Gullah. It is said that Books Wrenn can go anywhere up and down the Carolina and Georgia coast and speak with the local Gullah."

Liv turned off the recorder. "What is your opinion, Miz Sweet? What do you think is on this tape? I'm not asking for an interpretation of it—just your idea of what it is about."

"Your basement is home to spirits. Books Wrenn will call them boo-hags. I don't use that, but it all comes to the same—there's something there that is not human as we know human. I'd not lay claim to knowing the what of it, though."

"Granny, if we don't know what it is how can we deal with it?"

Miz Sweet rocked a few cycles. "Bambi, I think the why of it is what is needed. We can call those spirits by names that are familiar to us—and that serves nothing. But finding why they've come out gives us a path to travel."

Liv frowned, "A path?"

"Yes. Because at the end of any path is a goal. The spirits want something—if we can give it to them it might satisfy. Make more recordings if you can, and take them to Books Wrenn. You must do this." Sweetgrass took Liv's hand in hers and pulled herself close to her visitor.

Liv, startled by Miz Sweet's intensity, started to speak but was cut off. "Those spirits in your house are angry, very angry."

Books Wrenn's small frame house rested at the end of a long curving driveway through an old forest. The delicate yellow paint of the wood siding was set off by intense blue window and door frames. It was almost picture postcard pretty as it sat surrounded by giant trees that hovered protectively over it.

A stocky dark-skinned lady rose from her porch chair as her visitors got out of their car.

"Books Wrenn?" Bambi spoke up.

"Elethea told me you were comin'. She told of your problem."

Bambi was taken aback by the abruptness of the woman's manner.

Liv, sensing Bambi's surprise, rose to the opening presented by the sharp-tongued lady. "Yes. My basement has spirits, and Sweetgrass Weaver and Elethea both said they thought you could help."

"Help?"

"Sweetgrass thinks that we need to find out what the spirits want."

Books pointed to the chairs on her porch.

"I've brought a recording of their voices. Can I play it for you?" Books nodded her approval, and pointed her guests to chairs on her porch.

"These spirits are angry," Books Wrenn said after listening to Liv's tape recording. She motioned Liv to play it again.

"Can you tell what they are angry about?" Liv asked while resetting the recorder.

"Play that thing once more," Books commanded, pointing at the recorder.

She listened closely as her two guests sat in silence.

"Theirs' is a dialect strange to me. I can only touch pieces of what they say with my mind. I can tell you this, they are trapped in a place they hate, and they want out."

Liv looked at Bambi, and then to her host. "Miz Wrenn, I need your help. Will you come to my house?" Books Wrenn rose wordlessly from her perch, picked up a sizeable handbag, and stood waiting for her guests to gather their electronics.

"Stop the car. Stop." Books Wrenn stated firmly. "Stop here."

Liv stopped at the entry of her driveway and cut the engine.

Books Wrenn sat clutching the handbag in her lap. "I should not have agreed to come here—to this place." She sat rigid in her seat, her lips pursed. "I can't go in there."

Liv made eye contact with Bambi seated in the back. "Why, Miz Wrenn?"

Books Wrenn sat unmoving and rigid. She opened her handbag and drew out a tiny cloth bag and hung it from her neck by its long leather cord. "This is a place of much pain. A place of loss. I can feel longing and anger, no—rage. Yes, a rage so strong that it wants to kill." Books removed several amulets from her handbag and slipped them over her right wrist. She took out a small wooden figure and clutched it tightly in her fist. "I am afraid—and I am fearful of my fear."

Bambi leaned toward the front seat. "What are you afraid of, Miz Books? Books Wrenn didn't respond. Bambi continued. "Can you point to where the fear is coming from?"

Books Wrenn closed her eyes and lowered her head. "There." She pointed at the house, "is anger." She moved her arm and pointed a stubby forefinger aimed at the loblolly pine. "And there is pain and loss."

She pointed at the house. "What is on beyond the house? I feel a presence there. A powerful sense of longing of many."

Liv looked in the direction of Books' gaze, "Graves, we found what appear to be slave graves."

"Take me to them." Books commanded.

Liv started the car, "Okay, but you seem upset by what you've seen just by passing through the gate of the property. I don't know…"

All of a sudden, Books Wrenn snapped erect, and stared with widened eyes past Liv to the edge of the wood bordering the yard. She inhaled sharply, as though she had stopped breathing and was catching her breath. Her eyes bulged as she looked past Liv. She pointed with her whole hand. "There is the beast," she said in a voice hoarse with terror.

Liv and Bambi both swiveled their heads in time to see a dark shadow vanish into the undergrowth. Liv turned back to face Books as a sort of rushing sound came from her. Then she passed out against the car door, soaked in perspiration.

Bambi began wiping Books' face. "She's ice cold. Let's get her in the house."

The struggle to get Books into the house and on a couch was made difficult by her weight and the fact that she was shaking as though convulsed. Liv produced an armload of towels and blankets, then helped Bambi tuck them around their visitor.

Still wiping perspiration from Books' face and arms, Bambi said, "Tea. Make some strong tea—it might help when she comes around. But if she doesn't come about soon we better call 911." Books' breathing was strong and ragged. She began thrashing, but Bambi held her arms and talked soothingly into her ear.

Suddenly Books' eyes snapped open and she gave a loud gasp.

"He's here."

Bambi and Liv looked at each other. Liv began looking around the room. She moved to the gun case.

Bambi placed a hand on Books' shoulder and said softly, "Who's here, Books?"

Her patient sat up and looked about the room, and then down at her feet. As in a trance she raised an outstretched arm, extended a forefinger and slowly turned her wrist to point at the floor. "He is beneath us—and he wants out."

Liv had retrieved a handgun from the case and walked to the kitchen with it. She returned shortly without the gun, and carrying a tray of tea cups and a pot.

The strong plantation tea had a calming effect on Books as the three sat in the silence of their thoughts.

Halfway through her cup, Liv asked, "Who wants out?"

"A man, a young man; I can't see all of his face, but I know he is quite handsome—and angry.

"What is his name?" Liv asked.

Books drained her cup. "I don't know. But I know that his anger is directed at two beings. The first and greatest portion of his anger is directed at the beast that waits outside—the thing I saw from your car. It is an anger fueled by a flaming hatred that cannot be put out. His is a rage that is matched only by that of the dark creature in the forest." Books looked from Bambi to Liv. "When you take me from this place do not ask me to return."

Liv placed a hand over Books' hand. "I understand."

"No. You don't." Books pulled her hand away from Liv's clasp. "The other focus of his anger is you. Now take me home."

Liv rose from her chair as to carry out Books' command.

Books raised a hand. "Wait, there's more. There are others—others below, and …" She closed her eyes. "His name… his name begins with the letter 'M.'"

"Mongo." Liv said sharply. "Is his name Mongo?"

"Yes." Books looked up with a startled expression. "Mongo."

"Before you go, can you tell us what we need to do to make this—this—go away?"

"Yes. You must find and remove the sources of the anger of The Beast in your forest, and of—Mongo. You'll have no peace until you do so." She rose from the couch, casting aside the blankets.

"Oh." Looking out toward the salt marsh, Books raised both arms as though seeking the embrace of another. "There. There is the source of longing of many souls. Such sadness." Books' eyes misted over. "Take me to them."

A gentle breeze from the sound made poetry of Books' loose-fitting garments as she stood solidly, arms outstretched, facing the cluster of tabby capstones. Her face streaked tears as she stood and wept gazing skyward—and to the east. Several feet behind her Liv stood with a revolver on her hip, and Bob's leash in her hand. Bambi cradled Autis' 16 gauge pump in the crook of her left arm. Both women were occupied with scanning the forest to their left. They—and an alert Bob—knew they were watched. The sun was getting close to the horizon and shadows lengthened across the yard. The wind from the water came in cold and clammy.

"What lies there?" Books pointed to the north wood.

"Nothing," Liv said. "There's a neighbor, an older woman, Freedom Covers, lives there. She's been there for years—longer than any in the community can recall. Her house was here before there was a community."

Books walked a few steps toward the north wood. "There is a spirit—an unfriendly spirit—weak, but restless and filled with evil intent." Books took several steps in the direction of the Covers property. Liv and Bambi quickly looked at each other; Bambi shook her head. Books walked all the way to the edge of the wood, by that time her two companions were rapidly moving their head side to side in constant play over the surrounding area, weapons at a ready position.

"Covetousness, want, and a terrible longing. Oh, such sadness." Books pointed at the neighbor's house. She turned to the armed guard behind her. "Take me away from this place. Take me home." Books backed away from the wood as her companions moved with her. Bambi had her shotgun on her shoulder. Neither girl heard the soft growl from the shadows of a small cedar, but Books felt the rage.

Back at Books' house Liv and Bambi waited in their rockers as Books Wrenn prepared herbal tea.

"My heart is still pounding," Liv said, spreading her hand over her breast. I thought she was going to lead us into the wood."

"She'da gone without me then," Bambi fanned her face with a magazine. "I'm here to tell you, I was plumb scared."

Books came out to the porch with a tray of tea and oat cakes. "I felt your fear, and knew that we went as far as we should go."

Liv took a sip of tea. "If you'd felt my fear, we wouldn't have gone near that wood."

"The Covers house is a nexus for the evil on your land." Books looked at Liv. "I don't know yet what it is, but it does exert a force. However, you have other issues that you can, and must address." Books sat her cup on the side table. "You have graves to dig."

Chapter 39

"Dig them up?" Autis laid the daily mail on the roll-top desk they used as a work station. Then he set his briefcase next to the desk.

"That's what Books said. Dig them up and bury them with the others down by the edge of the salt marsh."

Autis dropped into the oak swivel chair that came with the antique roll-top. "Have you looked closely at that floor? Those are six-inch thick, cypress timbers laid tongue-and-groove and, if Sweetgrass is correct, stone pavers are under that."

"Books believes that Mongo, and those buried with him, must join the others at the marsh."

"How does that solve the problem with our friendly kitty cat?" Autis said. I mean, we can live with the spook in the cellar—as long as he stays in the cellar. But that panther is another issue—one that scares the tar out of me."

"Tar? You've got tar in you now?"

"I've been around your glass blowing friend too much—it's rubbing off. At any rate, the panther is dangerous and getting bolder—we're nearly in a state of siege. The state wildlife people have been out a number of times, but haven't had any luck—it's like the damn thing is a ghost. And you told me Miz Sweet insisted that the thing that attacked her was actually Alexander Maxton."

"I don't doubt her. I truly believe that we are dealing with some kind of demonic spirit."

Autis leaned back in the swivel chair and steepled his fingers in front of his face. "You know, this is getting to be too much, Liv. Let's put the house on the market, cut our losses and get the hell out of here. I don't like our lives being controlled by something that we can't even identify—and we have no power over."

"Cut and run? Is that you? I don't think so."

"It's not just me, Liv. We can't go out in the yard without being armed. When was the last time we went out on the dock at night? Remember how much we used to enjoy the moonlight over the sound? It's been weeks now since you and Bob encountered that cat in the yard. Since then we've been prisoners in our own home. We're not enjoying this house. Hell, I'd be afraid to have guests over. The only people we see are Bambi and Gar. He's taken to carrying that Ruger .44 in his truck, and Bambi's packin' heat in that monster handbag of hers. What do we tell people who want to visit? 'Sure, drop by, but come armed.' I say we sell."

"No. I say we stand and fight."

"I can fight. I'm fast, strong and good with almost any kind of weapon. You can make none of those claims. How do you plan to fight?

Liv poured a splash of Islay single malt for each of them. "I plan to fight with my head and my heart." She breathed in the fumes and took a tiny sip of the smoky liquid.

Autis reached over with his glass and gently clinked hers and then replicated her action. "Damn, that's a fine drink." He set his glass on the coffee table. "How are you going to 'head and heart' our feline friend out of our lives?"

"Books told me she couldn't help with what she called 'The Beast in The Forest,' but she claimed to know someone who could."

"Another Gullah shaman? Is this a club? What are they—like Masons?" Autis took another, larger sip.

"You know, Butthead, you really are a pain in the ass. Here I am trying to solve our problem, and all you can do is zing me from the bushes. Thanks a lot." Liv slammed her tumbler down onto the surface of the coffee table, spilling scotch.

"Okay, okay. You're right. I'm sorry. Tell me what you think should be our next move."

"Books has recommended a root doctor."

Autis didn't flinch, grimace, or make a sound. But Liv saw the knuckles on his clasped hands turn white, and his jaw muscles twitched. She continued, "She pointed out that the creature that appears in the form of a black panther is not of Gullah—it is a white man's beast and should be handled with white man root medicine." Autis sat impassive. Liv felt her face flush as her ire grew.

Autis sensed that he was in trouble. "Okay, there's a certain logic to that, completely defusing the tension. "But where do we find a white man's root doctor? That sounds almost like an oxymoron—white man's root doctor."

"On John's Island." Liv answered.

"John's Island—the land of overpaid professionals, retired millionaires, and Trustafarian grandchildren—that John's Island?"

"That's the one."

"Okay," Autis said with exaggerated patience. "How do we contact said root doctor?"

"He's in the phone book."

Autis squelched the desire to ask 'yellow or white pages.' "When can we get together with him?"

Liv looked at her wristwatch. "Well..."

Chapter 40

Finley Newman stepped out of the green Ford pickup that showed a sign on door the stating he was a locksmith. He closed the door purposefully, as though to tell it, "stay shut." He climbed the short flight of steps to Liv at the door.

"Miz Oakley?"

"Yes. Mr. Newman?"

"Most call me Finley."

"Come in. I'm Liv, and this is Autis."

Finley entered the foyer and exchanged handshakes with Autis. He ran his hand over slicked back salt and pepper hair. "Onct' had a friend who pronounced his name that way—Autis. Spelled it Otis. He was a boat-builder. Good man, him. The sea took old Otis in a quick squall one day. You related?"

Caught unawares by the slender old man's question, Autis stumbled over a reply. "Uh—I—probably not. What was his last name?"

"Foy. Otis Foy he was."

"No Foys in my family that I know of." Autis answered, gathering his wits.

"Steady friend, Otis. Mind if I smoke?" Finley asked.

"Let's go out on the deck," Liv said in answer. She turned and walked to the sliding doors that opened onto the deck. Finley followed with an ambling gait that indicated a short leg, or possibly a hip problem. He walked to the railing and lit a Camel. "Nice place. I like your view."

"Thank you. Could I interest you in a glass of iced tea, Mr.—Finley?"

"Tea would be fine." Finley brushed an ash off the front of his lightweight plaid shirt. As Liv departed for drinks, Finley turned to Autis. "Fish any?"

"No, we don't fish much. We both work and we've been busy fixing up this house that we bought less than a year ago—a never-ending job."

"See you got that long dock there going down to the pass. That'd be the place to fish. It's relaxing."

"I used to fish a lot. My dad took me when I was little. I still have some of his fishing gear. He preferred a fly rod."

"Lot of work there. I like to plop a bobber in the water and set and wait—gives me a chance to think." Finley climbed up onto one of the high stools that went with the tall metal outdoor bar. He crossed a leg and revealed a skinny pale shin, white cotton socks and black beef roll loafers.

"Your missus said on the phone that you all are having trouble with what might be a kind of creature from the other world."

Autis nodded and searched for a response just as Liv showed up with glasses of tea and a saucer ashtray.

"It's not sweet. There's sugar and slices of lemon."

"You got any Sweet and Low? I got to watch my sugar."

"Yes, I'll be right back." Liv spun away and disappeared though the doorway. Finley took a long pull off his Camel. Some people's cigarette smoke smells worse than others. The smoke from Finley's habit had a clean toasted aroma. He held his cigarette away, looking at it as though it was a different kind of thing that needed investigating.

"Smoked for over fifty years now. Started when I was fourteen. Smoked Old Golds, then Chesterfields. Went to Luckies, and now I've settled on Camels. Used to puff on a cigarette out of New Orleans called Picayune— right strong. Had to quit them. Reckon I'll quit before it kills me. Can't abide a filter." He took a final drag and snuffed out his smoke as Liv approached with a saucer holding pink packets of sweetener. The weathered man carefully field-stripped his cigarette, letting the breeze carry off the shreds of tobacco and paper.

Finley peeled open a Sweet & Low, poured the contents into his glass, stirred, and took a long pull at the glass. "Fine." He put his glass down. "Now what is your story? Start at the start."

It took an hour, two tea refills, three Camels, and one trip to the "facility" to get the entire story told. He proved to be an excellent listener, knowing when to talk, when to ask, and when silence served best. But most importantly, he knew when and how to respond to the emotions within the story. Liv told most of the tale, so Autis opted to start up a batch of wings on the grill while listening to her soliloquy, occasionally putting in a line or an aside. During the hour he added some garden vegetables off to the side, spritzing them with herbed oil as they cooked. He also had a pot of rice cooking on the side burner. Liv's story ended with the three sitting down to an early supper.

"Can't say as I've had better wings," Finley complimented with a lopsided grin. "She keep you on steady here?"

"She does. She's hard to work for, but the pay is terrific." Liv openly kicked Autis under the table.

"I really like those vegetables—the way you cooked them. I'll be sure to tell my missus about it. She's always on the lookout for making better fixin's."

"Thank you, Finley. Liv does most of the cooking, but she lets me take command over the grill—sort of feeds my cave-man instinct."

"Well, Og, while you and Finley finish your drinks I'm going to clear the table, and then we can get back to our critter problem."

Ten minutes later, Finley was halfway through a post-supper Camel. "What do you think is the problem?"

Liv and Autis glanced at each other. "Aren't you here to tell us?" Autis asked.

"Oh, I'll tell you what I think the problem is; I just wanted to hear your ideas on it first."

"Well, our lives are in danger from a large black panther that is getting bolder every day. I don't know what he is or why he is, all I know is that he is here and he means us harm. I want to eliminate that threat by whatever means necessary. I want to kill it before it kills us."

Finley thought a moment. "You speak your mind good, and you make good sense." After Autis nodded a 'thank you,' Finley looked to Liv with an inquiring raised eyebrow.

"I think we have a demon. A demon in the form of a panther. The demon has a reason for being—I'm not sure that it only wants to kill us. After all, what would it gain from our death? I think it wants something else. And like Sweetgrass Weaver, I think that demon is—or has something to do with—Alexander Maxton."

Finley snuffed his Camel, took a deep breath, and rose from his chair. "I see." He moved to the railing and gazed out at the forest. "I guess it's time to confront your demon. You want to show me where you think might be the best place for that?"

"Sure." Autis rose and moved toward the doorway into the house. "Come with me."

"Wait," Liv said. "You said you were going to tell us what you think the problem is."

Finley had started to fall in behind Autis. He turned to Liv. "I will. I've heard Autis' thoughts, and I've listened to yours. Now all that's left is to hear what the creature in yon wood has to say. Your demon."

Autis, cradled his 12-gauge pump as he led Finley down the front steps and to the F-150. Finley gave a low sharp whistle and a pair of ears appeared in the back seat of the cab. When Finley opened the door a multi-colored dog leapt from the seat to the ground and came to his side.

"What a handsome dog." Autis walked toward the truck as Liv descended the steps to join the threesome.

"Thank you. This is Tyro." Hearing his name, Tyro did a little jig and wagged his stub of a tail, but he never left Finley's side. "My Lil calls him

Tyro the tyrant but we know that ain't so, don't we, boy?" He reached down and touched Tyro's head.

"He's beautiful." Liv said. "What breed is he?" She came to kneel beside the happy dog and stroked down his back.

"A mix—Jack Russell Terrier and Australian Sheep Dog. That's why he's to have that riot of color—murl and tan and white, and that one blue eye."

Autis laughed heartily. "Jack Russell and Australian Sheep? Someone had a wicked sense of humor. Does he ever wind down—or sleep?"

"It takes right smart a workout for him to rest. He'd sleep on our bed if Lil'd let it be so, but she don't take to sleepin' with critters—'cept me, of course." Finley grinned. "I'm only quotin' her. But he is a handful. He weighs in at forty pounds, and it's all muscle, git and grit."

"I'll have to warn you—that cat has already killed a couple of hunting dogs and wounded our pointer pretty badly. He nearly killed a coonhound belonging to a friend of Liv's and doesn't hesitate to attack people. He's been shot a number of times, but then Liv's already told you about that."

"We'll be careful." Finley drew a stout walking stick from the seat of the truck."

"You're not armed?" Autis asked.

"No, I'll just take my cudgel here—it's right stout." Finley's cudgel was nearly head high and sported a carved handle.

"What kind of wood is that?"

"It's Mountain Laurel from up on the Blue Ridge Mountains. I cut it from a north slope—high up. The rings on it count near a hundred—I doubt you'll find a stouter wood anywhere. It's been my companion for some thirty year now."

Finley withdrew a set of coveralls from the truck and stepped into them. "Good protection from the briar."

"No offense, but that walking stick's no match for what's out there in the wood."

"I've got other protection." Finley said, drawing a canvas teardrop pack from the back seat of the cab. He unzipped the pack and withdrew a small cloth bag that was tied to a leather thong that he draped around his neck. He withdrew another tiny cloth sack and put it in his shirt pocket. He hung the pack over his left shoulder. "Well, I guess that's it then." Finley donned an Irish tweed hat, touched the brim to Liv and turned to the wood. "Where should I start?"

"I think we ought to..."

"We? There's no 'we' in this 'cept me and Tyro here. You stay."

Autis took a step back and looked at the slender man with the walking stick. "Oh, no. You're not going out there without a gun or a guide with a gun."

Finley leaned on his cudgel and looked at Autis with a very slight smile. There were several moments of tense silence between the two strong-willed men.

"Autis." Finley spoke softly, "Look at these gray hairs." He doffed his hat. "And look at these age spots and wrinkles on these hands of mine. Do you think for a minute I've not been here before? Do you suppose I look forward to dyin'?"

Autis didn't respond, but stood his ground.

"Autis, I go alone—with Tyro—or I don't go a'tall. I can pile up in my truck and leave if you want such. Or I can go out there and find out what kind of creature we're dealin' with. Why don't you stand ready with that scatter gun. If you hear me blow this whistle—you come runnin'." Finley pulled out a metal police whistle and blew it sharply. Tyro perked his ears forward, and Finley gave him a comforting pat on the head. "Now, where should I start?"

Autis turned to look at Liv, who nodded acceptance.

"Start at that loblolly. But watch out, there's lots of low branches and plenty of cover for a cat to hide in that tree."

"I'm glad to start there 'cause something is there. I don't know what, but there's a presence..." Finley turned to walk toward the loblolly. Tyro fell in at his left side, nearly touching the man he obviously adored.

When Finley disappeared into the low-hanging greenery of the pine, Autis turned to Liv. "That is either the bravest or stupidest man in the state."

Liv smiled. "Maybe he just knows what he's doing."

After a couple of minutes, Finley reappeared from under the pine and walked back to his hosts. "There's sumpin' there alright. I think I know what it is, and I think I know what the problem is." He withdrew a three foot long quarter inch steel rod with a wood handle from his cab, then went to the back of the truck and lifted out a short-handle spade. "You two might want to come with me."

Under the loblolly, Finley began probing the ground with the steel rod. After several deep stabs he hit a solid object. He probed around the object to determine its general outlines. "Dig here," he said to Autis. Some ten inches into the soft ground, Autis hit a solid object. "I think it's a rock."

"Maybe." Finley answered.

Autis quickly excavated the area around what they quickly realized was a granite headstone. They brushed away the dirt from the stone that was face down. With some effort they tipped the stone upright in its hole, and brushed away the soil from the face of the stone. Ornate lettering read 'Kathleen Jolly Maxton, wife of Alexander Maxton. Rest in Peace.'

"I believe we've found a graveyard under this old loblolly." Finley rose to his feet. "Why don't you probe out the rest of the stones while I go demon-

gathering? Liv, you keep an eye out while Autis probes—what we're dealin'
with here ain't dumb." He grinned at Autis. "Where should I go next, Boss?"

Autis pointed toward the front of the property. "Follow the tree line until
you get to a stand of cedar—turn in there. You won't need to go far before you
find what you might be looking for—or before it finds you. Keep an eye out."

"I'll locate the area you describe. I'll find a way to approach it with the
wind to my back. That way whatever is there can't sneak in and attack from
behind. Tyro has a keen nose."

"Of course." Autis began probing and hit another stone before Finley was
out of the perimeter of the old pine. He began probing for the outline of his
find.

Thirty minutes of work had yielded two more sites, marked for excavation, when Autis took a break. He turned to Liv. "Tell you what—how about
if you go to the house and come back with the 16-gauge? Let Bob out of
the basement, and bring him on a leash. Leave the 12-gauge. Oh, and bring
the Glock." Liv nodded in understanding, and she turned and hurried to the
house as Autis watched. He didn't return to his probing until she disappeared
through the front door.

By the time she returned with Bob and more armament, Autis had discovered two more stones. "That should be about it. What do you think?"

Liv ticked off her fingers. "That would be Jason Maxton, his wife, their
two sons, and Alexander's wife. Five stones. Sounds right."

Just then they heard a dog barking. They walked out from under the loblolly and toward the stand of cedars. They heard Finley's whistle. It sounded
again, and it became quiet. Autis raced to the stand of cedar. As he got to the
thick wood he heard a rustling from it. He turned to check on Liv's position.
Just as she caught up with her husband, Finley's back appeared through the
tangled forest of cedar. He was backing out of the wood. Tyro was at his side.

"I'm here." Autis shouted.

"Good. Keep an eye. He's close." Finley backed all the way out of the
wood before he turned to face Autis and Liv. The front of his overalls was torn
and red with blood. Finley had a deep scratch on his cheek. "Keep an eye."
Finley had his cudgel in one hand and a sheath knife in the other. Growling
came from the wood as Finley slipped the bloody sheath knife into the top of
the cudgel. The handle of the cudgel was also the handle of the knife that fit
into it.

Autis handed his shotgun to Finley. "Safety's off." Finley nodded as he
brought the gun to point. Autis unholstered the Glock. "Back away together.
Give me the leash, Liv."

Bob fought the leash—he wanted to attack. Tyro followed his master's
lead and backed up with Finley while watching the wood. No one seemed to

breathe until they had some fifty yards between themselves and the stand of cedar. The growling stopped.

Finley took a deep breath and exhaled strongly. "That's some spirit you got there. I'd of been in serious trouble if it weren't for Tyro." The dog wagged. "Ever time the cat came at me Tyro nipped him on the butt. He got plumb aggravated with that. Finally, he decided to ignore Tyro and keep comin.' That's what all this blood is about. I caught him good in the chest with my blade. Looks like he ruined my outfit though." Finley looked down at his torn clothing. Autis and Liv stood in stunned silence.

Liv tried to talk. "You—you were... I'm—I—I don't know what to say." She turned to Autis who stood shaking his head in silence.

"Now don't go thinkin' I do this all the time. This is the worst I've ever dealt with—by far. I was scared—pants-peein' scared. If I had this to do again—I wouldn't."

They walked quickly back to the house. "I need to get out of this bloody outfit. I can't let Lil see me like this."

"Autis will let you wear some of his clothes while I wash and dry yours." Liv said. "And we need to medicate that scratch."

"Okay, let's retrieve my probe and shovel as long as we're next to the pine here. Autis walked into the shade of the tree and stooped to gather his shovel. "I see you marked four more places to dig."

"Yes, that's five in all. I can take care of it later." Autis pulled the probe out of the ground. "This is a handy tool you've got here." He stabbed it into the ground and jumped when it hit something with a 'thunk.' He looked at Liv. "Another stone."

"Something wrong?" Finley asked.

"There's only supposed to be five stones," Liv said.

"Well, there's six," Finley answered.

The three stood around the probe stuck in the ground as the dogs sat on their haunches waiting for a command.

Finley broke the several moments of intense silence. "Do you have anything stronger than iced tea?"

Chapter 41

In the dusk light, Autis and Liv waved to the departing F-150. Finley waved back and Tyro watched them through the back window as the truck went down their drive to the roadway, where Finley turned on his headlights.

"That is about the most unusual man I've ever met," Autis said.

Liv nodded. "He's got my vote there too. Did you pay him for the torn clothing and his time?"

"He wouldn't take any money. He said normally there's a small fee for his services, but he wouldn't take a thousand dollars for today's experience."

"What—almost getting eaten by a panther? You men have strange ideas of fun."

"I think 'exhilaration' might be a better word."

"You want to explain that?" Liv cocked her head in puzzlement.

"If it needs explaining..."

"Don't give me that bullshit man-thing crap—just tell me why someone would feel a sense of exhilaration in a near-horrible death experience."

Autis frowned. "When you grapple face-to-face in a life-or-death experience with an enemy that wants—and is able—to kill you, you come away feeling that you are more alive at that moment in your life than at any other time."

"Even though you could get killed?"

"Especially though."

"As Bambi would no doubt say, 'You all are a different species.' And I agree with her."

"Really? How did you feel when Finley was backing out of the brush, and you could hear the panther growling."

"Feel? I was scared to death."

"So was I," Autis admitted, grinning.

"You ran toward the danger, though,."

"Finley needed help. You ran to it, also." Autis looked out at the wood with a far-seeing gaze.

"You're not going to go all Iraq on me, are you?"

Autis chuckled. "No, ma'am, those days are behind me." His hand strayed to the handle of the Glock in its holster. "It's just that ..." Long silence.

"Just that what?"

Autis pulled in a long breath before he exhaled mightily. He shook away the thousand-yard stare. "It's just that I sure could use a cup of your good strong coffee and a serious snuggle in front of an open fire. It's kind of cool this evening—strange."

"Mister, you sure know how to weasel your way out of explaining yourself." Liv turned to climb to the screened-in porch and a wagging Bob. "I'll start the coffee if you build us a small fire in the pub fireplace." Bob danced around Liv, followed her into the house, and then came back and danced around Autis as he entered the porch.

"To me." Autis said softly. Bob accepted the command and followed Autis down the stairs. He supervised the laying of the kindling and lighting of the fire before he went back up the stairs to Liv who was in the kitchen—where the treats were.

By the time the fire was past the kindling stage, and Autis had laid out blankets and pillows before the hearth, Liv descended with a tray holding steaming mugs of coffee and saucers of sorbet. "Bob is fed and making himself one with couch."

"He does that well." Autis smiled. "Hmm, does this smell like almond sorbet?"

"Reward for your courage, Braveheart." Liv lowered carefully, tray in hand, to the blanket.

"Brave?" Autis scoffed. I was scared out of my gourd."

He took the tray from her while she settled into a pillow nest, laid the tray between them and handed a mug to Liv. He hoisted his mug in toast. "To Finley Newman—truly a man for all seasons."

"To Finley," Liv echoed.

They clinked, and then sipped.

"Now that's a martini," Autis said in reference to a favored line from an old movie.

Bob barked as though in response. "See, Bob agrees."

Liv frowned slightly.

Autis leaned back with his mug. "Finley really liked this room, despite what he called a 'grave sadness' that hung about. He said he wanted to do his basement like this, but wasn't sure that his wife would approve." Bob's barking increased in volume. "He especially liked the way the doors opened out onto the ..." Autis looked at the door leading onto the patio, and his eyes widened as the lever handle on the right-hand door slowly dropped in a turn. "Oh shit, I didn't lock the doors after we came back in." He rose to his feet as the door slowly swung outward.

Liv, reading Autis' face, sat up and came to her knees just as the panther slunk into the room. It paused to look with lifeless yellow eyes at its' trapped prey. Bob was upstairs barking furiously and scratching on the door at the top of the stairs.

Autis glanced at the 12-gauge automatic that hung next to the doorway through which the panther entered. The great cat sat on its haunches as though contemplating who to kill first. Autis moved to the rack of pool cues and removed two of the heavy wooden ones. Liv had risen to her feet and moved to join Autis, who handed her a cue, and said softly. "You get the shotgun while I distract him." He turned to look quickly at Liv's pale drawn face. "No other way," Autis said. Liv nodded. Her lips were tightly pursed. She looked at Autis and saw that he had gone pale and was trembling slightly.

"I'm going to move forward and to the left. When he comes for me, you get the gun." Autis' breath came heavy, and his face was grim as he stepped toward the sleek black death. The cat fixed his eyes on Liv and seemed to pay little note of Autis—he wanted Liv. Autis stopped and turned to look at Liv, and then whipped around and leapt at the startled cat with a fearsome bellow. He was on the cat before it could gather itself to defend or attack. Liv watched in amazement as Autis rained blow after fearsome blow on the retreating animal, never once pausing to give it a chance to gather itself for an attack. She moved quickly to the gun, and arrived just in time to hear a loud crack as the pool cue broke, leaving Autis holding a foot-long piece of stick. Liv swung the automatic to the cat and at the same time pulled back on the ejector lever to jack a shell into the chamber. The lever didn't budge. She pulled it again—harder. Nothing. She squeezed the trigger. It wouldn't move. She watched in horror as the cat pounced on Autis, driving him to his knees. Autis drove the cue remnant into the neck of the beast, who screamed in pain and recoiled trying to pull the cue out of its neck. Autis rose to his feet and grabbed one of the oak bar stools just in time to meet another attack from the cat who drove him back despite the impact of the heavy stool. Liv reversed her hold on the shotgun and advanced on the cat, ready to use the gun as a club.

The cat and Autis met again. Autis crashed the bar stool on the cat's head, dropping him to the floor. He drew back to strike again, but the cat, with lightning speed, rose and delivered a rapid slashing blow to the raised stool, driving it against Autis' head. A corner of the stout wooden seat struck Autis on the temple. He collapsed in a heap. Then the glistening black feline turned to face Liv who stood with her "club" raised next to her head. The cat paused—much like a housecat might with a crippled mouse or bird—to watch the plight of his prey. He tensed and relaxed the great muscles that ran down his hind legs. His tail twitched and curled—he seemed to almost enjoy the moment. Finally he flattened to the wooden floor and laid back his ears. Liv was sure he was grinning, showing long white fangs and a pink tongue. He started to twitch his hind quarters. Liv had seen cats do that when preparing to pounce. She tensed still more as her hands tightened on the gun barrel. She knew at that moment she was going to die.

Then the cat inexplicably rose straight up into the air some six or seven feet and crashed down onto the heavy flooring. It screamed in pain. It rose again, this time squirming and spitting in rage. Again it crashed to the floor. Then some unseen force swung the animal by its tail and dashed it against a concrete wall, crushing a Miller Lite neon sign. The cat flattened to the floor and backed away from what Liv saw as a faint pillar of mist in the shape of a large man. The frightened angry feline snarled and then turned and slunk toward the doorway. As Liv stood aside to let it pass, it turned and made a wicked spat in her direction. Six inches of pool cue stuck out of its neck. And then it was gone. Liv slammed and locked the door, and turned to face the apparition that stood between her and the pool table. It leaned ever so slightly toward her and then it vanished in a swirl of mist.

Autis blinked his eyes and screwed up his face. As his vision cleared he was aware of two faces hovering directly over his. One of the faces licked him on the mouth. Liv placed a cool cloth on his head. He tried to rise but the pain in his head and Liv's hand on his shoulder stopped him. He opened his mouth and worked his jaw. Everything hurt. He dropped his head back down onto what he realized was a pillow. He squinted up at Liv's face—one eye closed. "What... Where?"

"Shh, shh. Don't talk."

He relaxed, took a deep breath, then another. "What was in that coffee?"

"Not funny. Not funny at all."

"Jesus, my head hurts."

"You want to go to the emergency clinic?"

"Hell no. I want a drink. Scotch."

"Stay here, don't move." Liv rose from the floor and went to the stairway. She was back in less than three minutes with a bottle of single malt, two glasses and a carafe of water. Autis was sitting up.

"I told you not to move."

"I was just checking for body parts." He took the proffered glass. "Thanks." He took a good drink, and another, and then lay back down. He stared at the ceiling. "Did you kill him?"

"No. He's gone."

"Gone? The last time I saw anything, you had the automatic and was pointing it at him. I figured ..."

"You figured wrong. I couldn't get that damn gun of yours to work."

Autis frowned up some pain. "Then how ..."

"It's a long story, and I'm going to have to tell it—all of it from the beginning. Drink some more scotch—a lot more." She poured his glass half full. "You're going to need it—and so am I."

Autis motioned to their circle of pillows. When they settled back into their cushions Autis took up the 12-gauge automatic. "What about this doesn't work?"

"I couldn't get the action to budge. I couldn't get a shell into the chamber."

Autis had a quizzical look. He handed the weapon to Liv. "Let me see."

Liv tried to tug back the bolt and it wouldn't move. "See. It's frozen."

Autis brought a fist up to his mouth to hide the smile. "Okay, now flip the safety lever on the left side of the action just above the trigger."

"Oh, shit. Safety." She pulled the lever back and let it go, slamming a round into the firing chamber. "I'm so damned stupid."

"We both know that's not true. You were under extreme stress, having to deal with a strange weapon—God, my head hurts. Anyone could have done what you did."

"Not you. You wouldn't have. You would have flipped off the safety, jacked a shell into the chamber and blown that black bastard to Kingdom Come—and then knocked off some smart-ass remark."

"I can't say that. There's no telling what people will do under really bad stress."

"I still can't believe that you did what you did. If the pool cue hadn't broken, you would have driven that cat out of the room. I mean, you had him going. I'll never forget the change that came over you—and all the while I was thinking you were a Clark Kent kind of a guy."

"Oh, you didn't see me slip into the phone booth? I guess I ..." It was just then that Autis realized that Liv was starting to shake hard. He moved to her and gathered her in his arms.

"I was scared, I was so scared. I thought we were both going to die. I just ... I wanted ..." She broke and started sobbing. Her face was flushed a bright red and her nose began to run. She started making small animal sounds from deep in her throat. The adrenaline was wearing off.

"I love you." Autis said. "And you love me." He held her closely. They sobbed in each other's arms. Kissing and weeping. The tiny fireplace flickered and died as Bob lay at their feet gazing in confusion over the pitiful sounds coming from the two gods he adored. It was his high-pitched bark that brought them around.

So un-Bob.

"Come here, boy," Autis said softly.

Bob burrowed between the two, heaved a huge sigh and fell immediately asleep. Autis and Liv laughed softly. Liv added. "Like the bumper sticker says: 'Lord, let me be half the man my dog thinks I am'."

The single malt was working its magic as the two stretched out, warmed by their pointer.

"Should I crank up the fireplace again?"

"I'm good." Liv snuggled into Autis' arms.

"I love you."

"You damn well better because you got me for life—unless…" There was a long pause.

"Unless …?"

"Like I'd said. I'm going to have to tell you the whole story—from the beginning."

"Okay. Start at the beginning."

"Right. But first I'm going to have to tell you that I think I've been unfaithful to you."

Autis took a good pull of scotch. "Okay, but I'm wondering how a sane lady can *think* she was unfaithful to someone she loves."

Chapter 42

Autis picked up his glass, started to take a drink, stopped, stared into the glass and then put it back down. "That was some story," he said softly.

"It's true and, I hope, accurate." Liv paused, I love you. I love you like the air I breathe. I love you more than everything else in my life—totaled."

Autis nodded with tiny nods. "Then we both love each other the same amount."

Liv burst into tears and hid her face behind her hands. "I'm so ashamed."

Autis reached out and pulled Liv to his chest. "I can't stand to hear you talk like that—to say such a thing. I love you and I want to protect you—to protect that thing called us. I think we should talk this out and get it behind us. What do you think?"

"I want to, but I feel violated, and I feel I have violated our marriage vows. How can I get past that shame?"

"I don't know yet. But you're going to have to if we want to keep ourselves together. I'm ready to do what I can to help us live past this, but I can't unless you're willing to work with me. You feel worse about this than I do. My feelings are for you, not for me." Autis took Liv by the shoulders and held her at arms length, looking into her eyes. "I want to help bring an end to this pain in you—that's what I care about. Nothing else matters much."

Bambi sat wide-eyed. "That's what he said? 'Nothing else matters much?'"

"Yes. He was trying to comfort me, but it only made me feel worse. It fully confirmed the fact that I'm a total shit."

"Of course you are, but you couldn't tell him that," Bambi said between sniffles.

"Of course."

"Dear Sweet Jesus, gal. Do you have any idea what kind of a man-size man you have? The broad and high of him? Hell, forget size of things—just think about the man's self-confidence. I'm here to tell you—he ain't human."

"If you're trying to help me feel worse, you're succeeding."

"I'm sorry. You're right. He's had two days to think about it and back out, and he's still around. You can help him the most by puttin' it behind you. He is that kind of man—a big man—and that's how much he loves you. You are one lucky lady."

"I know that."

"Good, then let's stop beating this dead horse, and go back to figuring out how to get rid of your haints and your furry friend. Nuff said?"

"Nuff said." Liv rose from Bambi's couch. "I'm going to go home and fix a giant steak for my 'big man,' and hope that we can find something interesting to do afterward." She started toward the door.

"Hey, Sis?" Bambi went to her friend and wrapped her arms around her.

"Don't forget, I love you—and I love your big man. Anything I can do ..." The two friends stood for a moment, looking into each other's eyes in a moment of unspoken love and acceptance.

"I know. Thanks, gal. I love you back. Thanks for the advice." Liv went out the door, and stopped to stroke the yellow tabby curled up on a porch rocker. "Bye, Spot."

On the drive home she noticed a particularly obnoxious realtor sign in front of a lovely small bungalow. Her mind went to her house: *Autis is right, we're going to have to sell.* By the time she got home, her eyes were red and swollen from tears. *Damn you, Alexander Maxton. Goddamn you to hell, you bastard.*

Chapter 43

Liv put down the phone and turned to Autis. "That was Finley. He wants to come over; he sounded very excited. He said we overlooked something last week and he has a hunch he wants to play out."

"A root doctor with a hunch—that sounds ominous."

"I told him to come right over."

Finley stepped from his truck and whistled for Tyro. He waved to his hosts as they descended the steps to greet him. Autis smiled as he realized that Finley was just like he was the first time they met: Same clothing style, same lopsided grin, same shambling walk. It would always be that way with the root doctor. What you saw was what you got—and the knowledge of that was comforting.

Finley touched his hat to Liv, and took Autis' handshake as Liv knelt to pet Tyro. "I've puzzled on this for two days now, and I think I know what we overlooked last week. I have a hunch I want to play out. But first we've got to exhume those stones." He went for his spade and probe in the back of the truck. "You got a good spade?"

Liv and Tyro stood guard as Finley and Autis labored to unearth each headstone, and pry it upright. Paired with Sally Maxton's stone was Jason Maxton's. After the space of a few feet, the two brothers, Elson and Ambrose, were paired side-by-side. Another space of a few feet and Kathleen Maxton's stone paired with the sixth and final headstone. It read "Alexander Caesar Maxton, April 10 1820." The date of death was blank.

"There it is." Finley pointed at the newly uncovered lettering.

Autis and Liv stood in silence.

The root doctor lit a Camel and leaned on his spade. He took a puff and studied the placing of the stones. "I'd say that cat critter is Alexander Maxton who wants to join his family. That means you're tasked with a wicked chore, if you want to live in peace on this land. You must find those remains, dig em up and place them, along with the grave dirt, under this stone." Finley stood over the hole that held Alexander Maxton's headstone. He stepped back from the hole and spoke to his Camel, then turned to Liv. He lifted his spade to his shoulder and that lopsided grin spread over his face. "Miz Liv, I'll wager you make a fine cup of coffee."

Chapter 44

Sweetgrass Weaver rocked slowly as she listened to Liv's telling of Finley's observations. The mockingbird praised-be-to-God several trees away from the front porch while Miz Sweet, Liv, Rebecca, and Bambi sipped tea and savored tiny bites of Royal Fronds.

When Liv was finished, she added to the story, "Miz Sweet, we need to know the location of that grave." Miz Sweet rocked and nodded. Bambi snagged another Frond.

"Autis and I have decided to put the house on the market. We've agonized at length; we love the place, but there…"

"I told you before he was buried on your property. I know right where his grave is," Miz Sweet said softly, and stopped rocking. "And so does Rebecca." The mockingbird was silent. She turned to look at her granddaughter who smiled and nodded slightly at the grandmother whom she loved with fierceness of heart.

Rebecca rose and went to stand against a corner column. "I remember the day Granny Sweet took me to that place. I was only twelve, but I know I can find it again. All I have to do is follow that dry creek bed, keep an eye for a clearing on the left, and 'watch out for moccasins.'" She smiled in sharp remembrance of her grandmother's admonitions.

Miz Sweet nodded and chuckled. "You were so full of yourself that day—all eyes and legs. Child, you have been tearfully beautiful since the day you landed."

Rebecca looked at Liv with a smile. "I'll be glad to take you to the spot. It's on your property, back off to the left as you're coming up the driveway."

"Thank you, but that would be a dangerous mission. That cat has grown bolder and smarter, and I could swear—larger. I wouldn't even try to go there with Autis and his shotgun."

Rebecca frowned and looked thoughtful. "There might be a way."

Miz Sweet frowned at this. "That cat is not of this world, child."

Rebecca reached to her grandmother's hand. "Clevis and his friends will see to it," Miz Sweet chimed in. It was as though she was trying to change the subject. "Bambi, let us see that new smile of yours."

Bambi blushed like a teenager, placed a hand over her mouth, and then dropped the hand to reveal teeth that, while still crooked, were just beginning to take on a semblance of order. "Granny, that dentist of yours is a miracle worker. I've got these braces that don't show, and I go in every two weeks for an adjustment. It will take about a year and a half to two years, but it will be worth it—being able to smile in public and all. I don't know what I can do to repay you for helping me get to that dentist.

"Hush, child. There's no talk of "repay" in this house. That smile is payment enough. It's going to let others see that it is the porthole to a soul of great beauty and passion. Let it come out, child. Let it come."

Minutes passed as the mockingbird went from *andante* to *adagio* and back again. Miz Sweet broke the silence. "Goody's coming back tomorrow. Dr. Andrews says he's in good shape and getting plenty of exercise with the other dogs at his clinic. Says he's near good as new. He's got some scars, but he's young and they'll pass with time. There's no bill, and I can't get the doctor to give me one—says it's 'taken care of.' Sort of got away with me. I assured him I was no charity case, and I paid my obligations. He told me there's no question of charity—says the bill's been paid."

"I've got to use the ladies' room, excuse me." Bambi rose and fled.

"That child just drinks too much tea." Miz Sweet said with a frown.

Liv and Rebecca briefly exchanged knowing looks.

Chapter 45

"Hell's Bells," Gar exclaimed. "We can find it. I know right where that dry bed is; and the clearing—Autis, it's that clearing where we lost the cat that time." The late morning sun made shadows on Gar's angular face. Autis noticed for the first time how handsome the man was.

"Right. I know where you mean." He handed Gar a cold Bud Light.

Autis took a pull from his long neck and came up with a satisfied smile. "I know that God loves us—he gave us malt and hops." He and Autis tapped their bottle necks, saying in unison, "Thank you, Jeezus." Liv and Bambi rolled their eyes in mock disgust.

"You two commune with your maker while I go get the shrimp," Liv said. "Is the grill ready there, Reverend?"

"Oh ye of little faith in the power of grain—the grill is prime." Autis lifted the grill lid to confirm his testimonial.

Bambi ran fingers through her mane. "C'mon, Liv, let's let these ne'er-do-wells practice their Bud suckin' pagan rituals in private. So many good men out there and look at what we got stuck with."

After the ladies left, Gar went to the deck rail and looked out over the salt marsh. A good breeze came in from the sound. "It'd be a good day to sail. We could take Four Aces out and have us a tumultuous time in the blue. She's good in a mild gale—she tacks into the wind beautifully, and when wind is abaft there's no stopping her. She gets a bone in her teeth and acts like she's ready to cross the equator. You ought to see her with a spinnaker—it's enough to make a grown man weep." He emptied his Bud and turned to Autis. "Come out with me sometime and I'll make a sailor out of you. I think you've got what it takes to make a fine sailboat man. And once it's in your blood, it's there forever."

"Sounds tempting. Tell you what, soon as we get our boo-hag issue settled, I'll take you up on it. We've had the house on the market for almost three weeks, and have not had a single offer. It looks more and more like we're going to have to deal with our problem ourselves."

"Word's out, Autis. Bambi says the house is hexed and everyone knows it. I don't think you'll sell this house for a long time—leastways not until the market turns around. Maybe some fool from out of town will come along and snatch it up, though. You never can tell."

"Maybe. But the realtor says she's obligated to reveal the house's history to potential buyers." Autis went to the cooler and pulled out a pair. "You ready for another?"

"Nah, not just yet. I'd like to take that cast net of yours down to the end of the dock and see if I can snag a fish or two."

Autis frowned. "I've got to stay with the grill. Liv will be back with the shrimp before long."

"That's okay. Your net in the usual place?"

"Yeah, but ..." Autis scratched the top of his head.

"What?

"I'm worried about our furry friend out there."

"Hell, Autis, it's morning, broad daylight and besides, the three of us can take care of ourselves just fine."

"The three of you?"

"Yeah, Me, and Messieurs Smith and Wesson," Gar said as he strapped his shoulder holster in place and patted the stout handgun nestled in place.

"Keep an eye," Autis said, still frowning.

"You got it." Gar started down the steps to the first floor landing. He quickly gathered up the net, slung it over his shoulder, and made his way toward the sand trail leading to the dock.

"Don't bring back anything too big to fit on the grill," Autis called. Gar waved a promise over his back and disappeared into the scrub just as Liv and Bambi returned with peeled shrimp and condiments.

"What's Friar Gar up to?" Bambi asked, still poking fun at the grain worshippers.

"Cast netting."

"In this wind?" Bambi said. "That's crazy. There's a good breeze here, I can only imagine what it would be on that dock."

Autis looked up with a startled expression that showed growing apprehension. "The wind ..." Just then they heard a pistol shot, and another followed by a loud shout from the direction of the dock.

Autis flew down the steps, vaulted from the railing of the first landing and hit the ground running toward the dock. Halfway across the yard he realized that the only weapon in hand was the barbecue fork. He shouted over his shoulder. "Shotgun!" Liv followed him while Bambi went for armament.

Autis sped toward the dock and rounded a curve in the sandy trail. He saw the panther crouched over Gar's prone figure. He had Gar's neck in his mouth. Autis raised what 150 years earlier would have been called a Rebel yell and bore down on the cat—barbecue fork held high for a killing thrust. The cat lifted its bloody muzzle and spat at the onrushing screamer. He turned unhurriedly to the brush and slunk away as though he had all the time in the world.

As Liv approached, she saw Autis kneeling beside Gar's prone figure. Gar was holding Autis by the shoulders and speaking to him. Just as Liv arrived, Gar collapsed with a strangling sound. Autis placed his hands over Gar's wounds to staunch the flow of blood.

"Call 911," Autis commanded. "And bring something to help me stop the bleeding. Hurry." Liv rushed back to the house just as Bambi arrived with a shotgun.

"Oh, God. Dear God. No! No!" Bambi's voice lifted to a shriek.

"I need calm here." Autis was crisp and matter of fact. "Go get the hammock—hurry!" He picked up Gar's gun from where it lay on the ground and stuck it in his belt, glancing at the trail from which the panther had vanished. Bambi turned and fled back to the house, screaming to Liv who was returning, cell phone in hand. "The hammock, he wants the hammock." Liv reversed course and went with Bambi.

In less than three minutes, Gar was laid on a canvas hammock. Autis dragged him to their SUV while Liv and Bambi tried to keep the loss of blood to a minimum.

They met the ambulance at the entry gate of the community, saving precious minutes of traveling time. The blood-stained threesome followed the wailing ambulance to the emergency entrance of the Medical University of South Carolina.

"It couldn't be helped. Even if I had been on site with my team I doubt we could have saved him. The damage was massive." The surgeon's fatigued face and demeanor left no doubt that he and his team had worked heroically for over two hours to repair the savage wounds while fighting the constant loss of body fluids. His smock was blood spattered. "I'm sorry. I'm so sorry. We tried everything. I doubt there is a medical team in the world that could have saved your friend." Autis and Liv stood facing the surgeon, Autis nodding and Liv motionless in tears. Bambi wept into her hands a few feet away. Sobbing and swaying, sobbing and swaying. Until the doctor's entrance she had prayed over clasped hand for the entire two hours, promising God everything: her earnings, fidelity, church attendance, chastity, sobriety—everything. There was no talking to her. Now she was lost in her grief.

Autis took the surgeon by the elbow and led him away, softly requesting "something" for their bereaved friend. Granny Sweet's grandson, Clevis, rushed into the waiting room and headed directly to Liv who stood slowly shaking her head. Clevis understood. His face shattered and he broke into tears. He and Liv went to Bambi and took her into their arms.

The doctor nodded. "I'll send someone here." Autis thanked him and turned to his friends.

Clevis turned and looked up at Autis. He spread a hand over his chest. "Clevis."

Autis nodded and did the same. "Autis."

Clevis shook with sobs. "He was the best … He was one of my best friends. We sailed…" He turned away, unable to speak, and then turned back to face Autis. "We sailed together. He was a good sailor. He was a fine man. Oh, God, why this?" He broke again as his face screwed up and he put a hand over his mouth and turned away.

A young doctor came in the room and spent very little time talking with Liv and watching Bambi before writing a prescription that he handed to Liv.

"I'll take it." Clevis said. "Granny Sweet said to bring Bambi to her house, and that you should go to Bambi's and gather personals to last a few days." Liv accepted this and handed the script to Clevis who turned, walked away and returned quickly with a wheelchair. "My car's parked near."

As Bambi was being wheeled out, she turned red-faced to Liv. She grabbed Liv's hand. "The last words he heard from me was a scold. I don't deserve to live. I want to die—I deserve death." She broke into a keening wail and bent over herself in the wheelchair. Clevis said softly to Liv, "Granny Sweet will know what to do—she's been there."

They drove home in silence. Autis parked the car. He walked around and opened the door for Liv. As she rose out of the car he folded her into his arms. She stood and sobbed onto his chest, wetting Gar's dried blood with her tears.

That evening, Liv and Autis drove to Sweetgrass Weaver's. Clevis and Granny Sweet were seated on the front porch when Liv and Autis pulled up. Clevis' eyes were red from weeping when he descended the porch steps to welcome the visitors.

"Bambi's sleeping. The prescription combined with the stress she was feelin' knocked her cold." Clevis walked them up the steps. Sweetgrass rose to Liv's approach. They hugged in an unspoken display of grief and sympathy.

"He was too young," Miz Sweet said, "too full of life to leave us so soon. I've only met him twice—Clevis brought him for lunch once, and Bambi introduced me to him—but I feel like I knew him as a friend. Bambi detailed his qualities to me, and Clevis has long told me of the man with whom he sailed, and I've heard others sing his praises. I knew him from afar as a man of worth and character; the world is not a better place for his passing. Maybe his tortured soul is at rest now."

"He was my best friend—after Liv," Autis said.

"So you are Autis." Liv's husband bowed slightly to that observation.

"Turn around, I want to see your back," Miz Sweet said.

With a puzzled look, Autis presented his back.

"Hmm," Miz Sweet looked at Liv with a grin. "I don't see wings. Bambi would have me believe that man of yours is an angel. You must only be a saint then—they lack wings, I'm told."

Liv smiled. "He is an angel—the wings come out when needed."

"Well, that's sure an angelic quality."

Autis marveled at the fact that the lady could muster levity in the face of terrible loss.

"Now, how are we going to preserve the sanity of that child drugged asleep in there?"

Clevis leaned forward in his chair as though to answer just as Rebecca drove up in her car. She stopped at the foot of the steps. "It's true then?" She dropped onto a step at the nods and took a tissue to her eyes. When she regained her composure she turned to her Granny Sweet. "Bambi?"

"The doctor gave her a pill and we put her to bed," Clevis said.

Rebecca stood and went into the house seeking Bambi. She returned shortly and joined a circle formed by Granny Sweet, Liv, and Clevis. Autis stood silently at the end of the porch, looking in the direction of his house. His arms were folded over his chest and none could see his clenched fists nor hear his heavy nasal breathing. His chest rose and fell, and his face was devoid of expression. There was that thousand-yard stare.

In half an hour Liv and Autis took their leave from Sweetgrass. She took Autis' hand between her hands. "Glad to finally meet you, but saddened that it is under such sorry circumstances." She did not release his hand.

"Thank you, we'll get together in a better world—or rather, at a better time."

"Yes." Sweet pulled his face to hers and, looking intently into his eyes said, "Be careful." He nodded and stood up, pulling his hand away. Sweet watched with an expression of sad concern as he walked away. Then she called, "Goodbye, Saint Autis." He waved from the car door he held for Liv.

Granny Sweet turned to Clevis. "That's a fine man, but I fear for him."

"Why is that, Granny?" Clevis asked.

"Just how do you think Mr. Oakley's going to spend the rest of the day?" Granny Sweet asked softly.

"Damn!" Clevis shook his head.

Chapter 46

"No. Hell no, you're not."

Autis didn't answer, but continued strapping on the gear he had meticulously laid out on the deck. Gun belt, sheath knife, canvas pack with ammo, water bottle, and first aid.

"This is insane—not alone. Others will go with you. Clevis will go, Granny Sweet's whole family will go—they adore Bambi and liked Gar. Call them up, they'll be here in an hour. You can't do this. If you love me at all, you will put away your toys and gather help around you."

"Toys?" Autis picked up his 12-gauge, jacked a shell in the chamber and clicked the safety to "on." He fed shells into a canvas ammo belt strung across his shoulder. "I'm going to find and kill that black bastard and I'm going to do it now—today—with this toy." He held up the shotgun.

"Please, please, don't do this—it's insane. Groups of men have tried to track him and failed, and you're going out alone. He will kill you."

Autis spun to her. He had a wildness in his eyes that Liv had only seen once before. "No, he won't. I'll kill him. He'll die in my hands. I'll hold his head in my hands and watch the light in his eyes go out, and when they do I will spit on his face." Autis pursed his mouth tight and breathed hard through his nostrils.

"It's an animal, not a person. What difference does it make that you spit on him?"

"Nothing to him. Everything to me—and Gar."

"Gar is dead."

"No, he's not. He lives in me, in you, in Bambi. He will always live in us. He lives."

Liv shook her head angrily. "Men are fools. You're all fools."

"Perhaps but this world, for better or worse, is made by us who have been and are—fools. Gar was not the least of us fools."

Liv, realizing that there was no turning him from his path, left the deck where Autis was gearing up. She returned carrying two tumblers with a half-inch of single malt in each. She had a grim countenance as she handed Autis his scotch. She raised a glass saying, "Hail, Caesar, we who are about to die salute you."

Autis touched his glass to hers. "Caesar." He took a sip and lofted his glass again. "Gar." After a second sip he slowly poured the remainder onto the grass beneath the high deck. He turned to Liv whose face was fixed in a hard stare.

"What did Gar say to you?" she asked.

Autis took a deep breath and stepped back. He tried to speak, "I—I can't..." He turned away, and his body convulsed as he fought back his emotions.

"What did he say?"

Autis breathed heavily, almost panting as he struggled to answer. "He—he—said. 'Tell Buff, he'll know what to do'."

"That's it? 'Tell Buff?'"

"No." Autis' breath was coming fast now. He took a very deep breath and exhaled fully. His breath starting coming in gasps, "He said to tell Bambi that..." Autis broke again.

Liv moved close to the man she loved. She looked into his distress—this man who had faced the panther with a cue stick.

He said, "Tell Bambi ..."Autis cleared his throat, "that—that he hadn't smoked in two weeks."

Liv took Autis into her arms and they wept openly under the vast puffy clouds laughing in the Carolina sky.

Ten minutes later Autis was geared up and ready to go. "Don't let Bob out," he admonished as he walked down the front steps. "I'm going to follow that dry creek bed until I find the clearing on the left. I'll wait for the panther there. I won't have to chase him, He'll come to me."

Liv stood at the top of the steps as Autis walked away from the house and toward—what?

"Good hunting, Saint Autis," she called when he was nearly out of ear-shot. He turned, waved, and faded into the brush.

Liv turned and went into the house. In the kitchen she dug out her crock pot, and a skillet, and began preparing a beef stew. An hour later, the seared beef cuts and large chunks of carrot, onion, potato and celery—all pre-heated— were beginning to simmer in the crock pot with assorted spices and broth. Then Liv went to the bedroom, stripped and began putting on hunting clothes. *I'll give him three hours. Then that goddamn cat will have to face the wrath of a woman and her hunting dog.*

* * *

Autis carefully followed the creek bed for a couple hundred yards before coming to a room-size grassy clearing about fifty feet to the left of the creek bed. He knew he was being watched. He went to the clearing and stood there, looking for places of advantage. Thick shrubbery grew on one side—the side opposite the direction of the wind. An attack would likely come from that direction. He looked at the large trees nearby, and found one suiting his needs. As he turned to walk to the tree, he spied a light colored slender object on the ground. He picked it up. It was a twelve inch long piece of a pool cue. The tip was still on it. He chortled to himself and held it over his head as though to display it.

"See this? I've got more." He heard a faint deep growl from the shrubbery. "Come on. Come and die. Come and die like the coward you were in life and are now." Autis jabbed the pool cue, tip up, into the ground where it lay. He unzipped his trousers, generously pulled out his member, and urinated onto the gravesite. "That's what I think of Alexander Maxton. Piss on you." Only silence and the steady breeze on the back of his neck surrounded Autis Oakley as he stood in a wide stance over his toilet, gun at ready, safety off. He zipped up.

After several minutes, Autis strode to a near tree and climbed to a big branch some twelve feet from the ground. He settled into a comfortable seat with the wind behind him, unsnapped the leather loop holding his large sheath knife and waited. Time did not pass slowly for him because he was constantly surveying the scene—thinking, planning and anticipating. He was here to kill the panther.

Occasionally he would hear a twig snap or a rustle of dry leaves. The beast was on the move. It moved continuously. Pale yellow eyes—eyes that would glow red by night light—fired from behind heavy cover, watched and waited. Time passed as the sun guided its shadowed forest panoply in an inexorable primitive dance practiced long before human feet trod those shadows. Autis could see his own shadow locked into the shadow of the tree trunk. He looked and listened, inhaling scents rising from the forest floor. He felt good. A woodpecker shouted from the distance as Autis watched. A single butterfly rose to investigate this interloper in the old oak. *A good day to die* he mused. *So this is what that means.* He watched his shadow on the forest floor—a shadow that, in effect, gave him eyes in the back of his head. He knew that the panther was doing the same thing he was doing—waiting for advantage. And then the wind died. *This is it. This is what he's waiting for.*

Autis heard a soft flurry of sound from his rear and turned to find himself staring directly into the face of the great cat. One leap was all it had taken for the panther to reach his perch. At once Autis plunged his razor sharp hunting knife into the panther's neck and slashed hard just before they both tumbled to the ground, Autis landing on top of his quarry. They each leapt to their feet and faced off. The shotgun was hung up in the tree. Bleeding and choking from the throat wound, the panther circled his prey, confident of the kill. Autis waited, poised and equally confident.

Soon, the cat tired of the game. He turned and took one step away as though to leave. Without warning, he whirled back and sprang at the man with claws outstretched. Just before those claws reached the man, Bob's powerful jaws closed on the cat's throat, and the two fell in a swirling heap at Autis' feet. Autis quickly dropped onto the panther and bent to his fearsome task.

Liv Oakley sat waiting at the top of the steps, holding a broken leash in her hand. Her 20-gauge pump stood against the step railing next to her. The allotted three hours was up and she was alone. She grasped the barrel of her weapon and used it to rise from her scrunched position on the brick steps. And then she heard a bark. Looking out at the scrub she saw Bob break into the open, followed by Autis. It was the closest she had ever come to fainting in her life. The gun served as a prop over which she swayed. She watched as Autis appeared with a confident step. Bob bounced at his master's side seemingly wanting to play. The sun was behind the approaching couple and so it wasn't until they got close that she saw the blood. She gasped and took a couple of steps down. Bob bounded to his mistress, *full'o hisself* in Bambi-speak. He had three deep scratches on his side and a wound on the left side of his muzzle. He didn't seem to notice as he jounced to the woman for whom he would unflinchingly die.

The entire left side of Autis' hunting jacket was glistening blood red. As he approached Liv, Autis took off his pack and carried it the last few steps by the straps. It was heavy. Liv didn't move.

Autis stopped at the foot of the steps, opened the pack and tipped out the head of the panther. Blood drained onto the paving stones of their driveway. He peeled off his jacket and laid it beside the gory, fanged object. He emptied the chamber of his shotgun and placed the butt of it on the stones at his feet. Standing erect with his feet apart, he began feeding unused shells into a loop of canvas strap. When he looked up, Liv could see he'd been crying in his rage. The Man cocked his head to the right and inhaled deeply. "Is that beef stew?"

Chapter 47

Autis applied ointment to the wounds of an unconcerned Bob as the athletic dog wolfed down a large bowl of stew and brown rice. A couple of times, Bob growled, almost in pleasure, as Autis gently applied the healing salve. Returning the cap to the ointment, he turned to his wife.

"Bob saved the day."

Liv nodded. "He broke his leash. I was waiting on the front steps, and was getting tired of restraining him. I tied the leash to a step railing post and went in for a glass of water. When I returned he was gone, taking part of the leash with him."

Autis patted their companion, who had just finished off some three pounds of food, and turned a grinning face to his master.

"I possibly could have killed the panther without him, but I would either have been killed in the doing, or I would have been badly torn up. He saved the day," Autis repeated, as he began peeling away his hunter clothing—all canvas and stiff with dried blood.

Liv lifted her head to the sound of a vehicle coming fast up the driveway. "Oh, shit, I forgot. I called Miz Sweet and asked her to find Clevis. I told her what you were up to. She didn't seem surprised; in fact, when I told her you'd gone out alone after the panther, she said, 'Of course.' Did you tell her your plans?" Liv started to the front door as Autis followed.

"I didn't tell her, but I think she knew—that is one shrewd lady."

They opened the front door to see Clevis squatting over the panther head. He looked up. "'Peers you don't need me." A wry grin spread across his face. He reached to touch the bloody trophy and suddenly leapt back. "Damn, it's still warm."

"It's only been dead a little more than an hour—and the sun's shining on it."

"Still—it should begin to feel death cold. It don't." Clevis wiped his hand on his pant leg and stepped around the head, giving it a wide berth. "What'd you take him with—shotgun?"

"No," Autis said. "My knife."

"Your knife?"

"Yes, but Bob helped—in fact I doubt I could have done it and lived, without that dog distracting the panther."

"Your dog and your knife." Clevis looked Autis up and down.

"Yes."

"Must be some knife." Clevis said

"Good dog, too."

"I'd say. Is he all right?"

"He's scratched some, but he'll do," Autis said.

Liv stood, mouth open, looking from man to man as she listened to the laconic exchange. Finally, she couldn't take it anymore. "Wait a minute—wait a minute. That damned cat has killed one of our best friends and damn near killed my husband. You two yahoos are trying so hard to do Gary Cooper that you completely miss the point that a very dangerous animal has been killed at great risk to the man who killed him."

Clevis looked down at his feet for a moment, and then up at Liv who was standing a couple of steps above the driveway. "Well, I ain't gonna hug him, Liv." Autis chuckled at this, and Liv rolled her eyes.

Clevis squatted next to the head and lifted one of the cat's lips. "Those are some fangs. Are you going to mount this?"

Autis thought a second. "No, I don't care for trophy displays. I've only taken one trophy in my life." He put an arm around Liv's shoulders and pulled her close. "And I've never regretted it a moment."

Liv choked and fought back a sob. She placed a kiss on her husband's cheek, made small dismissive gestures with her hands and fled into the house. Clevis grinned his best grin.

"You're welcome to it, though. You want to load it in the back of your pickup."

"I wouldn't put that in my truck at gunpoint," Clevis said flatly. "But I would like to take some pictures. Is that okay with you?"

"Help yourself."

Clevis went to his truck and withdrew a small digital camera from his glove compartment. "There's a lotta kin who'd want to see the head of this thing that tried to kill Granny Sweet."

"I'll leave it where it lay. You tell them they can stop by anytime tomorrow and look at it."

Clevis took several pictures from different angles. "You want to stand next to it?"

"That's not going to happen."

Clevis nodded. "You're a hard man, Autis."

"How's Bambi?" Autis asked diverting the topic.

"Pretty much as you'd expect. She really loved Gar—and I know he loved her. He talked about her ever time we got together. We used to sail and fish together. I don't know any ... anybody I enjoyed bein' around more than Gar. I'm sure gonna miss him."

"We haven't known him long, but Liv and I thought—think the world of him. I mean, what you saw was what you got."

"He was what he was," Clevis answered.

"We're going to have to have a service—soon. He told me to tell Buff Shellman. I called him and told him about Gar's passing. We didn't talk long because he couldn't. I'll try contacting him again."

"Another good man. He sailed with Gar and me a few times. There's no steadier hand at a storm helm," Clevis said.

"Well, it's a storm." Autis struggled with his composure.

"It is that—a terrible storm—for Bambi and the rest of us. But he told me what he wanted in this—this—situation."

Autis stood in silence.

"He..." Clevis' solid composure began to break away at the edges. "He wanted burial at sea with a sailboat coffin." Clevis cleared his throat, turned and took a few steps away. He raised his eyes to the sky and took several rapid breaths before turning back to Autis. "I think I know just the boat. Gar would have liked the choice." Clevis' eyes glistened as he looked up to the man standing at the top of the steps. Autis came down and put an arm across Clevis' shoulders. They stood in silence looking at the panther head. Liv watched from the kitchen window—hands clasped over her mouth.

Autis woke to the smell of fresh coffee being wafted under his nose. He sat upright immediately, almost spilling the mug that Liv held in front of his face. "Oh. Sorry. What time is it?"

"Coffee time." Liv handed him the mug, and sat on the bed beside her man. Autis took a sip, and another.

"Thank you," he said.

"Comes with the room, sir," Liv said with a coy grin.

"That action last night come with the room, too?"

"Any time it's needed, sir—courtesy of the house."

Well, hell, I think I'll just stay another night," Autis said over his coffee mug.

"I'll notify the help," Liv said, carrying on the levity.

Autis glanced at the bedside clock. "Damn. I never sleep this late—the morning's half gone. Must have been the stew—that was damn fine stew."

"I expect the dessert may have played a part in your peaceful sleep."

"I expect so," Autis grinned. "Love that 'courtesy of the house' custom."

"Welcome to the South, suh." Liv rose from the bed and headed to the doorway. "If'n you be needin' anything further, just ring for Georgia Mae— *Saint Autis*." She dodged Autis' pillow as she exited.

Half an hour later, Autis entered the kitchen, showered and shaved, barefoot, shirtless and wearing faded jeans. Liv looked at the muscular symmetry of his body and gave off a low whistle. "What a hunk. Come here often darlin'?"

"Only for the bacon." Autis filched a slice from a warming platter. He watched as Liv started the eggs.

"Do the toast." She nodded in the direction of the toaster.

The phone rang just as they sat down to eat. It was Clevis.

"Sure, send them over—no, wait a few minutes. We just started breakfast." Autis walked over to the window that overlooked the front yard. He glanced out the window.

"Wait a second, hold the line." He turned to Liv. "Did you move the panther head?" She shook her head.

"Let me call you back." Autis hung up the phone. "The head's not there." He walked to the front door and went down the steps to where the head had rolled out of his pack. The pack and his hunting jacket were still there. Liv came to the front door and watched as Autis visually searched the surrounding area. She came out of the door and down the steps.

"The head's missing. Do you suppose some varmint came and carried it off last night?" He looked inquiringly at Liv and saw that she had a look of near horror.

"What?" Autis asked.

"Your jacket, the pack. There's no blood on them."

Chapter 48

In less than forty minutes after Autis' return call, Clevis led a convoy of vehicles up the drive to Maxton Manor. Rebecca was in the front seat beside her cousin. Liv did a quick head count and set up a second coffee maker, and turned on the oven before following Autis to greet her armed guests.

She found Clevis and Autis, still shirtless and shoeless surrounded by over a dozen grim-faced men, each carrying at least one weapon. Two pick-up trucks held dogs in kennels. Clevis was holding Autis' hunting jacket. "This was soaked in blood yesterday evening, now there's only one or two places."

"That's my blood where the cat's claws broke through. Autis pointed to the injuries on his chest. What's missing is the cat's blood—and his head. Look at the pictures."

Liv realized that the men were looking at Autis with a mixture of awe and inquisitiveness that bordered on hero-worship. Autis seemed totally unaware of this.

There was a muttering among the ranks. A very tall light-skinned man bent to say something softly to Clevis who turned to Autis with an amused smile. "They want to see your knife." Liv turned to go to the kitchen, shaking her head. *Where's Bambi when I need her?*

Some twenty minutes later the men filed into the kitchen, each accepting a cup of coffee from Liv. Rebecca and Autis, now with shirt and boots, had led them to the clearing in the wood. There was no body. However, there were serious claw marks in the oak where the cat had leapt up the tree for what it mistakenly thought was a surprise attack. One of the men was carrying the broken cue tip. After being held by every hand in the group the broken tip was laid on the kitchen table next to Autis' sheath knife. Liv passed around a tray of fresh hot peanut butter cookies to go with the strong coffee. The men came back for seconds.

"You went up that tree and turned your back in the direction you thought the attack would come from?" An older man named Avery asked Autis incredulously.

"Yes. The cat had already shown us that we couldn't track him down. I wanted him to come to me."

"And it was your plan to kill him with your knife?"

"No. It was my plan to wound him with the knife and finish him off with a load of buckshot."

"Damn," exclaimed another man. "Weren't you just a little scared it might not come off like you planned?"

"I was a *lot* scared, but Gar was my best friend." This was followed by a soft mutter among the group. There was a quiet shaking of heads and glances of approving apprehension. Rebecca broke the trance.

"Okay, this is how I see it. The cat has just demonstrated that we can't kill him. Yet, somehow, we've got to rid ourselves of this—this demon. Books says that it is a white man's demon. I'm not sure she's totally right on that call, but we'll leave it at that for now. Finley Newman—you-all know him—says that it is a demon and he thinks he knows how to get rid of it. I think we ought to get Books and Finley to come help us work out something before this monster takes another life—and we need to do that soon." An affirming rumble followed that sounded almost like a growl. Liv raised a hand with an interjecting forefinger.

"Let me suggest that we all go down to the pu ... basement. There's more room, and almost enough chairs. Autis and I will tell you all the whole story. It'll take a couple of hours, but be worth the time. Autis has told me, more than once..." She rolled her eyes, bringing amused chuckles from the assemblage "... that if a problem can be stated it can be solved. We can tell you what we know, and maybe you can help arrive at a solution." There were low sounds of approval. "Grab up the kitchen chairs and follow me and Autis."

It took four hours—not two—because of the intense interest. Men were seated, standing, sprawled, but they were totally focused on the task at hand. There was laughter, anger, tears, fear, and joy. All this was held and woven tightly by a growing sense of closeness as the assembled individuals knitted into one being with a common history and a singular purpose. What Liv thought would be a presentation had become a spirited exchange of ideas and feelings.

In late afternoon, Liv took a break to order half a dozen large pizzas. The refrigerator in the pub was loaded with long necks. By evening the fridge was nearly bare and there was a stack of empty pizza cartons in the corner. Autis had opened the French doors and the group spilled out onto the lawn. Most went down to the edge of the marsh to see the grave capstones. There were prayers and no small amount of tears openly shed by men who would normally walk over coals to avoid a public display of weeping.

They had broken into discussion groups of three or four, standing on the lawn, sitting on the brick underlayment of the patio outside the French doors or perched at Autis' handmade bar. There were also bitter visitations to the Maxton gravestones. Angry thoughts ran amok and mean sound bites filled the air. No small amount of spitting occurred. One man had to be restrained from urinating on Alexander Maxton's headstone. "You'll not profane our hostess' grounds that way," members of the group scolded.

Slowly the group coalesced in the pub, back into a singular body.

"What do you think?" Clevis asked the assemblage.

After some muttering, there came a clear deep voice. "It's a hex and we need to end it." There was affirming body language and masculine approval sounds.

"Okay," Clevis responded. "Any ideas how?"

"Root it," came a positive assurance. "I say root it." A muscular man in his thirties stood to affirm his idea. "It's shown us it can't be killed—they's other ways." The man sat down to supporting sounds from the group.

One man suggested that Autis find and kill it again, but this time burn the body. Autis shook his head to this suggestion.

"Second time around I would be the one getting killed. I don't want to try that fearsome chore again. I can't. When I got up this morning and found that head and all that blood gone, something caved inside of me." Autis was sure this admission of fear and frailty would eradicate whatever feelings of admiration the men had for him. It had the opposite effect. *Only a truly strong man could make such an admission,* was the thought that passed among the group. Autis was totally unaware that he was at risk for being cast from the world of the merely mortal. Saint Autis.

A slender white man came unnoticed through the French doors and took a place in a corner while all eyes were on Autis.

Rebecca rose from her seat on the pool table. Wearing jeans and vest, her cowboy boots raised her height to just over six feet. Many of the men had grown up with her tomboy ways and had learned early on not to disrespect. "We have tortured souls here." She pointed at the floor under her boots. "We have tortured souls out there." She pointed through the open French doors to the capstones at the edge of the marsh. "Those in here want to join their own." She accompanied her comments with gestures. There were sounds of agreement from the group.

"And…there is a tortured soul in that clearing." She pointed in the direction of the site and was greeted with stony silence and grim visages. "I know—the man was a beast. He was a beast in life—and he is a beast dead." She paused to let this drive home. "As long as he remains a tortured, longing soul he'll stay a beast to us—and his power grows." Silence from the group. There is one here among us who has said he knows how to do away with the problem. I believe everyone here knows Finley Newman." She pointed to the man in the corner. "Finley, will you come give us your ideas?"

Finley Newman came from his lean against the wall and ambled to the pool table that proved to be the epicenter of the gathering. He started right in. "Before I tell you what I think of this problem I want to confess a crime." He had their attention. "When I was ten, Granny Sweet and a storekeeper by the name of Barnes caught me trying to pocket a box of .22 shells for my old single shot Remington. I could knock a squirrel out of a tree at a hundred yards with that rifle—but I lacked ammunition, money, and scruple. That move to eliminate my want was detected by Granny Sweet and Mr. Barnes at the same time. Well, Mr. Barnes had me by the arm and was ready to law me when Granny Sweet intervened. She knew my family and would see to it that justice was done if Mr. Barnes would see fit to release me to her care. To my great—and naive—relief, he did so. Granny Sweet proceeded to march me around to the back of the store where I was made to expose my hind parts to what proved to be the most skillfully applied hickory switch in the state."

This revelation brought laughter and "me too" kinds of remonstration. Finley continued, "That good Christian lady, having rendered me agreeable to anything she suggested,"—more sounds of understanding—"proceeded to march me back into Mr. Barnes' presence and proclaim that I had agreed to work free for a week in payment for my trespass. And that, furthermore, if I flinched as much as a single hour from that promise, he was to call in the sheriff to see that justice was done from that direction." There was a smattering of applause from an approving audience. "In short, Granny Sweet saved me from any aspiration to crime and, as it turned out, storekeeping. I owe the lady what I am today. I've agreed to come today—Liv called me earlier—because I pay my debts. I will do everything in my power to rid the island of that beast—and I think I know what needs be done." He motioned them forward with his hands. The entire group rose and clustered around the soft-spoken man.

Chapter 49

That evening, Clevis and Rebecca stood on the front porch steps with Liv and Autis to watch the last vehicles depart.

"That's some family you've got there, Clevis," Autis offered.

"They come when needed."

"You two aren't going *Gary Cooper* on me are you?"

"She always like this?" Clevis asked.

"Only when she's vertical."

Liv turned agape to her husband. "Did you just say what I thought you said?"

The two men broke into laughter.

"I don't know—did it bring an end to my 'Saint Autis' stature?"

"It sure as hell did."

"Then I said it—and I apologize, too."

Liv thought a moment. "Okay, apology accepted. And 'Saint Autis' is banished from my vocabulary."

"Good, mission accomplished."

Rebecca spoke up. "I like and approve of Finley's plan, but it's going to take a couple of weeks before we can pull it off—there's no small amount of preparation that needs doing. What are you going to do in the meantime? A beast is still out there that wants to kill you, has the ability to do so and is apparently getting stronger and bolder."

Autis raised a hand. "I vote that we move somewhere off the island until we can do what Finley recommends."

"No," Liv said. I won't cut and run. We can arm ourselves better and be more cautious."

"More cautious? Hell, we're living under a siege as it is. How can we be more cautious? Beside, we've got all these glass windows around us. It won't be long before the panther realizes that he can bust through most any window he pleases." The group fell silent. Clevis took a seat on the steps and was joined by the others. After a period of reflection he rose and looked out to the wood.

"I've got an idea. Goody is pretty much healed. How about if we let him out on loan to help Bob with guard duty? Before you nix this idea, let me finish. I got Goody from a friend who is a breeder. He specializes in Redbone Coon Hounds—like Goody. And this is a special breed with a good history. "When the British settlers came to this country they brought their dogs with them—foxhounds and such. They soon found that their hunting breeds couldn't cope with the great distances, deep woods, and vast swamps of this country. New variations of hunting hounds were experimented with and developed. Most fell by the wayside, but some few survived and became the kind of hardy long-distance runners that this country demanded. There was a man in Georgia by the name of Redbone who developed one such breed that was given his name. That's where we got the Redbone Coon Hound. It was a long runner that could work swamp and high ground alike, and was big and fierce enough to take on panthers and bears. That's what you've got in Goody—he's a powerful hunter, and fierce."

"He and Bob couldn't defend against that cat," Autis said. "But thanks for the education. I always thought their name had something to do with their color. Redbone."

"You're right, but if my friend were to loan you three more like Goody, you'd have a pack that could take on a lion. They are fierce in the hunt. They would keep the panther at bay until we can deal with him proper."

After a brief silence Autis said, "It's got my vote. We could turn the basement over to them at night, and set them out by day to patrol the area. That way we could move freely about the property—at least by day. The more I think about it, the more I like it. How about it, Liv—care to open a kennel?"

"It beats the heck out of living in a fortress," Liv asserted.

"I'll talk to my friend," Clevis said. "That's a good breed of dog. They hunt good and make great pets, too. Goody and Bambi are bonding like old friends."

"How is Bambi?" Liv asked. "She should have been here today. She would have particularly enjoyed the High Noon act you and Autis put on. You know—pathologically stoic."

"Nobody heals others' pain like Granny Sweet." Clevis ignored Liv's barb. "I wanted Bambi to come but Granny Sweet refused to let her get involved in all this right now. She asked that we wait a day or two more. Bambi's doing okay. Yesterday she said she feels like she's being reborn into the family she always wanted—especially as a child. I don't know what's happened to wound that girl so, but I sure would like to get my hands on the people who did it. I'd mean to put a serious hurt on 'em." Clevis gazed out into the wood a moment before he continued. "You know, this world would be a better place if more homes had Granny Sweets in 'em."

Rebecca "Amen'd" the idea.

"Gar's death hurt Bambi bad—real bad." The healin's going to take a spell, and I expect there'll be setbacks, but Granny Sweet will pull her through."

Autis cut in. "I'm ready for a drink. Do you all like single malt?"

Evening on the deck was one of Liv's favorite times. She put out a tray of light snacks while Autis gathered together the makings for cocktails for their guests.

"Damn, that is fine scotch," Clevis exclaimed. What brand is it? I've had single malt before but none that tastes like this." He took another tiny sip, savoring the deep smokiness."

"It's not the brand so much as where it's from."

"I thought all Scotch came from Scotland," Rebecca said.

"It's not that simple. This is single malt which essentially means that it comes from a single run not blended with other Scotch, nor with neutral spirits, like blended Scotch."

"Well," Clevis said. "The single malt I've had before didn't have this heavy flavor. I really like this. What's so special about it?"

"It's Islay."

"I-luh."

"Yes, like Island. Autis handed the bottle to Clevis.

"What's special about Islay?"

"I'm no Scotch expert, but as I understand, there are three areas that produce single malt Scotch, and they are called Highland, Lowland, and Islay—going from lighter to heavier flavored scotch. Some prefer the sweet mildness of Highland over the other scotches. Some like the heavy peaty flavor of Islay. Lowland is in the middle. It's all a matter of personal preference. Almost all Scotch was single malt until women started drinking whisky in the early 1900s and found it too heavy for their tastes. The clever Scots started adding neutral spirits to their single malt, and now most Scotch found on the American market are blends."

"Is the lecture over, Professor?" Rebecca asked. She lifted a glass of Islay and sipped. "Aw, Jeez. You drink that? I would clean floors with it—toilet floors. Tell the truth—it's gone spoiled and you don't want to admit it."

Liv cupped a hand behind her ear. "Listen. That hissing sound—it's—it's, why yes, it's the sound of deflating male ego. Music to the ears of us lesser mortals." The ladies burst into laughter.

"And they wonder why I've never married," Clevis said.

"Cuz, you've never married"—Rebecca poured her scotch into Clevis' glass—"because you can't find a woman dense enough to put up with your pig-headed ways."

Clevis turned to Autis. "See—she makes my point."

The doorbell rang. Autis and Liv looked at each other in fear. Autis picked up his shotgun and headed to the door. "Bad route for door-to-door sales I'd say." Rebecca quipped, and then she saw the look on Liv's face.

Autis returned with a short, sturdy-built man sporting a trim gray beard.

"Liv, this is Buff Shellman, Gar's friend."

Liv rose and shook his hand. It was firm and dry. She looked into clear gray eyes that truly twinkled. "Mr. Shellman."

"Call me 'Buff,' please. Hello, Clevis." The two men embraced, relaxed their hold and, without letting go, looked into each other's eyes. They both nodded understanding.

"This is my cousin, Rebecca Wells." Buff released his friend and received Rebecca's extended hand. He bowed very slightly at the waist and held her hand, "The fame of your beauty goes before you." He released the hand of the lady, who blushed like a girl.

Buff turned to Autis, Liv, and Clevis. "We've lost a friend. I've lost possibly the best friend I've ever had—or will have. It is not untrue to say that we were like brothers. I've known Gar for more than a dozen years. We served in the army together, and got discharged about the same time. I'd served eleven years and was discharged with a gunshot disability. Gar did his three and got out. He moved to the area because of my urging, and we've been sailing and fishing friends ever since. Because we were so close, I never bothered gathering other friends. For all practical purposes we were each other's only close friend—'til Gar met Autis." He took Autis by the arm. "Thanks for being my friend's good friend."

Autis poured Buff an inch of single malt. The gentle man took the glass and raised it to Autis' glass. "Gar."

He took a sip, looked approvingly at the glass. "Islay."

"Yes. McClelland."

Rebecca and Liv exchanged eye-rolling glances. "It begins," Rebecca said softly.

Autis laughed softly. "Philistines. They're everywhere." He added more to Buff's and Clevis' glasses.

Buff looked out over the salt marsh. "Gar would have loved this. He would have loved being here with us this evening."

Clevis smiled. "He *is* with us, Buff."

"Yes, of course. I suppose he will always be with us when we get together. The only one missing is Bambi. I just came from Sweetgrass Weaver's home. I'm glad that she's taken Bambi in. I think that dear lady is exactly what Bambi needs right now. Gar loved that girl like life. He was determined to prove himself to her. He stopped smoking, and was considering selling Four Aces. There was a teaching position in the Trident Tech College he was looking into."

"Professor Gar Hanson?" Autis asked.

"Math. He has a master's degree combination math and physics—very unusual. He was interested in Chaos, String Theory and plasma physics. I offered to foot the bill to help him complete his Ph.D. should he decide to do so. He had completely given up on the idea—until he got serious about Bambi. The other day he asked if that offer was still open. I told him it was. That was two days before he offered to sell me Four Aces." Buff's voice started to break. Autis placed a hand on his shoulder, and Clevis moved closer in.

Buff pulled a sheaf of papers out of his pocket. It was a will. "He left everything to Bambi—there was simply no one else. A couple of small items he left to me: fishing gear, some books, and a couple of statues I admired. I'm the executor, but I want you and Liv and Bambi to witness that I am not taking advantage. I want you three to act on Gar's behalf. I bought Four Aces. The money is in his bank account; fair market value. I bought it because I was afraid he was going to sell it off for the money. I wanted to keep it for him until he finished his Ph.D., and then I planned to give it to him as a graduation present—if Bambi approved. Oh, dear God!"

Buff sat down and dropped his face in his hands. Liv quietly went into the house, and came back with a glass of water. Buff took a long drink and sat the glass on a table. "Thank you." He stood up and took a pack of cigarettes out of his pocket and shook one up from the pack. After lighting it he took a long drag. "I haven't smoked in over a dozen years, but when I got your call, Autis, the first thing I did was go to Four Aces and take a pack from a carton that Gar had bought almost a month ago. When this pack is gone, I'll go another dozen years. I'd forgotten how good these damned poisonous things feel."

"I understand," Autis said.

Buff unfolded the will and laid it out on the table. "Gar wanted a burial at sea." There was silence. "Originally, he told me that he wanted to be buried in Four Aces, but as he worked on the craft and got it in nearly pristine condition, he changed his mind and said that an old sailboat on its last legs would suit. I never paid much attention to his thoughts on the subject because he'd usually had too much to drink when he went to that topic. It often took place somewhere out of sight of land, and we'd had a dozen beers each. He tended to get maudlin when he was tipsy. I suppose a lot of people are that way. I would humor him by listening and letting him go on. But, I never thought..." He had to take another break.

When he came up for air Buff continued. "I never thought he would go before me, so I just told him 'the same thing goes for me.' When I kick over, just bury me at sea—with or without a boat."

"Is that even legal?" Liv asked.

"Hell, who cares. As long as we don't endanger shipping or foul up the water, what's the harm. I'm sure there are a plethora of regulations against what we are talking about. My answer is, do it at night."

"I'm in," Clevis said.

Autis looked a Liv. "So are we."

Then Liv added, "Where are we going to get a boat? We don't have much time."

"Fortune smiles," Buff said. "I know where there is an old fiber glass yawl that can be picked up for a song. It belongs to an octogenarian who is living aboard until he sells it before going to a retirement home. He and his wife bought the craft when it was nearly new, and they lived the cruising life until she passed away a couple of years ago. He's just marking time and waiting to join his wife of more than half a century. I knew him back when they were a cruising couple. He's a good man, but the boat has gone into serious disrepair. It's only good for salvage. I asked him to sell me the boat, but when I told him what it was for—and who it was for he told me, 'The price is one dollar, and not a penny less'."

"Let me have one o' them smokes." Clevis lit up and turned to Buff, "You talkin' about old Larson's Pearson thirty-nine, aren't you?"

"Yes, I'm having the engine and reverse gear taken out today. You're welcome to them if you want. It's a Yanmar four cylinder, in decent condition. I can't speak for the reverse gear—you know how marine transmissions are."

"I'll buy it. Can I give the money to Mr. Larson?"

"I doubt he'd take it," Buff said.

"Maybe he knows a good cause ..."

"Maybe," Buff hesitated, then went on, "There's a clause: Mr. Larson wants to go with us to see his good girl off proper."

Silence followed. "There's symmetry in that," Rebecca said.

"Are we all in accord, then?" Buff asked. There were nods of approval all around.

"Okay, I'll take care of arrangements for the boats. We'll follow Mr. Larson on an early morning or late night out-going tide. That way we'll clear the harbor and jetties while it's still early. Unless the wind is absolutely unfavorable, Mr. Larson will be able to tack out. We can also hope for a land breeze like we sometimes get in the morning. If so, we'll have no trouble clearing the jetties. Worst case scenario—we can tie on to Mr. Larson and motor him out to where he can catch favorable winds. He's an experienced sailor, but some of us can go with him. I'll take the helm at Four Aces. Clevis, can you go with Mr. Larson?"

"You got it," Clevis answered.

"Can we have a wake?" Liv asked.

"Gar would like that," Buff said. "Would have..." He corrected.

"I would suggest Saloon Sandi. If that doesn't work, we can have it here. But we need to move fast."

"Will you take that on, Liv?" Buff asked.

"Of course."

"I'll look to the services," Rebecca said. "There'll be a preacher. Can we have a choir?"

"My thought is *yes*, but let's ask Bambi," Liv said.

"Okay then," Buff said. "I've asked for no embalming because there is to be a burial at sea. Gar will be kept in deep cold until the time is right. Let's stay in close touch and make this work. We want Gar to be happy."

Chapter 50

They caught an outgoing morning tide. But if Nels Larson had not had superb navigating skills, it would have been a difficult passage to the open sea. Buff said, "Thank God the tides are largely predictable because the goddamn wind *never* cooperates." Clevis had rigged a small outboard onto the stern of Nels' craft, but it was not needed. He would remove it when they arrived at an agreed upon location. Once they were clear of the jetties, Nels took a long tack to the north taking full advantage of the Gulf Stream. He worked his way outward as only a skilled sailor can do. Clevis was kept busy in the role of first mate, as Nels Larson worked sail and rudder to their best advantage. There was a quiet sure calm about the old man as he smoked his pipe and worked his craft.

By two o'clock they were well into blue water, and it was time to say farewell to Gar Hanson, who was safely tucked and tied into a lower berth.

There was a carton of cigarettes at Bambi's insistence and a case of Bud Light placed next to Gar. Bambi rode in the cabin with him, never once sticking her head out. As they approached the agreed upon location, Nels issued the orders to start taking in sail, and he watched canvas come down one last time. He had witnessed the furling and unfurling of his sails thousands of times. This time was special. Nels Larson, quiet, composed, stood in the full sun of day, keenly aware that his own light was at sunset.

All the unneeded rigging and hardware had been removed from the craft. The large, beautifully carved steering wheel had been loosened, and was to be the last item removed. Nels ran his hand over the wheel one last time, feeling the rudder below, as South Sea memories flooded his mind. A woman, his woman, stretched out on the bow as their wind-driven sailboat foamed its way through the islands. *She was so lovely.* He retraced the times they crossed the equator, toasting each other, loving each other. Nels Larson was beyond tears. He secretly wished that they would let him go down with "his girl" but knew they would not allow this act of mercy. He would go back to shore and die. Then their mixed ashes, after a long plane ride, would be cast into the South Sea by island friends. *It's better that way.*

At Nels' signal, an inflatable was motored alongside. Nels and Bambi carefully lowered themselves into it and were taken to Four Aces along with the carved wooden helm wheel. Then Clevis pulled the large plugs that had been cut into the hull —ten in all. He kissed Gar on the forehead and climbed up to the cockpit, and then onto the inflatable. By the time he was back aboard Four Aces, and the inflatable secured, Nels' yawl was noticeably lower in the water. Six souls watched as the yawl dipped lower, swaying slowly with the long summer waves.

Finally, just before the craft went under, Buff spoke up. "Gar had asked that the Breton Fisherman's Prayer be said at this juncture." He put his hands on a rail and struggled with his composure. Nels Larson set the example by doffing his battered captain's hat. Buff looked about at his companion seamen then began. "Lord, thy sea is vast, and my craft so small." Nels closed with "Amen." The group members looked apprehensively at each other until Bambi said, "Perfect."

Chapter 51

The following day, Autis took a break from pressure-washing the porch to have a glass of lemonade from the tray that Liv brought to 'the help.' Sitting on the deck railing with his feet hooked into a support rail below, he mused on the previous day. "'Thy sea is vast, and my craft so small.' How like Gar to have that as his favorite prayer. It doesn't ask for anything. It doesn't complain, or instruct. It simply acknowledges. I'm not one you would call a believer, but I could live by that prayer."

Bambi looked up from stroking Bob's large, well-formed head. "It sounds like Gar—him going his own way, never asking, never telling, just accepting whatever was around him. That's one reason why he was so well-liked. He was a man who didn't weigh and judge others. He just took folks as they were. That's partly why I fell for him—he just accepted me and didn't make requests or demands.

"I remember …" She was interrupted by the sound of a vehicle approaching up the driveway on the other side of the house. Autis went through the house to investigate. He returned in five minutes with Clevis in tow—and four identical Redbone Coon Hounds, one of whom went directly to Bambi and laid his head on her lap. Goody. Bob rose to his feet and put his tail straight up and rigid. He walked stiff-legged to the interlopers as Autis reached for his collar. Once the initial sniffing was done, everyone settled into the protocols of cordial body language activities seen in public dog parks around the country.

"Let 'em out," Clevis said.

"You sure?" Autis was skeptical.

"I'm sure."

Autis opened the wide gate and watched as Bob led the pack down the steps and out into the yard. Wagging games of tag commenced. Dogs dropped on their forepaws with their butts in the air, tail wagging—universal dog speak for "Let's Play."

As the 'play' unfurled in front of the deck observers, it became apparent that Bob was taking the role of Alpha Wolf. Autis and Liv marveled, as his demeanor went from affable, flappy hound dog to an alert poised sentinel of the pecking order. The sorting of hierarchies took only minutes.

"I reckon they'll do fine to take care of your feline problem until such time as we can work out a permanent solution—that incidentally is going to be ready in two weeks. When do you want to do it—pick a day."

Liv leaned against the railing. "I was thinking a Saturday would make sense because so many people work only half a day on Saturdays." There were nods all around.

"Saturday, two weeks from tomorrow." Clevis said.

"Saturday's good," Bambi said. "But I think we might consider Sunday."

"Everyone's in church Sunday," Clevis countered.

"Right," Bambi said. "We could make it a religious event. After all, it should be anyway. I can see a prayer meeting, hymns, a sermon—my God, what an opportunity for a sermon—covered dish luncheon. It's a wonderful opportunity not to just rid ourselves of an evil, but also to acknowledge the evil that brought us all together as fighters."

Liv stood open-mouthed at Bambi's eloquence.

Clevis smiled. "Now that's a powerful argument. I can go there." He paused and looked sheepishly at Liv. "Well, here we go, volunteering your place as a Sunday-go-to-meetin' ground. I'm sorry, that's rude."

Liv laughed softly. "You forget, Clevis, I'm family. I love the idea of tasking this on a Sunday. And two weeks from day after tomorrow is fine. We've got a lot of planning to do. However, if it's going to be a church activity, there'll be family and children. That's a major safety consideration in itself—and more than a little scary if you stop to think what the panther is capable of."

Clevis' eyes widened. "Have you seen him since—since…"

"No. But Autis has found fresh tracks. He's still around."

*   *   *

In the coming days the hound pack settled to the routine of being let out in the morning and put up in the pub at night.

"We can't let them out at night," Autis insisted, "that damn cat would wait until one of them separated from the pack, and then pick it off with a quick kill." Liv had bought several large canvas-covered foam cushions, which the hounds adopted immediately. Liv insisted that Bob be permitted to sleep upstairs in the living room. She laid out a pad for him next to one of the couches.

In three days, the dogs had settled into a daily hunt routine, making the rounds. The scent of the panther kept them close to the area the cat prowled, and each morning there was a fresh scent. From the deck late nights, Autis and Liv would hear the panther scream — an aspirant, throaty call of indignation.

Four nights after the hounds came, Autis and Liv were having a drink on the high deck. The gate was closed and the dogs were sprawled about before being put into the pub for the evening when the panther let out a call nearby. Five canine heads rose and turned in the direction of the call.

"Scream, you black bastard," Autis growled. "In about ten days you'll be history." At that moment, the door bell chimed and the phone rang at the same time. Liv went for the phone and Autis went to the door. The dogs went back to sleep.

Bambi stood at the door. "Hi, Bambi," Autis said. "You don't have to ring…" Then he saw her face. "What's wrong?"

At the same time, Liv came up with the phone in her hand. The moment she saw Bambi, they both broke out crying and fell into each other's arms. Autis stood dumbfounded until Liv turned from Bambi's tears.

"It's Granny Sweet." Autis nodded and turned toward the deck. He opened the sliding doors and said, "Bob." The pointer rose and came to his master. Autis spoke softly and the pack followed him to the doorway leading down the stairs into the pub.

On the way to her house, Bambi related that Granny Sweet had fallen down that day. Nothing was broken, but she complained of feeling very weak and took to her four-poster. It was pretty much the same message that Rebecca had given Liv over the phone. Granny Sweet asked for them to come.

The doctor was at bedside when they arrived. They were greeted at the door by Rebecca, who had been crying. Several family members rose to gather them in their arms. The sense of sorrow in the room was palpable. Autis found Clevis standing with a group of men and went to join them. No introductions were necessary; Autis would forever be remembered as "the man who killed the panther bare-handed with a knife."

"Gather yourself before you go in." Rebecca said to Bambi and Liv. "It won't do for Granny Sweet to see you all tore up like this." Liv and Bambi took several breaths and wiped each other's face with tissue.

Granny Sweet was sitting up in bed with children and grandchildren in attendance. She seemed very small and vulnerable. The faces of the ladies around the bed were tight and stern as the women clenched their jaws to fight back open expressions of grief. Everyone wanted to appear 'up to the task.' She beckoned the newcomers to her bedside with a wave. She pulled Bambi in close with a finger. As Bambi leaned over her she spoke softly, but audibly enough for all to hear. "Have you ever seen a meaner looking lot of women?" The turgid dam of tension shattered, and the ladies broke into tearful laughter that grew to such a volume that heads appeared in the doorway to be waved away by those inside who were feeling a joyous release of pain. Granny Sweet pressed Bambi's curly head to her chest. "Oh, child," she said. "You have miles to go. Spread your wings, sail high. Let the world sense your grace. Take me with you in your journey." Bambi sat up composed and dry eyed and said softly. "I promise, Granny, you'll be by my side—and from now on I will walk with you."

Granny Sweet nodded and pointed at a small woven purse on the bedside stand. One of her daughters handed it to her. Granny Sweet released the clasp that closed it and pulled out a tiny pouch held closed by string. She unlaced the bow knot and spilled a large yellow pearl into Bambi's hand. "I was cleaning some oysters once, when I wasn't much older than you, and this pearl lay there in one of them just for the takin.' I want you to keep it for me, and pass it on to your oldest daughter when she comes of age. Take it out during troubled times—for it is said that there is the wisdom of patience in a pearl." Granny Sweet retuned the pearl to its pouch and handed it to Bambi.

Sweetgrass took a deep breath and turned to Liv. "Where's Saint Autis?" she asked with a smile. Liv retrieved her man and brought him to Granny Sweet who took his hand.

"Seems I was wrong in calling you 'Saint Autis.' Word is about that you killed that panther with your knife. Clevis showed me the picture where you'd cut off his head." She mustered a slight smile. "Seems that you're more of a knight in shining armor than a saint—Sir Oakley." This brought a murmur of approving mirth from those in the room—and a short laugh from Clevis standing in the doorway. "Also seems that the job's not done yet." She raised her finger at Clevis. "I'm counting on you to finish it, Clevis. I don't reckon there's a banshee or boo-hag in the world that can stand up to you two, Clevis and Autis. I know you'll get the task done proper." She released Autis' hand and turned to Liv. "Olivia. Cousin. What a beautiful name—and how well your beauty matches it." She took Olivia's hands and pulled her face in close. "What a fine mother you will make." Sweetgrass looked deep into Olivia's eyes. "I want you to take good care of Sir Oakley here. The care and feeding of knights is a difficult business—but I understand the pay is good." Again, the soft smile.

The doctor said softly. "I think that's enough for right now, Granny. Let's let these folks take their leave to the next room. I need to check your vitals."

"I want a quick private word with Bambi," Sweetgrass said.

The doctor shook his head. "Okay, but be quick." He nodded to Bambi who stayed back as the others filed from the room. Each passed by Granny Sweet, touching and passing a word as they filed out the room and into the kitchen down the hall. Each person was silent in a mind of his or her own making as the doctor went last and softly closed the door.

Sweetgrass smiled. "Child, our time has come down to minutes." Sweetgrass pointed a slender finger at an aging dresser in the corner of the room.

"In the top drawer of that dresser find a long jewelry box and bring it to me." She patted a place on the bed. Bambi obliged, placing the box in Sweet's hand, and then she sat on the bed where Sweetgrass patted.

"This box..." Sweet pressed the item to her breast. "This box carries a story I want to share with you." Sweet leaned her head back against the pillow and took several long breaths, finally exhaling strongly. Her eyes took on a far away look as she gathered her thoughts.

"It was in Memphis, summer of '59—a bad place and time for people of color. My Mister had taken a high dollar dock work job down on the river docks and I followed him there, taking work cleaning offices for Lowenstein's Department Store. At first it seemed a good thing, but it quickly went sour. Wages were high but so, too, the cost of living." Sweet stopped and took a couple more long breaths.

"Granny, you don't need to trouble yourself on account of me..."

Sweet raised a hand to silence Bambi. "I do, and this wants telling," she caressed the jewelry case. "It was August hot, and August wet. I was on what they called my lunch break – thirty minutes of gobbling and rushing back so as to not upset The Man. On my way to the small park across the street from where I worked, I stood on a crowded downtown street corner watching for the light to change—along with a truckload of white people in suits and such. We were waiting there, sweatin' and trying not to notice one another. Of a sudden the light changed, and it read *Walk With Light*. I stood there looking up at that sign while everyone moved around and past me. *Yes!* My mind shouted inside my head. The light changed to red, I turned myself about, went directly to the office at Lowenstein's, and gave notice. The next day I was on the Greyhound going east. I never looked back."

Sweet coughed softly a couple of times and rested as Bambi reflected on what she had just been told.

"My Mister joined me here on the island three weeks later, and here we stayed. Since that time I gathered me about myself and learned to do what that corner stoplight in Memphis said." Sweetgrass opened the jewelry case and withdrew a slender gold bracelet with a small engraved plate. "Mister had this made for me. He scrimped for three years to pay it out of layaway." She held it up so a sun's ray fell across it releasing the beauty of the polished metal. The inscription on the delicate item read, *Walk With Light*.

"It's an ankle bracelet. I've never worn such, so I wore it on my wrist. After I lost it a couple times, I took to wearing it only for special occasions. I had thought to take it with me when I go to meet my Lord Jesus. But he knows more about such things than I do, and I couldn't stand the notion of this thing of beauty covered away in the dark. It wants advertising, and you, my child, are just the one to make it so." She handed the bracelet to her listener who was shaking her head while fighting back tears, her breath coming hard.

"There's no 'no' to this thing, Bambi. It's a favor I'm asking for, and a body can't turn away from such—not with the way we are to each other. Put it on. Put it on an ankle. I want to see it so."

Bambi's body was wracked with stifled sobs as she struggled to carry out the request, her vision blurred with tears. After several unsuccessful attempts, she stood, removed a sandal and placed her foot on the bed beside Sweetgrass. "I can't manage, Granny. Can you put it on for me?"

Sweetgrass expertly opened the clasp, wrapped the ankle and secured the clasp, and turned it so the statement faced out. She ended by patting the top of Bambi's tanned foot. "It looks even more beautiful than I imagined. I'm filled with joy to see my old companion where it belongs." She handed the jewel case to Bambi.

"You know what needs be done, and now you know how to do it." Sweetgrass relaxed against her pillow and appeared to fall asleep. Bambi regained her sandal and slipped quietly out to join others waiting at the door. She moved with grace, head held high. She Walked With Light.

The doctor returned to his patient.

In ten minutes he came to the door and asked for Rebecca. That night, Granny Sweet went to her maker, encircled by a loving family and holding the hand of her beloved granddaughter. Bambi stood among them, laying on hands and exchanging embraces, a source of solace and strength.

Three days later, driving home from church, Autis noted. "That was a short service."

"Yes, Rebecca told me the real service will take place on the day we put the panther to rest—for good. She said Granny Sweet asked that it be that way."

"Good balance to that." Autis said.

Chapter 52

"If this doesn't work, Mr. Newman, we might be doin' more harm than good."

"That's so, Miz Books. It just comes down to risk-taking. It seems to me that folks who believe in what they are about, are willing to take risks. Them that don't, won't."

Finley pulled a Camel out of his pack. "Would my smoking bother?"

"It would."

Finley returned the Camel to its pack and focused his attention to keeping his truck on the road to the Oakley's community. "I seem to recall, you were the one to call me, Miz Wrenn. How come you to get the notion to face up to this boo-hag neighbor of the Oakleys?"

Books Wrenn reflected on the question for a mile or so. "I sensed it to be weak. Neither the demon in the wood nor the spirit in the house were so. I thought we could attack the enemy at his most vulnerable spot."

"A strong thought but how come you to not bring the Oakleys in on this?"

"Belief, Mr. Newman. Belief. We—you and I—believe strong in what we are about. They, on the other hand, have doubt and therefore lack sureness. We need to be sure in our ways with this venture or we shall fail."

"I hope I have the confidence you seem to think I have Miz Wrenn—this sureness."

"Finley Newman, your reputation is known and admired. Some regard you as a force of nature."

"Now that just ain't so, Miz Wrenn."

"Maybe not, but there's many who think it so—and I number myself among them."

"Now how do..."

"That's it. That's Freedom Covers' driveway." Books Wrenn pointed at a dilapidated mailbox ahead on the opposite side of the road. "Let's pull over here."

Finley eased the truck across the road and came to a stop some 50 yards short of the mailbox with faded name and numbering.

Books turned to face her companion. "How do you think we should go about doing this—this confrontation?

"I thought you had a plan, Miz Wrenn."

"I do—you. My plan was to call you and ask you to come and call out this boo-hag neighbor of the Oakleys. And here we are. What do you propose?

"Drive up to the house and knock on the door."

"If they don't answer?"

"She won't."

"What then?"

"I guess you saw the sign on my truck door showing that I'm a locksmith."

"Isn't breaking and entering agin' the law?"

"I won't break—I'll unlock."

Books Wrenn frowned and looked at her driver. "Okay, say we're in the house. What then?"

"I'd have to say that depends on our hostess"

"Do you have your—equipment?

"I believe I have what is needed here." Finley touched the pocket of his jeans jacket." And this time I brought a weapon, it's in the glove compartment. Are you prepared?"

Books nodded. "Mr. Newman, let's go talk with the boo-hag."

No one came to the door. Knocking and clanging the mechanical door bell were of no use. Finley and Books exchange knowing looks. He reached into the breast pocket of his jeans jacket and extracted a set of folding picks. In almost the time a key would have worked, Finley had unlocked the door and swung it wide. The front door opened into a large great room that showed stairs winding to the second floor. The room contained a variety of furniture and overstuffed chairs. The back door of the room opened into the kitchen. If the shades had not been pulled the house would have been bright and clear. As it was, the majority of the light came from the open door.

Books Wrenn strode into the room and spoke up in a confident voice. "Freedom Covers, we've come to talk with you." No answer.

Finley closed the door and began moving about the room opening the roll-up blinds. By the time he got to the fourth blind, a voice came from the top of the stairwell. The voice of a frail woman. "Why have you broken into my house?"

"We want to talk with you."

"I don't know you. You could be thieves or murderers. Get out. I have nothing to say to you except get out!" The woman stepped out of the shadows at the top of the stairs—pale and beyond slender.

Finley walked to the bottom of the steps. "We don't rob or kill, Miz Covers. We've come to talk with you. We've come to talk about your neighbors and what you're doing to them. We want you to stop."

"You enter my home like a thief in the night and want to tell me what to do with my life. All I have to say to you is Get Out!"

"No. We're not going to leave." Books moved the center of the room where she could see her adversary better. "You are hurting our friends and we are come to bring an end to the hurt."

Finley climbed three steps and halted. "If there is no need to talk, there is only need to act."

"You. You little man. Little man. Little woman. Who do you think you are talking to? I commanded armies before your grandparents were born." Her voice began to change into that of a man. "I have no need to heed your wish." The frailness of her body seemed to pass and she stood erect, powerful and poised like a coiled cottonmouth. "You have overstepped your bounds." She raised her arms and looked out over the room. "You would threaten me with your will to act, little man? I—I am legion!" she ran down several steps and flung herself with a husky scream, near to a roar, at Finley Newman—and landed on his hand-held taser. The roar changed to a shrill scream that quickly became a pale cry.

Finley absorbed much of the assault by Freedom Covers, and Books, standing behind him, collected the limp body before it hit the floor at the bottom of the steps. They carried her, whimpering, to one of the overstuffed chairs. Books attempted to revive her while Finley stood by with taser in hand. She changed before their eyes into a wraith-like creature. She stirred and twisted and writhed, then opened her eyes looking back and forth at her captors. "Help me" They heard the voice of a child. "Can you help me?" It was a plea, a pitiful beseeching plea.

"Yes, child, we want to help. Tell us what we must do." Books took the frail claw-like hand into her own. "But you must help us, too."

"Yes, whatever you want," replied Freedom.

"Who are you?"

"Ask me who I was." The wraith-like woman shuddered.

"Who were you?"

"I was Gilly Beale, youngest of the four children of Charles and Ellen Beale of Chicago. All deceased. Murdered by Brutus Maxton in 1863."

"Maxton?" Finley leaned closer.

"Yes, eldest son of the Alexander Maxton who is buried on the property next to this."

"So, both of Alexander Maxton's sons didn't die in the war."

"Napoleon Maxton was killed in battle—lost because of his brother's cowardice. The same cowardice that caused their company to be captured and brought to that terrible federal prison in the swamps outside of Chicago where they were left to starve or rot. Brutus' own men tried to kill him and mistakenly thought they had. They disposed of his body in the swamp, but he wasn't dead. He survived and clawed his way out of the swamp, killing and robbing innocent people in order to feed and clothe himself." Freedom Covers began to return and Gilly Beale began to fade. The childlike innocence was disappearing and a snarling old woman returning.

"Stop!" Books commanded. She took a small leather pouch from a cord hanging about her neck and placed it on the breast of Freedom Covers. They watched as Gilly Beale returned.

Gilly Beale took a deep breath. I've helped you, now you must help me."

"What do you want? Books asked.

"I want you to take my life."

Books shook her head. "I can't willfully take a life."

"Then you can't help me."

"I can." Finley said. "Tell us more. Tell us about Brutus Maxton."

"He is a vile beast of a man. If you kill me you kill him." She looked from Books to Finley, and back to Books. "He kept a journal. I can give you his records."

"Where are they?" Finley demanded.

"Will you kill me?"

"I will grant your wish for death. Yes." Finley answered. Books looked at him incredulously.

"You must. I have lived under the spell of that Maxton beast for one hundred and forty-five years. I never married, never had children, lost all family. I have nothing. I am nothing—all because of Brutus Maxton's evil ways and greed to possess his father's property. He has robbed me of my life, my family, and my soul. I only wish to leave this earth. He occupied my life when he was alive and took over my body when he died. If you leave without killing me, he will reclaim my body—just as he is trying to do now—as we speak. He is raging inside of me, and I can't long hold him at bay."

"You've got my word." Finley laid a hand on her shoulder. Where are his journals?

Gilly heaved a sigh. "There's a doorway under the staircase. It leads to a study. The journals are in the lower right-hand side of the old roll-top desk."

Finley went to the stairwell doorway and returned in a couple of minutes with several large loose-bound books. He saw that the creature on the chair was fading back and forth between Gilly Beale and Freedom Covers as Books chanted and held her root bag over her chest. Finley went to his truck and returned shortly, carrying a snub-nose revolver.

"Tell me, how did you get the Oakleys to find this house?"

Gilly looked at the gun. "I—we didn't know about the Oakleys. We didn't know that Camille had changed her name to Jolly until this century—the internet did it for us. Once we discovered that identity, we sent brochures to all those we thought to be descendents of Camille Jolly. As it turned out, Janey was her only child, and we managed to track down her line. In the hope that we could cause a relative to move here, we contrived to keep the house on the market through the use of terror."

Freedom started to emerge once again. This time Finley withdrew his root bag and placed it on the forehead of their captive. "No." he commanded. "She is ours now and she will stay so." It was then that he looked through the kitchen doorway and saw a lit candle on the top of the refrigerator in the kitchen.

He turned to Books. "What have you done?"

"We need to get out of this house—now." Books stood and pointed to the kitchen. "Gas stove."

Finley nodded for her to leave first. "Leave the door open."

When Books was out of the house he turned to Gilly. He was wiping the revolver with a large red handkerchief. "There is one bullet in this gun." He cocked the hammer back. "A gentle squeeze and it will be over." He turned the chair around so it was facing away from the door he was to exit. He placed the revolver on the floor at Gilly's feet. "Close your eyes and let me hear you count to ten. He placed his palm over her forehead.

Gilly seemed to shudder from the pleasure of his touch. "Thank you. I love you." One...two...

And Finley was gone.

When they reached the mailbox they heard the report of the revolver. They did not look at each other until Finley had parked in front of the Oakley's house. Books was weeping.

* * *

Two and a half hours later the fire was under control enough that the firemen were able to safely enter the burn area. The Oakleys, Books, and Finley watched nearby as the firemen finished their tasks and secured the area around the charred remains of the Covers house. Autis held a shotgun in the crook of his arm. Bob pressed against Liv.

"As I see it, there are two things we need to do, Autis said grimly. We should give a sizeable contribution to our volunteer fire department. And I think we should claim the remains and see to it that what is left of Gilly Beale is properly buried with her family—it will take some research, but that poor child is due at least that small measure of respect. What do you think?" He pulled away from Liv to look at her.

"Yes, to both." Liv moved away and sought out the fire chief, Bob in tow.

"Books, Finley, you two have done a day's work, and it's only noon. That gas explosion was something I hope I never witness up close. It shook our house like an earthquake. I'm sorry to see the Covers house burn, it had a lot of potential, but I think burning it was the wise thing in light of Brutus Maxton's evil spirit. What do you two think? Are we rid of Brutus?"

Finley and Books looked at each other, nodded, and turned back to Autis. Finley cleared his throat, "Yes, he's gone"

"Won't that weaken Alexander's position?"

"Yes and no," Books said. "Alexander doesn't have the support of his son Brutus now, but this will surely send him into a blind rage. I caution you to great care; what we've done here will have filled him with a terrible resolve."

"We'll let Bob sleep in the bedroom tonight, and keep our weapons at bedside."

Finley nodded, "From what you told us about Mongo and the panther, you'd do better to sleep in the pub."

Chapter 53

The Oakley front lawn was filled and overflowing with vehicles of all description—pickups were the dominant species. At first glance, people were milling about aimlessly, but as you came closer you would hear the instructions being issued.

Clevis stood on the bed of his pickup surrounded by over three dozen strong men carrying shovels and weapons, mostly shotguns and handguns. The men were dressed for work—Carhartt overalls, canvas, and boots. Their faces were set for a task. "Listen up," Heads turned to Clevis and talk ceased. "You've all been a part of the planning. Each team leader knows what is expected from his men. We got a lot to do, and we're goin' to have it done by day's end." There was a mutter of assent from the group. "No one—I mean no one—goes off alone. Stay close to your group and stay alert. We don't want anybody gettin' hurt or kilt." He paused and looked over his audience. "There's water and first aid on the patio at the back of the house. There's all manner of tools in the parking area on this side of the house. There's spare gloves for those that need 'em."

Some of the men looked at their callused hands and smiled. *Gloves.*

"Any questions?" Clevis surveyed his dedicated army. No questions. "Okay then. Three men under the loblolly." He nodded in the direction of a small cluster of men who headed to the pine with shovels. They went armed. "The clear team"—he pointed at a larger cluster— "will give us a straight clean trail to the site." A group of six men armed with machetes and chainsaws moved in the direction Clevis pointed. "You know your task—make the trail wide enough so we can four-wheel in and out. You've got two hours, then report back to me."

He looked at the mass of faces looking up at him on his pickup bed pulpit. "Ten men at the saw grass." He nodded as a large party of men, each carrying shovel and shotgun, moved to go where the saw grass met the back lawn. One of the men was carrying a scroll, another, a folding table. "Watch out for fire ants," Clevis called. "The lawn was treated day before yesterday, but you never know." A couple of the departing men waved acknowledgement. Clevis turned his attention to the remaining group.

"The rest of you men—we've got a lot of hard work facing us. The teens have cleared out the basement, and the pool table's been moved off to a side wall." Clevis pointed at a tall, slender man wearing Levis. "Evans' team will take up the floor timbers where Books Wrenn shows em." Clevis waved them on to their tasks. "There's goin' to be a lot of pickin' up and puttin' down, but we got a lot of muscle and mind here. Timbers, stone, and dirt all have separate storage areas on the lawn. There's tarps laid down—use them. The timbers have been marked, so's we'll know how they go back together. Stack 'em so they will go back in reverse order to how they came out. Let's work so's the putting back together is easier than the takin' apart." Clevis paused and looked at the upturned faces of his kin and friends. "Pass the word—no one eats until we are done." He stepped down off the pickup bed and headed toward the doorway to the cellar.

Liv, Bambi, and Rebecca gathered over the large round deck table as they reviewed the plans. There were lists, maps, columns, and more lists. Autis, Finley, and Books stood in conversation at a corner of the deck.

"Granny Sweet would have enjoyed this," Rebecca said softly.

"She's here," Bambi took Rebecca's hand in hers.

"Yes, I feel her presence. She always loved a gathering. Mama says that Granny Sweet's always been that way. Some years ago she'd talked with some of the older women who remembered when Granny Sweet was young. Seems that she was a real rounder. Word was that no one could Charleston like Granny Sweet—and she did it 'til sunrise."

"Now why doesn't that surprise me?" Liv gave a mirthful chuckle. "I can just close my eyes and picture that scene." She rose from her chair. "I'm going to go check on the work under the loblolly." She stood erect and hung the 20-gauge from her shoulder by its leather strap. The weapon had become almost a third limb to her.

The digging under the loblolly was hampered by the extensive root system of the great tree. The men were sweating over axes and spades. They had off-loaded a wooden box and placed it near their excavation.

Liv approached the sweating men. "I'd offer to help, but I don't think I'd be much help with this kind of work. Can I bring anyone a glass of lemonade? This looks thirsty."

"Lemonade would be good, Cuz."

"I'll be right back." Liv turned away smiling. She had become "Olivia," following Granny Sweet's example. Some of the younger members of her new extended family seemed to enjoy calling her "Cuz" in recognition of blood. It was a compliment Liv did not take lightly. She was only just beginning to find out the number of weddings, christenings, anniversaries, Easter celebrations, and such that she was going to be invited to. Her life was on the cusp of a totally new turn. She had Family—and Family had her.

After delivering lemonade, Liv walked over to the wood framed object on the ground. It contained Maxton's tombstone with a recently added inscription:

Alexander Caesar Maxton
10 April, 1820—5 October, 1865
R. I. P. Forever

There were no embellishments on the stone—no flowers, no angels blowing trumpets. It was a naked stone of Georgia granite.

Caesar indeed. Liv turned from the stone and headed back to the house. At the edge of the overhanging branches of the pine, Liv stopped and listened to the men working their way to the site of the clearing. In a last-second decision she turned back to the wood and headed there to see how they were doing. It was then that she detected the game trail. It appeared to be a short cut in the direction she was heading. She un-shouldered the pump, jacked a shell into the chamber, flipped the safety to "on," and made a quick check to see that the wind was to her back. She stepped into the lowering wood.

Liv moved noiselessly through the tangle of briar and the dying attempts of lesser plants to survive in the dead shade of the overhead canopy. The heavy moisture pervaded everything: the air, the footing, the surrounding plant life of a southern hardwood forest. Liv moved with the grace of a young person in command of a healthy body, brushing aside cobwebs and hanging vines. What had once been ugly, repulsive environs had begun to take on a sense of beauty as Liv came to know the wood. She could hear the men talking in the distance and realized she was coming close to them. Apparently her choice of this path was sound.

There was a faint sound to her rear. She turned quickly, just in time to see a large hawk winging away from the branch where it had perched as she passed under it. She watched the great bird as it rose out of sight through the overhead canopy. She turned back to her path. The panther was sitting on its haunches about a dozen paces from her, pale yellow eyes focused on this interloper to its domain. Liv caught her breath and leveled the shotgun, switching the safety off. Her thoughts went to Autis' training with the weapon. Fire—pump another shell—fire—another shell. She was ready. She started to squeeze the trigger when the panther cocked his head as though curious to know what this strange creature was doing. Liv loosened her grip.

"What do you want?" The great cat flinched slightly at the sound of her voice.

Liv took a step toward the cat. "I'm not here to hurt you. All I want is for you to go away." She could swear the cat understood.

"Look, Alexander." The cat started. "Alexander, we're going to dig up your remains and move them to a gravesite under the loblolly. You'll be with your family." The cat seemed to almost relax.

"That's right, you'll be with your family. If we do that, I want your promise you will leave and never come back." Liv realized how ridiculous this appeared, but the cat bobbed his head once. *Damn, he's agreeing with me. He knows what I'm saying.*

All of sudden, the giant cat's demeanor changed, and Liv heard a low powerful growl that could have come from the bowels of hell. She realized that the sound was coming from her rear. She risked a glance. *Bob*. The powerful dog came to her side and was growling without stop. The two antagonists stared at each other with growing malevolence. The cat seemed to grow in size with its rising rage. Bob's growl grew even fiercer as he prepared to close with his nemesis.

Liv took a risk and removed her hand from the trigger of the shotgun and took hold of Bob's collar. "Bob, stay." She said firmly. She had control of the dog, but her finger was no longer on the trigger. She calculated how quickly she could release her dog and bring her hand back to the gun stock and trigger. "*Shit.*"

"Alexander, break it off. Go away. Let's not do this—we're all going to get hurt if you don't leave."

The cat rose to all fours and appeared to stretch. It turned away and slowly slunk into a deep bank of undergrowth. It was then that Liv realized she could actually hear her heart beating. She kept her grip on Bob as she knelt to his side. "Good dog." She put an arm around him while she removed her belt for a leash.

As she rose to continue her walk toward the working men, her mouth tasted like it had copper pennies in it. Blood taste. Bob seemed almost relieved not to have to close with a beast that would almost surely have killed him; he walked obediently beside his mistress. Liv breathed a great sigh of relief as she approached the several robust men clearing the trail to where Alexander Maxton's remains lay. She held tight to Bob's leash.

Clevis had come to check on the progress.

"Hi Liv, what are you doing walking around alone? Liv? Are you alright? You're pale as a sheet."

"I'm okay."

"No. Hell no you're not. Sit down over here." He guided her to a fallen tree trunk and took Bob's leash. He saw that Bob was trembling.

"You saw him didn't you?"

"Yes."

"Why are you…Never mind, you're okay." He sat next to her and put a strong brown arm over her shoulder. Liv took a deep breath and leaned against the gentleness of this powerful man. She fought back tears.

"It's okay, you're safe." Liv nodded silently in response.

"We've got a lot done. Everyone is doing their job to perfection. Buff is overseeing the disinterment of the…those in the cellar. His anthropology background has been a big help. The man knows what he's doing. I miss Gar. He should've been here."

The two sat for several minutes on the fallen log before Clevis broke the silence.

Liv felt her companion shudder as he struggled with his emotions. She sat up and placed a light kiss on his cheek. "Yes, he should be, but he's not and we are. Let's honor his memory and get this done." She stood up and took Bob's leash from her friend. "How are they coming with the grave sites at the salt marsh?"

"Good. Easy digging. We'll have the graves ready long before the bodies are dug up out of the cellar. I sure do hope we're doin' the right thing. Buff says it ain't legal, but it *is* right. I agree with him. He says we're breakin' all sorts of state and federal laws—he's lovin' it. He insists on takin' pictures and measurements all along the way." He's forever keepin' notes as fast as he can write. Even has a tape recorder. Always the scientist I reckon. He won't let a spade go in the ground without takin' note."

Clevis paused and thought a moment. "But he's one helluva fisherman."

Liv chuckled softly, then laughed out loud, starting a laughter she couldn't stop. It became one of those laughing jags that has to go on until you start crying. The digging crew stopped in astonishment as this white lady laughed so hard that Clevis had to hold her from falling onto the forest floor. He shook his head at the onlookers as Liv broke into tears. It was only then that Clevis fully realized what she has just gone through. Bob sat, panting. The very tip of his tail wagged in apprehension.

Chapter 54

"Lord." The Reverend raised his arms in supplication. He held them as the sounds from the congregation softened, then silenced. "Lord. Thy sea is vast and my craft so small." There came a chorus of "Amens." He looked out over his flock.

"What words? What words can tell?" The choir echoed his anguished plea for help and understanding. Gone were the Carhartts and bib overalls. Men stood in trim suits and ties—the women in colorful dresses and gowns. There was a pervading sense of being here, now.

The group stood at the edge of the sawgrass as the preacher related the story of Maxton Manor for all to hear—for all to remember—for all to never forget. He talked with eloquence and grace, pointing to the four new tabby grave caps. He lowered his voice with sorrow over the terror visited on their ancestors by the villainous soul interred under the spreading pine at the edge of the lawn. He spoke of forgiveness to stern faces showing tight lips and narrowed eyes. The choir stood in stilled silence, confirming the boundaries and limits of reaching with music. He returned to the fortune of the ancestors who now lay with their loved ones. Their souls could now return to the Home Country, bringing peace to them and to the cellars under Maxton Manor. Liv listened intently, arm in arm with Bambi and Autis.

After nearly two hours the Reverend brought his sermon-lesson to a close to the sound of a beautiful chorus. He ended his sermon with the repeated phrase: "Lord, Thy sea is vast and my craft so small." Then the supplicants broke as a tide to the waiting tables of comfort food.

In the late afternoon the congregation was gathered once again by the tabby grave caps, this time in remembrance of their beloved Sweetgrass Weaver. Testimonials were invited and given. The sorrow and joy was apparent to all. Autis Oakley stood in near astonishment at the accomplishments of this ninety-year-old lady who had pronounced him first a saint and then a knight.

As the testimonials grew to a close and the sun approached the horizon, there came a sound of beautiful sweet music from the high trees. At first one or two heads looked up, then gradually in a slow-moving wave, all craned to look high in the trees. "Marcel," a five-year-old great-great-grandchild announced clearly, pointing at the mockingbird. This brought first laughter, followed by tears. Those who had managed to keep their composure to that point now lost it. *Mimus Polyglottis* fluttered his one white wing in this final appearance and then sang his heart out to a weeping audience of partisans.

Chapter 55

The doorbell rang. Autis and Liv looked up from their respective books. Autis checked his watch. "Damn, it's 10:15. I didn't hear a car pull up, so it's not Bambi—unless she walked here."

"I'll get it," Liv said.

"No, hell no, you won't." Autis rose and headed for the front door, picking up his Glock along the way.

Liv stood, waiting for word from Autis. She glanced at the 20-gauge. It was over a week since they reburied Maxton and the souls in the basement. There had been no incident, and both Finley and Books pronounced their property free from "haints and hags."

Autis laughed softly then shut the door.

"What is it? Liv called.

"A black cat," Autis replied.

Liv moved toward her shotgun hanging beside the doorway to the deck. She got to her gun just as Autis reentered their living room. He was carrying a tiny black kitten with a startled look on its face. The two looked at each other and burst out laughing. Bob wagged his way to Autis by way of investigation, and Autis lowered the kitten to the dog's inquiring nose. The kitten laid a tiny clawed paw on the nose that was almost as large as its head. Bob wagged his tail.

Liv went to Autis and gathered the baby in her hands. It looked up at her with wide trusting eyes and began to purr when Liv touched her nose to its nose. She went back to the couch and sat with the kitten in her lap. Bob followed, laying his oversized head on her knees, and looked up with trusting eyes as she turned the kitten on its back and tickled its tummy. It responded by delicately seizing her fingers in four tiny paws. Bob reached in and licked the kitten on the face.

"Looks like Bob's got a buddy there."

"I don't know, maybe he's just tasting her," Liv answered.

"Her? How do you know it's a 'her'?"

"Look at that pretty face—it's got to be a girl." Liv said.

"We need some food."

"I'll fix something sensible to hold us over until we can call the vet tomorrow morning."

Autis put away his Glock. "I'll fix up a litter box. I've got some cat litter for oil spills in the garage."

An hour later a full kitten was exploring the living room and Bob. The pointer would respond to overtures from the kitten by rolling it over and nuzzling its stomach. The kitten responded with glee to these overtures. It sprang up and bounced around the big dog, arching its back and stalking stiff-legged as though it was about to pounce. Autis called it the 'Halloween cat mode.'

That night Bob slept on his side on the floor pad in the living room while the kitten slept curled up in a ball on top of her new friend.

The following morning Autis was wakened to the aroma of fresh coffee from the kitchen. In a few minutes Liv appeared carrying a tray, with the kitten trailing behind her. She sat the coffee tray on the bedside table and said. "Alex."

"Alex?" Autis said as he accepted a mug.

"Yes, that's her name." Liv hoisting the kitten onto the bedcovers. It curled instantly into a tiny ball.

Autis sipped his coffee and reflected. "Alex—it fits."

Chapter 56

Bambi looked up from the coffee table book about sea glass and gazed out over the lawn and salt marsh beyond. She pointed at the holstered revolver on the chair next to Liv.

"Gal. Are you still packing heat?" Bambi drew the revolver out of its holster and spun its cylinder. She checked the safety and returned it to the holster.

"Oh yes. It'll be a long time before I can comfortably walk around the property without a weapon."

"Didn't Finley and Books say it was okay now?" Bambi asked. She crossed her legs like a man and stroked the tiny gold plate on her anklet.

"Yes, but that doesn't matter. I know I'll never walk out on the pier un-armed and I'll never walk around the yard without Bob's company. That's just the way it is. I'm still scared. I can't help it—and I'm not apologizing."

"No need. It's understandable." Bambi shrugged. "No more voices in the cellar then?"

"No voices, no boo-hags, no demons. It's pretty quiet around the home-stead. About the most exciting things are the chase wars between Alex and Bob. I can't believe the two of them haven't broken a lamp or vase or some such thing. I mean they're all over the house, taking turns chasing and fleeing. Bob has lost weight keeping up with what Autis calls 'the beast.' But it beats televi-sion, and it's a never-ending show."

"I'll bet," Bambi said. She set her drink on the side table and glanced at her friend, frowning.

"What is it?" Liv asked. "You've something on your mind, I can tell it."

"You ain't wrong," Bambi said softly.

"Well, fess up," Liv leaned forward.

Bambi ran her hand over her face, looked up at the passing clouds and turned to her best friend. "A coupla things. First off, I miss Gar. I miss him so much I can almost taste it. I think I'll always miss him. In fact, I can't imagine not missing him. He was like a part of me—a part that's missing. Sometimes, I'm not sure I want to go on living without Gar in my life."

Liv took a sip of ice tea. "I think I understand. Of course I don't agree with your conclusion, but I know where you're coming from. There's no need for me to go into details about why such a conclusion is wrong; I think you already know them."

"Yes, I do. I also know time heals. I also miss Granny Sweet. We'd just got to know each other. I'd finally found a home—a place where I know I'm always welcome, a place where I was safe. First Gar, then Granny Sweet in close succession. I feel carsed. Everything seems like something trite or a clichŽ. When I'm alone I feel such pain. Such terrible black pain that I try to avoid being alone—and sober. If it weren't for Clevis and Rebecca and other members of Granny Sweet's family, I don't know what I'd have done. They've taken me in. They know how I feel and they involve me in family comings and goings. For the first time in my life I understand what it's like to have family."

"Yes, I know what you mean. They've taken me in too. There's so much love in that family. I'm really enjoying them, and they seem to like my company. And, of course, Autis has that god-like status with them that will last forever. Three generations from now, they'll be telling the story about the 'Giant of Wadmalaw who killed the panther with his bare hands.' The men treat him like he's the master of all things. They seek out his advice at every turn—my husband, Obi Wan Kenobi, I have to hand it to him—he's accepted his royalty with grace and humility."

"Of course he would, but that only makes it worse," Bambi said smiling.

"Of course," Liv agreed. "I mean, I fully expect someday to see a new mother bring her child to Autis for anointment. Poor guy, I think he really believes that if he ignores it, it will go away. What's really bizarre, though, is the way women treat him—I've never seen such idolatry. I'm surprised the men don't hate him for it, but they don't—and it just rolls off his back."

"Autis is a big boy. He can take care of himself," Bambi said.

"Yeah, I know. I'm probably envious."

"Maybe," Bambi frowned at her lap, and then took another long drink of Fly. "There's something else though," she refused to look Liv in the face.

Liv, sensed the intensity in Bambi's body and voice. "What is it, Bambi? You can tell me, you know we have no secrets."

Bambi sat up, took a deep breath, and looked directly into the eyes of the woman she loved. "It's you."

"Me? Have I done something to offend you? If tha…"

"No, no. That's not it. It's you. You're different—something has changed with you. This thing with the panther has really got to you. With me and other people, you often seem to not be here when you are here—you're somewhere else. You seem to be carrying a load wherever you go, and it's starting to wear you down. You even look different—right now your face is puffy and flushed. What's going on, Sis?"

Liv buried her face in her hands, nodding her head. Then she dropped her hands to her lap. "You've noticed then?"

"Yes. And I'm not the only one. Clevis and Rebecca ask about you, and want to know if everything is okay with you and Autis. They're worried. Please tell me what's hanging over you. You're kin now, and I have a right to know."

"It's simple, Sis. I'm pregnant."

Bambi's glass shattered on the deck boards.

The End

EPILOGUE

Camille Oakley hungrily pulled at her mother's soft breast while Liv relished the ethereal bliss of nourishing the child delivered from her womb. "Kissing the hem of Eternity" was the phrase that Sweetgrass had been overhead to say some years earlier as she had watched a recent new descendent nursing at his mother. When questioned, Granny Sweet answered that the mother and child were consummating a relationship that had been part of life from time eternal, and that "would likely continue to be such." Liv mused on the phrase as she watched four-month-old Camille watching her. Kissing the hem of eternity. Yes.

For Camille, the aroma, sounds, and sights of the salt marsh were coupled with the pleasure of mother's milk. Evening feedings on the dock had become a part of the mother and child routine. So much so, that Bob and his effervescent playmate, Alex, came to expect the pre-twilight sojourns. When let out in the evening they immediately headed to the long boardwalk that led to the dock.

Liv watched as the fog settled over the sound while Camille was secure in the crook of her left arm. Liv's right hand rested softly on the Glock holstered at her side.

The evening light approached the spectrum of silver and gray—much like an old tintype. Liv smiled as she watched Bob and Alex at her feet. Alex played her favorite game of attacking and killing a velvety hound ear. Bob, so accustomed to the game, had fallen asleep, unmindful of the mayhem being done to his person. Alex was rapidly, and gently, blapping the hanging ear, when she stopped in mid-blap, stood erect on all four, and gazed out at the salt marsh. Alex's intense purr caught Liv's attention, and she turned to look in the direction of the feline's fixed stare.

The water borne fog wafted toward the land, and would soon cover the marsh all the way up to the Oakley lawn. Liv saw a row of faint columns of mist moving from the land toward the fog. There were nearly a dozen and a half of the columns that leaned toward the fog. The last column was taller and larger than the others. It stopped and appeared to face back to Oakley Manor as the line of mist columns moved on. In the corner of her eye Liv saw a single column come from the loblolly pine and hurry to join the others. The tall one waited. The smaller column of mist stopped, appeared to turn and face in the direction of the pine. Then it turned back to follow the others and, like them, vanished in the fog over the Sound. The tall column turned and faced Liv. It leaned forward briefly, and then vanished into the mists.

In a few minutes, Camille finished nursing and was asleep in her mother's arm. Liv rose and led her pets down the boardwalk to the house. Just as she arrived at the lawn, Autis came out on the deck. True to form he was home on time, and true to form he had a fresh Bud Light in his hand. He dropped down the steps to join his family. Liv veered toward the loblolly pine and Autis turned to follow. They met about fifty yards from the tree where Autis kissed his wife and took Camille in his arms, and then followed Liv to the pine. Bob and Alex trailed along.

"I saw them leave—the slave spirits. But one of them visited here." Liv pointed to the pine.

"I wonder why they waited so long to leave?" Autis said.

"I think they wanted to see Camille." Liv led the way among the branches of the pine, stopped, and pointed to the graves.

They saw fresh marsh flowers on the graves of Kathleen Jolly Maxton and Sally Maxton.

Genealogy

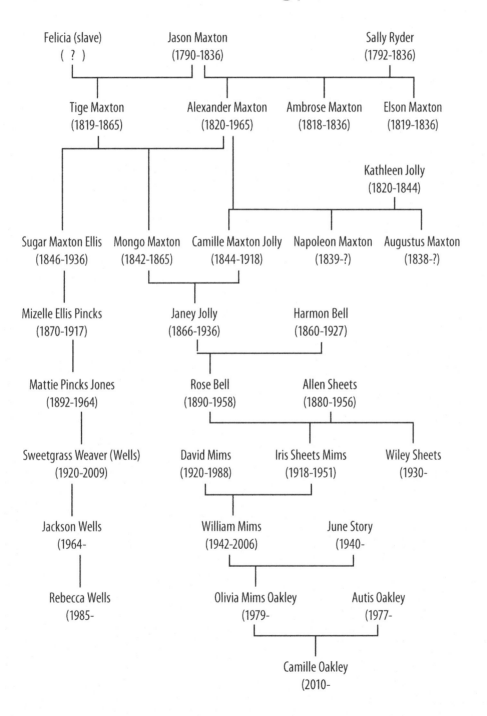

Bart Bare

Bart Bare brings a perspective both broad and deep to the written page. Bart retired as a college educator after twenty-seven years, and elected to follow an ancient Chinese adage which holds that the retiree, rather than stop  working, must take on a completely new life: New profession, friends, activities, and orientation. Writing is Bart's second life work, which he does in his home at Blue Moon Gap on the Eastern Slopes of Grandfather Mountain just west of Blowing Rock, NC. Bart and Caroline, his wife of thirty-nine years, enjoy their wooded mountain vista, along with a houseful of dogs and cats, and fields teeming with wildlife. His hobbies are bee-keeping, reading, and walking mountain paths with his wife.

Connect with Bart online at:

 BartBare.com